To my friends Angela H and Martin A, thankyou for your time and paticence with me. And a huge thankyou to my son as he was the one that weathered a lot of storms with me.

MARY D / MARIA THE IRISH COLLEN / PAGE 1

Maria woke up on her wedding day, hearing her friend Shelly snoring beside her .

She then heard the familiar sound of her Da stoking the fire.

At long last she thought its here a year of anticipating her wedding, that she had dreamed

about since she was a child.

Shelly stirred beside her , she had come over from England for her friends wedding.

My fucking head feels like its got dad`s army , hammering about in there! "she complained.

"I feel fine, but we did put a fair bit away last night well, you did at least, what with

Brendan Doyle chatting you up" laughed Maria.

"Oh, is that his name, he`s a bit of alright you know", said Shelly

"He`s that alright, only he`s married with about fourteen kids all over the village"

.

He likes to put it about our Brendan does". "Oh fuck I didn't did ?",asked a confused Shelly.

Maria laughing" No, you came home with me last night.Now on that note ,I`m getting up".

 She got out of bed and put her dressing gown on .

Shelly swung her legs out of the bed and said "Will I wake Mandy" Maria nodded looking

at her younger sister, snoring under the covers.

"I cant believe they served her last night, how old is she?"Shelly asked yawning.

"Fourteen, I had a word with Liam the barman who fancies her, she cant stand him."

"I thought he was a bit of alright" sighed Shelly.

"Look Shelly, you think anything in a pair of trousers is alright !" laughed Maria looking

fondly at her friend .

"Get lost", laughed Shelly. Mandy stirred.

"Good morning sis ,how is the head?" Smiled Maria at her little sister whom she adored .

Mandy moved her aching head. "Oh God"

" He won` t help you", said Shelly laughing at Mandy .

"Come on you two, I`m getting married today", smiled a radiant Maria

"Ok " smiled Mandy as she struggled out of bed.

Maria went into kitchen where her Da was making tea, "Here she comes THE GIRL" , he had called her that since she was a child.

That name made her cringe, as it triggered flashbacks of hidden secrets, which were under lock and key.

Looking coldly at him asking where her Ma was?

"Oh I`m here", said Catherine as she came out of her bedroom in her dressing gown.

"What`s the time ? Jesus it`s nine-o-clock !"said Catherine, "I`ll just go and wash my hair" Maria went and had a shower and her thoughts went back to her childhood.

They had never had a shower when she was little. Instead her and her younger brother Sean used to carry buckets of water from the pump down the road for drinking and for washing.

The next job was always to fill up the turf box by the range, as this provided the only heating in the house.

She was eight years old Sean was six and her baby sister Mandy was two who tried to help by carrying a sod of turf, they would clap their hands when she did this, she would stand there with a big dribbling smile on her face

She remembers the cold and lack of food as a way of normal life at that time.

This triggered forgotten memories for Maria as she remembered her Ma bringing home her youngest brother Paul.

For Maria life changed as her Ma ended up in hospital for a long period, after giving birth.

She remembers going to see her Ma with her Da it was a very long journey to Dublin.

When they arrived at the hospital Maria felt frightened she held on tightly to her Da `s hand everything seemed so strange .

Once she was inside the hospital the shear size with lot`s of big machine`s and strange noise`s going on, made her even more terrified. .

When they entered a room her Da went over to this strange woman and asked how she was feeling.

Her Da said " Say hello to your Ma ", Maria started to cry " That's not my Ma!" She screamed and ran out of the room.

Her Da followed her ,picked her up and said "This is your Ma", she stared at this woman who had a white face and looked like she was going to cry.

The woman said "Maria" and she realized this woman was her Ma.

"How is baby Paul?"asked her Ma. Little Maria was still crying and shocked as she held her

arms out to her mother.

"I`m sorry I didn`t know you", she sobbed

   "That's alright, I know I don't look very well but I`m on the mend and will be home soon, so don't worry about me, you look after Paul".

She looked at her Ma and through tearful eyes said " I`ll try".

She was just eight year`s old, and her Ma expected her to look after a new born baby.

             Suddenly a voice jolted Maria back to reality ," Have you drowned in there " shouted Catherine .

She had been so lost in thought she had forgotten where she was ,she turned the shower off

Putting her bathrobe on and went into the bedroom.

Her wedding dress and veil were hanging on the wardrobe suddenly Mandy burst in with excitement " The flowers have arrived !".

" Come here !", said Maria, as she held her arms out to her sister, looking down at her "I love you ", giving her a huge hug.

Hugging Mandy brought back memories of that magic day that her baby sister was born.

                         Chapter Two

She remembered she awoke to find Sadie their neighbour standing in the kitchen.

"Where`s me Ma and Da Sadie ?"

"They have gone to the hospital "

"What for ?".

"I don't know", replied an embarrassed Sadie .

"Yes you do I can see you know something, tell me " demanded Maria.

Even though she was only six , sometimes she behaved beyond her years.

All right then they have gone to get another baby" said Sadie reluctantly.

Maria`s brown eyes opened so wide and her mouth dropped that Sadie thought the little girl was going to faint.

"Are you alright pet?", said Sadie concerned.

Maria looked at Sadie in amazement. "What they`ve gone to get us a new baby ? ".

"Oh Sadie ,that is brilliant, are they getting a boy or a girl?" She questioned.

"Well, it will be whatever god gives them", replied Sadie, relieved to see that Maria had taken the news well.

Her brother Sean, who was four years then arrived out of the bedroom to see what all the excitement was about.

Maria went over and tried to lift him in the excitement, but instead they both fell over.

Sean hit his head on the floor and burst out crying.

Maria getting him up,trying to comfort him, Sean just pushed her away.

Sadie stepped in and picked him up and told him, "Maria is all excited because your Ma and Da have gone to the hospital to get a new baby".

Sean didn`t understand and just kept screaming.

Her Da `s car pulled up outside, Maria went screaming out of the house," Where`s our new baby ? Where is it Da ?".

"Calm down girl ! ",replied a very tired looking Tommy.

He had had a long night as Catherine still had not given birth.

" How is she" ,asked Sadie.

" Its taking a long time I need to go back in a few hours", he replied wearily.

Maria pulling her Da` s jacket," Where`s me Ma and where`s the new baby ?".

He picked her up and said " Your Ma is still at the hospital trying to pick one out".

" We can go and help her" she said excitedly. Tommy looked at Sadie for help .

"No Maria , that would spoil the surprise " said Sadie

"Now leave your Da alone and let him have a rest".

"Let`s hope Ma picks a baby soon ", said Maria as she skipped out the back door.

" Where are you going to ?" asked Sadie . Maria turned smiling " To my babby house ,where
else ?".

Sadie smiled to herself, thinking she will go places.

She had a very loving, caring and curious nature . You could not help but love her.

Sadie looked up at the shed, which was where Maria had her imaginary house, she played up
there for hours on her own.

That day seemed so long to her waiting for her Ma to pick a baby out, she lay on the shed
with her hands under her head , thinking hard it can be to pick a baby out.

Later that evening, Sadie called Maria in for her tea Maria stomped up the steps sighing

"Still no baby, how long did it take you to pick Sally and Paddy out ?" .

"A long time" smiled Sadie.

The next day Tommy arrived home to inform them that Catherine had picked out a baby
girl, who weighed only six pounds and two ounces.

 Sadie frowned concerned," Oh dear, everything ok Tommy".

He smiled and looked at her "Yes their both doing well but Catherine is very tired".

"She must be" piped in Maria its taken her three days to pick her out she sang .
Chapter Three
"MARIA you have gone off into that dream world again" shouted Shelly.

" Oh sorry Shelly, I was just remembering the day that Mandy was born ".

" Enough of the reminiscing ! Your getting married in a few hours ".

"Lets get these hairs done then " smiled Maria .

"Do mine first "demanded Catherine .

Maria had trained to be a hairdresser and turned out to be a very talented one.

She had come second in the all Ireland competition two years earlier.

She was eighteen years old then, and had left home at seventeen after having a row with her Ma.

 Since Paul was born, and her Ma having been so ill after his birth he had become the apple of Catherine`s eye.

She spoiled him rotten ,so did Maria.

In a way , Catherine and Maria , who was eight years old then were in competition over his affections.

Maria won hands down because while her Ma was in hospital Paul hand bonded with Maria .

When ever Catherine held him his little head kept looking for his sister.

Of course this brought jealous feelings Catherine had to the surface.

So any chance she got, she came down on Maria like a ton of bricks.

Catherine became very cruel to her, and if she back chatted her, she would, grab her by the hair, and throw her down the steps of the back door.

Maria would go flying down the steps, hit her head off the shed wall and pass out.

Catherine would then pick her up take her in her arms and dunk her head into a barrel of water to bring her round.

She would regain consciousness and her Ma would blame her for blaggarding saying that she fell down the steps on purpose .

Maria had learn`t to keep silent, because the last time she protested her Ma forced her head under water until she started to choke.

The shock of her Ma`s reaction to her protest terrified Maria  so much , she would leg it to Sadie`s for refuge and consoling .

She would cry her eye`s out and tell Sadie what her Ma had done, Sadie would comfort her and say her usual "Your Ma didn`t mean it ".

Sadie didn`t know what to think of the situation, Maria would arrive soaked to the bone.

Sadie would change her out of her wet clothe`s and give her a biscuit and a drink, and more than anything else she needed a hug.

She noticed that Catherine had got a bit short fused with Maria since Paul had been born.

"Earth calling Maria", squealed Mandy ,"Shit" smiled Maria.

"I have washed my hair" shouted Catherine .

"Ok Ma I`m coming".

Maria picked up her hair brushes and dryer and went to do her Ma`s hair.

" That colour looks good on you Ma it compliments the suit you will look stunning in it" .

"Ah shite, sure good looks run in the family" laughed Catherine.

Maria laughed with her Ma."Yes Ma, I suppose they do".

Since she had left home Catherine seemed to tolerate her a lot More which was nice for Maria.

"Your hair looks lovely" smiled Shelly as she came into the room

She looked every bit the brides mother in her lilac suit, cream blouse and matching shoes.

An excited Mandy bounced into the room in her bridesmaids dress ,it was a beautiful wine colour and matching shoes.

"Mandy you look beautiful !" said Maria with a lump in her throat.

It was now Maria`s turn to get dressed she had bought an off the shoulder satin white dress with long lace sleeves ,from the waist at the back of the dress flowed a train of silver and white lace.

On her head she wore a tiara . Mandy stood looking at her with tears in her eye`s,

 "Oh Sis you look stunning ".

"Come on Mandy you`ll ruin your makeup ! " Maria smiled as she looked at a picture of her and David.

Chapter Four

  A huge smile on her face she remembered the first time she had ever set eyes on David. It had been in a pub where he was the lead singer of a band her friend Rose was with her . Maria got them a seat and Rose got the drinks in, her favourite song came on as Rose returned with the drinks "By Jesus , he`s a bit of alright " she said nodding at the stage.

"I was just thinking that myself" replied Maria "I love this song go Johnnie go go go !" Maria sang and Rose joined in.

The two of were really enjoying their evening. At the interval the lead singer came over, asking "Would you two ladies like a drink?"

"Please" replied Rose quickly "Thank you, I`m Maria and this is Rose ,we work together".

"Hello I`m David" he said smiling.

"I think your brilliant"she said giving him her best smile.

 "Thank you but I would not go that far" he smiled .

He turned to Maria and said "Would you like to come out for a drink sometime"

"Christ you're a fast worker" smiled Rose.

"Don`t believe in wasting time" he smiled back at her waiting for Maria to give him an answer.

She flicked her hair and smiled and said "Yes that would be nice".

"You`ve got beautiful hair" he said cheekily .

"Thank you but since I`m a hairdresser, so it should look good".

"Oh where do you work ?" He inquired ."Studio 6" she smiled.

" Ah now I know where to get my next cut".

"Well I better get back up there," he said nodding in the direction of the stage," ladies are you staying to the end?".

" Well we are now " said Maria bursting out laughing,

 "Good you have made my night", he winked as he walked away.

"You lucky cow" Rose said to Maria enviously .

Jokingly Maria taunted Rose saying " Well baby some of us have it and some of us don't".

Maria was a very funny ,outgoing, confident young woman, full of life and loved to make people laugh.

David finished his set and joined the girls ."Do you play often David?" asked Maria. .

"Maybe one or two gigs a week"

"Is that your main job ?"

"No I`m a maintenance driver for the hospital."he answered, leaning over looking into her eye`s.

" So when am I taking you out ?" She looked back into his sexy blue eye`s feeling her heart miss a beat.

"How about Friday "she smiled.

"Do I have to wait that long Maria". he replied with a yearning in his eye`s.

"Yes because I work as a cosmetic rep and I also do modeling work in the evening`s and I`m really busy this week".

"Christ you do live a busy life, how about I meet you in The Swan on Friday for a meal I`ll book a table tomorrow if that`s ok".

" I`ll look forward to that thank you David" smiled Maria warmly.

Rose got up to go to the loo and nearly fell on top of David

" Oh dear, I think I might be a bit pissed just for a change" she laughed as she staggered off

to the loo.

Maria offered to go with her "No" slurred Rose "I`ll be alright "

Maria looked at David and laughed " She`s a smashing girl but she cant take her drink ".

"There`s quite a few like that around here pet", joked David as he gazed around the room.

" Right I`m off " said David and I will see you on Friday night about eight.

"Looking forward to it " she said giving him one of her sexy smiles.

David bent over and kissed her on the cheek Maria looked at him thinking I wont be kicking

him out of the sack.

A staggering Rose arrived back from the toilets "Come on we`ll go home"

said Maria .

Hiccuping Rose followed Maria out of the pub taking by the arm, they got back to Maria`s

flat and Rose threw herself on the bed and passed out.

Maria sighed as she took Roses shoes off and climbed in beside her, Rose snoring Maria lay

there thinking about David.

She eventually nodded off and awoke to the alarm going off oh my fucking head she

thought as she looked at her friend dribbling beside her.

She gently shoved Rose who groaned " Jesus I`m going to be sick " as she rushed to the

bathroom.

"Fuck we are going to be late "shouted Maria, Rose poked her white face around the corner

of the door and said " I cant go to work today".

"Ok fine one of us has to do it" snapped Maria..

"Sorry " said a very sheepish Rose.

Maria stormed out of the flat and headed to work.

She heard a van tooting looked around and saw David drive by waving at her he pulled in and opened the passenger door.

"Hi baby, want a lift " asked David . " I`m only just going around the corner", smiled Maria.

David opened the door and said "Come here" in a humorous way.

"Why", smiled Maria.

"Just come here".

Maria bent over and David slid over to the passenger side and taking her face very gently in his hands kissing her on the mouth.

Maria was very surprised at the gentleness, she pulled away a little flustered.

"You ok? " smiled David."Yes I just was-" David put his finger gently over her lips and whispered" I wanted to kiss you the minute I saw you " Maria blushed, something she did not do very often.

"You're a very sexy lady and I am over the moon that you have agreed to come to with me. me"

" Honk Honk " a car blew behind him, "I better move the old banger, I`ll see you Friday, cant wait" he smiled. .

She got out of the car and watched him pull away, Butterfly`s going on in her tummy, as she wandered off to work thinking of the kiss.

When she got there feeling very pleased with herself.Finding Joe her work college in tears.

Joe looked at her" I`m leaving home cannot take the stress of Kevin" he sobbed.

Kevin was Joe`s brother, who was right up his own arse, Maria didn't have any time for him.

" Your dead right" replied Maria."Now wipe those tears we have work to do".

Maria adored her work ,Joe and her were the top two stylists in the salon.

They got on like a house on fire and worked really well together.

They both also enjoyed a bit of competition. They were always trying to out do each other in who could take the most money, on the odd occasion, Joe would out do her, much to her annoyance.

Her competitive personality sprung from her childhood. Never getting any attention from her Ma, or if she did it was the wrong kind.

So anywhere she could find someone that gave a little praise or a bit of love she grabbed it with open arm`s.

As a little girl in the summer Maria`s life was spent in the bog land.

The bog was an area of land were over the millennia that vegetation had turned into peat.

It was very soggy land little Maria found it very hard to walk in ,her feet would get soaked.

She learned to use a spade to cut the turf, it was then left to dry and weeks later would be brought home.

She worked the bog with uncle Pat and cousin Seamus who felt sorry for her .

She was only a little thing far to thin, undernourished , as Seamus`s mum Francis used to say.

Even though she was small she was well able to work along side the lads.

Francis always packed a lunch for Maria she would sit on a clump of turf and devour the sandwiches and biscuits.

The three of them would sit in the sunshine , Pat would sing a few songs and Maria would join in.

They would work until dark and travel back on a donkey and cart with the turf`s.

After unloading the turf ,Francis would give Maria a bun and a cup of orange.

She was very grateful and wished her Ma was like that. Francis knew the look and would give her a big hug.

She felt sorry for Maria she as knew everything was not up to scratch at home.

Maria loved the sympathy and attention something she never got at home.

Chapter Five

After work that day Maria had a modeling job ,which she did with two friends.

They met in the their local, The Swan it was very upmarket , the three of them loved it there.

They walked in as if they owned the place, ordered their drinks and Brendan the barman welcomed them with a smile.

"Good evening ladies your all looking rather tasty" said Brendan. " You make us sound like burger and chips" laughed Maria.

"How are Sarah and the twins?".

" They are all grand but why wouldn`t they be, they got me" . laughed Brendan .

"Your to big for your boots" laughed Martina.

"My boots fit me fine "he laughed.

Martina gave him a deadly look, Maria heard the door go and turned around to see David walk in. .

Her heart missing a beat, she waved at him, seeing her he went straight over .

"Hi David , fancy seeing you here,"

"Well hello to you too" he smiled, "Can I get you a drink,"

 Shaking her head "No thank you were just a modeling job."

"Christ he`s a bit of all right" smiled Martina as she nudged Susan.

"I

"Would you like to come "Maria asked.

"I would love to come and see you modeling" he smiled "Where is it?"

"Its in Clara at 8pm "replied Martina."I suppose I have to introduce myself"

Maria stepping forward saying "If you would give me a chance,"

" David, this is the sensible one Susan, "

" Hi David "she smiled kissing his cheek.

" And this is the cheeky one Martina".

" Well hello there, and where have you been hiding all our lives? " chirped Martina giving him a peck on the cheek.

"Oh I have just come out of the woodwork to meet Maria" , he smiled as his blue eye`s sparkled at her.

Martina turned and said to Susan " He`s got it bad ".

Maria overheard tossing her long dark hair and replied to Martina " Jealousy will get you nowhere girl," teased Maria .

"You just got lucky" Martina replied .

" Come on girls we have to make a move are you coming David" asked Susan .

"Oh yes I`m looking forward to it, anyone want a lift?".

" I`ll come with you" said Maria,

" How many have you got room for ?" asked Susan.

"The three of you if you want" he said.

"Done I`ve got fuck all petrol" said Susan gratefully.

They all piled into David`s car, Maria jumped into the front, as they laughed and chatted about the evening to come.

Martina started giggling " Its me nerves " .

"There is always something "sighed Susan.

"Your dead right there" said Maria and turned around and giving her friend a friendly shove,

"Behave yourselves girls " said David jokingly .

"It's the next right up here" said Maria,

" Where here ?" asked David.

" Yes " smiled Maria.

He looked out of the corner of his eye seeing her mischievous sexy eye`s .

God she does things to me, he thought David indicating to turn right .

He pulled into the village hall and Maria showed him where to park.

They piled out of the car.

Maria directed him where to go,

 "Thanks baby" he said giving her a peck on the cheek.

The girls headed into the changing rooms ,checking out the attire, it was summer wear they

were modeling .

Maria picked up her size ten fire red swim suit that was trimmed in gold sequin`s it was cut

up high on the thigh, which enhanced her figure .

Susan who was six foot was in a black swim suit, with a silver trim, she was very slim and a

very beautiful woman.

She had six children but to look at her you would not have thought she had any.

Martina was in a lemon swim suit,

All three of them loved, the job modeling .

David got a seat in the front row with the rest of the village.

Jackie who organized it all, did the introduction`s .

First one out was Susan , she looked stunning with her blonde highlighted hair, blue eye`s

and beautiful smile she had a lovely elegant manner about her.

As she approached the catwalk Brian who was Susan`s husband whistling as he saw his wife

step out.

Maria was next in her high heels ,long dark hair, she looked stunning.

As the two of them paraded up and down the stage Martina joined them.

They were a joy to watch David could not believe his eye`s to see these three looking and acting so professionally .

The show finished and they headed backstage , Maria invited David .

Jackie asking" Who have we got here?"

" Oh it`s her new bit of stuff",sniggered Martina.

Maria ignoring Martina introduced Jackie to David.

"Very pleased to meet you " said Jackie flirtatiously.

Jackie looked him up and down. Maria could see this made him uncomfortable , so she playfully pushed Jackie back.

David looked at her gratefully , he adored her brown sexy eyes and she knew how to use them.

"Cor he`s a bit yummy , you have got a looker there girl", said Jackie.

Susan looked at her watch,saying

 "Christ is that the time, we will have to make a move soon".

Martina looked at him, "Your not bad, I suppose", she laughed jokingly.

They got in the car, about chatted about the evenings events.David smiled to himself, listening to the banter.

Susan got dropped off first, thanking David for the lift , said her goodbyes, and headed in home.

The headed back into town, "Fancy a quick drink, before you head off?" giggled Martina

"Sounds like a plan", smiled David, took his wallet out, and handed Maria some money," Get the drinks. There`s a doll,I `ll just go and park the car"

She smiled gave him a peck on the cheek, "See you in there " Martina sliding her arm through Maria`s.

 "Well your in there girl, he is gorgeous and generous "Martina said smiling.

Chapter_____

Maria remembered her first love Liam.

They had met when she was sweet sixteen, at Bogeys Disco where her and her best friend

Sally ,went every Sunday night .

Her and Sally were dancing ,when two lads joined them.

"Hi I`m Liam ",This blonde haired lad with brown eye`s said to Maria .

" I`m Maria " she replied smiling .

"Do you come here often ?" Asked Liam. " Every week " she replied " Do You?".

" No this is about my second time here " he replied .

They were dancing to a rock and roll song and Liam started to jive with her.

Maria loved jiving and they danced well together her. The band switched to slow music.

He shyly put his arms around her, she could smell his aftershave and recognized it as Brut.

It was one of her favourites, she put her arms around his and laid her head on his shoulder.

As the band sang out Lady in Red, Liam pulled her closer, she liked the way he was holding

her.

He held her as if she was a china doll.Maria looked over at Sally who was dancing with

Liam`s friend.

He was holding her closely, they winked and smiled at each other. They were both having a

ball.

After the music stopped, the went to the bar to get a drink, Liam`s smiling brown eyes looked

at her,

She could feel her heart beating ninety to the dozen, "What would you like?"

"An orange juice" she smiled "Two oranges please" he said to the barman "Where would you

like to sit?"

"Lets go over to the balcony so we can have a nose", she smiled Liam led the way and

grabbing some seat`s.

They sat down and Liam asked" Where are you from?"

"Kincora" she replied,

"And you" she asked feeling a bit nervous.

"Rahan" he smiled back at her.

"How old are you?" She asked,

"I`m seventeen, you? "

"I`m sixteen" she smiled.

" Are you still at school ?" He asked. " No I`m training to become a hairdresser".

The night was nearing an end they left the bar hand in hand and went to find Sally and Joe .

The found the two of them snogging in a corner .

" Hi Sally don`t eat him " laughed Maria .

Joe looked up and winked at Liam .

" Right We shall walk you two girls back to the bus "asked Joe.

They walked back to the bus laughing and joking , when they got there Liam took Maria into

his arms and held her closely.

" When can I see you again ?" asked Liam "

"You live said you live in Rahan" she said.

"Well a bingo bus goes from Kincora to Rahan on a Monday night so I could meet you

then."

" I`ll be there " he smiled . Sally and Maria got on the bus home two of them excitedly

gossiping about the evening they had, had .

" Are you meeting him again ?" asked Sally .

 " Monday night outside the Bingo hall in Rahan" she replied.

" So am I " said Sally " Meeting Joe I mean, Maria do you believe in love at first sight" asked

Sally with a far away look in her eyes .

" I don`t know " replied Maria " Why ?"

" Just asking " sighed Sally closing her eye`s with a huge grin on her face.

Maria shut her eye`s and could see Liam`s handsome face in front of her.

The bus arrived back in Kincora at 2am . The two of them danced home .They were high on life or love or what ever you want to call it.

Chapter Five

"Maria where the hell have you floated off to now ?" said Shelly

Maria blinked hard trying not to cry. She could not believe the amount of emotion that was going on inside of her.

Mandy arrived in the bedroom and gasped " My God Maria, you look beautiful ! ".

Shelly put her arms around her friend and said, " No second thoughts". Maria shaking her head,smiling "No"

"Well, its is nearly time to go. Your Ma, Sean and Paul have already gone to the church",

 Shelly said that, the car arrived to take her and her Da to the church.

"You and Mandy can go in Seamus`s car" said Maria .

She looked out of the window to see all the neighbours from the surrounding houses out waiting for her to appear .

She came away from the window and looked at her Da in his pin stripped suit gazing at her.

She looked at him and said coldly.

Taking his arm and he turned to her and said " This a very proud day for any father ".

 They got into the car with all the neighbours waving and cheering at her,feeling like a queen.

They pulled off slowly and headed for the Church as they approached she saw her beloved

David hurry into the Church followed by her relations and friends .

The car stopped her Da got out first and went around to help his daughter out.

She got out of the car and looked at her Da, thinking I would rather have a tinker give me away.

But then hidden secrets harm.

Maria taking her Da` s arm and headed towards the Church door there were flowers everywhere .

Maria started to tremble as she heard the Wedding March begin to play .

Feeling her heart beating nine to the dozen.

As they began the slow march down the aisle she could see her David at the end of the Church waiting for her.

As David turned to see his bride approaching he could not believe his eye`s.

In front of him was the most beautiful vision he ever seen in his life.

As she got near him their eye`s met and she could feel a tears welling up .

She wanted to put her arm`s around him but instead Mandy took her flowers and David removed the veil from around her face .

They stood at the altar holding hands taking their wedding vow`s as they became man and wife.

 As the services finished, David gently taking her face between his hands and kissed her.s

As they did this the guests applauded.And David and Maria started their walk up the aisle smiling.

 They looked lovingly at each other as they started their new life as Mr and Mrs Kelly.

Getting in the wedding cars guests smiling and cheering as threw confetti at them, the headed for the reception.

.It was held in a local hotel called The Tree Lakes, the grounds were beautiful ideal for photographs.

David helped his bride out of the car, the rest of the guests arrived, had their photographs taken and headed for the reception.

As they headed through the doors, David looked at her and said "I`m so proud to call you my wife, and you look beautiful".

"And I`m very proud to be your wife, and you look very handsome", she smiled back , they kissed.

They went through the reception doors to a huge applause, from their family and friends.

They sat at the head table with their parents ,after the meal and toasting of the bride and groom, came the speeches.

They music started as they danced to "Woman" their first dance as Mr and Mrs Kelly.

David held her in his arms as if she were a delicate flower, whispered into her ear.

"I Love You".

David and Maria had a wonderful day.with their family`s and friend`s

After the guests had gone, they went to the bar and toasted each other. They then headed to their room.

David taking his brand new wife in his arms, started to undress her, with the greatest care he removing her wedding garments,

Then removing his own clothe`s.

He put her on the bed and started to kiss her mouth, neck.Then he ran his tongue down between her breasts.

He started to caress her and as they two of them became one, their bodies shook with excitement.

As they lay in the aftermath of their lovemaking ,he looked at his new wife,

"You are the most beautiful, gorgeous, precious woman, I could ever have asked to be my wife, and I don't just love you, I adore you."he smiled down at her.

Maria turned to look at him, stroking his face gently with her finger .

Tears in her eye`s she said to him "An I adore you darling, and will be the best wife any man could ask for".

David looked at her proudly " I could not ask for more than that ".

He lay back with her in his arms thinking what the hell else could man ask for ? .

He fell asleep in her arms and Maria lay there listening to him gently breathing .

Thinking to her self how lucky she was to find someone to love her .

Because all through her life all she ever wanted was for someone to love and care about her .

She eventually fell asleep . David woke her up the next morning with a coffee , they went and sat on the small balcony.

Maria stretched and looked at him lovingly , " When we have babies I want them to look like you." he said suddenly.

She almost choked on her coffee " David we haven`t been married twenty-four hours yet and your twittering on about babies. We have got loads of time for that lets enjoy the next few years".

" Take me to bed ," she whispered, climbing into bed he gently started kissing her neck, licking her breasts until the nipple`s were erect, slowing guiding his tongue to her special place.As she was about to climaxed slowly he entered her, teasing her, until she could take no more and pulling him to her, screaming out his name, as she climaxed.

Afterwards Maria falling asleep in his arm`s. He lay there never having felt so content in his life.

Waking to a rumbling in his tummy grabbing the phone he ordered breakfast.

Waking her to a fry up she looked at him smiling saying "Just what the doctor ordered".

"I did not realize how hungry I was" David said as he washed the last of his breakfast with a cup of tea.

"Mmm I was famished" she answered smiling at him.

"Lot`s of exercise can do that to you "

Picking the pillow up throwing it at him.

"I`ll have you for assault" he laughed, holding his arm`s up to protect himself.

"Oh yes you`ll have me for assault will you", she laughed.

Laying back they fell asleep in each others arms, David woke first it was early evening he

Slipping out of bed so as not to disturb his beautiful wife.

He got in the shower thinking how much this woman had changed his life.

Before her there had been lots of girl fiends but nobody like Maria .

She was so different from all the other girls he had gone out with for starters she was a

beautiful looking woman with long dark hair brown eye`s and always smiling.

There was never a dull moment around her .

So unpredictable and such an aura about her that anybody who met her could sense this she

wasn`t just a pretty face either.

She was very artistic which was very good for her job she also had a very vivid imagination

she could walk into the most dismal place and immediately see the potential .

He adored every inch of her, to be honest he could hardly remember his life before her.

He had the band which he loved singing in he had his football which he idolized his job he

didn`t particularly like but it paid the bill`s.

The shower started to run cold he grabbed a towel and rapped it round went back into the

room and Maria was sitting up in bed smiling at him .

" I`m just going to jump in the shower" she said to him

"Ok darling " he answered as he grabbed the a coffee and headed out on to the balcony.

He heard her scream " David its fucking freezing " he went inside " Sorry darling I must have

used all the hot water up , give it a few minutes and I`m sure it will warm up ".

Maria gave David one of her looks which meant he was in trouble .

He put his arms out to her , she went straight into them.

She looked at him with her brown sexy eye`s and he just melted into. .

Wrapping his arms around her to warm her up looking down at her saying" I`ll get you a

coffee darling".

She sat on the balcony sun shining in her eye`s he went over, passing her a cigarette.

"It has been perfect, worth all the effort" she with a satisfied sigh.

Holding her hand "It was darling" he smiled kissing her finger`

" What time are we meeting Shelly tomorrow at the airport " She asked. " 2 O`clock

darling"

Chapter Six

Their friend Shelly had invited them to London for their honeymoon .

They had met her when they had been living together before they got married.

The house beside them had been empty since they had moved in.

Maria arrived home one day to see some washing hanging on the line next door.

She opened the back door to find a very attractive blonde lady, in the garden.

"Hi I`m Shelly" she said in an English accent, "Hi I`m Maria, nice to meet you".

" Have just arrived over from England, this is my grandmothers house and I`m hoping to rent

it out" she explained.

"Oh I see, it`s been empty since David that is my boy friend and I moved in" smiled Maria.

"Fancy a coffee" "love one" said Shelly, as she jumped over the wall.

"How long are you here for" asked Maria asked she put the kettle on.

"Oh, as long as it takes ,I needed to get away, and thought Ireland is as good as place as any,

how long have you lived here," she asked as she looked about the place admiringly

"Just over a year, do you take sugar," Shelly nodded "two please, did you decorate this

yourself?"

"Yes I love decorating`"she answered. "You have done a bloody good job, I was thinking of

doing a bit myself next door, just to spruce it up a bit before I rent it out" said Shelly.

"I have never been inside, what`s its like?" asked Maria curiously."just let me finish my coffee and you can have a nose."smiled Shelly.

They headed next door, and when Shelly opened the door the smell of damp hit them.

There were sacred heart pictures and crucifix`s all over the place and wallpaper hanging from the walls.

The place gave Maria the creeps.

"Jesus Christ, Shelly you can` t stay here, you`ll end up getting ill, why don't you stay with us until you get the place livable"

Shelly looked at her`" That`s really kind of you but what will your boyfriend say?"

"Oh he won`t mind he is just like me easy going" she smiled "Grab your stuff and come on next door"

Shelly grabbed a bag and headed next door ,Maria showed her the spare room and

Saying "Make yourself at home".

"Do you know your so kind just like my mum and dad, Next door is where my mum grew up and Nanny lived there until she died two year`s ago,  no one has lived in the place since, that`s why it`s run down"

"Your Ma is Irish" said Maria.

 "Yes and my Dad " replied Shelly.

  The front door went and David walked in "Hi darling we are in here."

Maria went and kissed him and introduced Shelly to him.

"Hi, you didn`t tell me he was a dish" said Shelly, holding out her hand flirtatiously.

David held out his hand ,"Pleased to meet you".

Maria watched as Shelly flirted with David, she didn`t mind because she knew that it was only banter.

Anyway what was the point in jealousy it only led to unwanted rows .

Maria explained the state of the house next door and told David that she had invited Shelly to stay with them until she got the house sorted out .

"Hope that's ok , I promise I shall not be any trouble ".laughed Shelly.

Shelly had forgotten her cigarettes so she popped next door to get them.

"She`s a one" said David when she disappeared. .

"She`s ok her parent`s are Irish " she smiled at him.

"That is one of the qualities of I love about you nothing is ever to much bother".

He kissed her on the neck, "I`m just off for a shower to get myself cleaned up before dinner."

" Alright " she smiled as she pinched his bum . "Ouch " said David as he walked off to the bathroom turning asking " What`s for dinner ?" .

" Bacon cabbage and boiled spuds " She replied . " You certainly know the way to a man`s heart ".

"Off with you and stop talking shite " laughed Maria and she finished off peeling the spuds .

Shelly arrived back with a bag " This is for afters " she smiled as she put a bottle of Vodka, Southern Comfort and cans on the side .

David appeared out of the shower Shelly gave him a wolf whistle " He scurried into the bedroom .

Maria set the table and Shelly asked would she like a drink " After dinner " she smiled .

" Mind if I have one ? " asked Shelly " Help yourself darling I`m not going to tell you again make yourself at home ".

" I feel like I`ve come from one home to another " Shelly smiled as she opened the bottle..

David came out of the bedroom and sat down to dinner , the conversation was flowing.

"Oh shit we have ran out of lemonade" said David, "Ill just pop over the shop"

   "Is David your first love Maria?" Shelly asked Maria .

Swallowing the last of her dinner she shook her head , and a glazed look came over her

eye`s

,"No there was Liam,"

"Well go on don`t just leave me hanging" smiled Shelly settling back in her chair

"Well I was fifteen and my friend Sally and I used to go to the central nightclub every
Saturday night, " smiling as she remembered her first love.

New Chapter

Her and her friend Sally had just hung up their coat`s and their favourite song came on,
heading to the dance floor ,when two lad`s joined them.
"Hi I`m Liam" this blond haired lad with brown eye`s said to Maria.
"I`m Maria " she answered bopping away.
Maria looking at her friend , who was chatting away to the other lad.
The music slowing down and Liam shyly putting his arms around her, she could smell his
aftershave and recognized it as Brut, it was her favourite, she put her arm`s around him and
laying her head on his shoulder.
As the band played out Lady in Red, he pulled her closer, holding her as if she was a china
doll.
Maria looking over at her friend they both smiled and winked at each other.
They were both having a ball.
After the music stopped, they went to the bar to get a drink.Liam`s brown eye`s smiling at her.
She could feel her heart beating nine to the dozen.
Asking what she would like to drink .
"An orange please " she replied.
Getting the orange juices they headed over to the balcony.
"Where do you come from" he asked .
"Kincora " she smiled sipping her drink."And you?"
"Are you still at school?"
Shaking her head "No I`m training to become a hairdresser".
They sat looking over the balcony.
The night ending they left holding hand`s, finding Sally and Joe snogging in a corner , near
the bus that was taking them home.
"Don`t eat him" smiled Maria at her friend.
Joe grinning at Liam said"Shall we walk these two beauty`s back to the bus.

LIAM STORYNew Chapter.

"What about you ,have you have you ever been married?" Maria asked. David walked back in from the shop to find the girls in a very deep conversation.

She shook her head and answered " Nah nearly did once "

. " Oh what happened ?"

"It`s a bit of a story " Shelly replied sadly .

"Go on I`m all ears " said Maria . David looked at Maria and said "I`m going to pop up my Ma`s and leave you two too gossip."

"Ok darling tell her I can do her hair on Saturday morning" she said." see you later".

Maria got up poured the drink`s ,smiling at Shelly, "Right go on I`m all ear`s."

" Ok his name was Simon, we met in a pub surprise, anyway we got hammered and ended going back to his place".

Maria I didn`t fall in love with him ,I adored him we were together six months when he asked to marry him".

"Of course I said yes, well we set a date for three month`s later on Valentines Day , a month later I found him shagging my best friend in our bed".

" You what " said Maria, Shelly with tears in her eye`s and bottom lip quivering ,

She was choked up taking a deep breath continued,

"I came home from work one day after buying us a curry and bottle of wine, thinking he was at work,"

"I went in laid the table and then thought I`d put fresh sheets on the bed , Opening the bedroom door and there they were" .

Maria was snow white listening to this she was trying to imagine if this happened to her and David.

It sent shivers down her back to thinking about it.

" My God Shelly what did you do " asked Maria shocked .

"Oh I`m so sorry to have upset you" she had a lump in her throat and tears in her eye`s as she watched Shelly feeling her pain.

" I just stood there and screamed , I did not think it was me screaming because I felt as if this was not happening, it felt as if I was watching a horror film ".

" The next thing I knew I had a knife in my hand ".

" I don't remember going to the kitchen to get the knife, nothing ! ".

" The next thing I know there's blood all over my hands, I looked at the blood and then at Simon ,I had stabbed him in the ankle " she sobbed .

" God almighty Shelly that's unbelievable " sobbed Maria putting her arms around her.

Shelly put her head in her hand's, looked at Maria with tear's running down her face.

"You don't have to go on if it's too painful" handing her some tissues.

She shook her head and sniffled "No it's just that I have not spoken out loud about it for a while"

Maria could see that she wanted to continue ,she wiped her own eye's, and said "Go on".

I ran out of the flat and home, my Dad caught me as I fell through the door,

 "What's wrong ?","I was sobbing ,could not talk, he took me inside and poured me a brandy.

I was shaking from head to toe, eventually I calmed down and explained what had happened.

He shook his head at me, and asked "How badly hurt is he?",

"I don't know",

"God almighty, I knew you had a temper, but this goes beyond it all" he shouted.

" I'm going around there now " he shouted and stormed out, I just sat there and shook.

He wasn't long gone ,he came in and said" He's alright nothing more that a cut he'll live ".

"Oh Da what have I done" sobbed Shelly " Nothing more than he deserved ".Snarled her Da.

Shelly looked at him eye's red raw from crying and nose running.

" Oh for Jesus sake Shelly clean yourself up " sighed Patrick , as he passed her a hankie .

She took it and blew her nose " Is he calling the police ? " she asked tearfully .

"Nah he`s not that stupid a bit shook up , but it`s like I said to him what did he expect you to do, offer him a cup of tea ?".

She let out a little laugh he looked at her " That's better now go and put your face on or what ever it is you do , and we`ll go round there ok ? "

She nodded went to the bathroom put some lippy on, coming out her Dad handed her another brandy and said " Ready ? ".

 Shelly downed the brandy in one and nodded , they jumped in the car and drove round to Simon`s .

When they walked in Amanda, Shelly`s best friend couldn`t look at her.

Simon was in the kitchen with his foot in a basin of water. " Shall I put the kettle on ? " asked Patrick sarcastically .

 " What ever " replied Simon .

" Don't get smart with me boy or I might just finish the job Shelly started " shouted Patrick .

Simon looking at him, could see the anger in his face.

Shelly looked at Simon and the rage erupted inside her. She went for him pulling his hair and scratching his face.

Patrick went and pulled her off of him , " Jesus Christ Shelly calm down " he said .

"Calm down Dad" she screamed " Calm down your asking me to calm down after he`s slept with my best friend ?" screamed Shelly .

Amanda came into the kitchen , " Shelly I`m so sorry it just happened " sobbed Amanda .

" Get out of my fucking sight or you never know what I might do ? ". she screamed blue in the face with temper.

Amanda grabbed her coat and fled the flat sobbing . Shelly screamed after her " You fucking slag this is not over yet ".

Patrick grabbed her horrified to see his daughter in so much pain .

He looked at Simon and said " If I were you boy I`d get out of town because when I tell my lads what`s happened ,lets just say they wont be happy " .

"Dad help me " Shelly was on her hunkers in a corner of the room gasping for breath.

She looked at Simon ,choking said" I hope you die in hell you bastard ".

Patrick picked her up and took her towards the door, she looked back at him sitting with his feet in a basin of water looking totally ashamed and pathetic.

She wanted to drown him in that basin of water as Dad led her out through the door.

He got her to the car sobbing her heart out, he put his arms around her and hugged her tightly .

She had always been the apple of his eye, his baby girl .

" Come on me darling you`ll get through this you're a strong colleen ".

His heart was breaking seeing his daughter in such a state, they got home and Shelly drank the rest of the brandy, went to bed where she stayed for three days.

" But I am still here to tell the tale " sighed Shelly as she finished.

Maria slouched back in the chair and said " My God that is unbelievable , where is he now ? "

"He`s still in London , moved a few miles from where we lived , I still see him now and again ."

"My heart still does a little somersault but its not racing like it used to , I`m coming to terms with it"

David walked through the door to see two pair`s of tear stained eye`s staring back at him.

He went to the kitchen to pour himself a drink but both bottles was empty.

"See you girl`s have been busy" he smiled holding up the empty bottles.

"Christ have we finished it" said Shelly.

"Yes I`ll just pop over the shop" he said grabbing his wallet.

When he came back he was glad to see the mood had lightened . Maria was on one as she telling one of her stories .

Shelly looked and saw what David had in the bag . " Now there`s a man after my own heart "

smiled Shelly.

David put the bottles on the table and smiled at Maria asking " What would you like ?" .

" Do you have to ask ? " she replied .

" Not really but since we have a guest I thought I would be polite " he smiled back at her .

" Do we have ice " asked David .

"Yes Hun in the bottom draw of the freezer ".

David bringing in the glasses, ice with the brandy and vodka, put an ash tray on the table

with a bowl of crisps and nuts .

Shelly watched in amazement , " My God has he got a brother ?" .

"Yes " smiled Maria " he`s got three ".

" Are they married ? " laughed Shelly.

" Two of them are "

" What about the third ? ".

David replied " Gerry he`s a chef in Waterford , we don`t see much of him "

" That's a shame ? " said Shelly " Does he look like you ? ".

" I don't know I never thought about it " he smiled as he poured the drinks .

Chapter 5 .

" Do you remember the first time we met Shelly ? " asked Maria .

" How the hell could anyone forget that? " replied David.

" Do you know on a time scale we have only known her three months ? But it seems like we

have known her all of our lives ".

"Yes it seems that way, but she is a bit like my darling wife , you get addicted to people like

you and Shelly, you cant get enough of them ".

" What shite are you talking now ?" asked Maria curiously .

" Just like I said, Shelly and you have got personalities that people love being around , your both fun very unpredictable and bloody hell ! You never know what`s coming next . Your different your not the usual run of the mill and you both say what you mean whether its what want to hear or not," he grinned.

" Ok I agree with that " Maria answered smugly .

 " Oh God that will swell your head even more "smiled David jokingly " Come here to me woman ."

He took her in his arms and gently kissed her and they made love ,falling asleep in each others arms.

Maria awoke, she gently slipped out of bed so as not to waken David, showered, wrapping herself in a towel,she headed out on the balcony, sat there with a coffee and a cigarette enjoying the morning sun.

She was thinking how good life is, David appeared kissing her neck, she smiled up at him.

"I`m going for a shower"

"Ok darling, you carry on" she replied. Finishing her coffee, going back inside to pack.

She looked at the time again, it was 7.30am."David what time are we leaving for Dublin at?"she shouted.

He had just got out of the shower and put his hands over his ears jokingly.

"Christ I might be hard of hearing, but I`m not deaf" he laughed.

 " I thought you were still in the shower""

We can have breakfast and then head to Dublin" he answered.

"Ok" she replied and started to get dressed.she put on a long white dress with a slit up the side that reached the thigh.

,

She looked stunning in it, David turned and whistled, saying "My God wifey, you look stunning"

"I know", she replied, cooking her head to one side, He grabbed her and started to tickle her.

"Get off," she screamed,

"I have to your far too cocky" he laughed.

"No I'm not ,I'm one of the most modest woman you could meet", she laughed.

"What you? Who are you talking about?" he asked standing back, looking about the room his face looking very puzzled.

This made her laugh, he picked her up and swung her around the room.This made her laugh even more.

He gently laid her on the bed and made mad passionate love to her, falling asleep peacefully in each others arms.

David woke up with a start, looked at the clock ,nudged Maria," Darling wake up, we have

to get going."

She sat up rubbing her tired eyes, smudging her make up, looked down at the crumpled dress on the floor.

"Christ David I can't go looking like this" as she pulled a pair of leggings and top out of the case.

She pulled a pair of black boots on, looked at David as he stood there shaking his head.

"What"? she asked, getting annoyed, "Nothing just Ms Vanity peeking her rare little head out again.

"Oh come on , you know what I'm like ,I cant got to Dublin to get on a plane in a creased dress."

"My God almighty, that would be breaking one of the ten commandants" replied David

sarcastically.

"OH shut up" she said as she gave him one of her annoyed looks.

"Oh, come here to me", he said as he held his arms out to give her a hug.She stormed off .

He sighed "Oh come on don't get all moody on me, come on Maria, please."

She turned around and looked into the blue eyes and wilted. She hugged him.

"Sorry for getting upset but, I do have principles"

"Oh God I know all about your principles, they come big, small ,little and large" he

laughed.

Maria burst out laughing at this description of her principles , David picked up the luggage .

They headed downstairs to pay the bill " Did you have an enjoyable stay ? " smiled the

receptionist.

" Everything was spot on , thank you very much indeed " replied David .

"Yes it was lovely " smiled Maria opening her purse and giving a her tip .

" Thank you Madam " smiled the grateful receptionist . " Your welcome ".

They picked up the suitcases and headed for the car . They started their journey to Dublin .

As they pulled into the airport , they could see Shelly waving madly at them .

Maria got out of the car and David went to find the long stay car park .

He joined Maria and Shelly in the bar after he'd checked them in.

Shelly had already got the drinks .

" What time do we board " asked Maria , Shelly answered " We have over an hour yet ".

" Have you got the tickets " asked Maria " Yes darling I have got the tickets " said David

impatiently .

" Well you can remove that attitude Mister " smiled Maria

" What attitude ? " he smirked.

Maria gave him a playful box on the head . " Oh I`ll have you for assault" he giggled. .

" Will you two love birds leave it out " laughed Shelly .

Maria headed to the loo , " It is lovely to see you two so happy " sighed Shelly .

" Do you know I could not believe it when she said yes " said David.

"Why" she asked a curious look on her face.

"Because she could have had any man she wanted " he replied .

" Yes but she didn`t and now she`s your wife " said Shelly matter of factually .

Maria came back from the loo and asking

 " How long will it take to get to London ?".

" Just over an hour " Shelly replied .

 "I`m exhausted" said Maria as she leaned her head on the back of the seat,

"You know what`s wrong with you, It's the come down the anti climax " said Shelly .

" Do you know I think your right what with a huge build up ,now its all over I feel like a

deflated balloon all the airs gone out of me " sighed Maria .

They had another drink and then heard their flight being called and headed for departure.

They boarded the plane , Maria slept on David`s shoulder most of the way.

CHAPTER SIX

They landed at Heathrow just after 3.10pm ,grabbed a taxi and an hour later were outside

Shelly`s flat.

They got inside, "God this is lovely "exclaimed Maria as she wandered about.

The living room was very nicely decorated, with a bay window overlooking the park.

 There was a beautiful Welsh dresser with some Waterford crystal in it.

The carpet was a pale pink, which matched the corner suite, in the center a glass coffee table.

"Is it ok to look around the rest of the flat Shelly?"asked Maria, beginning to come to life again.

"Christ you have woken up" she smiled,

 "That`s what she is like" sighed David;

"She gets the stuffing kicked out of her, give her an hour`s rest and she is back in full swing".

Giving her a hug, "Don`t you darling".

Maria gave herself a tour of the flat, and fell in love with it. The bedroom`s were beautiful,

The main bedroom was decorated in cream, lovely thick carpet with matching bedspread and curtain"s.

The smaller bedroom was decorated in peach. Maria presumed that this would be their bedroom.

She went and found Shelly in the kitchen, "Oh Shelly I love it" she smiled, "Did you find your love nest?" "Is it the peach one?" She nodded.

"Is it ok for you?"

"Ok it`s like being in the Hilton", Maria smiled.

"I would not go that far" replied Shelly, "Did you decorate it?" Shelly shook her head .

"No my sister lived here before she got married, she had impeccable taste."Shelly replied.
"She certainly had, it`s like a palace", "How long have you lived here" David asked.

"Coming up a year now and everything is around me, there` takeaway`s the offie most

important" she laughed.

"Right how about some food, I`m famished" said David."Well downstairs, there`s Chinese or a fish and chippy"

"What do you fancy darling?" "I`m easy" she answered, "Oh yea" David smiled pinching her bum.

"Get off" Maria snapped, "Oh getting a strop on are we, I was just having a laugh" David growled back."Oh come on you two, I fancy cod and chip`s" said Shelly,

"That sound`s good to me" answered David, "I`ll go and get them, then I`ll pop to the off license, Do we need cig`s?"

"No darling we bought 200 in duty free "laughed Maria.

"God I`m losing it as well ,""he smiled as he popped out."Are you ok ? You don`t seem yourself, "asked Shelly.

Maria looked at her "Oh I just need to recharge my batteries, I`m physically, mentally and emotionally drained"

"You`ll be ok get some grub inside you a couple of drink`s, some sleep `and you`ll be as as rain in the morning"

"I never realized how much this wedding lark has taken out of me" she sighed.

"Well I don't know, but I can imagine ,I know when my sister got married she told me she spent the first day of their honeymoon in tears. She had no idea why",   "

"I`ll be ok tomorrow, just need a bit of me time, David can be a bit smothering at times"

"I thought you liked being the center of attention" ,said Shelly looking at her surprised.

"I do but sometimes I feel suffocated by him, I like to be able to breath by myself" she sighed.

"Look were two very independent women, And whatever man try`s to tame us, well he will have a job on his hands" They both creased up laughing.

David arrived back to find the two of them in much better spirits, much to his relief.

He dished out the fish and chips for them, and poured them a drink."You're an angle "smiled

Shelly.

"I know only things missing is the wings" he replied cocking his head to one side.

The ate ravenously " Christ that was just what the doctor ordered "said Maria as she burped.

"Pardon me" she sniggered.

"You are pardoned Madame, want another drink" asked David.

 Shaking her head, "No darling I`m done in I`m going to bed"

Giving Shelly a peck on the cheek, and kissing David she made her way to bed.

"Goodnight darling " said Shelly and David in chorus, They laughed.

She got into bed and no sooner had her head hit the pillow, she fell asleep.

"Do you think she is alright" David asked Shelly as soon as she was out of ear shoot.

"Lord David all you have to do is look at her ,you can see she is worn out"

"I`ll have one more and the I`ll retire myself ,if that`s ok"?

"I`ll join you" Shelly answered.

He poured them another, and the chatted.He finished his drink and said "I`ll hit the

sack"

Looking at him "You two just make yourselves at home and enjoy yourselves"

"Thanks Shelly you're a good friend"

"So are you goodnight David"

Shelly wandered off to bed not long after.

David went into the bedroom where Maria was snoring her head off.

He got into bed and cuddled her and drifted off to sleep, he still could not believe

how lucky he was to have her as his wife.

 Next morning David awoke first, kissed Maria on the cheek and slipped out of bed gently,.

He wandered into the kitchen ,Shelly was already there "Morning, how is sleeping beauty?" she smiled

"She is still asleep", replied David in a surprised tone."I have never known her sleep for so long, she is normally up with the lark."

"She was knackered" Shelly smiled.

"What`s the time?"

Shelly looking at her watch replied "It`s 10 30".

"What`s the plan for us today?"he inquired as he poured them a coffee.

"Right today I thought we could pop into town, grab a bit of lunch ,and just have a stroll around the shop`s."

"Yep that sounds like a plan, Maria will enjoy that "he answered.

"Maria will enjoy what" inquired Maria as she wandered into the kitchen.

"Morning darling" said David as he went to kiss his new bride.

"I did not hear you get up" she said smiling.

"Oh I was just asking Shelly what we were doing today "

"And the verdict ?" she asked.

"I thought we would have a wander into town, grab a bit of lunch and a wander about the shops" answered Shelly.

"That sounds good too me, Christ Shelly that bed is so comfortable, I dropped off the minute my head hit the pillow."

"Yes it is I used to sleep in it, when I stayed with Karen" replied Shelly.

"Where is she now?"asked Maria yawning." I`m not used to sleeping that long"

Oh after she got married ,she moved to a town called Stevenage, its on the outskirt`s of London",

"Right while you two are nattering, I`m going to have a shower" said David.

"Coffee" ,Shelly asked Maria?

"Please" she nodded Maria went and put her arms around Shelly.

"What`s that for?" Shelly asked

"Because I appreciate all your doing for us"

"Look I`m just returning the hospitality show you shown me" she smiled.

"I love you girl, I knew the first time we met , that we would be friend`s"

"So did I" smiled Shelly, David came into the kitchen, all showered and spruced up

"Mm you smell nice," Maria smiled, "Right my turn" she said giving David a kiss.

  Shelly had already, showered and changed turning to David she said

"When Maria is ready I have just rang me Dad and he has agreed to lend me his car to go into town"

"That`s handy" said David, "Where do they live?"

"Just up the road, you can pop up and meet them before we head into town"

Maria arrived out, David turned and said "Were going to meet Shelly`s parent`s"

"Great, and then head into town?"

 "That`s the plan" replied Shelly.

So they headed off , it was just a stone`s throw up the road from the flat.

 Shelly opened the door and shouted" Mum, Dad were here",

Patrick Shelly`s dad was the first to greet them, "Jesus come in it`s a pleasure to meet you"

Biddy came into the room, "Ah at long last, Shelly told how good you were to her when she was across the water"

"Be God she did and a friend of her is a friend of our `s, now what can I get you to drink?

"I have Brandy, Whiskey, Vodka or Guinness,"

"A whiskey sound`s good" smiled David.

"Be Jesus you're a man after my own heart" smiled Patrick as he poured him a large one.

"And what is your tipple Maria?"

"The same as mine" said Shelly,

 "What a vodka?"

"Yes please" he poured them to large one`s,

"Now Shelly don`t forget your driving" said Biddy, taking note of the measure.

"Oh for God`s sake, stop nagging" laughed Patrick, Biddy had a tea towel in her hand which she playfully hit him with.

"Do you see what your letting yourself in for David? You need to show them who`s boss" Biddy swung the tea towel at him again as he jumped out of the chair, escaping to the kitchen.

They all laughed as Biddy followed swearing at him.

"Do you know they have been married 34 years and it`s always been like this"

"It`s lovely to see the still got a sense of humour to share, let`s hope were like that" smiled David.

"I`m sure you will" replied Shelly as she poured herself another large vodka.

"Cheer`s" she said as she raised her glass, "To us darling" David said as he clinked glasses with his wife.

"Yes to the newly wed` s" said Patrick as he came back in the room in a very cheerful mood.

He sat down, and started singing, "Oh God here we go " said Biddy pretending to be mortified.

He belted out the good old tune Danny Boy, they all joined in.

Maria getting in the mood started singing A Group of young soldier`s. Patrick joined in.

The crack was in full swing, the never did get into town that day instead they drank lot`s.

danced and sang into the early hour`s of the following morning

Next morning Maria and David awoke ,they had no recollection of the evening

before.

And no idea where they were, she looked at him through misted eyes,

"Where the fuck are we, I can`t remember a God dame thing"

"Jesus I`m going to be sick" he answered he rushed out the door.

Luckily he found the loo before he threw up.

Maria was not feeling much healthier than her hubby, He arrived back from he bathroom.

Looking half dead.

"Where is they loo" she gasped, "Straight in front of you" he panted.

She was ill and feeling very shaky, as she headed out of the toilet, looked up and saw a

 vision of what looked like Shelly appeared in front of her. ,

Shelly with her mascara halfway down her face hair matted together. She looked how Maria

felt like death warmed up.

"Shelly where are we" she squeaked. Shelly looked at her and burst out laughing.

"My God you're a sight for sore eye`s" ,Maria squinted at her and said,

"You don`t look like no oil painting yourself"

Shelly squinted in the mirror turned to her and said, "We look like the horror sister`s"

Maria looking at her and asked again "Where are we?"

"Were in my mum`s" she said coughing.

"Where did you think we were", she asked as she tried to catch her breath.

Shaking her head "Had no idea,".

Going into the bedroom were David lay white as a sheet.

"Were in Shelly`s ma`s house" explained Maria,"

"Oh God I never want to see another drink as long as I live" said David trying to lift his

 head.

"Come on get your bit`s and well head back to mine" said Shelly.

"Oh no I can`t move" croaked David.

"Well you stay here ,can you remember your way back to mine?"

"No I`ll come with you" he groaned."what `s your Ma and Da going to think"

"Well me Dad is still half pissed downstairs and Mum is snoring her head off in the other room"

"It`s not the first time they have got themselves like this and it won`t be the last" Shelly half smile.

The three of them half staggered, half walked back to Shelly`s.

It was Shelly`s turn to be ill, which she did very unladylike on the pavement.

Which in turn made Maria and David ill again.

So there stood all three of them on the pavement being ill. What a sight that was'

They held on to each other and staggered the rest of the way back to the flat.

Luckily it had started drizzling so they did not have to worry about cleaning up.

Shelly started laughing, and all of a sudden was collapsed on the ground.

Maria and David picked her up and between them half carried her home.

They got her inside and she headed straight to bed ,were she stayed most of the day.

David went to bed for a few hour`s and Maria just lay on the couch watching telly.

A few hour`s later David emerged from the bedroom to find his wife asleep on the couch.

He grabbed a duvet off the bed and covered her with it. She moved a little and then went back to sleep.

David went for a walk and realized that he was outside Patrick and Biddy`s house.

He went and rang the doorbell, a very hungover looking Biddy answered the door.

"Christ it`s you David, where`s the girl`s?"

"There both asleep" he said.

"Christ where my manners gone, come in lad"

"Thanks where`s Patrick?"

"Oh he is gone to bed ,Lord knows how I made it upstairs last night"

"Is he bad" David asked."

"Bad ? He is as drunk as a skunk from yesterday"

"How are you feeling?" He asked politely.

"Like a bear with a sore head, Jesus I have had hangover`s in me day but this take`s the biscuit."

David started to laugh, "It`s not funny I have been sick in the toilet and look at me hand`s their shaking like leaves"

"Would you like a drink, or a cuppa" she asked.

"Tea would be lovely please"

"Sugar"

"Two please"

"There you go" said Biddy as she passed him the cup.

"How are you feeling? ".

"Well apart from being ill this morning, sleeping half the day, and as you said shaking like a leaf. Not too bad, I`ll tell you something you and Patrick are mighty crack. I have not enjoyed myself so much in year`s. I`m sure Maria will tell you the same."

"Well now I`m going to tell you something, no nation in the world know `s how to enjoy themselves like the Irish .And where would we be without the bit of crack?"

She got up and put the kettle on ,"Would you like another cuppa?"

"Why not" he answered smiling.

"Why not indeed, I am glad you enjoyed yourselves, you make a lovely couple, and I hope you will be very happy together" said Biddy very sincerely.

"Thank`s right Ill head back make sure that my two girls are ok"

"Make sure you pop around before you go back" he said smiling opening the door for him.

"We will and thanks again" he kissed her as he left.

"Good luck lad" he turned smiled and waved.

Biddy thought to herself as she closed the door, if I were a few years younger,

And then laughed to herself and thought, the old body might be withering, but the mind is

still very young.I wonder if Patrick is up?

David arrived back to find the two girls still asleep.He popped to the shop and bought a few

things he thought they might need including aspirin.

He got back upstairs, to find Shelly rutting through the cupboards.

"Looking for these" he asked as he held up the aspirins.

"Oh thank you" she said gratefully, "Why do we get ourselves into such state"

"Seems like a good idea at the time" he smiled.

She looked as if she was going to be sick again, she swallowed.

"Never again" she answered as she ran for the bathroom.

David looked up to heaven.

Maria came into the kitchen, "Jesus I think I`m going to be sick again"

Shelly came out just as Maria was making her way there, "Good job I was finished" gasped

Shelly as she headed back to the bedroom.

Maria arrived back, grey in the face." Are you ok darling?" David asked concerned.

"Jesus do I look ok, stop asking stupid questions"

 "Ok clam down, it`s not my fault"

He answered looking hurt. "Oh baby I`m sorry" she regretted what she said.

Shelly appeared out of the bedroom, "Feeling any better" David asked.

She shook her head, "Just came out for some water" she whispered.

"Well at least I had a narrow escape" said David jokingly.

They both looked at him with a puzzled look on their faces.

"Oh I just meant it got me out of the shopping trip." Shelly threw a tea towel at him.

"You and your mother are bloody dangerous women, I popped into see them today" he

added.

Shelly looked at him surprised, "Did not know you had gone out" piped in Maria.

"Well the two Madonna`s were nursing their hangovers, and I felt like a bit of fresh air,

So I wandered by and recognized house ,so I knocked on the door and had a cuppa with

your Ma."

"Bet she was pleased to see you" said Shelly. This seemed to perk them up a bit.

They went into the living room and Shelly looked at Maria and said," Do you know what

would perk us up?"

Maria was sitting with her eye`s closed," What"? She asked opening one eye.

"A hair of the dog" she answered, pulling out a bottle and pouring herself a small one.
s
"Want one," she nodded ,"Just a tiny one" Maria went into the kitchen to David staring out

the window,

"Are you ok darling" "Yes I`m fine, just thinking about when we get back"

She hugged him saying, "And what wonderful thoughts are you having?"

He turned to her kissing her cheek, "I think when we should think about buying a house"

"Good idea for when we get back. But at this moment were still on honeymoon"

He looked at her "I love you" he smiled, taking her in his arm`s.

"I love you too" she said looking up at him with those wonderful brown sexy eyes.

"Oh leave it out I feel sick enough already" Shelly said in a very envious voice.

Grabbing bottle of vodka, from underneath the cupboard and wandered back to the living

room.

"Oh dear I think we have upset her" said David.

"No I think she is still getting over what his name, Simon"

"Hungry darling" he asked, She nodded, "Shall I get us a Chinese?"

Maria wandered into the living room where Shelly was sitting looking very sad.

"Are you ok hon?"Maria asked looking at her concerned.She looked up and nodded.

"Yes I was just reminiscing, when I saw you and David it still hurts, just thinking about

what might have been"

Maria went and cuddled her, "David is getting a Chinese, fancy some?

"Yea that sounds good" "David came into the room, "Right my two angles what can I get for

you".

They gave him their orders, "Ok your wish is my command" he smiled as he walked out.

"How are you feeling now" Maria asked,

"As rough as fuck, but at least the cure has lessened the shakes" she giggled.

"I know is it sad when you have to have a top of alcohol to sort us out" smirked Maria.

Shelly laughed, "Well these things have to get done, and we did have a top nosh day"

"Oh yes, "replied Maria," Your parents are brilliant."

"Yes they are,do you know, when we where growing up, on a Sunday after lunch, we would

sit in the living room, my Dad with a whiskey in his hand and my mum standing beside him

with a gin and tonic, singing the Irish ballads.My dads favourite is Danny Boy, that is

probably why I detest the song"

"My favourite is A Group of young soldiers" Maria said."Well go on give us a bar then"

"I sang it yesterday"

"I can`t remember so go on" encouraged Shelly.

She started singing "A group of young soldiers one night in a camp,"

David coming up the stairs could hear his wife singing.It made him smile.

He arrived in with the food, dished it up and took it into the living room.

Maria looked up at him, her eyes smiling, he looked down at her and could feel the hairs

stand on the back of his neck.

He adored everything about her, as he listened to her finish the song.

Shelly and David clapped as she stood up and taking a bow laughing,

He passed each of them their food," Thank you "she said a tad out of breath,

Shelly looked at her and said "That was absolutely beautiful"

"Glad you enjoyed" she smiled flicking her long hair.

"Mm this is really good" Shelly said as she tucked in.

"Oh its delicious" said Maria "I`m beginning to feel human again"

"Glad your enjoying it" replied David nearly choking.

"I keep telling you not to talk with your gob full" scolded Maria.

He looked at her and smiled, "Ok goby ,I`m not a child"

She threw a cushion at him ,nearly knocking the food out of his hand.

"Ouch" he laughed, "Come here you silly sausage" as he pulled her towards him.

She went to him and he held her as if he would never let her go.

Shelly looked at them feeling very envious."You two are so lucky" she sighed.

"I know" smiled David, as he kissed her. Shelly held the bottle up, "Too you"

David took the bottle from her, she seemed a bit pissed.

Maria and David looked at each other, "Right were going to call it a night"

Shelly looked at them, "Go on then spoil sports" she slurred.

"Ill just finish this and Ill retire myself"

"Good night Shelly" "Good night my two love birds" she waved.

They laughed as they headed into the bedroom.

Maria turned to David and he kissed her passionately.

He then slowly began to remove her clothes. She lay on the bed as his tongue very ,very slowly ran down her tummy and slid between her legs. She moaned loudly.

She was about to climax when he pulled his away.She screamed, "Don't stop"

He looked at her and gave her a teasing smile.He then put his tongue back to finish what

he had started.Pulling the pillow over her face, she screamed as she climaxed and her body fell back on the bed exhausted.

David then came up to her with his erect penis, she slowly started to lick it and as her tongue slipped over his penis she could see the sperm shining at the top of it

She wiped some of the sperm from it and put it in her mouth to taste.

She looked at him and could see the pure lust in his eyes, she then put the whole of his penis in her mouth as he gasped.

The sensations running through his body were breath taking.

She slowly removed it from her mouth and guided his now throbbing penis inside of her.

There love making came to a very passionate end.They lay in each others arms exhausted.

They fell asleep, Maria awoke a while later needing a wee.

She slowly untangled her body away his and got out of bed. On her way to the loo she heard snoring.

She stuck her head into the living room to see Shelly stretched out on the couch, half empty glass in her hand.

She went to the loo ,then pulled a quilt out of the cupboard out of the and put it around her friend.

She climbed back into bed, were David lay snoring, she wrapped herself around him, and was soon sleeping.

David awoke first and turned over, admiring his beautiful wife, he could feel a tingling in his groin remembering the passion of the previous night.

Maria awoke and could feel his erect penis in her back.She turned over and started to massage it. He moaned his as he slipped his fingers inside of her,! "Your soaking "he said.

"That`s what you do to me" she sighed with that gorgeous smile of hers.

He melted inside of her as they climaxed together.

It felt as if they were both breathing with the same pair of lungs, sharing the same heartbeat they felt totally one.

The feeling was excelling and they had never felt so close. He looked at her and said,

"You my beautiful gorgeous wife are the best and I love you with every bit of my being".

She looked into the blue sexy that she had fell for," And I adore you darling"

She had never felt happier in her life.

They heard Shelly next door showering. .

"She was sparked out on the couch last night when I went to the loo".

"Well that's what topping up with vodka does for ya" he answered, "Would my darling wife like a coffee?"

"Oh that sounds wonderful please "she said beaming at him,

She watched as her gorgeous husband left the room, she snuggled back under the covers.

Thinking how lucky she is," Its ready darling" she heard him call.

She got out of bed and went into the kitchen, put her arms around him.

He looked down at her and kissed her."Do you two ever leave it alone?" Shelly asked.

"We are on our honeymoon, darling" Maria grinned."Oh I know don`t rub it in"

She went over and hugged her ,"Right I`m off for a shower; by the way what are we doing today?"asked Maria.

"Well I will tell you one thing we are not doing, and that is consuming alcohol "answered Shelly .

Maria did a little dance as she left the room," She`s on one today" smiled Shelly.

"That`s the effect I have on women" smiled David his blue eyes sparkling.

Shelly looked at him fondly, thinking it probably is.

"So what surprises have you got in store for us today?"

"How about we get a bus into town and take in a few of the sights "she suggested.

"That sounds good" David said as he gave her a hug."What was that for?"

"Because it felt right"

"Oh whatever" Shelly tutted.

Maria appeared in a beautiful red dress, with red high heeled sandals, hair and make up done to perfection.

David looked and gave her a wolf whistle, Shelly turned around,

" You look fab, right I`m off to make myself look more beautiful than you, " she said as she headed off.

"I have just made you a coffee "he smiled as he pinched Maria`s bum.

"You are good to me" she smiled "where are the cigarettes?"

"There on the living room table "he answered.

He watched her walked through to the living room.

God she is one sexy woman, he thought,

She sat on the balcony enjoying her cigarette and coffee. He joined her.

"Happy" he asked as he sat beside her.

She looked at him before she answered, "Do you know this is the first time in over a year, that I have actually sat with a coffee and a ciggy and actually relaxed"

"And yes darling I`m very happy "she bent over and kissed him.

"Good that's what I want, my darling totally relaxed, and enjoying herself."he smiled.

Shelly arrived in the room, dressed in a black jumpsuit; and ankle boots, with the hair wild and wonderful,

"You look"

"I know amazing" Shelly answered before Maria got a chance to finish her sentence.

"Vanity or what" laughed Maria,

"Well when you got it you got to flaunt it" Shelly sang as she did a little dance.

They all laughed."Right my turn now" said David as he danced .He headed off to the bedroom to grab his wallet.

"He is great" Shelly as she headed into the kitchen to make some coffee.

"Yes" as she followed her into the kitchen,"what time are we leaving?"

 Shelly passed her coffee.

"As soon as David Bowie is ready" Shelly said as she lit a cigarette.

They sat on the balcony enjoying the morning sun, David joined them all spruced up.

"Christ you scrub up well", smiled Shelly enjoying the view.

Maria went over to him, she loved the smell of him, kissed him and said,

"Yes he scrubs up very well, and Shelly he is all mine ,to smell, to lick or do whatever else comes to mind" Maria joked.

"Your disgusting" replied Shelly as she shook her head, "Right are you guys ready to get this show on the road?"

"Right lets do this" said Maria as she lead the way out.

The bus stop was only outside the flat. The jumped on the number 8 that took them into the center of London.

David and Maria were overwhelmed by the size of the buildings and the mass of people.The got off the bus in Oxford Street, Shelly decided that Trafalgar square should be the first stop. They stood there amongst the pigeons having their picture taken.

Next stop on their tour was Big Ben.

"Fucking hell" .Maria screamed as her angle went from under her in her high heels.

"I`m going to have to get some flat shoes, my feet are killing me".

"That's ok darling, where is the nearest shoe shop?" David asked Shelly.

Shelly pointed across the road ,Maria looked and saw the longest line of shop's she had ever seen in her entire life.

Crossing the road, and Maria tried a pair of red mules on."Christ that's better" she sighed in relief.

David paid for them as Maria did a little skip out of the shop.

"That better?" asked David, "Oh yes thank you"

They three of them then walked to Madame Toussauds, they were totally enchanted.

Maria could not believe the life likeness of the mummies, she found it totally fascinating.

After this amazing experience, Shelly took them to a quant Chinese restaurant where they had lunch,

"That was delicious" said David patting his tummy. Maria agreed "Yes it was just what the doctor ordered."

David picked up the bill, and the next item on the agenda was to see 10 Dowling Street.

By this time they were beginning to feel very fatigued, between the heat and all the walking.

"I think it's time to say goodbye too London for today" said Shelly.

She looked at them and they nodded in total agreement.

David had undone, the top buttons of his shirt, and lost the tie. Maria had tied her hair up as the sweat was running down her face.

They caught the bus and were back in the flat within the hour.

"Oh Shelly that was wonderful! I absolutely adored Madame Tusords.I have had a day that I shall remember forever"

"Yes thank you Shelly, We had a lovely time " said David as he fell on the couch.

"Well I'm glad you enjoyed it ,and I'm glad we were able to make it.The state of us yesterday we would not have been able to wipe our asses if our lives had depended on it" she laughed.

"Never a truer word said", yawned David. .

"What time is it" asked Maria,

" Time you got yourself a watch" he replied dryly.

"Oh piss off and stop being so smart" she snapped back at him.

"Now children there is no need to quarrel", laughed Shelly "It`s 6 30 darling"

"I could murder a drink "Maria said as she kicked her new shoes to one side.

"Oh that sounds good" replied Shelly as she slouched in the arm chair, "David do the honours"

"Oh bloody hell, just let me get changed, and I shall be at your beck and call",\ he sighed.

Appearing in a bath robe he poured them a vodka each" Ice "he shouted, "Please" they shouted in chorus laughing.

"Shelly is there any whiskey left, "David asked "No were fresh out" shit he thought as he made his way into the bedroom to get dressed,

"I`m just popping down the offie, want anything"

"Oh be a darling and grab some Tortilla chips" Shelly said.

He popped down to the Offie got his whiskey and the Tortilla chips and ran back upstairs with the goodies

The two girls were settled in the living, with their drinks.David gave them their Tortillas.

"Thank you "smiled Maria with that mischievous look in her eye`s; he looked at her replied raising his eyebrows "It's a pleasure".

Shelly looked at them and said" I`m popping around my mums, do you fancy it?"

Maria looked and saying "If my poor little pins have to take another step they will go from under me"

"No we`ll take a rain check on that but tell Patrick and Biddy we will pop around to see

the before we head back to The Green Isle".

"Ok you two enjoy and don`t do anything I wouldn`t do" she laughed

"Well that is leaving the gap wide open" Maria shouted after her laughing.

"We will be good", David reassured her .Shelly put her jacket on and left.

David poured them another drink, and Maria put her head on his shoulder.

"I have really enjoyed today" she sighed."It`s not over yet "he whispered.

He took her in his arms and kissed her on the neck, this sent tingling sensations

down her.

She guided him to the bedroom, were they gently undressed each other.

David took control, and laid her on the bed and started to kiss her feet and ankles.

His tongue gradually smoothly glided up the inside of her thigh, until she was morning.

He by passed her special spot and gently licked her nipples until the were standing up erect.

She was getting inpatients, so she started to push his head towards her special spot.

He put his tongue on her clit and played there until she was soaking wet and screaming with

pleasure.

He was taking her to heights she had not realized existed.David then entered her and they

both climaxed .

Afterwards they lay locked in each others panting, absolutely exhausted.

"That my darling was the best" he sighed as he lay back with a very contented grin on his

face.

"I know darling" she smiled as she stretched out on the bed, purring like a Cheshire cat.

David lay stroking her hair, they fell asleep. And were awoken by Shelly returning.

"I`m getting up" she said as she pulled a black satin pyjamas.David pulled on his jeans and t

shirt.

They went into the living room, "Hi, wonder what you two have been up too?"she smiled.

"Look what I bought for us" as she held up a bottle of vodka."There`s half a bottle in the kitchen" said David.

"Oh don`t worry it won`t go off" David got the glasses and poured the drinks.

"Thank you" smiled Maria," Yes thank you "said Shelly you're a gentleman.

Maria looked at him and thought, yes what an amazing man she had married.

He held his glass up and toasted to friends."Yes to friends"

David looked at Maria with his sparkling blue eyes.She kissed him.

And whispered "To us" Shelly saw this but did not say anything; just looked the other way.

Maria clocked this and went and gave her friend a hug.

"Don`t worry sis there is someone waiting out there to sweep you off your feet"

"It`s ok ,its just that when I look the two of you ,I can`t help remembering what Simon and I had."

"Oh Shelly your still raw ",said Maria sympathetically as she went and hugged her.

"I`ll never forget what happened, the intensity of the pain he caused me" she sobbed;

"Sometimes I can hardly breath, and when I see him I do think my heart is going to stop"

"Oh Shelly, It will ease. " said Maria as she knelt in front of

She looked at Shelly and said" Do you know your one hell of a strong woman, you have got this far, you will get the rest of the way.I love you and we will be friends forever"

Shelly hugged her back, as she whispered "You know that don`t you"

"Yes I do" she half smiled back at her friend.David always felt award in these situations.

"Come on you two, your getting far too sentimental" interfered David.

"Oh piss off," Shelly snapped," I`m just saying what I feel"

David a bit shocked with this reaction, He apologized,

" Oh come here "said Shelly feeling bad at her reaction,hugging him.

"Oh my hubby, cannot handle raw emotion" said Maria trying to lighten the atmosphere.

"Oh well, I 'm afraid David but emotions is what makes the world "sniffled Shelly.

"Oh lets have a drink, and forget about the toe rag, "suggested David

"Good idea "answered Shelly, as she blew her nose.

Shelly headed to the loo, David turned to Maria and said" Put my two feet in it there"

"Don`t worry darling, we all need a little outburst now and again"

"I just hate upsetting anybody "

"Oh for Gods sake just forget it" Maria snapped.

"Now what have I done?" He asked looking puzzled.Maria put her eyes up to heaven.

She poured herself a drink, "Want one "He nodded looking like a little lost boy.

She started to laugh, Shelly came back from the bathroom, "What`s funny?"

"Oh look at the little face, he hate`s upsetting anybody ,and now wants to be forgiven"

He decided to play the game, put his finger in his mouth and started sucking on it.

Shelly went and sat beside him," Oh I`ll show you how nice I can be"

"Now come here to me pet, and Auntie Shelly will let you have a little drinkie poos"

"Oh you want to play that game, do you as he started to tickle her"

"Oh no she screamed, get off me"

"See two can play that game", he laughed as he drank his drink.

They then decided to watch a bit of telly.The bottle disappeared quickly.

Shelly stood up and waddled to the kitchen, hiccuping on her way.

David looked at Maria and said "I`m done in, I`m going to hit the hay"

"Ok darling I won`t be long",

" Take your time " he said as Shelly arrived with the vodka.

"Oh your not going to bed David"

 "I have had enough for today" He kissed her ,then Maria.

"Sleep well" said Maria as she blew him a kiss.Shelly poured them a large drink.

"Trying to get me drunk?"asked Maria. "Look this bottle has been the best friend and

painkiller, since" she hiccuped "Well you know"

Maria diverted the conversation away from relationships.With Shelly talking shite by now,

she decided to go to bed.

She got the quilt out and put it on the end of the couch, "What are you doing" slurred Shelly.

"Just in case you get cold" replied Maria as she kissed at her goodnight.

They rest of the week flew by. They went for a walk the evening before the headed back

saying goodbye to, London holding hands.

Maria was lost in thought, "Are you ok darling". She looked at him, "I think we should move

here"

David looked at her in total disbelief, "What you want to leave Athlone and our family`s"

She nodded "Yes why not" she answered "It would be a whole new adventure in our lives"

"Well because I don`t want to leave our life back home or our family`s"

She could see she was getting his back up ,"Ok we can talk about it another time"

she answered sadly.

He looked down at her and could see the disappointment in her eye`s.

"Oh come here to me "he said as he put his arms around her, "Let`s just go back home

and start our married life before we make any rash decisions"

She looked at him thinking he`s right, you always` s have to run before you can walk, she

scolded herself.

David held her and said, "Let`s just get home" she smiled "Yes let`s go home"

That evening they went and said their goodbyes to Patrick and Biddy.

"Your always welcome here" said Patrick as he kissed Maria and shook David`s hand.

They headed back to Shelly's, Maria packed their stuff, they enjoyed a few farewell drink's

And soon they were saying fare well to `Shelly. Taxi arrived, The girl's looked at each other

with tear's in their eye's.

"I'll miss you" sobbed Shelly she hugged her friend, David was putting the suitcases in the

taxi,"

I'll miss you more" said Maria with tear's running down her face.

"Come on you two" said David with a lump in throat.He hugged Shelly and thanked her for

the amazing time they had.

She hugged him back tears running down her face,

"It was a pleasure ,right I'm going back in, I hate goodbye !s, you take great care of each

other",

She ran back into the flat.

 They got in the taxi as the pulled away, Maria looked up at the window and could see

Shelly waving like mad.

Maria waved at her until they were out of sight. She sat back and looked at David

Saying "We have had a wonderful week."

 He put his arm around ,"Yes, it was great."

"I would really love to move here" she sighed as the headed to the airport ."OK lets get home

and see what happens" he answered as he kissed her head.

CHAPTER 7

"Ok" she smiled and snuggled up to him"

There flight was on time, so the arrived back in Dublin on schedule.

The got their car and headed back to reality.

David parked the car outside the house and carried his bride over the threshold

"Oh it feels good to be home" he said as he put her down.

She looked around and smiling answered "Yes hon it does" He went and parked the car.

"Where do you want these?" He asked as he brought the suitcases in.

"In the bedroom darling ,Coffee?" "Could murder one "he answered'

He came into the kitchen, put his arms around her and said" "This is the beginning of the rest of our lives"

She smiled at him, "Yes it is" as she put her two arms around him .

Maria headed to the bedroom and started to unpack. "Darling shall I get us a chip supper"..

"Oh a chip supper," she smiled "that would be very appealing" He grabbed her to tickle her.

But she knew what was coming and ran out in the garden.He went and got the fish and chips'..

She had set up the garden table, with some candles ,and a bottle of wine.

He brought the plates, as the sat in the evening sun, eating "The clinked each other"
He looked into those beautiful blue sexy eyes ,as she said," I don`t think I have ever been this happy"

"Nor I, my adorable wife" he smiled, She looked at him and could see such emotion in his gorgeous blue eyes.

She kissed him gently on the lip`s, "Its getting nippy" ,They cleared the table and headed inside.

"I`m shattered darling" "Me too "he smiled ,They went to bed and slept soundly in each others arms.

She awoke first, and turned to see David snoring gently beside her.She gave him a kiss and went into the kitchen and put the kettle on.
She jumped in the shower, put her dressing on, David came out of the bedroom, sneaking up on her and grabbed her by the waist.

She screamed, "Christ, don`t do that, you nearly frightened the shit out of me" she scowled.

"Oh I`m sorry sweetheart", They went into the living room, David turned the telly on.

"Well we are back to work tomorrow hon", "Yes" she sighed."What`s up?"he asked.

"Nothing I just cannot believe it all over, all the months of anticipation ,stressing, that everything went so smoothly"

"Well sweetheart it all went really well, you looked beautiful, and I`m so proud that you're my wife"

She looked at him" I cannot believe how lucky we are" she smiled.

He put his arm around her," Well I do" he whispered as he starting kissing her neck.

She responded, he lifted her up and carried her into the bedroom, were they made love. Afterwards they fell asleep in each others arms.

David woke up first, he gently pulled back the covers and slid out of bed. Went into the kitchen and put the kettle on.Maria woke and followed him and giving him a kiss said" I love you David".

He looked down at her and holding her in his arms replied "I adore you, my darling"

They cuddled, watching the kettle boil.He made the coffees as he passed it to her she looked at him and said" I don't want to go back to work"" Neither do I but unfortunately were back in reality."

"That we are hon", Maria unpacked the suitcases and got their work clothes ready for the following day.

Watched some telly and soon it was. time for bed.

Soon the alarm was going off ,Maria switched it off and called David as she pulled the curtains.

The morning sun hit him straight between the eyes."Christ that sun is strong "he complained.

"Yes" she sang "It's a beautiful morning" "How can you wake like that?"

"Like what" she sang jumping on the bed laughing.

"I`m going for a shower" he said as he threw back the covers.

"I`ll make us some coffee" she said as danced out to the kitchen.

She was waiting outside the shower, for him with a kiss.

He kissed her back, "I`m going in the shower, coffee`s on the side" she smiled.

He was ready to go to work when she came out of the shower.

"I`m off darling" he said giving her a kiss" Oh by the way, don`t cook tonight"

"Why" "Because I`m taking us out" "Oh anywhere nice?"

"The Swan, so I can show my new wife off" he smiled.

""Whoo" she smile

."Oh and do me a favour, wear that little black number I bought you in London"

Giving her a wink as he left. She headed to work shortly afterwards. She had brought

photographs to show everyone, of the wedding and the honeymoon.They mooned over them.

Then their clients started coming through the door and it was back to work.

After work she went for a drink with the girls, and in away was glad to be back.

She headed home to find David with a pile of paperwork on the table.

He looked up as she walked in" Hi darling, I have cooked us something to eat instead of us

going out. "

"What`s all this" she asked?

"Well, I popped to the estate agents today and picked up some property leaflets" ,he smiled.

She was very surprised, "Christ you don`t waste time".

"Look there is some here that are in our price range" he smiled."

Ok then lets have a peek" she smiled.
They browsed through," Oh I like that "she said getting at excited at the thought of them
owning their home.

"So do I" he agreed, nodding his head.

"I`ll ring the estate agent and make an appointment, to go and view it".

"Oh darling, us owing our own home," she said hugging him.

He hugged her tightly, as he kissed her head, saying "It`s the next step".

He got on the phone and made an appointment for the next day.

"Oh I cant wait" she said as she did a little dance.He laughed he loved the way she expressed things.

"Lets go for a walk and have a look", she said," Lets eat first I`m starving darling" he said.

They ate their meal, and then took a wander to see the house.

It was not far from where the lived.She held his hand tightly as the house came into view .

"Oh David look" she smiled," It`s lovely" leaning over the wall, it had a lovely garden.

It was an end of terrace, had a driveway and new double glazing.

"It look`s empty so that means we could move in straight away" she said getting over excited.

"Now stop running before you can walk" he smiled, "we will see the inside tomorrow and then we will decide"

She turned and kissed him and said, "We will love it, I just know we will "as she skipped ahead of him.

He looked at her "There is three that are in our price range"

"I know but it will be this one that we are going to buy" she sang.

They walked home with her talking ten to the dozen. He loved her energy.

Next day they went to the estate agents, "Hi I`m Declan ,I believe you're here to look at 43 Treetops` estate."

"Yes ,that's right" replied David.They shook hands."Ill just grab the car keys, and we`ll be off"

"It`s a three bedroom semi detached property" he said as he lead them to the car.

"We had a walk to see it yesterday, it looks lovely" said Maria.

"You know the area then?"

 "Yes we live just at the front of the estate"

"That's great " he smiled as he opened the car door.They were soon at their location.

As they entered ,there was a long hallway, Declan showed them the living room first.

"As you can see there is double glazing, this is a nice size living room",

Maria looked at David and winked, he smiled back at her, next was the kitchen.

The kitchen was huge ,it had a dinning area, "What`s the asking price?"David asked.

"£18,500" replied Declan, Maria was looking out the back window, David let out a slow

whistle.

"That's a bit more than we were budgeting for".

"Let me show you the rest of the property, and then you see what your getting for your

money" replied Declan.

He showed them upstairs, there was the master bedroom, with built I wardrobes a nice sized
second bedroom and a box room.

"This would make a lovely nursery" said David.

Maria looked at him," Your jumping the gun a bit""

"Just thinking out loud" he answered.

"Right " said Declan "Ill leave you two to wander around, Ill be downstairs"

"I love it" said Maria as soon as she knew he was out of ear shot.

"Don`t you think we should look at the others?"asked David.

" What for?" She answered.

He shook his head and knew there was no point in arguing.

"Ok Ill go talk numbers with Declan" "I love you", she smiled as she kissed him.

"No you just love getting your own way "he smiled as he went downstairs.

She stood in the bedroom imaging the colour scheme, what carpet the would pick.

Downstairs David put an offer in, and as Maria came back downstairs she saw them shake

hands.

"Ill get back to the office, put your offer to my clients and have an answer for you by the end

of the day" Declan said as he locked the door.

"Great " said David, "speak to you later" They waved as he drove away.

"Oh David I`m so excited" she said as she jumped up and down.

"Clam down the deal is not sealed yet"" Lets go for a drink" she said squeezing hand.

She was so excited that as soon as the got to the Swan, she blurted out to Brendan the barman

their news.

David shook his head," Can you never keep that closed" pretending to be cross.

"That's great news" smiled Brendan, as he poured their drinks.

"We have just put an offer in there is nothing concrete yet"

"It will be soon you know, when you just know the result before it happens" she smiled.

 Brendan shrugged smiling" I`m sure the result will be positive".

"What time have we got to phone him?" "A few hours" he answered.

They finished their drinks, and as they walked by the estate agents on their way home.

"Lets see if they have an answer yet" Maria said as she pulled him by the arm inside.

"You have absolutely no patience at all" he said, Declan looked at them.

"I was just about to ring you", he smiled" I have just got off the phone from the owners and

they have excepted".

"Oh my god, you're a diamond" she screamed, as she ran around the desk to hug him.

Declan a tad taken back by this outburst, looked a little embarrassed.

David noticed," Excuse my wife she gets a little over excited"

Maria looked at David and replied "I`m a woman that's my job".

They laughed, "That is amazing news" said David, "where do we go from here?"

Declan explained the procedure, as Maria chatted to one of Declan`s team.

They got outside and she kissed David ,saying "Thank you darling"

He looked at her and smiling said "You make me so happy"

She put her arm through his and said "I want us always to be like this"

He looked down at her "Snap so do I you're the best thing that ever happened to me"

"This is the beginning of the rest of our lives" she said as her brown eyes twinkled back at him.

She sang beside him the whole way home.She had never felt so happy in her life.

The next day after work ,they headed to the estate agents to fill out the paper work.

Declan shook their hands and congratulated them, giving them a date to pick up the keys.

Maria thought about kissing him but decided against it. David saw the look and took her arm and escorted out of the office .

Outside she hugged him dancing on the street singing" We done it" A celebration drink is in order" smiled David.

"Definitely" she smiled. They held each others hands tightly as the headed to the Swan .

Brendan knew without either of them saying a word, that there dream had come true.

"Looks like congratulations is in order" he beamed at them.

"Who told you" asked Maria a little shocked since they had just found out themselves.

"Your face told the story as usual"" Please and one for yourself" said a very proud David.

"He looks like someone who`s got the cream "Maria said as she leaned on the counter.

"Well he has" said Brendan a bit envious, "He`s married to one of the finest bits of stuff around town and now the two of you have bought a new love nest"

He passed their drinks, "What more could a man ask for?" "Money" laughed David.

"Money cant buy what you got" he replied as he went to serve the next customer.

David had a grin on his face after these complements.The ended up staying their the rest of the evening celebrating.

New chapter 8

The weeks flew by, and soon the were in their new home and all moved in.Maria got busy

working, decorating and buying furniture. David was back doing his own thing, after work

he was either playing football or out with the band.

After the decorating was finished, Maria went back to modeling a few evenings a week.

And then selling Oriflame cosmetics which brought in extra money. David had weekends off.

But his time was filled up with Friday and Saturdays nights out with the band, and Sundays football.

Maria worked Saturdays and normally had a parties on these nights selling her cosmetics.

Plus she had her modeling, to say the least they both lived very busy lives.

Before they knew it , it was nearly their first wedding anniversary.

David took Maria out that evening and wined and dined her, and bought her a beautiful eternity ring.

Through the meal the florist arrived with a beautiful bouquet of Maria`s favourite flowers.

Her eyes filled with tears, as she looked at David with those sexy brown eyes.

She bent over and kissed him ,he looked at her and said "Anything for my princess"

She looked at him and said "Christ I nearly forgot" as she pulled his present out of her bag.

He opened it to find a beautiful signet ring inside, with both their initials inside.

"Oh darling its perfect "as he hugged her.

They strolled home slowly hand in hand, enjoying the evening breeze.

David made love to her that night, afterwards she lay panting beside him.

"Do you know I cannot remember the last time we made love".

He leaned up on one elbow saying" Oh come on its not that long"

She looked at him and said, "Can you remember?"he lay back down and shrugged his shoulders.

She sat up in the bed and said "Actually we hardly spend any time together"

"What do you mean?"he asked yawning.

"Precisely what I said, look think about it, we both work during the day"

"Yes that is correct" he answered, She gave him one of her looks.

"Oh God now what have I done?" "Will you take me seriously" she snapped.

"What do you suggest, we both work, you have your modeling and your cosmetics party`s" she sighed.

He continued" And I have my work, football and the band.So where do either of get this spare time?"

She thought about their situations looking at him, and answered slowly,

"Well maybe one day a month we should designate, just to you and I you spending together"

"Yes that sounds like a plan" he replied rather absentmindedly kissed her turned on his side and went to sleep.

She listened to him breathing, and dosed for a while herself.

Next morning, as she made their coffees, he came up behind her kissed her neck.

"Right I`m off "he said as he grabbed a piece of toast, "Oh I`m out with the band tonight don`t wait up"

Maria sighed, she seemed to be doing a lot of that lately.

She sat and looking out on her garden, now in full bloom.

Her mind wandered back to this time last year, the fairy tale wedding, the honeymoon in London.

They had never had so much fun or been so close. Since they arrived home they seemed to be drifting apart.

Then she scolded herself, come on they could not stay on honeymoon forever.She went showered, got dressed and headed off to work.

On her way to work she was still trying to pinpoint why she was feeling like this.

Gone was the attentiveness the magic. This made her feel very sad.They were only a year married.

The week continued and on Friday she suggested, that they might spend Sunday together.

He apologized, but he had football and a gig on Sunday night."Sorry darling" he said as he got his football kit together.

She looked at him saying" David we have to find time for each other"

He took her in his arms, "Darling we will but right now I`m late".

He was gone.She felt like she was banging her head against a brick wall.

Feeling a bit low she rang Joe, when he heard her voice he asked what the matter was.

"Nothing except I was just wandering what your up too" "Well nothing I was going to wash my hair" he giggled.

"Fancy going to the pup?"she asked, "No not really, we have got an early start in the morning"

"Oh Christ I`d totally forgotten about that, good job I rang" "Ok see you in the morning"

She rang off.She went to the shop and got a bottle of vodka and some cigarettes.

Headed home put a video on and curled up on the couch.Poured herself a drink and settled in for the night.

She looked at the clock it was well after midnight, no sign of David. She went to bed.

Her alarm was going off before she knew where she was.David was snoring beside her.

She got out of bed , she had not even heard him come in.Showered and dressed she headed off to work.

 Joe was there with a coffee ready for her, "Hi Doll" he said as he heard her running upstairs .

"What time are the due" Marie asked, "Any second now" he answered as they heard the chitter chatter coming upstairs.

Maria welcomed them, got Nora to shampoo ,who was the new Saturday girl.

Maria chatted away to the bride to be, as she compared notes on weddings.

Soon all the wedding party was ready and off the went. They wedding was in the Bridge House.

Maria and Joe were invited to the evening reception, so as they wished the bride good luck and promised they would see them later.

After work Maria had taken a little black number with her ,so she changed in the salon.

The two of them headed off after work.It was in full swing when they got there.

"What`s David up to tonight?"asked Joe, "There playing in Mullingar tonight"

Good thought Joe who was not overly fond of David," Why" "No nothing, I was just wondering if he would be joining us later"

She shook her head, "Can`t even remember if I told him I was going" she sounded sad.

Joe gave her a cuddle, he had always thought Maria too good for him.Always thought David a bit stuck up his own arse.

They had a really good evening, with some bloke, called Johnny doing his best trying to chat Maria up.

"I wouldn`t have said no" said Joe looking at the quirk little bum heading to the bar.

"Behave yourself,"" I am" he sniffled as he headed off to the bar.

"Coming to Spiders?" asked Joe as they bar was closing.

Why not she thought, David wouldn't be home for ages.

They headed to the nightclub arm in arm and ended up getting hammered.

Maria woke up the next morning and couldn`t remember a thing. They looked at each other both suffering.

Neither of them could remember getting home and they both woke up hungover.

It was Sunday so Maria didn`t have any work that day but David had to go to football.

She wrapped her arms around him, pleading with him to stay.

He unwrapped her from around him saying" I`m sorry darling I have to go it`s coming up to a cup final"

She started sulking, "Well go then, I might just have to find someone who might pay me some attention"

He got up from the bed giving her a filthy look, got dressed and left without even a goodbye.

She fell back to sleep.And woke up feeling very delicate after the night before.

She showered dressed and walked to the local.Went in there was the usual crowd.

"Hi Maria "waved Nick, she strolled over to him."Where`s David?"

"Oh he is right beside me, spending quality time with his wife" she answered sarcastically.

He looked at her puzzled, this was not the Maria that everyone knew and loved.

She looked at him, "Sorry Nick I`m just having a bad day" she could feel her voice choking up, with tears stinging her eyes.

"He`s at football" "Is everything ok? "he asked getting concerned.

"Oh come here to me" sighed Nick putting his arms around her. She went into her friends arms.

Nick looked at her thinking how could any man put a game in her.

He gently kissed her brow in a friendly way."Usual pet?" "Please" she hi cupped.

Nick called the barman" Two large vodkas and coke please Ollie"

"Coming up Nick" he smiled.

She gulped her drink down," Another one" she asked Nick.She ordered the drinks and headed to the loo.

As she peered in the mirror, she did not think a lot of what reflected back at her.

Looking back at her was two bloodshot eyes and dull skin.Turning away she thought, your heading down the wrong road girl.

The band had set up when she returned to the bar and were playing her favourite song.

She started dancing, Nick joined her and soon she was back in the swing of things.

She ended up getting very drunk and again she couldn`t again remember getting home.

Following day she woke up, there was no sign of David.She crawled out of bed.

Looked at the clock it was 1.00pm.Her head was banging, her mouth as dry as sand.　　　 ,

she half staggered to the bathroom.

 Brushed her teeth, trying to see if she could discard this undesirable taste from her mouth.

She sighed, went downstairs thinking to herself David must be at work, searched the

cupboards for some painkillers.

Went and lay on the couch, hoping that the headache would subside.She dosed off.

David arrived home to find her asleep still in her dressing gown.

She opened her eyes, he looked at her with total disgust on his face, walked out of the room.

She heard him put the kettle on, and called "David can I have a cup of tea please"

 He came into the room with a cup of tea for her."Thank you" she said in a very small voice.

He sat beside her and said "Maria this has to stop".

"Stop you were as drunk as I was on Saturday, and yesterday when you stormed off, what

was I supposed to do" she asked crying.

"Oh nice one so I get the blame for you going out and getting totally rat arsed ".

Maria was totally taken aback at his outrage, she could feel her bottom lip begin to quiver.

He looked at her and just walked out.

She heard the front door slam, and looked out the window to see him drive away in their car.

Tears of frustration appeared in her eyes as she looked out the window.

She went upstairs showered and got dressed.Ringing her friend Martina.

When she heard her voice, Maria just burst out crying.

Martina said "I am coming over give me half an hour."

She went into the kitchen, trying to pull herself together she heard Martina`s car pull up.

She opened the door and immediately Martina saw how upset she was.

"Whatever`s happened"?

 "Oh Martina it`s all my fault" she sobbed.

"I went out last night ,met Nick and ended up getting hammered, I don`t even remember coming home, he was gone when I got up, when he got back I was still in my dressing gown. He just glared at me and then shouted at me for getting pissed"

"What, and that is it, he get`s pissed often enough ?"

"Well he just walked out" she was really upset.Martina put her arms around

" Oh Maria what`s the matter really, There`s more to this than you getting pissed last night"

"Yes there is, I feel like we are growing apart, He is either at football or with the band in the evenings, so I filled up my time with the Oriflame and I do two or three nights a month modeling."

"Well look you have just pointed out the problem, so all you need is to talk and make time for each other simple."Martina sighed.

"Do you not think I haven`t tried that?"she sobbed.

"Oh come here " she said as she hugged her.

 Martina sighed "No one can do this only the two of you, I`m sure you know that already"

Maria nodded as she blew her nose.They heard the door went.

"He`s back " whispered Martina.

David walked in," Hello Martina saw your car outside what`s she looking for? Sympathy"

She looked at him and in an annoyed tone and answered ,

"There`s no need to speak to her like that, you can see how upset she is".

"Oh I can see that all right" he smirked "want a cuppa?"

"Na just had one" she replied, "Right I`ll be off leave you two to talk"

She gave Maria a kiss and whispered phone me, "See you soon,"

She went over to David" Go easy on her and talk but you most of all listen ok" she pecked him on the cheek and was gone.

Martina got in her car thinking The two of them needed their heads banging together everything going for them health, good looks a lovely home.

Ah well it was down to them at the end of the day she sighed as she drove away.

Back in the kitchen Maria looked at David saying "We really need to talk"

He put his hand up "I haven`t got time , I`ve got band practice tonight" he said as he put his jacket.

With fresh tears in her eyes she looked at him" Oh David please we have to sit down and work through this"

He pecked her on the check and was gone.

She sat there sobbing, I have had enough for one day she thought and headed upstairs to bed.

Later she heard the front door go looked at the clock, it was 11.00pm. She went downstairs to find David and two of his friends there.

They were as pissed as arseholes.

"Hi Maria, do you want a drink?"hiccuped Brian at her.

"No thank you" she answered.

David stood up unsteadily "Isn`t she gorgeous lads? And do you know she is all mine" he slurred.

He made a grab for her but she stepped back as he fell clumsily on the floor.

Brian and Eddie finding this very amusing and started laughing hysterically.

.Maria went to help him up from the floor and looking at the lads said "I think you better go home"

"Oh no you don`t " snarled David at her "Your not calling the shots."

She backed out of the room and flew upstairs.They carried on downstairs until the early hours.

 Eventually the left he somehow made his way upstairs and staggered his way in beside her.

She was still awake, she climbed out of bed, between the odour of drink and the snoring she thought she would go mad.

She went down stairs into the living room, opened a window to let the smell of booze,

Looked at the overflowing ashtrays and the empty can and bottles.sighed tidied up got a cup

of tea.

She eventually dosed off was woken up by the milk man.She looked at the clock it was
6.30am.
She went upstairs to have a wee, as she was sitting there David arrived in the bathroom with

his hand over his mouth.

She made a very quick exit, sat on the bed until he had finished being ill. He arrived back in

the bedroom looking like death warmed up.

"Is this your way of getting even?" She asked.

"Oh don`t start" he groaned as he stuffed his head under the pillow.

"Where`s the car?"

"Maria just go away, I`m dying here "

"I want to know where the car is " she said raising her voice.

"He looked at her, his eyes so bloodshot, they looked as if they were going to pop out of his

head. "I can`t remember"

"Oh for Christ`s sake David" she screamed.

"Piss off" he shouted back at her.She had enough.She got dressed went downstairs grabbed

her bag and jacket and flew out the door banging it as loudly as she could.

She went in search of the car, eventually she found it parked at the back of the pup.

She got in it and headed to Martina`s ,she was outside cleaning her windows.

She looked up when she heard the car, smiled and waved at her.

"Hello" Maria looked at her."Oh dear things no better then come on in".

Maria shaking her head, nearly in tear`s.

Going inside, Martina put asking "What`s happened now?"

" Jesus Christ things are going from bad to worse, "she said as Maria filled her in on the night before.

Martina looked at her and sighed.

"Do you know I was just thinking yesterday as I left yours what a lovely couple you make, you both have your health, your young, got your own home and here you are mucking it all up. What is it with you two?"

Tears in her eyes "When we got married, we had a fantastic honeymoon we had never been so close, but since we got back and especially the last few months, we just seem to have drifted further and further apart"

"Yes but Christ Maria you have just been married five minutes, are you going to give up already?"Martina sighed as she passed her a cuppa.

Maria was a tad taken aback with the abruptness of Martina`s attitude "No I`m not I`m" Martina putting her hand stopping her in mid sentence,

"Look I`m telling you how I see it you know I don`t mince my word`s "

"I think your both being pathetic and need a good kick up the arse, don`t look at me like that, you know I`m right"

"I know your right but it doesn`t make it any easier" said Maria drying her eye`s.

"Well I`m sorry but there is no magic answer, as `I said to you yesterday there is only two people, that can sort this out, and that is the two of you "

Maria nodded "I know but any time I say to him we need to talk he is always too busy"

"Well then you will just have to give him the ultimatum, don`t ask him, tell him you have to talk".

She hugged her saying "Come on your stronger than this"

Maria hugged her back and said "Thank you my friend" Martina smiled at her saying,

"What the hell are we all here for if we can`t help each other out"

"Now go on off with you, get yourself sorted, think positive girl and I`ll see you real soon"

Martina watched shaking her head as she dove off.

As she drove home she was going over in her mind what she was going to say to David.

She pulled up outside the house and her heart sunk as she saw one of David`s friends cars parked outside.

As she was going in her neighbour Francis called to her "Hello Maria your garden is looking good."

"Thank you Francis" her mind else where, "Fancy a coffee" "No thanks, things to do" she replied inattentively.

."Another time" smiled Francis.Maria smiled at her as she opened the door.

The noise nearly deafened her, she could hear David shouting at the telly.

"Come on you stupid bastards, kick the fucking thing".

She opened the living room door to a fog filled room of cigarette smoke.

As she went in, David looked up at her and said "Here she come`s my lovely wifey"

He went to put his arms around her, she shoved him off, saying "I`m making some tea anyone want some?"

"Na were all right" Ollie replied holding up a can.she closed the door on them, went into the kitchen. Where she sat drinking tea.Thinking now what do I do!

She continued on as she normally on her day off , cooked dinner, caught up on the washing. Pretending they were not there.

She sat on her own eating her dinner, not feeling really hungry.She poured herself a drink.

By the time David`s friend`s left, his dinner was ruined and she ended up binning it.

He staggered into the kitchen slurring, "I`m off to bed"

She just looked at him with disgust ,took her drink into the living room and watched some telly.She could here him bumping about.Sat there thinking what a disaster, if this is his way of getting even ,well he has made his point.

She eventually wandered upstairs.to find David lying on his back, snoring his head off.

She did a double take and went into the spare room.

She awoke up the following morning to the sound of David being ill down again.

Lovely she thought and headed as she headed downstairs to make a cup of tea.

He arrived down and stood beside her looking very ill and embarrassed.

She put a cuppa in front of him as he sat staring out the window.

"There`s no point in asking how your feeling, I can see " He looked at her asking

"What is happening to us"

She sighed thinking has the penny dropped at last?

"Look we really need to talk, and I mean talk not just skimming around things"

"Ok" he agreed," lets do it then", Shaking her head "No the timing is all wrong"

"Why" he sighed, "Mainly because you have a hangover and I`m majorly pissed off with

you".

He put his head in his hands and started to sob, Maria felt no pity for him, she knew the

feeling-hungover, ill, feeling sorry for yourself.

She went to the fridge to make herself a sandwich, asking if he wanted anything to eat.

The look he gave her answered that question."I`m going to bed" he said as he got up from the

chair knocking it over.

She picked it up answering "OK"

The next few day`s passed, Both of them working, David going to band practice and his

football.

By the weekend they were tired of the silence.Maria turning to him asked "Don`t you think

it`s time we put an end to this atmosphere?"

He looked at her and nodded."Yes it is getting a tad tedious" She put the kettle on and sat at

the table.

"Well where do we start" she asked?"How has it gone so terribly wrong?"he asked.

"Well the reason I went out the other night is because I'm fed up of being on my own in the evenings"

"Well that's not my fault" she put her hand up before he got time to finish,

"Look if were going to start blaming who done what we might as well not have started this conversation"

"Well you started it " he answered in self defence.

She could feel her bottom lip trembling, she didn't want to cry.

"I was just saying ,why I went out" she answered crying.

"I just feel you don't want me anymore" "Oh darling that was never my intention" he was crying now,

David put his arm's around her as she clung to him. They two of them crying he took her in his arms and brought her upstairs,

They made love like the hadn't for a long time.Afterwards they held on to each other like their life's depended on it.

They lay there crying for a long time, looking at her as he turned on his side, tears rolling down his face.

"I don't ever want to loose you, my baby girl" he said as he held her closely.

"Or me you" she answered hiccuping. They stayed in bed David apologizing profoundly.

She looked at him saying "I need to apologize as well"

David smiled and sniffled "Apology accepted, I love you so much"

"And I love you " she replied as she snuggled up to him.

"All we need to do is too make time for each other" she smiled as she looked at him.

He just melted into the brown eyes, his heart doing a little flip.

"Yes and we will as he took her in his arm's and started making love to her again".

They fell asleep.He woke up and sighed a sigh of satisfaction glad they were back on track.

He looked at the clock, it was five am. Went downstairs and made a cuppa.

Maria awoke and stretched out in the bed, feeling warm in the aftermath of their loving making.

She got out of bed and found him staring out of the window.

She put her arms around him kissing his neck. He turned to her "I love you"

He took her in his arms and made love to her over the kitchen table.

She smiled at him, kissing him "I love you too" she looked at the clock it was seven am.

"I'm just going to shower, and get ready for work"" Ok "he smiled as he smacked her bum.

He could hear her singing in the shower, it was music to his ears, after the silence of the last week.

She came out of the shower, and he went in kissing her nose.

The phone rang, she answered "It was Joe saying that she could have the day off as the had no water.

"Ok will we have water tomorrow?" "I bloody hope so" he said, "OK doll I1ll see you tomorrow"

David asked "Who was that?" She explained what had happened.

"Oh by the way I have got football practice tonight, it will be a late one".

"Ok darling Ill see you later" she kissed him as he left.

It wasn't often she had a day to fill, so she decided to give the house a good spring clean.

Satisfied that the house was now speck and span she decided to go and do some shopping.

 She bought some fillet steaks, onions rings which she knew was David's favourite,

She set the table with some candles their best cutlery, that she had put away for a special occasion, thinking this was a very special one.

The phone rang it was Martina, "Hello doll how is it going?"

"Good" she replied, "Every thing is back on tract."

"Oh darling I'm am really pleased, is David with you" "No he's going from work to football practice"

"Well the girl's and I are going to the pup tonight if you fancy us"

She declined saying "That she was going to do her best to make her marriage work."

"Good for you ,if you change your mind" "I won't ,see you soon" she hung up.

Looking at the clock she poured herself a drink, thinking David should be back any second.

She settled herself on the couch, a while later she went and cooked dinner, took a cheesecake out for afters.

Looking at the clock, thinking he should be home by now. "She rang the pup asking if he was there"

She got the reply she wasn't hoping for.He got on the phone, "Hello darling"

"Don't you fucking darling me" she swore down the phone."What's up?"he answered.

She totally lost her patience, "So much for wanting our marriage to work, You stay with the lads"

"Maria stop going into one, I'm just having a few pint's and then I'll be home" he sighed.

"No' no" she screamed down the phone, "Stay where you are with your football cronies and enjoy yourself"

"Right I will" he answered, she slammed the phone down.

Tears in her eyes she ran upstairs put on her black dress and black high heels and headed to the pup.

As she walked in Martina looked at her very surprised."Maria let me get you a drink you look as if you could do with one"

Brendan the barman looked at her" Usual Maria" she nodded "Make it a large one" said Martina.

"Christ what`s happened?"asked Martina? Maria filled her in on the evening before, how they had talked and made love, thinking every thing was back on track.

"So give a guess where he is now?" said Maria thinking I`m going to choke here trying to hold back the tear`s.

"Where "asked Martina."In the bloody pup" Maria answered her voice getting louder

"Ok doll clam down" Martina didn`t like to see anyone get into such a state.

She turned to Martina saying "I shouldn`t be here" "Why not?

"Because two wrongs don`t make a right."

Feeling uneasy she drank her drink and headed home hoping David would be there.There was no light`s on to her disappointment.She went into the kitchen looked at the table that she had so lovingly set earlier.

The steaks were still on the pan, she looked at the clock it was eleven pm.

What a prick she thought and the sad part was that she had thought that they had turned a corner.

She heard the front door go and went into the hallway to see him nearly fall through the door.

She screamed at him, and gave him a wallop across the face. He fell over at the sudden impact.

She managed to drag him into the living room where he passed out.

She went into the kitchen poured herself a drink lit a cigarette and sat staring into the garden.

 She honestly didn`t know whether to laugh or cry.

She went and had a shower, as the hot water hit her body she wept.tears of disappointment.

Got out of the shower, wrapped herself in a bathrobe and got into bed. She fell asleep.

A while later was awoken by the sound`s of David been ill in the toilet.

She got up , and headed downstairs made a coffee, she went into the living room sat and watched telly for a while.

Soon it was morning, she heard him wander downstairs, she followed him into the kitchen, He was looking very white and ill, Serves him right she thought.He got a drink of water and immediately threw up in the sink.

Bloody lovely she thought, as she looked at him with pure disgust in her face.As he turned and looked at her he spotted the look on her face "What are you looking at me like that for?"

"Because obviously the chat and the making up we did yesterday, meant sweet fuck all to you."she screamed at him.

She could feel her bottom lip quiver, thinking I`m not going to cry.

She walked with her coffee into the living room, sitting on the couch feeling totally deserted and alone.

She heard him being ill again in the kitchen.

She could feel the tears slide down her cheeks and she knew that what she felt for David was beginning to crumble.

She knew that she was to blame as well, but something inside her was dying.

He poked his head around the door and said "I`m going back to bed" "Fine" she snapped back at him.

She heard him wander upstairs and close the door.

She went out in the garden and started to prune her plants, she loved nature watching things grow.

After she went inside she went upstairs opened the door to get some clothes.

He was lying on the bed snoring and farting and the odour in the bedroom leaving a lot to be desired.

Banging the door closed in rage.She then rang work ,Joe answered, "I won`t be in for the rest of the week" she said.

"Maria are you ok?" Joe asked concerned."Just a few problems, nothing I can`t handle" s
"Well if you need me you know where I am" "Ok" she hung up.

She made herself a cuppa turned the radio on, and started on a pile of ironing.

She went upstairs to hang her clothes up, he stirred as she entered the room opening his eyes

he asked "What time it was"

"The bloody clock is right beside you" she answered in a raised voice.

He sat in the bed, looking at her and said "Don`t start, I`m not in the mood"

"Fine "she shouted and stormed out.She went downstairs and made herself a sandwich.

She heard the shower being switched on. He came downstairs and put the kettle on.

Maria gave him a look, "Look I went a bit over the top, had one too many, so can we just

forget it.

"I don`t believe you" she answered as she grabbed her coat and went for a walk along the

canal;

She took deep breaths and looking at the trees blossom.

Feeling more clam she headed home.

He was in the living room watching telly, "Hi Ya" she smiled through the door.

He got up "Sorry" he said simply."Want a cuppa" she asked, He nodded "Please"

He followed her into the kitchen, she passed him the coffee," Ta "he sighed" Not going to

work today"

She shook her head "No I have taken the rest of the week off" "Why?" He asked looking

rather surprised.

"Because I`m in such a state mentally and emotionally that I am unable to deal with people."

"What do you mean?" He asked looking puzzled.

"Exactly what I said" she snapped.

"Look that attitude won`t get you anywhere" he snapped back at her.

She looked at him and sighed, "Right if you have got all the answers, where do we go from

here?"

David looked at her as if she had two heads, "Don`t look at me like that" she said in a raised voice.

"Darling what wrong?"he asked totally bewildered.

"WRONG!" She was screaming hysterically at him,going towards her.

"Don`t "she sobbed as she moved away, "Did you not here a word we spoke yesterday"

"Well yes but at the end of the day this is us" "This is us!"she said weeping.

"Stop being so hysterical" he said, She took a deep breath before she answered

"Well start listening" David was a bit taken at the sharpness in her voice.

Taking another deep breath she continued, her voice still quivering.

"Ok yesterday after we had made love and talked, I felt so much better, you went off to football, I really felt we were back on tract"

"Yes" he nodded" and I felt the same" "Please listen" she asked patiently.

He heard the undertone in her voice, so apologized.

"I had all this energy so I cleaned the house from top to bottom ,went shopping bought your favourite steak and onions ," she was sobbing again."You never even rang me to tell me you were going to be late"

She stumped around the kitchen pointing at her head.

"Because inside my stupid head, I thought you would come home from football and we could have a nice evening together, but instead, well the rest is history"

He sat looking at the floor, "Where is the David gone that used to make me feel I was the most important person in his life "she asked more calmly.

He looked at her and answered "Baby you still are" She was finding it impossible to keep it together.

She put her head in her hands tears sliding down her face.He took a step towards her.

She put her hand up "We used to have respect for each,and share everything"

She was sobbing again, looking at him she asked in a very soft voice "Where is it gone?"

"It`s not gone ,we can get it back the thing is we are both burning the candle at both ends"

"Oh no you don`t " replied Maria with fire in her eyes, "The truth is the minute you walk out that door, in your mind your single it`s ok for you to go drinking with the lad`s"

"No I don`t" he butt in, "Shut up and listen you stay out half the night.I didn`t marry you to be your doormat".

"Alright then why did you marry me?" He shouted.

"Not for this "she screamed "Do you know I spend most of my life At the moment either in tears of pure frustration, or just feeling totally alone."

"Oh baby I`m sorry for shouting at you" he apologized.

"Christ if I hear that word sorry again I`ll bloody scream"

"What else can I say "he asked feeling totally helpless."Nothing "she replied as she marched out of the room.

The next few days went by, the strain between was getting worse.

Maria went back to work, Martina popped in to have her hair done.

"Hello doll, how are things?" Maria just shrugged her shoulders.

"No change then" sighed Martina."How about we go for a drink after your finished here".

Maria nodded, "Yes that sounds good"

She headed to the pup after she finished work, filled her in on the going`s on.

Martina shaking her head said "That's not good"

Maria looking at her "I`m at my wit`s end, I honestly don`t know what to do next"

"Do you know your both a silly pair of fools, you need your heads punched together"

Maria looked at her surprised, Martina was always so sympathetic, but then she realized she was right,

"Oh Martina I have been so selfish, I haven`t even asked how Andy and the kids are"

"Oh there fine, look I don`t mind listening, but if you want your marriage to survive you two are going to have to talk".

"I know" she sighed as she sipped her drink.The door opened and David walked in.

Looked saw them and without acknowledging them headed to the bar with his friends.

,"Now that is God dame ignorant of him "said Martina really shocked at his behaviour.

"I`m going to have a word" she said as she got up from her seat.

Maria took her arm and said "No don`t bother" "Yes but by him behaving like this is only making things worse." She sighed as she sat back down.

"Yes but he is showing his true colours",Martina looking in his direction, shaking her head, "No your wrong, I think he is embarrassed and doesn`t know what else to do."

"Do you think so?" answered Maria "Yes" snapped Martina she was getting a tad pissed off with their lack of communication.

Maria sensed this and said "Shall we join them?" Martina thought that's better.

"Yes why not" They got up and went over to where they were sitting.

"Hello" smiled Maria, David looked up as if surprised to see her.

"Oh hello darling, get you a drink" he asked.

"Thought you would never ask" smiled Martina trying to lighten the atmosphere.

David smiled pulling chairs out so they could sit down.

He came back with the drinks and sat next to Maria, grabbed her hand squeezed it.

She looked at him and smiled, Martina saw this gesture and gave Maria a wink.

They all had a good laugh and a few drinks later they left.

David and Marie walked home hand in hand. He stopped and pulling her towards him,

Whispering in her ear "I love you" She looked at him and answered "I love you too"

They stopped at the shop on they way home and David buying them a bottle of southern

comfort.They got home and he opened the door to the living room, saying

"You go in baby and I`ll fix us a drink"

She put some music on, he came back with the drinks and the snuggled up on the couch,

He put his drink down and taking hers put them on the table, took her face between his hands

and kissed her.

As she responded he slowly started to undress her, he made love to her with such a passion

leaving them both breathless.

In the aftermath of their lovemaking he held her as if she was a china doll.

They wandered upstairs and fell asleep in each others arms.

They awoke the next morning to the sun shining through the window.

Maria jumped in the shower first, as she came out David was waiting for her,

He grabbed her gently and smelt her, he adored the scent of her.She smiled as she kissed.

"Let`s stay on tract this time" He nodded ,and smiling said "I have got no intentions of losing

you baby girl"

"I don`t want that either, but we were heading down the wrong road" "I know" he whispered.

gazing at the ground "I was wrong"

She went over and gently held his face I her hands, saying "I don`t want anything to spoil the

way we are now"

He smiled at her and reassured her that nothing ever would.

"David look at what we have, I`m only twenty one and your just twenty, see all we have

achieved in just over a year."

"We have our health, good jobs a beautiful home and each other" she smiled.

"So are we going to save some time for us That is the question?" "Well of course" he said.

"Well it is easy to say that now but," then her eyes lit up as they always did when she had

something ticking inside her head.

"I know I`ll give up my job with Oriflame that will give me a few evenings a week free."

David nodded and replied "Ok I`ll tell the band that I`m leaving"

"Oh no you can`t do that" she knew how much he loved the band.

"Well what then? I can`t give football up at the minute because were in the middle of a league" he sighed.

"How about if we dedicate one weekend a month to us" he picked her up and kissed her saying "you're a genius"

As weeks turned into months they had managed to find one weekend to spend together. Slowly the whole situation started to slide back to how it was.

This time Maria didn`t bother to point out the obvious.She just took life as it came.

David was hardly home at all, she had given up her part time job as promised. Which left her with time on her hands.

She had decorated the bit's she hadn`t bothered with in the house when they had first moved in, the garden was immaculate.

When she returned home from work in the evenings, she would find David packing his

football kit or getting ready to go out with the band.
He would greet her and be gone.She would eat alone and most evenings just watch some telly or read a book.

She didn`t think too deeply anymore about her marriage to David, he still told her he loved her and that was supposed to make everything better.

She would walk away from him thinking words as he went out.

The phone rang, she answered it was Martina, "Hello doll what are you up too"

"Well nothing David`s gone out as usual"

"Right get your glad rags on we are going to a strippers night in the Swan"

There was silence on the phone, "Are you there" "Yes " she answered, "well are you coming or what"

Maria had not been out in such a long time, "Come on girl your turning into a recluse"

"Ok what time" "An hour see you there" she hung up.

Running upstairs she showered ,did her makeup and pulled a little black number out.

Happy with the result she headed to the Swan. Everything was in full swing.

Martina waved at her smiling "You look great" "Thanks " she smiled, "Christ there is loads of

talent here" she smiled starting to feel the most relaxed she had in ages.

Martina was so pleased to see Maria with the glint back in her eyes. She hadn`t seen that for a

while.
As the strippers appeared, the women went wild, shouting screaming really egging them on.

As the act continued, Martina and Maria joined in the swing of things having a fantastic

evening.

There was this one lad showing a lot of interest in Maria, he introduced himself as Johnny.
Buying they two girls a drink, turning he asked Maria "Where have you been all his life"

"Oh I have been about" she laughed, "Not on my watch you haven`t" he grinned back at her.

She looked into the greenest eyes she had ever seen, and could feel her tummy turn over.

Something her tummy used to do when her and David got together. But not anymore.

"Is there any chance that I could take you for a drink sometime?"he asked.

For the first time since she had met David, had another man turned her head,

She looked at him and regrettably said "Under different circumstances I would love to but

I`m married,"holding her wedding finger up.

She could see the disappointment in his eyes "Oh".

"I had not noticed" he said so honestly that Maria wanted to hug him.

They definitely had a connection and both of them could feel it.

"Who`s the lucky man then" he questioned?

She was just about to tell but at that moment, David arrived at her side.

She hadn`t noticed him come in, "Are you trying to chat up my wife" he slurred.

Only then did Maria notice how drunk he was. She had never felt so embarrassed.

Johnny was taken aback "You're the fella out of the band "Shocking"

"That's me," slurred David as he held on to the counter to keep himself upright.

Johnny looked at him and in an admirable voice, "I love your music "David raised his glass at him.

"Look's like you like my wife as well" he hiccuped, Maria looked at Johnny wishing the ground would open up and swallow her.

Johnny could see how uncomfortable she was in the situation ,giving her a smile and wandered to the other end of the bar.

."Right darling don't you think it's time we went home?" Martina watching on thinking what a prick.

She could have had anyone she wanted.And David at this moment in time was no catch

David turned to her and said thickly, slurring "I'm having another drink"

Maria with plenty of practice knew how to humour him,

"Ok one more and then we will head home"

"Brendan get us another round in" David shouted.Brendan looked at Maria who shook her head.

"I think you have had enough" David staggered back and snarled at Brendan "No one tells me when I have had enough."

He came out from behind the bar, grabbed David by the arm and escorted him off the premises.

Maria followed him out, called a taxi and twenty minutes later they were home.

With the help of Tom the taxi driver the managed to get him indoors, got him upstairs where he collapsed on the bed.

She turned and looked at him, her tummy turning over, the sight of him making her feel sick.

She went downstairs put the kettle on, while waiting for it to boil she could feel the tears prick the back of her eyes.

She stood looking around her beautiful kitchen and felt like throwing everything out of pure frustration.

She took her cuppa into the living room, turning the telly on sat holding the tears back.

She dosed for a few hours, waking up she stood up stretching and headed upstairs.

She showered and went into the bedroom to get dressed for work.David was in the same position as she had dumped, snoring loudly.

She shook him saying "David you`ll be late for work" He opened his eyes putting his hand over them and groaned.

Maria was losing patience with him pulled the covers off him screaming, and hitting him ; Shouting get up you drunken good for nothing.

He jumped out of the bed and headed for the toilet, she could hear him spluttering and vomiting.

Charming she thought as she headed off to work.

She could hear Joe singing as she climbed the stairs, this brought a smile to her face.

"Morning doll, coffee?"he asked. "Please" she answered as she hung her jacket up.

Joe being very observant, "What`s up" he asked as he passed her coffee.

She let a huge sigh and filled him in on the previous evening.on what had been going on"asked Joe.

"I bloody well hit him over the head, do you know I felt sick looking at him this morning."

"Come here " Joe gave her a big hug."It`s not working is it?" She shook her head.

"Look if your not happy you know where the door is" he said simply.

"Yes but it`s not as simple as that", she sighed.

"Oh yes it is life is very simple it`s people that complicate it" he smiled.

The conversation finished as their first client appeared.

The day flew by, Joe giving his opinion on everything to his clients.

Maria loved Joe, and working with him was a laugh a minute.

After work the headed to the local, Brendan was serving" usual" he smiled.

"Please darling " said Joe, "Where is he" asked Brendan looking at Maria.

"The last time I saw it was this morning, with it`s head stuck down the toilet"

The finished their drinks and headed home.Joe kissed her saying "Sort it out doll"

She smiled nodded ,wondering what would be waiting for her.

As she put her key in the door she heard a car pull up, She turned to see one of David`s

friends pull up .

"Hello Maria David about ?""Got no idea" He walked up the path" We were supposed to go

for a couple of games of pool tonight"

She opened the door shouting "David" She heard a movement upstairs looked up to see a

ghost peering over the banisters , Paul looked up the stairs, looking at David said " Fucking

hell you look like shit"

Maria went into the kitchen, want a cuppa Paul, "No I`ll be off thanks anyway"

She let him out, as she walked back inside she looked to see a very sheepish David making

his way downstairs.

Ignoring him she went and made herself a coffee,hearing him run back upstairs being

ill in the toilet.

She went upstairs the odour of stale booze hit her, She opened the windows, changing the bed

cover`s.

David appeared out of the bedroom, looking like death.

She walked by him, cleaned the bathroom pouring bleach down the toilet.

Spraying air freshener, she went downstairs and put the kettle on.

David appeared beside her, he opened his gob to speak, putting her hand up, saying "I don`t

want to hear it".

She grabbed her bag and keys and walked up to Martina`s.

Knocked on the door ,Martina opened it looked at Maria`s face and said.

"Come in",putting the kettle on and turned to her "How was he this morning?"

Maria filled her in,

 "He didn`t go to work then?"she shook her head.

"Anyway I`m not here to talk about him" Martina looked at her with a surprised look on her face.

"How do you feel about a weekend away?"Martina raised her eyebrows "What`s brought all this on"

"I just feel if I get away for a bit it would do me good"

"So I`m going to organize a weekend maybe Killarney, and just wanted to know if your up for it."

Martina grinned at her saying "You go for it and count me in"

"How is work going" she asked, "It`s busy Joe is great, sometimes I do think that if I didn`t have my job I`d go mad"

"Well you do, and the customers love you, and you need to do what you got to doll "

"What do you mean?" She asked Martina questionable.

"Look sometimes in life you can be hitting your head off a brick wall" she smiled.

Maria still wasn`t getting her meaning.

"Look Doll what I`m getting at is, I have seen you try really try over the past  month`s,

you have bent over backward` s to make a go of thing`s,but as far as I can see you have been

hitting your head off a brick wall maybe I`m using the wrong word`s," she sighed

"Let me rephrase that, I have seen you put lot`s of effort in trying to make your marriage

work, and to no avail, and David hasn`t either been listening or he is totally thick, or he does

not care."

Maria nodded "Well that's why I thought a break away would do me good, a bit of space"

"Now let's get back to the target at hand" smiled Martina.

Maria hugged her , Martina hugging her back said "You're a lovely doll and that's how you should be treated, like a piece of china, not somebody's doormat"

The bought laughed at this description. "Who are you planning to invite?"

"Joe of course and Declan, Rosie Brenda and I'll put the feelers out, just need about ten"

"Why is that?" asked Martina, "To get discount of course" she smiled back.

"Your not just a pretty face now are you" "Na right I'm off and I'll see you soon"

As she was leaving she turned to her friend "Thanks for last night."

"Ya it was good,"Martina smiled.

Martina stood at the door watching her as she wandered home.closing the door thinking she is a fighter.

As she opened the door ,she could hear the snores coming from upstairs.

Putting her eyes up to heaven she went into the living room and taking the telephone book, started looking at possible hotels.

She then wrote out a list of who to invite.Then rang the hotels and got some prices.

David appeared at the door, looking a bit more human.she put her lists away.

Got up and went into the kitchen, "Tea " she asked, he followed her and as she was putting the kettle on he went to put his arms around her.She shrugged him off.

"Oh come on darling, I know I have been out of order, lets kiss and make up"

He grabbed her arm "Get off of me" she shouted, he was taken aback.

"You make me sick" she screamed.

David looked at her shrugging her shoulders headed upstairs.she heard the shower going,

She sat down to finish her list, started to circle some of the hotels that she thought were promising,

She heard him come downstairs and then heard the front door go.She looked out the window

and saw him head towards town.

She sat thinking Joe is right whatever makes you unhappy in this world, get rid.

She picked up the phone, and ringing some of the hotels started comparing prices'

This took up the rest of her evening, she wandered into the kitchen and poured herself a drink.

Sitting at the kitchen table thinking at least I`m doing something positive.And it`s something

to look forward to.

She went to bed in the spare room that night, looking around the room admiring it.

She was glad she had spent a few bob on its décor, she had painted, one wall in green the

other walls in a cream and carpeted in a dark green.

She had bought a new bed and picked a green and cream duvet covers and pillow cases.

Yes she was definitively glad she had done, it as she had a feeling she would be spending a

lot of her nights here.

As she got into bed she heard the front door go, she got up headed down stairs.

David looked up," Want a coffee "he asked she nodded, as she followed him into kitchen.

She watched as his hand`s shaking spooned the coffee into the cup`s.

 His neck and face were soaking with sweat.

David I have seen you with hangover`s but this takes the biscuit, your lucky  you haven`t

ended up in hospital with alcohol poisoning"

He looked at her, his eyes bloodshot and nodded ,looking down he answered "I know".

"David if this keeps up your going to have to get help"

He looked at her in disbelief "What" "You heard" she replied.

"Christ I had a few too many and your saying I should get help"

"Yes I am, this has been going on too long " she answered raising her voice.

He looked at her as he grabbed his coffee shouting at her" Don`t start on me, I`m not in good place to listen at the moment"

"Fine" she sighed as she could feel a lump coming in the back of her throat.

He heard the quiver in her voice and looked at the brown eyes welling tears.

He felt a wave of shame run through him, "Maria I`m sorry"

She looked at him tears sliding down her face, "I can`t go on like this"

She sat in the chair her head in her hand`s "David look around you we have got everything ,

A lovely home, car we both have good job`s were not stuck for money"

Taking deep breath carried on "Were on our way out" she said and looked up.

But he wasn`t there , she could hear him being ill upstairs.Fucking hell I have been talking to

Myself, she thought.

Maria feeling very foolish went into the living room and put the telly on and just sat there

staring.

The living room door opened, he put his head around the door and said I`m going back to bed.

"Ok" she went upstairs and got back into bed in the spare room.

Woke up to here him in the shower looked at the clock, it was 6.30am.

She wandered downstairs put the kettle on. She felt him come up behind her.

Turned around, he was looking bit more human."How are you feeling?"

He shrugged "Not great I`m going to ring work and tell them I `m not coming in for a few

days"

"Good idea, they can always `s put it down as holiday`s "As she looked out the window

The sun was shining brightly and her plants were looking thirsty'

Heading out the back door, with a bucket of water, watered her babies coming back inside.

She said "It`s a beautiful day" He nodded "I`m going back to bed, I still don`t feel a 100%"

"Ok" she smiled, "I`ll see you after work "

      She headed off to work, filled Joe in on the weekend away she was planning.

He came up with some extra names to add to the list."How are thing`s at home?"

She smiled shrugging, "Usual, changing the subject quickly"

Joe could take a hint, the day flying by.Going for their normal beverage after work.

They were talking ten to the dozen about their trip when Martina walked in.

"Hello want a drink" she smiled."Hello Martina no you come and sit here and I`ll get them in" said Joe.

"You're a gentleman" "More of a queen " he laughed as he did his walk the walk to the bar.

Looking at Maria she asked "How is things" Maria looked at her shaking her head and replied, "No magical change"

"To be honest I`m not even thinking about it ,I have got far more important thing`s going on up there" she laughed pointing to her head.

Martina was glad that she wasn`t sitting around dwelling on things. Joe arrived back with the drinks.

"There you go dollies" he said as he plonked his bum on a chair.

"Are you joining us on this over 21s weekend?" Martina asked laughing.

"Joining I`m the cabaret" he smiled, they all burst out laughing.

"I `m off got thing`s to do and all that" said Maria, "Ok doll see you tomorrow" the two of them said in chorus.

Maria walked home her heart feeling a lot lighter,walking through the door she could here the telly in the front room.

She stuck her head around the living room door, "Feeling any better "He looked at her shaking his head.

"Fancy some dinner?"He pulled a face saying "Maybe later" "Ok" she went upstairs to their bedroom to get some clothes.

Opened the windows to let a bit of air through, she lay on the bed thinking about the over 21s weekend.

Only Martina could come up with a name like that, she smiled to herself.

She could feel her eyes closing, she fell asleep.

David came upstairs and walked into the bedroom, seeing his gorgeous wife lying on the bed.

Her long dark hair spread over the pillow, he lay down beside her listening to her breathing.

Putting his arm's around her ,she didn't move.He fell asleep.

When she woke up, she could hear David snoring behind her.She gently got out of the bed so as not to disturb him.

She went and showered, wrapping a towel around her she went back into their bedroom.

David was lying awake on the bed naked.Staring at her with lust in his eyes.

Going toward's him dropping the towel and laying beside him.Gently stroking her face he made love to her.

Afterwards they lay in each others arms out of breath.He held on to her as if he was never going to let her go.

Breathing into the back of her neck and telling her how much he loved her.

She lay beside him listening to the words thinking no you don't mean a them.Just because they had sex or made love whatever you wanted to call it, everyone had needs.

It always' s amazed her how easy people could use these word's, it was like as if the said them , it made everything ok, no matter what the other had done.

You should never have to say sorry to someone you love.

She turned and asked if he would like a coffee, laying back with a huge grin on his face.

"Ya go on then" she got out of bed pulled her dressing gown on and headed downstairs.

Putting the kettle on he came up behind her , pulling her towards him, looking deep into her eyes.

"I really do love you, and I'm really sorry for my behaviour, can we put it behind us and start afresh."he asked with hope in his eye`s

"Yes I`m willing to try if you are" she replied smiling up at him.

Holding her close he whispered "Thing`s will be different ,I promise" and deep down he believed that.

The weeks went by and David true to his word, came home straight after football or a gig.

Thing`s settled down into a nice pattern, David was back to being the attentive loving husband.

She told him about her over 21s weekend she had organized, expecting criticism.

Much to her surprise ,telling her she deserved a break and to go and enjoy herself.

Things were good between them and Maria was starting to trust him again,

One evening David had just gone to band practice, Maria was in the garden chatting to Francis over the fence, when her phone rang.

She ran into answer it, her sister Mandy was on the other end sobbing.

"Mandy what`s the matter" she asked down the phone, she couldn`t make head or tail of what she was saying.

"Right Mandy are you listening to me, I`m coming to get you, I`ll be there in a half an hour"

Grabbing the key`s, jumped in the car, and pulled up outside the house where she`d grown up.

Knocking on the door she heard her Da shout come in.

Walking in there he sat King of his castle, sitting in his thrown by the fire.

He looked up and seeing it was Maria, got out of his chair.

"Well Christ it`s the girl ",It gave her the creeps when he called her The Girl. It ignited too many fires in her mind that she needed to keep extinguished .

New Chapter10

When Maria was two years old her brother Sean arrived. Maria slept with Cathrine and Tommy at this point.

A lot of the time Cathrine slept on the settle bed in the kitchen saying Maria kicked too much.

When Sean turned two, Maria and him were put in a bed of their own.

But now and again Cathrine would put Maria in bed with Tommy, and she would get in with Sean.

Saying she couldn`t get any sleep with their Da` s snoring.

She was only four years old and she still remembers the warmth of the willy and bits on her back.

She could see his willy and bits swinging underneath the shirt as he approached her.

She would hide under the blanket and pray to saint Anthony. He was the saint everyone prayed to when they were in trouble.

He would climb into bed beside her and start prodding and poking , as she lay still her eyes closed, waiting for it to stop.

He would then kiss her on the forehead calling her The Girl.

She was four years old, she started school. It became Maria`s sanctuary even thought she got beaten on the back of the hand`s and leg`s by the nuns, for trivial mistake`s not remembering a prayer or getting her sum`s wrong.s

She wet her knickers on one occasion, where she was frightened to ask where the toilets were and Sister Una put her kneeling in front of the statue of the blessed virgin, for the remaining of the day.

Maria was always hungry, she would have one piece of bread and jam and a bottle of water.

She would sit beside the other girl`s, her mouth watering as she watched them eat cheese or ham sandwiches, packets of crisps and bottles of orange.

Whatever leftovers the girls didn`t want the would give to Maria, who would except and devour, gratefully.

Her Da would sometime` s be waiting outside the school for her, she hated him doing this.

He was thirty odd year`s older than her Ma, so was a lot older than the other girl`s `Da`s.

He always` s wore his postman uniform and would stand there with his head held high like as if he was someone really important.

Maria would feel ashamed.

Next day the girl`s would tease her taunting shouting name`s at her saying" That`s your grandad and you got no food, your like the tinker`s"

She would retaliate, by pushing them out of her face, they would then spit on her and push her to the ground kicking her.

She would pick herself up and try and stand up for herself, by fighting back they all talked about her, but she didn`t care.

She would not cry and let them see they had won.

She would then arrived home from school with cut knees and had got blood on her socks her Ma would give her a hiding and tell her money didn`t grow on tree`s.

She got it from all corner`s.

At Christmas her Ma got vouchers so she could have a pair of new shoes.

And when summer was approaching her Ma would cut the toes out of them to make sandal.

This made the girl`s real ammunition to take the piss out of her.

But she still held her head up high and her and Sally would skip home.

Sally was her next door neighbour and her best friend in the whole wide world.

The told each other everything.Sadie was Sally`s Ma and Maria loved going to their house.

She would sit beside the open fire with Sally and her Ma on the cold winter evening, drinking tea and Sally would read them stories.

She would stay there until her Ma called for her saying, "Lord Sally you have the patience of Joeb putting up with this one."

"Ah sher she is no trouble at all" Sally would reply, "You don`t know her she nothing but trouble that one"

"Come on home with ya" Cathrine would shout at her."Sitting there like Lady muck"

"Ah go easy on her Cathrine, sher she`s doing no harm"

"I sent her out to get the turf" Cathrine would protest "And here she is rambling."

Maria would get a clout from her Ma and would be sent on her way.

Six years old her new baby sister arrived, Maria loved her with all of her heart. She was called Mandy.

By the time Mandy was four, Maria was like a body guard around her.Making sure that she was never left alone with her Da.

So when Mandy was put to bed, her Ma would go to play bingo, Maria and Sean would stand and sing to her Da.

When the singing was over he put Sean to bed and taking Maria to his bed playing with his willy beside her.
Sometimes he would put them between her legs ,this would hurt and she would cry.He would put his hand over her mouth and say "If you make any noise you will waken Mandy and then there will be trouble,"

She would push her head into the pillow to stop the sounds coming out,
Chapter 11
"Want a cuppa girl?"Shaking her head, "No thank` s where`s Mandy"

Cathrine arrived in through the back door" Oh Hello what are you doing here?"

"Christ that`s a nice welcome Ma" smiled Maria.

A tear stained Mandy arrived out of the bedroom, "What`s wrong with you?"questioned Cathrine in a snappy voice.

 Mandy started crying again. Cathrine looked at her giving her daggers.

"Oh for fuck`s sake your always `s been the same, making mountain`s out of molehill`s"

Maria looked at Mandy and went over and hugged her, Mandy hugged her straight back.

Cathrine watching said "Yea that`s it spoil her like you have always` s done"

"I hate you" Mandy screamed at her Ma.

"Your nothing but a spoilt little bitch" Cathrine shouted back.

Maria turned to her Ma saying "Ill bring Mandy with me for a few day`s"

"You can fucking keep her, she get`s on my nerves "snapped Cathrine back at her.

"Ok Ma have it your way, Mandy get your stuff you can come and live with me"

"She is not taking anything out of this house" ",Cathrine snapped spitefully.

"Fine, Ma considering I bought most of her clothes, come on Mandy let`s get out of here".

Marie said giving her Ma a pitiful look."Lord God what in the name of Jesus is going on"

asked Tommy.
"Oh that`s it take her side as you normally do" answered Cathrine getting extremely annoyed.

"Now why don`t ye all clam down" said Tommy," All this trouble is no good for my blood

pressure ".

Maria heading out the back door with Mandy beside her, when their mother shouted,

"Go on off you go Mandy with that black headed whore!"

Maria turned around and very calmly replied "Ma I am not a blacked whore, and I am not a

child anymore, you can bully"

"Oh off with ye!" said Cathrine nastily "And she`ll be back you mark my word`s with her tail

between her legs"

Maria took Mandy by the hand and led her to the car, she was crying her heart out.

Out of the corner of her eye she could see Tommy standing at the gable end of the house.

She started the ignition and drove away."No need to tell me what`s happened, I know what

she`s like."

Mandy calmed down, "What`s David going to say?"

Looking at her sister said "You have nothing to worry about, your safe now, and David

won`t mind"

Mandy let out a sigh of relief and settled back as Maria put some music on, blasting out Cher If I could turn back time. The two sister`s singing the whole way back to Maria`s.

It was getting late by the time they got back, David was back from his band practise.

Maria opening the door shouting "Hi honey"

 "I`m in here "he called back from the kitchen.

As she opened the door she was very surprised to see Johnny sitting there.She hadn`t set eyes on him since the stripper`s night.

David went and kissed her, "Darling this is Johnny" "We have met" she answered.

Mandy wandered in ,David looked surprised to see her, he looked at the teared stained face.

He went over and put his arm`s around her "What`s the matter "

"Oh me Ma just upsetting anything that does not move, she`s staying with us" Maria replied.

David nodded "That`s not a problem, you stay as long as you want and remember your safe now"

She smiled she loved being with her sister. Maria looking at Johnny sat at the table,

"I did not know you and David were friendly."

 "Well I have always followed the band and earlier I was in the shop and we got chatting so here I am"

"Right "said David rubbing his hand`s "I think we deserve a drink"

"That sound`s good" smiled Maria.

David got the glasses out and asked what they were all having, "What have you got?"asked Johnny.

"Beer, vodka, whiskey, wine" smiled David, "A whiskey would be great" he replied.

"Maria" he smiled "Now do you really have to ask" he gave her a wink and smiling,

"Na but you know how polite I am,"

"Oh just get on with it" she laughed.

"What would you like Mandy" Looking at him she said "I'll have whatever Mandy's having"

"Right two screwdriver's coming right up" Maria went over to Mandy put her arm around

"Feeling better now" Mandy looked at her and with a grateful look in her eye's said "Yes"

Maria smiling raised her glass and made a toast to happy time's and new beginning s.

"Right on that note I think a few sound's are in order" smiled Johnny.As he picked up his

guitar.

They all sat with their drink's and sang along."Nothing to cheer the heart up as quickly as a

few tune's" smiled David as he poured a few more drink's.

While the lad's were tuning in Maria took Mandy upstairs to her bedroom.

She had just decorated the box room, Mandy walked in

" Oh Maria it's lovely" she smiled.

She had done it out in a pale cream paintwork, with yellow curtain's and matching bedding.

And a pastel pink carpet.

"Well it's yours sis, so make yourself at home" as she hugged her.Mandy since she'd been a

little girl had always felt safe in those arm's.

She stood back and said Maria "I have got no clothes,"

 "Oh don't worry about that I have plenty "

She took her into the spare bedroom where Maria kept a spare wardrobe.

Looking at her "You can have what ever you want out of there" took a bag down and handed

it to her.

"There is some new underwear inside I bought for you "she smiled.Mandy put her arm's

around her "You're the best sister ever".

Maria got her a spare nightdress and a bathrobe smiling at her "Job done"

Mandy looked done in "Why don't you call it a night baby sis you look tired"

"Yes it's been a long day, say goodnight to David and Johnny for me"

"Ok pet you sleep well and don`t worry about a thing", smiled Maria closing the door.

When she arrived back downstairs Johnny was leaving,

"Thank you for you hospitality." He smiled at her Maria giving her a kiss on the cheek.

"Thank you David glad I bumped into you, it`s been a lovely evening"

"It was a pleasure and now that you know where we are don`t be a stranger"

David watched as he ran across the estate, closing the door,

He turned to Maria "He is a nice fella, I noticed he has been at a lot of the gig`s that`s how I recognized him"

Smiling she said "Yes he does seems like a nice lad" she didn`t bother to mention about the meeting on the night of the strippers.

"Fancy a night cap" he smiled , she nodded "Why not" as she took his arm and they headed into the kitchen.

They sat chatting ,Maria filled her in on her trip home to pick Mandy up,

"I cannot believe how nasty your Ma can be."

"Well when you live with someone like that all your life, you don`t come to expect anything else"

David yawning said "I`m going up" "Ok Ill be up in a moment just clear up here"

She heard him go upstairs, tidied the kitchen poured herself a drink and sat looking out the window.

What a day.she thought having to rescue Mandy and then arriving home to find Johnny in her kitchen .

She finished her drink and checking everything was secure she headed to bed, opening Mandy`s door she heard her gently snoring.

Went into their bedroom David was snoring, she got into bed and was soon asleep.

She woke up to the sound of the shower going and Mandy singing.

David was still sleeping, she quietly got out of bed, and headed downstairs.

Putting the kettle on she heard Mandy come in behind her .

"Morning sis" smiled Mandy. "Did you sleep ok?" asked Maria.

"I was out like a light that bed is really comfy"

Taking the frying pan out of the cupboard, looked at her and said "Fancy a fry up"

"Oh yes please, Ill just nip up and make my bed" Maria nodded.

David arrived in the kitchen putting his arm`s around his wife`s waist said,

"Something smell`s good"

He started to kiss her neck, Maria wriggling away as she heard Mandy coming back

downstairs.

She turned and said "Darling we have company" as she looked at Mandy.

"Oh don`t mind me it make`s a change to see someone happy in the morning`s instead of

shouting"

Maria dished up breakfast putting her arms around Mandy`s neck repeated "Your safe now"

 meaning this in more way`s than one.

Chapter 12

 Maria had left school at fifteen and started a hairdressing apprenticeship.

Which she loved and was very good at.

A huge argument with her Ma had ended up with her Ma telling her to get the fuck out.that

she was nothing but a black headed whore, when she had just turned seventeen.

She had bullied and abused by her Ma since she could remember.

So leaving the house she hitched to Athlone, there was no other means of transport,

As there was only one bus a week from the village.

Athlone was the nearest town near to her ,it was the capital of the county .

She was lucky that day the second car that she waved down stopped.

It was a neighbour that lived just up the road ,so they chatted and half an hour later she was dropped in the middle of the town.

Looking around her she felt panic setting in, here she was in a big town where she didn`t know anybody .

There were lot`s of people about, everyone seemed in such a hurry, and so much traffic.

.And she couldn`t take in the amount of shops that were all together.

Pulling herself together she asked directions to local post office.

Since she had started work her Ma had always` s taken her money from her, but she had managed to save some, from doing people`s hair after work, and on the odd occasion someone would tip her.

As she was heading to the post office, walking past a butcher`s she saw an advert for a bedsit.

Going inside she asked the butcher, about the advert in the window .

"It belong` s to me ,if you hold on a minute I`ll take you across the road so you can have a gander at it" he smiled.

"By the way my name is Pat" he introduced himself.

"Hi I`m Maria" she smiled back.

A few minutes later she was standing in a room that was shaped like a fifty pence piece.

It was small consisting of a single bed a sink and a wardrobe, and that was the room full.

She asked the price,

"It`s £10 a week and I`ll need a week` in advance"

"Ok, I`ll take it ,I just need to go to the post office"

"Right I`ll see you in a few minuets then" he smiled and headed back to the butchers.

She headed to the post office and taking all the money she had in the whole world out ,which was £39.

"Went back to Pat and gave him £20 "

"Well it`s a pleasure doing business with ya",giving her a rent book and the key`s.

Feeling very grown up, she asked if there was any job's in hairdressing

about.

Looking at her he said "Well it must be your lucky day, if you walk around the corner there's

a hair salon, It was only yesterday I was walking past and I seen an advert in the window

looking for someone"

She smiled "Thank you very much"

"No trouble at all" he answered "And if there is anything I can do , just shout."

She waved, and walking around the corner saw the Salon with the advert in the window.

Taking a deep breath she went inside, It looked very posh, There was a very well dressed

attractive looking woman sitting at the reception desk.

She looked up "Good morning can I help"

Maria looking down at her attire feeling very scruffy, compared to this lady in front of her.

Looking at her said "Hi my name is Maria Daly and I'm here about the job"

The woman stood up and introduced herself as Elizabeth Robert's the proprietor.

Looking at one of the staff she said "Ursula can you take reception, please"

 Smiling at Maria she said "Come with me" As she climbed the stair's to the staff room.

"Tea or coffee" she asked.

"Coffee please" said Maria feeling very apprehensive.

Elizabeth sensing this from her asked "Where she was from"

Maria told her and smiling at her she informed her she had a sister that lived there.

She started to relax as Elizabeth passed her the coffee.

The interview went well, Maria telling a few porkies as she went along.

Mainly about her age and the amount of experience she had.

But it worked and she got the job. Starting the next day.

Leaving the Salon she was feeling elated

She then went to a second hand shop and bought a black skirt and a copper blouse.

Wanting to fit in on her first day, at work.

Then went and bought some basic`s with the little money she had left.

Heading back to her new home feeling very adult.

When she got there she realized she would need some bedding and

a kettle .

Hanging her new clothes up in the wardrobe she looked around deciding that her first wage

packet after she paid her.

 She then hitched back home.

Her Ma sitting at the kitchen table glared as she walked in.

"You still here ?" She mocked.

"I`m just back to get my thing`s" Maria replied definitely.

"Oh and where are you off to" she jeered.

She gathered her stuff and when her Ma wasn`t paying attention she nicked a tin opener

And a few bit`s of cutlery.

Tommy walked in and seeing her packing asked "What`s going on?"

Maria now brimming with confidence and feeling very sure of herself.

Looked at him with contempt saying "I`m leaving."

Tommy stood there rooted to the spot.

"What have you got to say about this Cathrine?" He blurted out in shook.

"Good riddance to bad rubbish" she scowled.

"Now hold on a minute there is no to be hasty" he replied.

"Hasty , she`s nothing but trouble" said Cathrine outraged.

Tommy walked away shaking his head.

He arrived back from the bedroom holding a clock, handing it to Maria saying,

"This light`s up in the dark, so if your frightened it will give you a bit of comfort"

Maria looking at him thinking ,You will never know how many time`s I have looked at that clock for solace.

She looked at him saying" That is from your bedroom, no thank you"

She noticed her Ma`s baffled reaction to the comment.

Tommy quickly turned away to avoid any eye contact with them, and busied himself putting turf on the fire.

Her youngest brother Paul, who was eight year`s younger than Maria, came into the room and asking where she was going?

She looked at him, and replied "I`m going to Athlone to live"putting his hand`s in his pocket`s, asking if he could come.

She sighed and hugging him said "Maybe when your older you can come and visit me"

Cathrine overhearing the conversation shouted "Get out "to Paul,

As he walked out of the room, looking at Maria, holding his head down he said to Cathrine "Ma I don`t want her to go"

Cathrine looked at him and said "Let her go she is no good to man or beast" Maria stared at her Ma,

"What are you looking at me like that for" she uttered fiercely. As Maria turned away she noticed Mandy out of the corner of her eye under the kitchen table crying.

Her heart nearly broke, ignoring her Ma she went over to Mandy and said "I won`t be far away as soon as I get myself settled I`ll write to you and you can write back to me"

Mandy was sobbing, and clinging to Maria" Don`t go please,"

"I have too" she answered .

"Well go on then you fucking black headed whore, get out and don`t come back", swore

Cathrine.

Maria gave Mandy a kiss and whispered "If you ever need me ,you write to me"

Mandy nodded not really understanding. Sean walked in asking "Where are you going"

Maria had a lump in her throat that she thought she would choke on if she didn`t get out of the house soon,

She picked up a plastic bag that she had put her worldly good`s ,in tear`s rolling down her

face she walked out.

Cathrine was standing with a cigarette in her hand, shouting at Mandy and Paul to stop

whinging.

As Maria looked back over her shoulder her only regret was having to leave Mandy and Paul

under these condition`s.

chapter14

"Darling that was just what the doctor ordered" David smiled as he got up from the table.

"Yes " smiled Maria as Mandy she asked "Can I have the last sausage"

Maria burped, smiling "Excuse me of course you can". David washing his hand`s asked

"What are you two up to today" he asked.It was Monday so Maria had the day off work.

"Well I`m going to the school to see about Mandy getting in there so she can finish her

education" said Maria .

"Christ I didn`t think about that" said David, "Right I`m off to work you two have a good

day"

They two sisters cleared away the breakfast dishes, sat having a cuppa and planning their day.

"Right I`m going to shower and then ring the school" said Maria.

Mandy hugging her said "Thank you" Maria looking into her eyes answered "There is

nothing I wouldn`t do for you"

Smiling Mandy replied "I know," "Well lets get our arse into gear and get this show on the

Road laughed Maria, as she pinched her bum.

"Ouch, that hurt" squealed Mandy as she ran after Maria up the stairs.

Maria went into the bathroom laughing.She showered and got dressed.

Mandy showered and soon the two of them were ready to hit the town.

Maria had got an appointment at the school for later that afternoon.

They headed for the clothes shops, were they kitted Mandy out in shoes .

That was the only area that Maria couldn`t help Mandy out in because she was two shoe size smaller than her sister.

Mandy sang as they walked the streets, she had never felt happier in her life.

 The relief and freedom of being away from home, that`s if you could call it that, where her Ma found fault with everything she did and a shouting match went on everyday.

And her Da had gone right into himself since Maria had left, hardly saying a word or taking any notice of anything that was going on,

Mandy had found him looking at her on occasions in a strange way.

But she was away from all that now,having lunch in the Swan.

Mandy had never been out to lunch before, she felt all grown up and posh as Maria introduced her to Brendan the barman.

He smiled at her shaking her hand saying "Pleased to meet you ,you're a looker just like your sister"

This made her blush, Maria noticed this and said to Mandy, "Take it as a complement he doesn`t dish them out easily."she laughed.

"What would you like to eat" asked Maria as she watched her sister trying to take it all in.

It was a totally new world, as Maria new having gone from a bog land girl to a town girl herself.

Mandy looked at her and answered "Ill have whatever your having"

So she ordered them egg mayonnaise for starters, followed by cottage pie.

They got a table and Eileen, their waitress brought over their food.

"Hello Maria not working today",

"Hello Eileen, no it`s my day off, this is my sister Mandy"

"Chris doesn`t she look like you" said Eileen."well enjoy your lunch"

Mandy looked at Maria and said "You know everybody". "Well I have lived here a few years"

Maria looked at the time "We better get this inside us, our appointment is in an hour"

They finished their lunch, "That was lovely" smiled Mandy

"Good glad you enjoyed it, come on or we will be late" she paid the bill and they headed to the school.

The met the head Mr Burke, Maria explained that her sister had moved to live with her and was looking for a placement.

Mr Burke, took Mandy`s details and said she could start next week.

"That is great " smiled Maria , as she got the information from him about school uniforms and times.

He showed them around the school and smiling at them said" We will see you Monday "

They strolled home arm in arm, Mandy starting to feel a bit apprehensive about the new school.

Maria reassured her there was nothing to worry about, and said that they would buy her uniform,on her lunch hour tomorrow.

Maria got dinner going when the got in, Mandy helped, afterwards they went into the garden With some crisps and lemonade and sat munching.

They talked about their Ma and discussed how unkind and nasty she could be.

 "I think it might be how she was brought up in poverty and neglect" said Maria.

"Yeah but we didn`t have a lot and I would never be nasty to anyone ,cause it`s not there fault"replied Mandy wisely,

"Neither would I " said Maria "but different times brings different things"

David appeared at the back door smiling he said "Hello and how did my two girls get on today"

Maria filled him in as Mandy made him a coffee. "Oh thank you Mandy so your all set for next Monday" he smiled.

She nodded saying "I`m a little bit nervous" "Oh don`t worry you will be fine"

"Let`s go and eat " said Maria as she went inside laid the table,

They chatted after dinner, and David got up from the table saying "I`ll see you both later "

Kissing Maria on the head, as he headed off to band practice.

Mandy started clearing the table ,and as her and Maria washed up she said,
"It`s lovely to see you and David so happy",

Maria looking at her answered" Well we have been through a rocky patch, but I hope it`s all sorted now"

Mandy stared to yawn, "I`m tired" "So am I " said Maria stretching.

"What time does David get back?"

"Christ it could be anytime, fancy a nightcap?"

"Why not "smiled Mandy feeling very grown up.

Taking there drink`s into the living room, they watched a bit of telly.

Mandy yawning said "I`m off to bed".

"Night sis. oh if you want to earn a bit of money , we need someone at the salon " said Maria.

"That would be great" she smiled. "Night" she waved.

"Night baby"

Maria went up not long after her.

Next morning Maria awoke to the alarm, David was snoring beside her.

She got out of bed thinking I didn`t even hear him come, showered she woke David," Hello sexy" he said as he opened his eye`s.

Smiling at him as she dressed, "What time did you get in last night?"

"Just after 11" he answered, "And you my darling were snoring your little head off"

"I didn`t hear a thing"

"I did try waking you but all I got was a grunt" he laughed.

 "Mandy is coming to work today with me"

"Well I suppose I better get my arse into gear" he said getting out of bed.

"Have you got anything on tonight?"

"Just an hour of training after work, why?"

"Nothing just wondering what time to do dinner for "she said smiling as she closed the

wardrobe door.

 Coming up behind her ,kissing her "I love you "

Turning she kissed him and ducked under his arm.

"I`m going to be late, got a wedding coming in this morning" she went and woke Mandy.

She was up and dressed.

They grabbed a cuppa and the two of them headed off.

"See you later David" she shouted as she closed the door.

They got to the salon Joe was there, coffee in his hand.

"Morning doll" he smiled as he heard Maria arrived with Mandy.

"Morning" she smiled and explained to Joe that they didn`t need to advertise for a new junior

as she they had Mandy.

"Great " he said as he flicked through the appointment book.

Mandy went over beside him asking "Busy"

"Chocker block doll" he smiled. As his first client appeared.
The day flew by, The salon was heaving, Mandy couldn`t believe the volume of people in
and out.

By the end of the day her feet were killing her.

Maria cashed up and the three of them headed to the Swan for a drink.

"I`m just going to phone David" said Maria..

"Ok I`ll get the drink`s in" said Joe.

Joe and Mandy headed to the bar, got the drink`s and grabbed at a table.

Maria arrived back with a puzzled look on her face.

"What`s up "asked Mandy?

 "Can`t get hold of David" she replied.

"Oh don`t worry he will be around like a bad smell" said Joe.

Joe didn`t like David mainly because he found him to be right up his own arse.

And also he wasn`t a very nice drunk, he had seen him kick off a few time`s

in pub`s where he had been playing.

                  They sat gossiping about the day , Joe asked Mandy how she was

adjusting to her new home.

 A huge smile on her face "I love it".

Johnny walked in spotting them he walked over and smiling, "Hello gang"

Maria looking up a spark seemed to fly between them.

Joe spotted this and gave Maria a wink.

She ignored him.

Mandy thought Johnny was lovely, so Maria encouraged it.

Half an hour later David walked in hardly able to stand.

Mandy spotted him first and nodded to Maria, Looking up she couldn`t believe her eye`s .

Her back went straight up and Joe saw the anger in her eye`s.

He put his hand on her` s whispering "Clam down".

Brendan the barman looked over at Maria who shook her head at him.

David was so drunk he didn`t even see his wife as he staggered to the bar.

Johnny seeing Maria`s reaction went up to him, asking if he was all right.

"I`m fucking fine" he slurred back.

"Ok, ok " replied Johnny shaking his head as he returned to the table.

As he sat down Maria looked at David trying to hold himself up at the bar.

As tear`s appeared in her eye`s she whispered "God almighty here we go again"

Mandy heard and asked in a concerned voice, "What`s the matter?"

"I told you the other day that we had been through a rocky patch, well this was the start of it

the last time"

 Mandy put her arm around her sister trying to comfort her.

Patting Mandy`s arm she said "I`m going home"

 "I`m coming with you"

She had ,had a hard day at work, and tomorrow being Friday would be even more hectic.

This was all she needed David sliding down the wrong path again and especially with her

baby sister living with them.

Joe said his goodbye`s looking at Maria said "You got my number doll".

"Yes Ill see you the morning, thank` s" she smiled.

Picking her bag up she said to Mandy "Come on let`s go"

"What about David ?" She asked as she looked over at him falling asleep on the counter.

"What about him wanker" Maria spit back at her, immediately sorry she snapped at her.

"I`m sorry sis" she apologized.

"Don`t worry Maria it`s ok" she said putting her arm through her `s.

They headed home.Mandy didn`t say a lot .

They got inside and Mandy with a worried look asked" What will happen when he get`s

home?"`

"You don`t worry about it sis I`ll deal with him, you go and get some rest, it will soon be morning and we will be back at the grind stone"

Mandy yawning put her arm`s around her gave her a kiss on the cheek said

"Goodnight" and headed upstairs.

Maria let out a sigh, made a cup of tea, not long after heard a car pull up outside.

Went into the living room looking out the window to see a taxi driver helping David out.

She opened the front door as David nearly fell through it.

The taxi driver looked at her, asking can you pay me or I`ll just have to go through his pocket`s.

Looking very embarrassed she went back in and got her purse,

"Where shall I put him" asked the taxi driver as he was still holding him up in the hallway.

She opened the living room door and said "Just throw it in there"

Paying the driver she thanked him, turning he said "You got your work cut out there my love"

Closing the door she was getting a splitting headache, she looked into the living room.

He was collapsed out on the sofa, dribbling and snoring.

She banged the door shut, and then realized Mandy was asleep upstairs.

Sat with a cuppa in her hand, tears of sorrow running down her face.

Thinking well there`s the last few month`s gone down the pan.

New Chapter14.

The next few weeks flew by, Mandy started her new school where she settled in quickly.

Maria working looking after the house and Mandy, and doing her odd modeling job.

David doing his own thing,

Maria felt they were drifting apart again, but this time she didn`t care.

She still went home to see her brother`s once a month.

Mandy refused to go with her.

One Sunday, leaving Mandy in charge of dinner,

She sang as she drove toward`s her parent`s house, thinking about the following weekend away with the girl`s.

Killarney here we come.She smiled as she unpacked the groceries which she always`s bought for them every time she visited. Smiling even more, as she looked up the road to where a childhood friend, remembering the first day Regina Doyle,who had befriended Maria And one evening she invited her to tea at her house.She was six year`s going to Regina`s for tea well it was a huge thing,in Maria`s world.

Getting there wearing her best dress which was blue, that her next door neighbour had made for her out of out of some scrap`s of material she had.

Going in the house was huge ,there was a driveway, with lawns and flowers, as she entered there was a huge hallway, Regina and her skipping along into her bedroom.

Maria couldn't believe that all this space was her`s,she had her own bed, a big cupboard that she hung her clothe`s in a big box with more toy`s in it , than Maria could ever imagine.

Her Ma calling them saying tea was ready.

Maria walked into another room which was bigger than Regina`s bedroom, to see a table with flowers on, more food than the shop had.

There was banana`s,boiled egg`s cheese bread one brown, and white,butter, a plate with different meats on tomato`s and green stuff in a bowl that Maria had never seen before.

Sitting at the table feeling well out her depth, Regina`s Ma watching her ,who had come from a very poor background , knew the look.

Smiling at Maria said "Tuck in sweetheart,"

Watching what Regina did , she copied.

Having a banana first followed by , brown bread butter cheese and ham.

Her Ma then bringing a big cake through, Maria`s eye`s nearly popping out of her little head.

After having some cake ,her tiny stomach not being used to so much food at any one time, she thought she was going to blow up.

Going home telling her Ma about the feast she had just had, her Ma looking at her giving her

a slap across the face telling her she was getting too big for her boot`s.

Saying that ,that was the last time she was going there.

So that ended Maria and Regina`s short friendship.

She always` s remembered being hungry, so now that she had her own few bob, she would

bring them biscuits, cakes, tinned fruit and veg,

She did this especially for her two brothers.

Knocking on the door, "She heard her Da shout "Come in"

"Oh it`s the girl" sitting back down as his God was on telly.Football.

She put the bag`s on the floor cringing at the name, her brother Paul walked into the room.

"Hi Paul" she smiled at him.

"Hi ya want a cuppa" he asked.

Hearing a huge sigh coming from The Thrown, Paul put the kettle on.

"How`s is Mandy?"

"She`s doing good, settled in at school and making new friend`s" answered Maria in a hushed

voice,

"For Jesus sake I can`t hear a bloody thing with all this racket "he shouted.

Maria looking at Paul put her eye`s up toward` s heaven.

Handing her the cuppa, he turned to his Da and asking if he wanted one.

"For the last time I`m trying to watch football".

"Fine" snapped Paul.

Maria finished her tea, said "I`ll be off then"

Her Da waved at her from The Thrown.

Paul walking her to the car, "Ma`s next door"

Tell her I`ll catch her next time.she said giving him a kiss on the cheek.

Paul nodded as he walked back into the house, it was lonely since his two sister`s had moved out.

She arrived home to find ,David half pissed, Johnny playing his guitar.

Mandy looking after dinner,and Joe had arrived "Have you seen the state of that in the front room"She shouted in anger.

Joe gave her a big hug and whispered "Stay Clam Doll"

She looked at Mandy smiling asked" How`s the chicken doing"

Mandy smiling replied "It`s fine kept an eye on it while you were gone."

"How are they"

"Usual" said Maria as she burned her finger`s on the oven.

"Fuck" she shouted.

"Are you ok" Joe asked,

Looking at him with tear`s of frustration in her eye`s she snapped,

"Yes I`m fine apart from arriving back to a half drunk husband, I asked him not to do this,

I just wanted to have a nice Sunday dinner, but Na Can`t even have that"

Joe taking a bottle out of his bag said "Sit down Doll and have a drink"

Shaking her head she said "No I want to get dinner finished"

Johnny came into the kitchen asked "Do you need a hand Maria?"

She looked at him shaking her head smiling "Na everything is under control"

"Can you set the table Mandy?" "Sure"

Maria went and stuck her head around the living room door,

David was snoring his head off.

Looking at him with disgust, left the room.

She put the finishing touches to dinner and served it up.

"What about David?" asked Mandy

"Fuck him the snoring pig, carry on, now where that` bottle Joe?" She asked trying to lighten the mood.

Joe poured the drink`s and they all sat down to dinner.

Johnny giving her a look that could melt a piece of ice.

Said "This is gorgeous Maria"

The eye contact between them did not go unnoticed by Joe.

Dinner over Johnny picked up his guitar and they sat around the kitchen table singing.

The door opened David appeared looked at the table, seeing the drink grabbed a glass and helped himself .

This put a damper on the evening and they watched David drink himself into oblivion.

Johnny helped him upstairs to bed as Maria and Mandy did the washing up.

Joe sitting at the table, giving his penny`s worth about the situation.

Maria looked at the half empty bottle on the table, getting her purse out asked Joe if he would go to the shop.

Mandy said "I`ll come with you after that big dinner"

As they walked out the door Maria shouted "Get me some cigarettes"

Putting the dishes away she turned to find Johnny beside her .

Smiling she said "Christ you frightened me there".

"That`s the last thing I`d want to do " he said with a mischievous grin on his face.

She let the tea towel fall, and the to of them bent to pick it up they bumped heads.

They burst out laughing.

He looked at her and the next thing she knew they were kissing.

It was a kiss full of affection and passion.

She felt it from the tip of her toes to the top of her head.

As she pushed away, he very gently pulled her back by her long dark hair and kissed her strongly on the lip`s.

They heard the front door go Maria nearly jumped out of her skin.

Joe and Mandy arrived in laughing, Maria busied herself making coffee as Johnny picked up his guitar started to sing.

Soon they were all having fun singing laughing and dancing.And Johnny finished the evening off singing Lady in Red. And Christ could he sing.

Maria nudged Joe as she looked over at Mandy, who was a bit tiddly at this stage, and was gazing at Johnny, with eye`s that were half shut.

Maria going over to her suggested that she should go to bed. Nearly falling from the chair she nodded.

After attempting to kiss everyone she made her way upstairs.

"She`s turning out all right" laughed Joe.

Maria answered with a far away look in her eye "Yes she will be fine"

"What did you say it like that for ?" disturbed a little by the tone of her voice.

"What do you mean?" replied Maria a little unsure.

"Come on doll spill the bean`s" said Joe.

Maria started shaking and sweating, holding her head in here hand`s she started to cry.

Joe got up and put his arms around her. "Hey what`s the matter" he asked softly.

She looked at Johnny and he took this as his que to leave.

Grabbing his jacket, he kissed Maria gently on the head and thanked her for a lovely day.

She didn`t even look up.Joe saw him out and coming back into the room saw Maria just staring out the window.

Chapter new15.

Joe poured them a drink and patting the chair beside him indicating for her to sit.

Maria taking a deep breath sat and put her head in her hand`s.

She hadn`t realized the effect seeing her Da had on her. Especially now that Mandy was out of that hell hole.

She didn`t even know why she bothered going back to see them, duty or maybe she felt responsibility toward` s Sean and Paul.

As they were the only one`s left behind.

"Oh doll what`s the matter?" Joe asked concerned.

She looked at him with the saddest eye`s he had ever seen in his life.

He passed the drink to her, "Come on you can tell me, after all you know all about my secrets." he smiled trying to encourage her to talk.

"Is it David and his behaviour of late".

Shaking her head, the tears rolling down her face.

"Johnny?"

"No" she sobbed "It`s nothing to do with either of them"

Joe knew whatever she was going to tell him was serious.

"I went to see me Ma and Da today" she was crying now holding her stomach.

The pain inside was so intense, she didn`t know where to start or even if she wanted to.

She had never voiced to another human being about the dark secrets of her childhood He went over and bending on one knee softly said "Doll what is it?" he prompted

She looked into his eyes and knew she could confide him, without any worry`s.

Pushing her drink gently towards` her he said "You can trust me"

Wringing her hand`s together tear`s pouring down her face, trying to find her voice.

"When I was a little girl"

"No no I can`t go down that road " she burst out.

Joe was totally bewildered.

"What is it oh Maria your really worrying me"

"I`m sorry Joe but I can`t tell you" she sobbed.

"Oh darling it can`t be that bad"

"Bad, Bad if I told you ,you could never look at me the same way again"

"Maria your not making sense "he said looking totally confused.

She looked at him with a total worn out look on her face, she was tired oh so tired.

She started to scream at him "I`m not making sense, you want to be inside this" hitting
herself on the head.

He was starting to feel panic inside as he had never seen Maria in such a state.

He had not got a clue what to do next.

"Shall I call Mandy?" He stammered. Joe always` s stammered when he got nervous.

Maria looked at him as if he had grown ten heads.

"Have you lost the plot totally" she shouted.

"I have protected her from that malignant demon, all of her life and you want to get her down
here to see me like this"

"Maria `Ill be honest "he stammered, "I have never seen you behave like this and your
frightening me" .

She was exhausted with the pain and confusion that every so often hit her brain like a bomb
going off inside of her head

Looking at Joe she said "I`m so sorry Joe " she was beginning to clam down.

She felt so angry, let down, disappointed and now lashed out at the person closest to her

Which had never happened as she never let anybody get that close.

But Joe was different, she felt as if she had known him all her life, they jelled together.

Joe saw the anger and hatred that had been in her eyes earlier subside.

He poured himself a large drink, looked at Maria asking "Do you want one"

She nodded, her head pounding, she suddenly blurted out "HE abused me"

Joe pouring the drink`s looked and said "What, who abused you?"

She took a huge gulp of her drink, lit a cigarette and blowing the smoke out through her nostrils very calmly answered "My Da"

Joe looked at her with a stunned expression on his face.

Swallowing trying digest in what she had just said, "He what" he replied in a high voice.

In between the sobbing she blurted out "He had sex with me"

"Jesus Christ" he answered shaking his head, totally shocked.

Squeezing her hand " Carry on sweetie"

"You haven`t been to our house?"

Joe shaking his answered "No".

"Well it was very basic, four room`s in total" she was getting more composed.

"Three bedroom`s and a kitchen, there was no heating or running water, no toilet facilities"

He nodded seeing the distance look in her eye`s.

"When I was a little girl I used to sleep with my brother Sean, we used to cuddle up together to keep warm" she smirked at him as she was remembering.

"On occasion`s me Ma would take me from the bed and put me in with me Da and she would get in with Sean, saying that she couldn`t sleep with his snoring",

Joe looked at her with a puzzled look on his face interrupting he said "Wasn`t she doing that a bit arse about face"

She looked at him uncertainly "What do you mean"

"Well if she was getting away from your Da `s snoring, why didn`t she put your brother in with him and she get in with you".

"I have never thought about that" she answered calmly.

Joe poured them a drink, sitting opposite her held her hand giving it a squeeze.

Taking a deep breath, she looked at him and said "This is hard"

Joe smiled saying "Take your time doll"

Tear`s in her eye`s she continued "I would climb in beside him, he would put his arm`s around me "She stopped, started to tremble, Joe sat next to her and cuddling her whispering "It`s ok"

"I would feel his willy warm in the bottom of my back, he would then put his hand down and start playing with it" she said choking.

Joe was near to tear`s as he could feel intense pain flowing from her.

"He would sometime` s put it between my leg`s and God would that hurt"

Tear`s pouring down her face, Joe got some tissue`s.

Very few thing`s shocked Joe but this confession, was making him feel sick to the pit of his stomach.
                    "Did your Ma know" Joe stammered.Maria looked at him nodding.

"Oh yes " she replied sharply.
Joe was shaking his head in total disbelieve, looking at her he said, "And you have never told anybody "

"No", she sniffled blowing her nose,"Who was there to tell"

"Not even David?"   she shook her head.

"To be honest I don`t even know why I`m telling you" she said looking baffled.

Joe smiling at her and gently kissing her on the forehead "Maybe because were friend`s?"

Looking at him she said "It feel`s like a bit of the strain has been taken away by telling you"

Holding her hand, stroking it gently, he slowly answered, "I can understand that"

"I know there is no comparison but when I had to admit I was gay" squeezing his hand.

He poured them another drink, handing her the glass, she said "Nothing can be compared"

He nodded in agreement.

"My darling friend and you are that" she said trying a smile,

"That is why I lost it a bit because when I went home today, HE was sitting in his chair like,

a lord of the manor, when I walked in he looked and said "Here she come`s THE Girl"

"That is all he ever called me, THE GIRL" she repeated.

"IF you ever heard him talk to someone, you would think what a gentleman, a caring loving

father an absolute pillar of society."

Knocking her drink back she hissed "I despise him"

Joe was speechless, "What about Mandy"

She sat waving her finger "No NoNo ,I was six when she was born, I protected her, made

sure he was never alone with her"

"That was until I left home, if he had done anything I would know she would have told me"

"That`s why now she is living with us it`s a relief, I don`t have to worry about her."

"I need another drink" Joe said getting up and bringing the bottle to the table.

Sitting down opposite her, "Your Ma knew".

Nodding "Yes I remember being ill and off school, I was in bed and he came into the

bedroom, sitting on the side of the bed he removed his trousers, climbing in beside me"

Joe shivered, lighting them a cigarette he passed her one.

As he got in I got out and went into the kitchen where she was she turned around and asked

"What are you doing up?"

I answered "Because I`m feeling better"

"Get back into that bedroom, your not staying here in my fucking way" she shouted.

"So back in I had to go" she sighed dragging in her cigarette.

"She then would punish me, by throwing me out the back door down the concreate step`s and

hitting my head off the wall then I would passed out" Joe was looking at her speechless.

"She would then carry me to a barrel of water, dipping my head in it to bring me around"

Joe was shaking his head, "My God what bloody cruelty" finishing the last of his drink"

Maria shook her head" If I protested, she would pull me by the hair calling me a black headed whore or just lash out at me."

She stared at him crying "I never got any love or sympathy, just abuse. It`s a wonder I`m still here" she sobbed.

Joe was totally lost for word`s, he stared at her as she rocked in the chair.

.She got that glazed look in her eye`s "I had a little dog he was a stray that just wandered into our yard one day, I adopted him. He wasn`t allowed near the house, so I kept him in the shed at the end of the garden."

Letting a long sigh out she continued "I loved him with all of my heart, I called him Tiddle` s he was my friend" a tear ran down her face, as she remembered.

"I would run the whole way home from school and he would be there waiting for me, tail wagging as soon as he saw me,"

"I`d walk him every day through the field`s .He would jump up on me ,He loved me.I`d rob some scrap`s from the butchers, sit watching as he devoured it"

"One day I ran home from school got to the gate I couldn`t see him, normally he`d be barking wagging his tail as soon as he saw me come through the gate`s"
S
he poured them another drink, passed Joe his, "What had happened" asked Joe curiously.

"I ran into the house in panic" and asked me Da if he knew where Tiddle`s was.

He looked at me and in a matter of fact voice said "Yes I took him to the river and drown him"

I started to scream my Ma came out of the other room "What the fuck is wrong"

Me Da looking at her said coldly "I got rid of the fucking dog, only a fucking nuisance"

"Jesus Christ I thought someone had died" she answered looking at Maria.

"I screamed at them I HATE YOU, and ran out the door. Something died inside of me that day"

        "Christ I don`t know what to say" he paused.

"There is nothing anybody can say" she answered calmly.

They heard movement upstairs, Joe looked up, "That`s David" said Maria trying to compose herself.

"I`d better go " Joe in a very quite voice.

She got up and as he looked at her he saw a very worried look on her face.

Putting his arm`s around her he whispered "Your secret`s are safe with me Angle"

She hugged him closely, and there was a lot of affection in that hug.

"Thank you" she said.

"I`m always` here for you Doll, cause I for one Love you"

Walking him to the door she waved him off.

Joe looked back at the closed door thinking "How does she do it?"

He knew she was a a very determined woman, but he couldn`t put his finger on what had kept her going or how she had survived.

        Maria went back inside, feeling a release, that at long last she had put into word`s what had happened,

She collapsed on the sofa ,exhausted, and fell asleep. Next thing she knew Mandy was sitting beside her on the sofa looking a bit worse for wear.

Maria opened her eye`s and smiled at her baby sister.

Asking her as she stretched out on the sofa "What`s the time?"

"It`s midday"

"Bloody hell" smiled Maria.

"Why did you sleep down here?"

"Oh Christ Joe and I were talking until Christ know` s what time, so after I let him out I came back in here and conked out"

"I don`t remember going to bed" smirked Mandy.

"Well you did have a few sherbet`s last night" smiled Maria back at her.

They could here David being ill upstairs. Mandy lay beside her sister and put her head on her knee`s

.

She started stoking her hair, "I love it when you do that" smiled Mandy as she looked up at her"

They rest of the day the two of them just chilled out.

Going into work the next morning Joe was standing there, the kettle on for a cuppa for the two of them .

"Morning Doll" he smiled.

"Joe before we start work, I just want to thank you for the other night."

Smiling at her he said "Think nothing of it, I am glad it was me you confided in"

Hugging her saying "If you ever need me I am always` s here for you"

Hearing the salon door go They headed downstairs.
"The main conversation that day ,was about their trip to Killarney, which was coming up next weekend.
NEW CHARTER

The week flew by, and soon it was Saturday morning.

Maria had packed everything the night before, she awoke early that morning.

Mandy heard her and went downstairs making her a coffee before she went away.

Kissing her Maria telling her to have a great time.

 The Swan where they were all meeting

When she arrived Joe, Martina and Susan were already there.

Joe was there wearing black leather trousers and a loud yellow shirt,

"Well good morning Doll" he smiled.

"Hi ya " she smiled.

"You look very refined" laughed Joe.

Laughing she answered "These are my traveling cloths you want to see what`s in here"

Martina laughing said "At least she doesn`t look like a fucking tiger on the prowl."

Joe looked at her "Oh fuck off, your only turning green with envy" he said as he minced,

swinging his shoulder bag about.

Rosie arrived looking like Liz Taylor, "Coo look at her" said Martina.

"I like to do things in style" she said shaking her blond hi-lighted hair.

"Who else is coming?" asked Susan.

Declan Joe`s "friend" arrived. Joe introduced him.

Smiling with a gold filling sparkling tooth. .

He was wearing pink jeans and a black silk shirt.

Martina nudged Susan who nearly chocked trying to hold back from laughing.

His hair was high lighted to nearly white in colour.

"Hi girls" he said in a husky voice.

"Which of you is Maria" he asked ?

"I am "

"Well I have heard so much about you " he said taking her hand and kissing it.

Maria had never met him but had heard lots about him from Joe.

"And me, you and now that I can put a face to the name, I`m really pleased to meet you"

Declan was as camp as the got.

Joe then said "I love the jeans"

"I know pink to make the girls wink" he sniggered.

Next to arrive were they twins Una and Rita, who were clients of Maria`s and got asked to

make numbers up.

Joe shouted "Here comes the bus".

"Who else is coming? "asked Susan impatiently

"Here thy are " said Maria as Nick and his wife Liz arrived.

The bus driver, said "Good morning ladies and gentlemen, my name is Sean Bracken and I`m your driver for the weekend,"

Martina whispered to Maria "He can drive me wild anytime he likes" she pointed to the wedding band on his finger.

Martina just shrugged and said " We all got our crosses to bear".

Maria playfully shoved her "Your terrible"

Martina turning to her said "I know that`s why they love me"

 Sean said "If your ready, lets hit the road"

They bus started, and they all got comfortable and as they pulled away the started singing

"It`s a long way to Tipperary it`s a long way to go, without your granny"

Everyone in high spirit`s, Declan produced  bottles of drink, passing around some paper cup`s.

"Oh be Jesus that`s a man after my own heart" smiled Rosie as she poured some whisky into her cup.

The arrived at their destination, all a bit pissed.

Maria booked them in, most of them staggered to their room`s.

Maria told them to be in the dinning room at eight.

Maria Martina and Susan were sharing, decided to have a little siesta.

Maria awoke first , showered, made a coffee went sat on the balcony, lit a cigarette, sat admiring the view.

The balcony of the hotel over looked the three lakes of Killarney.. It was spectacular.

There were boats on the lakes with tree`s over shadowing it.

Susan appeared beside her.

Looking up "Beautiful isn`t it" she said.

"You can see now why it cost's so much to stay here" Susan replied.

"It's only money what's it is there for, we bloody work hard enough for it" answered Maria.

"True and when we pop next door, we can't bring it with us" smiled Susan.

"I love the way you describe death" said Maria offering her a cigarette.

"Cheer's Doll, but it is true we will all see each other again,"

"What are you talking two talking about?" Asked Martina as she appeared beside them.

"You" they both laughed.

"I'm off for a shower" said Susan.

"Ill have one after you "said Martina.

"Coffee" offered Maria.

"Na I am going to indulge in a Bacardi and coke" Smiled Martina as she waddled off.

"We are on holiday" she smirked as she poured her drink.

"Fuck it " said Maria as she stood beside helping herself to a vodka and coke.

Taking their drink's out on the balcony, They sat down looking at the view.

"Christ it's beautiful here" Martina sighed as she sipped her drink.

"We should do this more often" smiled Maria as the clinked their glasses.

"It's lovely to get away from everything" sighed Maria.

"Yes " answered Martina "I know things haven't been easy for you lately"

"No they haven't, that's why I thought we could do with a break and I'm not thinking any

negative for now"

Martina hugged her and said "It will all work itself out in the end"

Maria nodded "I'm sure it will but we all make our own destiny."

She sat back thinking.This is what I want to be surrounded with people who care, peace and

tranquillity. Not the mayhem and the chaos that life had become.

Like a light being switched on, it dawned in her that she was allowing men to dominate her life maybe that was why she felt sometimes like damaged goods.

Susan arrived back from the shower , "Showers free" she shouted.

Martina went and showered and the three of them got ready to hit the town.

They were dressed to kill, "Right lets do this" smiled Martina.

Heading out the did the grand tour of Killarney, no pub was spared of infectious antics.

They were having a ball, heading back to the hotel, singing dancing in high spirits.

Walking into the hotel to see Joe and Declan on a karaoke, singing together ,

"Tainted Love".

The crack was mighty.Declan singing was totally pissed , and was trying to put the microphone up Joe`s arse.

Maria who loved karaoke got up singing "These boots were made for walking"

She ended up on a table with the microphone swinging it and dancing and singing her heart out.

They whole lot of them ended up on the tables, dancing.Joe removing his shirt and Declan removing all of his attire, just leaving a leotard skin printed knickers in view.

The night porter refused to serve them anymore to drink and told them he was going to put a complaint into management.

Everyone of them pissed ended up knocking tables and chairs over much to the night porters annoyance.

Next morning, Maria awoke to the sounds of Martina snoring in her ear.

Pushing her off of her she went and got a glass of water feeling totally dehydrated.

Susan arrived out her hair standing on end, make up stains on her face, looked like a scarecrow.

"Christ can`t she snore" Susan grumbled.

"Fucking hell my mouth feels like sandpaper and my head feels as if a symphony orchestra

is tuning up in my brain."complained Maria.

"Here is some aspirin " said Susan.

"Fucking good night last night" smiled Maria.

"Did you see Declan trying to put the bloody microphone up Joe`s bum." She laughed.

Maria looked at her going into hysterics "I know, did you see the leotard knickers that's

something we won`t forget in a hurry"

Gathering at the breakfast table , Una and Rita looked as if they were going to die,

In fact the whole tribe, looked as if they had been on the razz for a week.
                        Because of their antics the night before the manager called Maria aside
and told her that they had an hour to leave the premises.

Standing there absolutely gob smacked, She apologized, The manager was not having it

telling her it was their policy to remove disruptive guests who`s behaviour affected other

people staying. Especially the two gentle men who were insisting on lets hide the microphone.

Smirking as he walked away.

Fuming Maria went back to the girls and told them what had happened.

"You two fucking arseholes" said Martina, gutted they had to leave looking at a very sheepish

Joe and beetroot faced Declan.s

"What are we going to do now" Nick asked?

"Well I`ll just have to get hold of Sean, tell him what`s happened and go home" said Maria
not happy at all about the situation.

Finding Sean, she explained the crises they had on their hand`s.

Laughing his head off, he said "Right just give me a few minutes and I`ll be ready."

                        They headed upstairs and packed, and soon they were on their way home.

Joe and Declan, kept apologizing to everyone.

"Oh look we had a good night and at least we have something to talk about" said Nick.

They arrived home a few hour's later. All of them nursing hangover's and feeling a bit brain dead.

All of them disappointed at being home, that their adventure had been abruptly cut short, By the antics of The Yellow Shirt and The Pink jeans.The were falling about the street laughing.

Joe mincing in front said, "It wasn't all our fault was it?" he said to Maria giving daggers.

Laughing Maria answered "Minor detail's"

Joe taking her arm laughed "Well we won't be going back there again, do you know why?"

Maria laughing shaking her head said "Why"

"Because we are The Destroyers" he said hysterically.

Nick said "Well at least we won't be forgotten"

Arriving at the Swan Brendan looked up to see them come in,

"What are you doing back?" he asked.

"Because these two nob head's were trying to get a fucking microphone up each other's arse's" said Martina with a total look of disgust on her face.

Brendan holding a glass in his hand, nearly let the glass fall laughing.

Joe ordered the drink's "Well we might as well finish off what we started "

Holding his glass up."To the destroyer's "

They all fell about laughing,

The destroyers leaving, singing, Brendan looking after them thinking no wonder the manager threw them out.

Joe looking back swinging his handbag, and Declan mincing beside him,

Shouting" The Destroyers will return"

Brendan shaking his head thinking, God almighty help us!

Maria said her good byes to Declan and Joe,

Joe stumbled as he went to kiss her,

Laughing she said "Ill see you Tuesday" as she watched the Queens wander down the street.

Opening the door she heard Mandy in the kitchen, "Hello " she shouted.

Mandy hearing her walked into the hallway" Fucking hell what are you doing back"

Maria filled her in on the drama`s, she nearly wet herself laughing.

Laughing she asked "What`s your name`s?"

"The Destroyer`s" Maria answered, throwing her eye`s up to heaven.

"That is fucking amazing" she laughed.

"How has David been?"she asked.

"I haven`t seen him, heard someone moving about earlier" she answered.

Right I`m going to have a lie down, I`m bloody so tired I could sleep on a bed of nail`s"

Heading upstairs.

Went in to see David snoring.

She went into the spare bedroom, got into bed and was soon asleep.

She awoke a few hour`s later, Mandy was cooking dinner.

"You're a diamond" she said .

They chatted about The Destroyers weekend or rather overnight stay.

Mandy was creased up,

They heard movement from upstairs.

David arrived in the kitchens, "Hello thought you weren`t arriving back until tomorrow"

"They Destroyers were kicked out " laughed Mandy.

"The what" David asked.

There was a knock at the door. "I`ll get it " said David.

They heard a male voice in the hallway.

Mandy looked at Maria questionably .

She just shrugged.

David came into the kitchen with his brother Gerry behind him.

"Hello Maria," "Gerry hello" she answered.

"Want a cuppa"

"Na were heading out" David butted in.

Gerry looking at Mandy said "Your Maria`s sister I remember you from the wedding"

Mandy nodding smiled .

"Yes nice to see you again" she answered.

They left,

Maria and Maria ate dinner ,"Don`t suppose there is any point in leaving some for David"

Mandy asked.

Maria shook her head,

"I`m going to go to shop and get us a video out" smiled Mandy.

"That sound`s good, here get me some cigarettes" giving Mandy some money.

The phone rang it was Joe" How are you doing Doll"

They chatted "Fancy meeting up for some lunch tomorrow?" He asked.

"Yes that would be great" she answered.

Mandy arrived back with "Ghost"

They spent a nice girly evening together Mandy really pleased to have her sister home.s

"Joe has asked me out to lunch tomorrow, fancy coming?"

Smiling at her sister she nodded.

They went to bed, and in the early hours, Maria heard noise coming from downstairs.

Getting up she found David with Gerry pissed up.

"Can you keep it down?"

"Oh dear her worship is back" David sneered.

"Oh just keep it down" she snapped.and headed back to bed.

NEW CHAPTER

The next morning she woke up to David being sick in the loo.

Home sweet home, she thought, and then started laughing to herself, at the antics of Joe and

Declan .

Hearing David leave the bathroom, climbed out of bed showered, and headed downstairs

putting the kettle.

Hearing a noise behind her ,turning Mandy was behind her, "Morning sis " she smiled "want

a cuppa?"
Mandy nodding said, "What was all that bloody racket last night?"

"Them two idiot`s " she answered nodding towards the front room.

"What time are we meeting Joe at?"

"About one"

Drinking her coffee she said "I`ll just go and shower, in a second".

"Oh I almost forgot, there`s a present in the bedroom for you" smiled Maria.

Mandy ran upstairs, coming downstairs with a beautiful black jumpsuit in her hand.

"Oh Maria I love it " she said hugging her.

"I`m going to wear it today, just going to shower"

A few minute`s later she arrived back looking stunning in the new jumpsuit.

Oh Mandy that look`s beautiful on you" smiled Maria.

Gerry wandered into the kitchen, Mandy looked at him and asked if he wanted a coffee.

Shaking his head he answered "No ta David and I are going to football game"

Mandy nodded looking at Maria who had a face like thunder.

David arrived in the kitchen, looked at Maria`s face, turned and said to Gerry "Lets go"

"See you later " smiled Gerry as he walked out the door.

"Did you have a think about you and him" asked Mandy.

Maria looking at her said "Not really , but I do know that I cannot go on living like this"

Mandy said "I don`t blame you, I`m just popping over the shop"

Sat at the table light a cigarette and started thinking about what she had confided in Joe last week.

She felt relieved to have spoken about the dark hidden secret,that she had been buried inside her for year`s.

And she knew that her secret was safe with Joe.They had hit it off from day one.

Mandy arrived back with a box of chocolates for her.

"Oh sis you didn`t have to do that"

"Right let`s go meet the destroyer`s" Mandy said with a huge grin on her face.

They went to the Swan as soon as they went walked in Joe stood up shouting her she come`s " They Queen of The Destroyers ".Brendan stood watching, smiling shaking his head.

Maria turning replied, "There is only one lot of queens here ," as she ruffled Joe and Declan hair.

Mandy was creased up laughing.

Grabbing some seat`s, Joe got the menu`s and they ordered

Maria heard her name being called.

Turning around she saw Johnny."Hello " Mandy said, "How is the most gorgeous girl`s about town" he smiled staring at Maria.

"Were grand" she replied looking into them sexy eye`s.

"Can I get you a drink?"

Shaking her head she answered coldly, remembering there kiss the week before" No thank were just having a bit of lunch"

"With the destroyers" smiled Mandy

Johnny a bit taken aback by her cold attitude said "Ok, suit yourselves" and walked off.

Mandy puzzled by her sister`s aloofness asked "Why did you speak to him like that ?"

"I didn`t " she snapped.

"Yes you did " answered Mandy really annoyed.

"You Fancy him" smiled Mandy.

"I do not" she snapped back a bit too quickly.

They all sat eating their lunch Joe looking at Johnny`s bum commented

 "Very nice arse" Declan swallowing a mouth full of food nodded in agreement.

Declan finishing his lunch looked at his watch said "I have to dash or I`ll miss my train"

Joe finishing his drink answered "I`ll walk with you"

Kissing Maria and Mandy he said his farewell`s and they were gone.

 Johnny passed them as he was leaving.

"Johnny" Maria called.

 He went over to her looking at him apologized "I`m sorry I was so off with you earlier, It`s

just that I have had a hectic weekend, me The girls and Joe have arrived back from Killarney.

I`m not feeling a 100%".

Johnny looking into the sexy brown eye`s smiling said "Forgiven, Drink?"

She nodded smiling, "Please a coke", "Mandy" he asked.

"Ill have the same" she smiled.

Both sister`s stared at him as he headed for the bar.

"Yes he does have a nice bum" Maria commented. As Mandy giggled in agreement.

"Do you like him?"

"Yes he`s nice, but I do like Don" she replied swallowing the last of her fish.

Maria feeling a bit relieved laughing said "Don Egan you mean"

She nodded feeling a bit confused as to why her sister was laughing.

Maria knew she shouldn`t be feeling like this so covering her track`s answered "I used to fancy him before I got with David"

Mandy looking a bit surprised "Did you".

"Well you can`t go there now" replied Mandy with a smug look on her face.

"Nope" laughed Maria,

Johnny arriving back from the bar, passed Mandy her coke, "Thank you" she smiled "My pleasure"

To Mandy`s delight Don walked in, Johnny shouted over "Don come and join us"

Don a tall ,handsome fella with blondish coloured hair and a gorgeous smile.

Maria could see why Mandy was attracted to him, He was very well dressed, Maria thought not short of a few bob either.

"Hello " Don smiled, "This is Maria and her sister Mandy,"said Johnny as he introduced, the girl`s "Hello I know Maria David`s wife, is that right?"

Maria nodded said "Yes that`s right"

Then smiling at Mandy said "I haven`t had the pleasure"

Mandy feeling very shy stood up and shook his hand,

"Drink" he asked Maria looked at Mandy`s face, she immediately replied "Yes that would be nice"

Mandy gave her a grateful look, and settled back in her seat relishing in the company of Don.

Johnny looked at Maria," I really enjoyed last weekend."

"Yes it was a nice evening" she replied feeling a bit embarrassed thinking about the kiss.

"Where`s the man himself?"he asked.

"He is gone out with his brother Gerry" replied Mandy.

Johnny looking at Maria said "Do you know he can`t drink"

"Oh he can " replied Maria sharply.

"Well" replied Johnny lying back in his chair with his arm`s folded, "Yesterday he had six maybe seven pint`s" And I nearly had to carry him home".

Maria nodding agreed "But he is only topping up"

"What do you mean?" Asked Johnny.

Maria sighing replied "Well Friday he went to football got pissed, came home did his usual party trick`s, puked up and went to bed."

"So you see he is just topping up all the time".

"Oh right I see "replied Johnny "The man`s an idiot"

Mandy was a tad shocked at the tone in Johnny`s voice.

Maria twigged her sister`s reaction, and turning to Johnny in a raised voice ,asked "What did you say?"

"All right then if you want to stand up for him" Johnny replied in a disappointed voice.

"When did he last put his hand in his pocket to take you out?"

Maria nodded understanding what he meant, smiling "Point taken"

Mandy looked at Maria asking "Everything ok"

Maria smiled at her reassuringly her.
                    Mandy`s eye`s were on focused on Don.Maria seeing this smiled to herself.

Don sitting next to Mandy, she was soaking up every word he said.
They were laughing and joking , the crack was great,

Mandy looked up as the door opened and saw David and Gerry walk in.

She nudged her sister.

Maria followed her Mandy`s stare, to see David standing there.

Maria waved as David walked over.

He looked like shit, very hungover, eye`s all puffed up and bloodshot.

She looked at him with pure disgust on her face.

"What`s up?" He half spat in her face.

Standing up she whispered "You look like shit".

Half staggering standing back, He replied "Charming" as he half walked ,half staggered

towards the bar.

Maria sat back down beside Mandy, shaking her head.

Mandy taking Maria`s hand squeezed it, seeing her sister was upset.

She looked as if she wanted the ground to open up and swallow her.

Mandy aware of this, looking in David`s direction, wondered why her sister ever married him.

Don distracting her from her line of thought, as he asked if he could take her out sometime.

Giving him a huge smile answered "Yes"

Johnny taking the scene in between Maria and David, putting his hand gently on her `s asking

if she was ok.

She nodded holding back the tear`s.

David half staggering walked out of the pub.with out even a goodbye.

Maria finished her drink, saying" I`m going home."

Mandy got her bag saying "I`ll come with you."

Shaking her head Maria said "No need you stay and enjoy yourself"

Mandy asked "Are you sure"

Nodding she said "Of course, I`m going to have a lie down, when I get in, you have your

key?"

Mandy giving her a big smile nodded and hugged her said "Ok sis I`ll see you later"

She gathered her thing`s said goodbye to everyone, and was gone.

Johnny looking at his watch finished the last of his pint saying "Shit is that the time

I should have been somewhere an hour ago" pulling his jacket on he half ran out the door.

He saw her turning the corner, and legged it after her.

Catching up with her, she turned around in surprise to see him by her side.

"What are you doing following me?" She asked half smiling.

"Just thought you could do with some company" he answered simply.

"Fancy a coffee?" She knew he didn`t live far.

"Ok, why not" she answered.

It was just two minute`s around the corner.

Getting his key`s out, and the walked in.

Maria was pleasantly surprised at place,

There was a guitar in one corner, with a music stereo unit .

Coffee table and a comfortable looking couch.

"Would you like a tour" he asked as he noticed her checking the place out.

Smiling she nodded.

.As she wandered around "I`m quite surprised" she said.

"At what" he asked.

She shrugged and smiling at him."At nothing really"

  "Bet you thought I lived in a pig sty"

"No Oh don`t mind me my head is all over the place at the moment"

"Make yourself at home" he said as he went into the kitchen.

She sat down and he brought the coffee`s through.

Sitting beside her he said "See you weren`t very impressed with your other half today"

Turning to face him "No I wasn`t"

She got very emotional, and with a lump stuck in her throat ,looked at him and said "What am I going to do"

  Putting his head between his hand`s, he said "Do? well if it was me ,married or not, if it wasn`t working I`d walk"

She was shocked at his reply, "Why did you say that" she asked sharply.

"Look you asked me a question, and I`m answering you honestly,"

"I know you two haven`t been married long, but even I can see , especially by you that your

not happy"

She lowered her eye`s looking at the ground answering "Your right"

Putting his arm around her he went to kiss her, she pulled quickly away.

 "What`s the matter"

"I`m not in the right place right now, I have to go" she answered simply.

He stood up putting his arm`s around her, "I`m here for you always"

 She looked at him and smiling said "Thank you"

"Now that`s better " he smiled back.

 Helping her into her jacket like a true gentleman. She kissed his cheek and was gone.

When she arrived home she found Mandy there with Don.

"Hi sis were in here" Mandy called as she heard the door go.

 Making her way into the kitchen, "Where have you been"

"Oh I went for a walk" she answered quickly

Mandy was making some sandwiches for them.

"Would you like some sis"

Shaking her head she said "No ta, I`m not hungry"

"Is David home"

"I don`t know , haven`t heard him" as she passed Don his cuppa.

Smiling she said "I`ll just go and check.

 Running upstairs` she opened the bedroom door, the odour hit her she went and opening the

window`s.

There was no David.

Sighing she stripped the bed put clean sheets on thinking why am I doing this.

It was automatic with her, she had always liked thing`s clean and tidy.

She quickly hovered and sprayed the room with air fresher.

Headed for the bathroom opening the door she found David passed out.

She let a scream, there was vomit all around him.

Mandy and Don hearing the scream ran upstairs, to see Maria trying to pull him out of the bathroom.

"Jesus Christ here Ill do it" said Don taking over. "Fucking hell what are you doing to yourself"

"Out of the way" he shouted to the girl`s.

Mandy was crying, Maria said "I`ll call an ambulance" as she noticed there was very little movement.

Running downstairs she quickly dialled 999.

Went back upstairs and noticed blood on Don`s hand`s.

"Oh Christ" said Maria as she looked at him, his breathing was shallow and he was yellow in colour.

Don looking at her said "He must of cut his head when he fell",

Open his eye`s as the jerked around his head, he was sick again.

Don turning him on his side, saying to Maria get a towel.

Knock at the door "That`s them " she said as she ran downstairs to open the door

They ambulance crew were on the ball and had him on a stretcher and out of the house in no time.

The ambulance man turned to Maria and said, "You were lucky we were in the area."

Don looking at the two sister`s Mandy crying hysterically, Maria in shock "I`ll go to the hospital with him."he said.

Maria taking her sister back inside, put the kettle on.

Mandy sat at the table shaking from head to toe.

"Is he going to die?" sobbed Mandy.

That thought hadn't even crossed Maria's mind.

She went upstairs and started cleaning the bathroom, seeing the blood on the floor, she started to cry.

Sitting on the bed she was wondering how they had got into this mess

Heading downstairs she said to Mandy,.

"I'm going to the hospital". The Phone rang.she answered.

It was Don telling her that he was going to be fine, That he had poisoned himself with alcohol and he was getting his head stitched at the moment.

"Are they discharging him" she asked. "His not giving them any choice"

"What do you mean?"

"He refusing to let them admit him" he answered.

"See you soon" he hung up.

Maria wandered back into the kitchen, shaking her head.

"What" Mandy asked beginning to clam down.

She filled her in on what Don had told her.

"Fucking idiot" she added.

Mandy looked at her and said "Well at least he is going to be ok"

She sat at the table, thinking,

She had loved David with all her heart or as much as you can love somebody.

All I'm doing is crying and wondering what is coming next.

Wondering if he is going to be sober or drunk, and this evening just took the biscuit.

Hearing the door go she ran downstairs to see a very embarrassed David coming through the door.

Don helping him she opened the living room door and said to Don "Drop it in there"

Doing as he was told he put David in the living room.

Following Don into the kitchen he handed her some tablet`s "There in case he dehydrates"

"Thank you" she said.

Nodding he said to" Mandy fancy going for a walk."

She looked at Maria who nodded.

"Before you go could you give me a hand to get him upstairs, I need to bath him?"

Don said "Of course you get a cuppa and I`ll help up"

Don headed into the living room to find David crying.

Looking down at him said "It`s a bit late for that don`t you think"

.David could hardly move he felt so weak.Trying to stand up he fell back down "What have I done to myself."

"Glad you realize that it`s you that has done this and nobody else"

David looked at him and said "I think I`m going to be sick"

Don grabbed him and got him out the front door just in the nick of time.

Maria hearing the commotion opened the kitchen door shouting "What` s going on "

Don turned around and shouted back "He is being sick"

"Serves the bollock`s right" she screamed back.

Don getting David back inside, Maria ran upstairs and ran the bath.

"Get him up here please Don"

Don half dragged him upstairs, got him outside the bathroom door.

"I`ll take it from here" she said looking at Don.

"Mandy and I are going for a walk"

She nodded.

"Mandy" she shouted downstairs "Can you throw some bleach outside"

"Yes" replied Mandy.As she was cleaning outside she was thinking (what the fuck is he playing at,? My sister will not put up with this) and she didn`t blame her.

Maria getting him into the bath, looked at him, and said "How low can you get?"leaving, banging the door.

Don said "Are we going for that walk I need to get away from all this madness" Mandy wasn`t sure she didn`t want to abandon Maria.

With that she walked back into the kitchen."Are you ok " asked Mandy.

Maria looked at her as if she had grown a head, "What do you think? A fucking drunken husband to contend with that gave himself alcohol poisoning and cut is head in the process" she shouted.

Don turned to her and said "It`s not her fault"

Maria burst into tear`s sat on the chair and sobbed.Looking at Mandy and Don she apologized bent over holding her stomach "I`m so sorry for taking it out on you, I`m just so fucking angry "

Don went over to her holding out his arm`s she went straight into them, .

Looking down at her "Calmed down now?,"he asked gently.

She looked at him and nodded, sniffling she said "Thought you two were going out for a bit of air"

"She didn`t want to leave you" he answered nodding at Mandy.

"Oh baby I`m not your responsibility" she said hugging her."But I`m not taking much more of this"

Mandy standing back said "I don't blame you, and I can see why your so angry"

"You two go on I left the thing in the bath" she half smiled at them.

"Ok "said Mandy "We won`t be long"

Maria headed upstairs to see what remains where left in the bath.

Opening the door she could still smell his sick.

"You're a bloody idiot" she said looking at him with so much anger he thought she was going to finish him off.

"Come on get out" she shouted as she held the towel up to him.He struggled to get out of the bath. She ended up throwing the towel at him, running out of patience.

She went in and sitting on the bed he arrived in the bedroom dripping wet.

She left the room went downstairs picked up his tablets, got some water and brought them up to him.

He was sitting with the towel half hanging off him, sobbing in both shame and self pity..

She handed him the tablets and water. He looked at her the whites of his eye`s so bloodshot you could hardly see the pupils.

He looked at her and went to apologize.

"I`m sorry Maria"

Putting her hand up screaming "What for David, For drinking so much that you had to be hospitalised or for ignoring your wife, making her feel as if she`s a nothing well come on big man which is it, I` M WAITING",she screamed at him they tears were running down her face with temper.!"

He had seen her angry before but never like this He knew he had crossed the river of no return and had no idea how to get back to shore.

"Jesus David we are not even married three years yet and on a slippery road to nowhere"

He nodded, lay back on the bed, his stomach turning. His head and mouth felt like the bottom of a sewer. How had he been so stupid, he could have killed himself.

"I have had enough" she said simply walking out of the room.

She heard the door go downstairs.

Mandy looking upstairs called "Are you ok"

.Wiping her eye`s she composed herself and went downstairs.

"How is he?" Mandy asked.

"Still breathing" Maria answered flatly.

"Cuppa"

She nodded.

You could cut the atmosphere with a blunt knife.

She took a deep breath thinking it`s not worth getting yourself into such a state over a man.

"Did you have a nice walk?"

Mandy gave Don a look that said everything.

"Yes, we had a lovey walk" she answered with a twinkle in her eye.

Maria kissed her "I `m glad" .

 She liked Don at least he seemed to have a level head.

"Yes we had a good old chin wag, didn`t we my little Doll"

"Less of the little" replied Mandy.

They all laughed.

David could hear them laughing as he lay with his whole body aching.

"I`ll just pop up and see the old boy" said Don.

"Well go on tell me" said Maria as soon as she knew he was out of earshot.

"Oh Maria he is so lovely" she answered with a glazed look in her eye`s.

"I really like him"
"I never noticed" answered Maria dryly.
Hugging her baby sis she realised she was becoming a woman.
"I`m really pleased for you"
"So am I" said Mandy with a grin on her face, like the cat who got the cream.s
Up stairs Don went into the bedroom, finding David laying on the bed sobbing.
"Well you have made a right dog`s dinner of thing`s this time"
David looked at him nodding as tear`s poured down his face.
"If I was you I`d grovel, cry, buy flowers, chocolate, whatever it take`s, It`s time you grew up.

And started looking after your wife because if you don`t well I don`t have to spell it put for you".

Heading out the door he looked back at the snow white face on the pillow, Shaking his head he walked out.

Don arriving back downstairs, Maria looked and asked "How is it"

"Not too good" he replied.

"Oh dear what a shame" said Maria sarcastically

"Coffee" Mandy asked.

Shaking his head "No thanks baby, I`d better be going"

Taking Mandy in his arms, he said "How about I take you out tomorrow evening"

She stared at him, and nodding her head smiling "Oh yes please"

"Great pick you up about seven" he winked as he headed towards the door.

Giving Maria a kiss on the cheek, He said "Take it easy" throwing his eye`s towards the ceiling.

They went back inside, Mandy skipping beside her like a little child,

They heard a yell from upstairs, Maria putting her eye`s up heaven, said "Stay there and make us a cuppa"

Finding David with his head down the toilet, "You yelled sis" she said sarcastically.

Looking down at him she could see he was finding it hard to breath.

"Jesus Christ" she said pulling his head out of the toilet.

She was getting worried now.

"Mandy bring me up a bowl and a jug of water" she shouted.

"David can you get up?"

"Here lean on me" she managed to get him up and into the bedroom.

Mandy arrived with the bowl and jug."Fill the jug up with water"

She got him into bed and putting the tablets in her hand. Mandy came back with the water.

"Come on take the tablet" she coaxed.

"I don`t know if I can keep it down" he cried as tears and snot ran down his face.

She passed him some tissues.s

"Fucking hell David how have you managed to get yourself into such a state" she sighed helplessly.

Sitting him up in the bed, "Look come on take the table and wash it down with water"

David looked at her thinking how can she be so nice? Doing as he was told Mandy watched on as her sister looked after him thinking if that was me I`d leave him to rot.

"I cant go to work, this week I`m going to ring in and tell them I`ll take it as holiday."

"Why" asked Mandy.

Maria looked at her and answered, "Because I need to sort this out"

Mandy was very taken aback by her sister`s calmness.

Maria looked at her and asked "What`s the matter/"

She shook her head and said "I just cannot believe how calm you are"

"Well if I rant and rave, where will that get me?"

"I`m going to try and get some sleep" said Mandy.

"Good idea"

They headed upstairs, Maria looked in on David who was asleep.

Went into the spare room thinking I cant deal with this for much longer.

She woke up a bit later looked at the clock and went and rang work.

Joe answering the phone heard her and asked "Is everything ok"

Hearing her best friend`s voice on the phone, She blurted out what had gone on.

"Oh Doll you cannot go on like this, Christ you deserve better a lot better, he is an idiot of a man"

Listening she could hear the disgust in his voice.

"I`m going to Dublin later on after I get back I`ll pop up and see you, and you just remember your better than this"

"Ok " she whispered down the phone.

"Maria I love you" he said with such warmth in his voice she could almost touch it.

"And I love you Joe" she whispered back.

Going into the kitchen, thinking how lucky she was to have a friend like Joe.

She started thinking he is more than that a lot more than a friend more a soul brother.

She heard stirring upstairs and heard David being sick in the toilet.

Christ she thought is this going to be the story of my life, Joe is right nobody should have to live like this.

It`s not my fault if David has a drink problem.

The door opened and Mandy walked in hair standing on end.

This made her smile.

"Morning Sis"

"Morning " Mandy yawned.

"Coffee" asked Maria as she stood up from the table.

She nodded.

Making the coffee David walked in, looking like death warmed up.

Mandy gave him a filthy look.

"What`s that look for " he asked.

She just shrugged,

"Now you listen to me this is my house and as long as your staying here you will show me a bit of respect" he said in a raised voice.

Maria turned on him, "Who the fuck do you thing you are shouting at her like that"

Mandy turned and ran upstairs in tears.

"After your antics over the weekend, your are one of the most selfish men I have ever come across in my whole life".

He stared at her ,went to say something, she put her hand to stop him in mid stream.

"I don`t want to hear it "she screamed at him.

David almost jumped out of his skin with the anger she that was in her voice.

He made a quick exit upstairs.

She sat staring out of the window, thinking this cannot go on,

Then she thought why am I putting up with this unreasonable behaviour.I don`t have to take this.

Mandy arrived into the room sniffling. Putting her arms out to her.

She went into them,

"He has gone over the line now" said Maria she stroked her hair.

"Joe is popping around this evening"

"That will be nice, I like Joe" answered Mandy as she got up put the kettle on.

"He is the best friend a Gal could have"

"Cuppa" she asked her sister who looked deep in thought.

"Maria" she said a bit louder.

"What"

"Do you want a cuppa"

She nodded getting up from the table.

"What time is Joe popping around at" said Mandy yawning.

"Well he is gone to Dublin this morning so I presume later this evening"

"He be able to meet Don" said Mandy dreamily.

Maria smiled hoping that her dream would not shatter .She never thought in a million years that her and David`s dream would even crack never mind shatter .

But then that was life, or at least hers.

Looking at Mandy she said "Lets do a bit of shopping so when Joe and Don arrives we can have a few nice nibbles on the table and a bottle of something make the place look welcoming and warm for them"

"Yes " smiled Mandy "that sound`s wonderful, But Don he is taking me out"

"Well you can have something when you get back, he can look at it as thank you for all his help last night"

She started to sing getting a little over excited, "I`m going to shower"

Nodding Maria said `I`ll have one after you"

Sitting at the table scary thoughts running through her head, she saw the door open and David appear like a ghost.

He looked at her like a naughty school boy.

"Maria I think we need to talk" he said in a very small voice.

Looking at him and thinking about the past months, how he ignored her, making sure that he was ok and not a thought for her.

Drinking excessively, being sick everywhere, and her cleaning up after him.

She got up from the chair looking at him answering "There nothing to say, how long have I been asking you to talk?"

"Well bloody answer me" she shouted.

 Mandy arrived down ,David looked at her ignoring her and headed back upstairs.

"Ill just jump in the shower " sighed Maria won`t be long.

She came back down and the two of them headed off shopping.

David was downstairs when they arrived back, with a drink in his hand.

Maria seeing this went for him, removing the bottle and pouring it down the sink, she went towards him and hitting him across the face, he went reeling across the room , screaming at him asking" Are you on a death wish"

Mandy couldn`t believe her eye`s, David getting up from the floor, unsteadily holding on to the chair , stared at Maria in disbelieve. You could cut the atmosphere with a knife.

Looking at Maria he shouted, "What do you care?"

"Care it was her that looked after you, "Mandy shouted.

"This is none of your business" he shouted glaring back at her.

Maria sat on the chair, tears rolling down her face, Mandy went over and said

"Come on sis, he is not worth another tear" hugging her.

Looking at the clock she said "Are we going to get these nibble`s done Joe and Don will be here in a while"

"Oh that bum boy" snarled David.

"He is not a bum boy" snapped Mandy.

"Yes he is a fucking poof with a capital P"

Maria had had enough, "If you want to keep your teeth you will keep your trap shut" She screamed at him.

"Well I`m out of here, if the Bum Boy and Don are dropping by"

"Do whatever you fuckin want, were finished" Maria said in a clam voice.

Stood up and started unpacking the shopping.

"Whatever " he answered and headed upstairs.

They heard the shower going, Mandy turning said to Maria, "How can he be better"

Maria answered "He`s not, but I do know this me and him are finished"

"What do you mean?" She asked looking at her shocked,
"Mandy do you really think I married him to share a life like this with him?"
She said as she buttered some bread."Not knowing what I'm arriving home too,
His drinking is getting totally out of control, and it's not just that, he used to make me feel as
if I was the most special girl in the world , these day's he doesn't even notice that I'm
breathing , never mind pay me complaint's" she sighed, "I feel more like a lodger than a wife,
and that's in my own home" s
                    Hearing a car pull up, Mandy ran into the front room, looked out the
window and shouted" Don is here".
Opening the door with the biggest welcoming smile on her face, "Hello" he smiled at her.
Following Mandy into the kitchen, he greeted Maria,
"Hello Don Just doing a little spread for us" she smiled.
"How is his nib's?" he asked.
"We went shopping earlier and came back to find him drinking" blurted Mandy.
He stood there shocked "You are joking"
Maria looking at him answered "I wish she was".
"I recon he has lost the plot" The phone rang."Help yourself" smiled Maria as she went to
answer the phone.
Mandy heard Maria yell, went into the hall, to see her curled up on the floor, crouched down
with the phone still in her hand.
"What's the matter" she asked taking the phone from her.she could hear someone still talking
on the line.
"Hello, who is this, Who my God, I'm so sorry Mary, if there is anything we can do"
Mandy looking down at her sister and bent down holding her, " Maria I'm am so sorry," she
knew what Joe meant to her.
David walking downstairs, Looked down "Now what's all the drama's about?"
Mandy looked up and said! "Joe is dead"
David in a sneering half drunk voice, "What the Bum Boy ,Oh well good riddance"
Maria looked up at him, The anger welling up inside of her shouted "I wish it had been you
fucking bastard, Joe was my friend and I Loved him" she sobbed.
Picking up a glass vase she threw it at him , just missing him by a fraction.
Don hearing the commotion came into the hall, seeing the broken glass looked at Mandy who
was crying her eye's out.
Looking at David who was half pissed ,"What's happened" putting his arm's around Mandy,
And picking Maria up from the floor.
Maria was just staring didn't utter a word,
"Can someone tell me what's the matter?"Don asked in a very concerned voice.
"The Bum Boy is Dead " sneered David as he balanced himself on the banister's.
Maria slowly rising her head very slowly, looked at David as she was going to kill him.
Screaming at him, "You bastard he was my soul brother not that you would understand what
it's even like " They tears were running down her face she went to punch him Don catching
her fist just in time./
Her heart breaking she sobbed as she went in the kitchen.
Don looking at David said "I think you have said enough,"
  Swaying from the banister "Don't you go fucking telling me what to do in my house". he
slurred.
Don giving him a look of total disgust, and said "You want to learn a bit of respect"
 Taking Mandy by the hand he brought her into the kitchen.
Maria was sitting just staring out the window, Don sat beside her with Mandy on his knee.
Taking her tiny hand, in his He said "I'm so sorry"

There was no reaction, Mandy looked at him worried.

He gently removed Mandy from his knee, "I`m just going to make her a sugary drink, she is in shock"

He made her a tea with lot`s of sugar in it, Mandy taking it from him, took it over to Maria. Bending down beside her, saying "Here sis drink this".

Maria looking at her said "Joe`s gone "Mandy feeling her pain, put her arm`s around her.

"I know" she answered sadly.

Tears running down her face, "What am I going to do without him, he was my soul brother"

"You have me" said Mandy wiping the tears from her face.

"I need a drink " she got up to go to the cupboard and finding two empty bottle`s.

"I`m going to kill that bastard" she said her face white with anger.

"It`s ok Maria I`ll go to the shop" Don said seeing the grief in her face.

Looking at him, she nodded. "Ok"

"Ill come with you" said Mandy.

They headed to the shop.

"I can see this pushing her over the edge" said Mandy as she walked beside him.

"What`s make`s you say that?"

"Well you have only seen a tad of what as been going on with David"

"I have seen enough" he answered.

"She really loved Joe" said Mandy sadly.

Getting to the shop they met Johnny, "Hello" he smiled.

He looked at Mandy`s face "What`s the matter"

"Joe is dead" answered Mandy filling up with tears.

"Joe that work`s with Maria" he said totally shocked.

"How, when?"

"Car accident, outside Kilbeggen earlier on this afternoon"

"Bloody hell, how is Maria?"he asked looking very concerned.

"She is totally devastated," Mandy replied.

"She is in a state of shock at the moment hence this" Don said showing him the bottle of vodka.

"I`ll pop over and see her" said Johnny.

Mandy nodded thinking maybe a friendly face might help her.

On the way back Mandy filled him in on the antics of David over the past few day`s.

Johnny with an angry look an his face answered "That man need`s his fucking head examined"

Don nodding agreed.

They arrived back at the house to find Maria in the garden looking up at sky, with such a sadness surrounding her.

Johnny went out to her.Shading her eye`s from the light, to see who was approaching.

"Johnny," she cried, sitting beside her, she fell apart.

Holding her in his arms feeling her tears through his shirt, she held on to him as if her heart was going to break .

He looked up at Don bringing the drinks out.Shaking his head, he passed her a drink.

"Here darling " he said in such a gentle voice.

Don looking on thinking this should be her husband consoling her, looking up at the bedroom window .

They couple few day`s were a blur,

David sobered up or at least attempted to.

Mandy did her best to make sure her sister ate , she had never seen Maria fall apart, she had always` s been the strong one.

The funeral was four days later.

Maria went with Mandy and, Don to Joe's house where the wake was.

Joe's body was in a coffin in the front room, with his grief stricken Ma and Da his two brothers and sister

His Ma looked up at Maria as she walked in and just burst into tears.

Hugging Maggie, Maria couldn't talk with grief,

Looking in the coffin she went over to Joe's body and touched him.It was cold very very cold.

Kissing him on the forehead, hers tears falling on his face.

She said her goodbye's.

Mary Joe's sister took Maria into the kitchen, she made a cuppa.

Looking at her said "This seems like a nightmare that Ill wake up in the morning and he will be there arguing with Kevin."

Maria nodding, "I know" she had a lump in her throat since it had happened that wouldn't move and a emptiness inside her heart that she knew no one could fill again.

The body was removed from the house and after the service, Joe was buried beside his Grandmother and grandfather.

Maria went back to work the following week.It was so strange without him.

Life just went on as she found out.

Her and David hadn't spoken since the day Joe died.

Mandy was spending as little time around David as possible, seeing Don every opportunity she got.

So Maria was left feeling very alone, and was missing Joe dreadfully.

Arriving home from work, one evening to find David sober and cooking dinner.

Hanging her coat up, walking into the kitchen, turning giving her a smile.

He said "Hello I have got dinner cooked".

"So I see" she answered, she was feeling exhausted, work was busy and there was still client's ringing up wanting to book in with Joe, who didn't know he had died.

So every day was a challenge at the moment, she couldn't talk about Joe's death without choking up,

"Maria I'm am so sorry for my behaviour, especially over Joe's death".

Looking at him so coldly, "That was unforgivable, and I have had enough of this sham of a marriage"

David looked at here feeling panic set in, "What do you mean,"

"I have been thinking about this for a while now, But let me put in simple terms for you"
 Standing with a fork in his hand prodding the spud's "I'm listening "

"I want out" she said simply.

He looked at her his head spinning, Feeling sick to the pit of his tummy.

"Maria we can sort this, please" he pleaded

"What with a magic wand" she snapped back.

Mandy walked in, "Hi sis, I'm just off out"

"Ok darling ,see you later"

"Do you want some dinner?" David asked, this was the first time he had spoken to her in weeks.

Shaking her head, she said "No"

"No thank you would be nice" he said sarcastically.

Mandy turning her head sharply, replied "Don't talk to me in that tone"

He turned going red in the face, "Don't fucking speak to me like that" pointing the fork at her.

She had ,had enough of David, seeing how he was treating her sister.

"What are you going to do hit me with it" she sneered at him.

"You bitch, don't fucking look down your nose at me" he answered walking towards her.

Maria seeing red went straight for him shouting "How dare you" she hit so hard across the face that it left her hand stinging.

"He is a dickhead" answered Mandy.

She looked at Mandy with anger in her eye`s and said "You go on I`ll deal with this"

Mandy nodded and left, hearing her sister shout "What the fuck are you playing at".

He slumped on to the chair, and started to cry, "I don`t know" holding his head in his hand`s

Tears rolling down his face her looked at her and asked "How has it all come to this"

"Do I really have to spell it out? All I know is I don`t want this anymore" she shouted.

Looking at her with pleading in his eye`s he whispered "I love you"

She stared at him and realised she did not feel a thing for him.

The love they had shared had died, gone never to be rekindled.

Mandy returned back into the room saying "This is all my fault, I`m sorry"

Maria turned and looking at the sad face hugged her and said "None of this is your fault"

"We were ok before she came to live with us" he said in a broken voice.

Maria glared at him "Do you want another slap? We are finished you ignorant moron! Do you understand finished!"

Shocked at her display of anger, he nodded wiping the tears.

He looked defeated.

Anger appearing in his eye`s, "Fine you go your way and I`ll go mine" he said in a childish loud voice.

"It`s not as simple as that "she answered, the anger subsiding.

"We need to sort out finance issues, and the car, who`s going to live where" she answered him coldly.

"You do what you got to do," he said, glaring at Mandy as he headed out the door.

Mandy looked at Maria and knew it was the end between them.

Tears in her eye`s Mandy looked at Maria, "Are you ok"

Nodding she said simply "Yes, I`m going for a shower," as the hot water hit her body tear`s of frustration, disappointment ran down her face her heart feeling heavy and her mind exhausted.

This was not a decision she had made lightly, as she knew apart ending her relationship with David, there would be repercussions from their families and the community.

Put her bathrobe on and went downstairs putting the kettle on.

There was a knock at the door Mandy answered it.

It was Johnny and Don standing behind him.

She beamed when she saw Don."Is Maria in" Johnny asked.

Nodding as put her arms around Don.

"Is it ok to go in" he asked.

"Of course" she smiled at him.

He wandered in calling her name, "Maria"

"In here" she answered.

She was spooning coffee into a cup as she turned to see Johnny there , he went over and stood with his arm resting on the worktop.

She was conscious of her nakedness under the bathrobe.

She tightened the belt.

Mandy popped her head around the door and said "I`m just popping out with Don"

"Ok"

"How is things?"Johnny asked.

Shrugging she said "I told him it`s over"

Johnny was a bit taken aback.

He noticed tear`s appearing in her eye`s as she squeezed the dish cloth, wiping the side`s.

"Need a hug" he asked holding his arm`s out.
Nodding she went straight into them. She was very petite.
He felt as if he was holding a little girl.
He adored the smell of her.
Actually he adored everything about her.
How she smelt, how she looked, but most of all in this tiny little package, there was a generous, kind ,caring and very strong woman.
The qualities that ticked all the boxes for him
They door went and she pulled away from Johnny.
Mandy arrived in Don behind her, she pulled out a bottle of drink that Don had bought for them.
"I`m just going to put some clothes on" she smiled excusing herself.
"I`ll just pour the drinks" Mandy smiled looking at Don adoringly.
"Ok Doll" Maria answered as she ran upstairs
She pulled out a pair of red leggings and a red top, looked at herself.and thought what the fuck are you doing?
Her sister and boyfriend downstairs and her husband could walk back in at any minute.
Even if they were splitting up, and here she was dressing herself up to impress Johnny.
Idiot, she pulled off the red top and put a long t shit on.
Her head was totally messed up.
                    Mandy had her head in the freezer looking for ice, "Have we got any ice?" She asked as Maria appeared.
Shaking her head "No I defrosted it earlier and forgot to put the ice cube maker back in."
Mandy smiling at Don asked "If it was ok without ice"
He went over to her and taking her in his arms looking down at her "Of course it is "
Maria looked at Johnny shaking her head smirked.
Johnny looked at her giving her a wink.
"Young love" Maria said smiling at her sister.
Blushing Mandy replied "Oh shut up"
Johnny always carried his guitar, and was sitting at the table strumming a few notes.
"I`m only jesting" she smiled hugging Mandy "It`s lovely too see you happy"
Soon they were all singing ,having a drink, and then the door went,
Mandy looked at Maria, she stood up as David walked into the room.
"Well aren`t we having a nice cosy time" he slurred.
"Want a drink?" asked Don.
"Why not " he answered as he half staggered over to the table pulling up a chair.
  He sat there and said "I suppose she has told you the news?"
Maria stopped him "David this is not the time or the place to wash our dirty linen"
Looking at her through blurred vision, "And where would you like me to air our wonderful news darling"
Don sensing an atmosphere looked at Mandy and said "I better be going"
She gave David a look "You always have to spoil everything" she half cried at him.
Pointing his finger at her "Your fucking sister is responsible for this one my darling sister in law" he said in a sneering voice.
"That`s enough David " said Don in a very stern voice.
"This is my fucking house and I`ll do or say whatever I want , and if you don`t like it you know where the door is" he half slurred at them.
Maria had had enough and went over and hit him straight across the face much to everyone`s surprise.

MARY D / MARIA THE IRISH COLLEN / PAGE 165

Half raising his hand going to hit her back, Johnny stepped in, grabbing him from the chair and dragging him upstairs.
He shoved him into the bedroom saying "Your totally out of order.If I was you I would stay there."
David sat on the bed in a total dazed state, started to cry so loud that they could here him downstairs.
                    Maria looked so distressed, Don looked at her "What`s the matter baby" he asked her gently
Putting her head in her hand`s she started sobbing "Everything"
He nodded to Mandy to get her a drink.
Johnny arrived back downstairs, "I don't think" he stopped in mid flow when he saw Maria so upset.
He put his guitar in the corner and going over to her kneeling beside her holding her hand .
She looked at him and sobbing said "I miss Joe so much, and he was right I don`t deserve a life like this I have had enough,"
Her hand`s shaking her heart breaking she looked at him and asked "Why am I here? "
She looked so lost and her eye`s so sad "I drowning" she thought.
Mandy passed Don a drink,
Shaking his head he declined.
She looked disappointed.
He hugged her and said "I have to go an early start, I`ll pop by tomorrow evening"
 "Maria you're a strong woman, you will get through this" he said in such a kind voice that she cried harder.
"Johnny looking at him said "You go on I`ll look after them"
 Mandy looking back as she walked Don to his car said "I told you she would loose it"
Holding her in his arms he said "She will be fine with the support from us she will be ok"
"Now you have got to be strong for her ,just like she has been strong for you in the past" he said as he kissed her gently on the mouth.
She looked at him and answered "Yes your right, it`s pay back time"
He looked at her and putting his hand gently under her chin,
 He said "That's my baby girl"
She waved until he was out of sight and went back inside.
"He always ruin`s everything" whinged Mandy when she went in.
Maria looking at her "Well it won`t be for much longer sis"
"What do you mean?" Mandy asked looking at her anxiously.
Jonny looked at her doubtfully.
She said "It`s decision time, I am at a crossroad`s in my life , for once I`m going to control my own destiny"
Mandy asked, "What about me"
Smiling she answered "You don`t need to worry, you will be coming with me"
"What are we moving"
"Obviously, I am going flat hunting tomorrow on my lunch hour."
She yawned, Johnny took this as his cue to leave.
"If you need any help, you know where I am" kissing them both, he left.
Mandy looked at her sister and said "What your leaving all this"
Nodding she said "It`s just material thing`s, and you and I together can make a life for ourselves away from all this madness"
Seeing a look of trepidation on Mandy`s face, hugging her said "This is going to be a new beginning for us both"
Mandy got their drink`s and smiling handing her the drink, said" To our new adventure"

NEW CHAPTER

Maria was finding it very hard to stomach David, as his behaviour to her after Joe's death she found appalling.

She had so much going on that she didn't know what to focus on first .

Her first priority, was to find somewhere for her and Mandy to live.

She spent the next week visiting the local estate agent's and trawling through the local paper's for suitable accommodation.

Eventually she found a two bedroom ground floor flat with a nice garden.

Making an appointment, her and Mandy went to view it.

It was two nice sized bedroom's, good sized kitchen, bathroom and living area.

Maria smiling discussed the rent with the estate agent.

Looking at Mandy asked "What do you think?"

She beamed at her and answered "I love it"

"Can we decorate it" Maria asked .

Nodding the estate agent, Mr Delaney, said "Yes you can do as you like"

"We will take it" beamed Maria.

Heading back to the estate agent's Maria signed the tenancy agreement, leaving the office with the key's the two of them were overjoyed.

Mandy looking at Maria squeezing her hand" Sang we have done it" as they walked towards the Bridge House for a celebratory drink.

Don and Johnny were in there, Mandy went straight over to them revealing there new' s.

Don grinned at them raising his glass saying " The gob shite is in for a bloody big shock "

Johnny looked surprised, and going towards` Maria ,said "You have done it then".

"Why are you surprised?"

"I am" he replied honestly.

"Why?"

"I just did not think you would leave him" he replied simply.

Mandy overhearing ,put her penny` s worth in.

"And what is she supposed to do? Put up with his bullshit and drinking for the rest of her life" she said in raised voice.

"I thought he was going to hit me earlier" she added.

"He what "Don snapped stepping in.

Maria intervened, "It's ok Don, I have dealt with it."Giving Mandy a very annoyed look.

"Ill fucking kill him! threating to hit woman especially his sister in law" said Johnny who was livid having overheard the conversation.

Maria looked at him and said, "Now clam down, I told you I have dealt with it"

He looked at her in disbelief.

"Don't look at me like that, I have got enough going on without you making wave's"

Johnny nodded answering "Point taken but I cannot abide men who threaten women"

"What about the other way around?"she asked.

"What do you mean?"

"Well women hitting men, because that is what I did when I thought he was going to strike my sister, I walloped straight across the face" she sighed.

"If I had seen him attempt to hit Mandy, well it wouldn't have been a wallop he would have got" replied Johnny.

Don who was a very level headed fella, raised his hand seeing how annoyed Maria was getting, said, "Ok enough we get the picture."

Maria smiled and looked at him gratefully.

"I'm sorry" said Johnny" But that man just makes me so angry."

"I totally agree with you " answered Mandy in a whispered voice,

"Look at her Johnny you could not meet a nicer person, what goes on in his head?"
He shrugged.
"Football, the band and where he is going to get the next drink from" she said sounding so bitter.
Finishing their drink`s Maria said to Mandy "We better get home and start packing"
Don kissed Mandy and said he was off to Dublin for a few day`s and would be in touch as soon as he got back.
Johnny offered his help and his van to help them move.
"That will be great" Maria answered as she gave him a kiss on the check.
He walked out of the Bridge House with them, and watched as the two of them walked up the street.
What a dick head he thought.
Walking towards the house they saw the lights were on, "Oh Christ it`s home" said Maria, taking a deep breath.
As they opened the door the got the smell of bacon cooking,
Heading into the kitchen Gerry was sitting at the table reading the newspaper and David standing by the cooker frying .
Gerry getting up said "Well hello there"
Maria looking at him said "Hello"
Mandy looked at Maria ,as she knew that there had been very little communication between them.
David looking over his shoulder asked if either of wanted anything to eat?
They both shook their heads, answering "No thank you"
"David can I have a word when your finished eating" she asked politely.
Looking at her he knew it was serious.
"Bro can you take over here".
Gerry putting the newspaper down said" Of course"
Mandy making herself scarce said "I`m just going upstairs"
Maria nodded and headed into the front room.
The stink of smoke and beer in there ,made her gag.
 She opened the window, and sat down.
"What s the matter "David asked as his stomach turned over.
Looking at him she bluntly blurted out "I`m leaving you".
He sat back in the chair laughing said "Christ and I thought this was serious"
His mouth was drying up and he started fidgeting which he always did when he was nervous.
She looked at him "I`m not joking"
She saw his bottom lip tremble, and tears well up in his eyes.
Looking at her in disbelieve "I have been a total arse hole" he choked.
"Yes " she answered simply, totally emotionless.
"Mandy and I will be moving out tomorrow" she added so coldly.
Standing up she went to leave the room, he caught her hand and with pleading in his eyes,
"Don't go please "he was begging."I am so sorry, Maria I can`t loose you"
She walked out without another glance.
Gerry was in the kitchen still cooking the bacon.
Turning as he heard her come into the kitchen,
"Everything ok" he asked as she approached.
"Fine" she answered shortly.
David following her into the kitchen.
His hand`s waving about the air ,his face red with anger.
"Fine is it ,Gerry she is leaving me" he said as the anger draining from him.

He looked at Maria and knew immediately it was true.

He was speechless, Gerry knew there was problem's but to finish?

David looked at her all the anger gone pleading with her,

Tears in his eye's he said "I know I have been an arse hole, but please give me a chance to fix this ".

She looked at him with a coldness in her eye's.

"Oh please don`t do this, I love you" he cried.

"I can`t live with you anymore, you destroyed it" she answered and went upstairs.

Mandy had heard overheard most of the conversation.

Maria looking at her said "Have you packed were going now "

She nodded "Are you sure".

  "Never been surer about anything more in my life" she replied taking a suitcase out of the cupboard.

"Maria" she heard Gerry calling her.

"In here" she called.

Walking in he saw the suitcase, "I know it`s none of my business, but he is my brother"

Maria continued packing without even giving him a glance.

Looking at her with a pleading in his eye's "I have never seen him so devastated"

"I just don`t want you to do something that you will regret."he said.

She was packing quilts and pillows, grabbing towels.

She stopped packing and looking at him said "Gerry how do you fix something that is broke?"

He turned and answered "Well you can`t"

"Exactly so what`s the point in wasting time or trying to repair, something that will never look or feel the same again?"she answered as she zipped the suitcase up.

Gerry stood watching her, "I see".

"So there is no point in wasting your breath, put your energies into helping David come to terms with thing`s".

"Tell him I`m taking the car" she said as he walked out of the room.

Mandy helped her put the luggage in the car.

She was just putting the key in the ignition and she remembered her toothbrush and toiletries, and the spare kettle.

Going back into the house running upstairs she grabbed the bag.on her way into the kitchen she heard Gerry call her.

Sighing, she rapidly running out of patience.

"Yes " she snapped at him as was returning from the kitchen.

Meeting her in the hall, "I don`t want to see you break up" he said simply.

Standing with a bag in one hand and kettle and some mug`s in the other she asked "And what can you or I do to fix this?"

Gerry shrugged, "Tell him he has been a naughty boy and slap his hand" she said.

Pushing him out of the way she stuck her head around the living room door,

"I`ll be back tomorrow to pick up the rest of my stuff" she said to David.

 He was sitting as if in a trance his world falling apart.

He nodded.

Getting back in the car beside Mandy, "Ok?"

"Yeph" she answered driving away without a backward glance.

            Arriving at the flat handing Mandy the keys, "You open up"

She was just getting the bag`s from the car, when she heard her name being called.

Looking beside her was Johnny.

"Let me give you a hand" he offered.

Heading into the flat he saw Mandy coming out of one of the bedrooms.
"Hello Johnny " she smiled.
"Mandy be a doll stick the kettle on" Maria shouted as she carried the last of the bag`s in.
"So you have done it then" Johnny smiled.
Looking at him a sad look in her eye`s."Yes" she said simply.
Johnny looking around the flat said "Christ this is quite spacious."
Mandy answered "Yes and it is ours".
She was feeling so relived to be away from the house, and that it was just her and Maria.
They had there tea and Johnny leaving said he would be with them first thing in the morning with the van.
  Mandy wandered about making plans about how they were going to decorate the flat.
Maria was feeling very strange, fatigued relieve and sad, her emotions where all over the place.
But at least she knew deep in her heart that she made the right decision.
                    Next morning, Johnny arrived at the flat with the van.
They had a cuppa and headed up to he house.
"Will he be here ?"Johnny asked.
Maria shook her head ,"No he should be at work".
Pulling up in the van she noticed the bedroom curtains twitch.
"He`s home" she said.
Getting out of the car, taking some boxes from the van they headed in.
David standing at the top of the stairs, Gerry appearing out of the living room.
Ignoring them Maria leading the way into the kitchen, giving instructions to Mandy and Johnny as to what she wanted them to take.
Gerry called Maria into the hallway and looking up at his brother, who was sitting with his head in his hands sobbing.
"You cant do this" he said.
She looked at him and said "Pardon"
"He love`s you and he is genuinely sorry, for all the mistakes he has made, I had a really good talk to him last night" he answered with a glimmer of hope in his eye`s.
She looked at him coldly thinking of all the lonely nights she had spent here waiting anxiously to hear his key in the door.
They lack of respect and disgusting behaviour when Joe died, which she found unforgiveable.
The excessive drinking, the obnoxious person he turned him into.
"Look I have made my decision, which wasn't an easy one by any means" she answered.
Shrugging his shoulders, he went back into the living room.
David over hearing the conversation, came downstairs.
She totally ignored him.
Following her into the kitchen, seeing Mandy and Johnny there packing their stuff a wave of anger overtaking him.
Johnny was removing the telly, David stood in front of him blocking his pathway.
Maria went and pushing him out of the way saying "What the hell are you playing at? I thought you would have been at work".
"I`m having a few day`s off" he replied wiping the snot from his nose.
"You won`t have a job to go to soon" she muttered under her breath giving Johnny the nod to remove the telly.
"And that is your problem?"
Mandy looked at Maria uncertainly, Maria seeing this said "Carry on"
Mandy and Johnny headed out to the van
David left alone with Maria looked at her tears pouring down his cheeks,

"Please don't go" he begged.
Feeling nothing apart from pity, "It's over ,I'm leaving and I'm not coming back, so get used to it."her voice almost frozen.
He couldn't believe the coldness, it was like looking at a stranger.
"What about the house?" he said anything to delay her leaving.
"You can buy me out or we can sell, no big issue" she replied hauntingly.
"I cant afford that" he answered furiously.
"Well your left with only one option then and that's to sell" she answered as she walked out.
Turning her head she said "I'll be in touch" She felt as if she was closing a business deal not a marriage."
The other two in the van "Got everything" she asked looking at Mandy.
 She nodded, Johnny starting the van she looked back at the house that had been full of hopes and dreams to see David looking out the window.
Letting a huge sigh of relief she turned to Mandy "This is the first day of the rest of our lives" she smiled, squeezing her hand.
                    Arriving outside the flat, the three of them got stuck in and was unpacked in no time.
Maria looked at Mandy's face, she was like a little child with a new toy, over excited.
Johnny saw her staring at Mandy, "Everything ok "he asked.
Smiling at him answering "It is now"
"Mandy could you make us a cuppa please "asked Maria.
"Sure sis" she smiled as she came out of her bedroom.
Making the tea, Maria wandered into the kitchen with some boxes.
She looked at her asking "Maria can I paint my bedroom pink?"
Maria looking at her seeing the over excited look on her face.
Smiled and answered, "It's all yours to do as you want"
She went over to her giving her the biggest hug, "You're the best"
Well that's her happy she thought as she walked into the bedroom to see Johnny put the bed together.
Looking at her he said " I thought you would like your bed under the window, so you can have your wardrobe there and your chest of drawers here and that way it makes the room more spacious."
"You're a really lovely man" she said smiling at him.
Looking back at her she replied cheekily "I know"
She threw a pillow at him "Big head"
Moving the furniture in position, taking her new bedding out he helped her make it.
They then started on the black bags.
Opening one she saw it belonged to Mandy, calling her, she came skipping and singing into the bedroom.
"Oh this looks lovely" she said as she picked up the bag leaving humming.
Maria looked at Johnny and smiled.
"She's happy" he said.
"Yes I think she is as relived that it is over as much as I am".
He nodded "Yes I don't blame her the way he was picking on her".
"Yes " she answered him sadly thinking where had the old gentle David gone.
She could feel herself welling up, so she quickly left the room and went into the kitchen to make a cuppa.She didn't want Johnny seeing her upset.
It wasn't that she was regretting what she was doing, but she was closing a chapter on her life, that she never thought would end
Johnny coming into the kitchen asking "Where's the table and chairs going?"

"In the bathroom" she laughed.

Johnny grinned looking at her loving her sense of humour, actually there was not anything he didn't like about her.

Maria treated them to a takeaway to thank Johnny for all his hard work.

Mandy called them into her bedroom, showing off her handy work.

"Christ it look`s great" said Maria and Johnny together.

"Pinch for you surprise for me " she giggled as she pinched him.

Mandy looked at them saying "Your like two kid`s" walking back to finish her bedroom.

"When are we getting the phone in" she shouted from the bedroom.

"I`m not deaf, tomorrow".

Looking at Johnny stretching she said, "I`m done in" as she took a twenty pound note from her purse, handing it to him.

Looking at her gratefully he said, "Maria I would not normally take it, but I`m skint"

"Nonsense" she smiled, "Without you Mandy and I would be still up there"

Putting his jacket on, she kissed him on the cheek, and looking at him said "Thank you you're a real friend"

He left and waving he shouted "I`ll see you tomorrow".

Closing the door behind her she was thinking how much she liked him.

Come on girl your not jumping out of the fire into the frying pan.

Going into the kitchen she was rather surprised at the job Mandy had done.

"Sis this looks great" she smiled.

"I think so" she answered, standing back to admire her handy work.

"Can`t wait to paint my bedroom" she smiled at Maria.

Maria tickling her promised to buy the paint soon.

Mandy pulling away said "For the first time in my life I feel at home"

She sighed looking at her and replied" I know that feeling that`s how I felt when I moved into the house".

"Do you feel sad about leaving the house?"

She nodded as she felt stinging tears at the back of her eye`s.

"Oh don't cry sis" said Mandy.

"Well it`s the end of a chapter of my life that at one point thought would be forever." She half smiled wiping her eye`s.

Mandy went to the cupboard, taking out a bottle, smiling at Maria she said "Thought we could toast to the future."

The two of them raising there glasses, clinked and smiling together toasted "To the future"

The next few months were filled with decorating the flat, work and the two of them settling in.

NEW CHAPTER

David couldn`t face the reality of the situations, living in his ever deepening alcoholic haze.

Wandering about town blaming Maria ,to anyone and everyone that would listen.

Maria coming from a deeply religious and conservative background.

Knew that she was going to be judged by others for her actions of ending the marriage.

She thought she was prepared for this, but was shocked by the negative reaction of people.

The postman whom she met every morning ignored her.

Going back to the house picking up the rest of her stuff, her neighbour Francis,

Looking at her said "How could you do this to David ,you have broken him"

"If I had stayed the two of us would have been broken" she said simply.

Maria knew she would have to weather this storm, no matter how windy it became.

S   Everyday Maria had to endure snarky comments being thrown at her by people that she thought should have know better.

This began to wear her down.

She started thinking that her only escape would be to pack and leave.

She couldn't continue to live in this continual atmosphere of blame.

 Mandy sensed her distress with the reaction of certain people around her.

, Mandy having cooked dinner for Don and Maria, the door knocked.

Don looked at a Maria and said "Ill get it "

Opening the door finding a very drunken David, "I want to see my wife" he slurred.

Maria hearing the familiar voice , went to the door seeing the state he and said "What the fuck do you want?"

Holding on to the door frame he asked if he could come in.

Shaking her head she said "Piss off", closing the door in his face , going back into the kitchen looking at Mandy and Don saying"

That's all I bloody need. "

"What did he want?" asked Mandy.

Shrugging her shoulders she sat back down, in tears "I need to get away"

Don asked "What do you mean "

"I thought I could weather this storm but I`m not dealing with it very well".

Mandy looked at her "Get away where?" She asked feeling panic.She didn't want to move and have to leave Don.

"Oh don't worry sis I`m just feeling a bit pissed off with everything at the moment".

Don looking at her asked "What`s the matter?"

"It`s just since David and I split up, people well there judging me, disregarding me and making me feel like an outcast." She explained.

"Just ignore them", said Don sympathetically.

"That's easy to say , your not the one that people are nudging at in shop`s, staring at on the street, I knew it was not going to be easy, but I wasn't prepared for this humiliation" she answered sadly.

Don went over to her and hugging her said "You will be ok".

                    The following week she rang David asking if they could meet up.

She heard a glimmer of hope coming into his voice as he answered her "Yes"

Immediately she picked up on the vibe she reassured him it was business only.

Hearing the disappointment in his voice, he answered laughing" Of course I didn't think it was going to be a reunion."

Hope not she thought , you would have two chances nil and none.

Especially after he had been telling people that the breakup had been her doing by having an affair.

 This had come out in the salon by one of her clients, Who thought it was fair that she should know what the rumours floating about town about her.

She didn't react and laughed it off in her professional way, "Oh well at least I`m giving someone else a break. " she was exploding inside with anger.

                    Saturday couldn't come quick enough for David, getting up early morning, not having had a drink for three days.

At least the shakes had subsided and he wasn't sweating so profoundly.

He showered and had bought a new shirt and jeans for his" meeting" with Maria that day.

Wearing old spice aftershave her favourite.

Having had a haircut the day before, looking in the mirror was pleased with the appearance that reflected back at him.

Since his wife had left him eight months earlier, he had gone to pieces.

Lost his job , not being able to face up to reality hit the bottle, his Ma and Da were helping him out financially, but even they were getting pissed off with his behaviour.

Making a coffee he looked around the kitchen good old Francis he thought, he had told her that Maria was popping up that day and there might be a chance of a reconciliation and had asked if she would give him a hand to tidy the house up

The day before while he hovered she had swept through the place like a tornado. ,leaving no stone uncovered it sparkled like a new pin.

Hearing her car pull up his heart racing as he went to answer the door.

Opening the door she stood there the dark hair shining in the sunlight and the brown eye`s staring at him.

"Hello come in" he smiled.

Shaking her keys at him "That's very kind of you considering I own half of the house" she answered him sarcastically.

A bit taken aback by her unwelcoming attitude.

He stepped aside and let her in.

Walking in she was very surprised at the shape of the place.

She didn't comment.

"Coffee" he asked in a hope full voice.

Shaking her long hair "No thank you, look I want to make this as painless as possible for both of us"

Placing some paperwork on the table, pointing at one of the sheets said"Your behind on your share of the mortgage payments".

Looking embarrassed "Yes well I lost my job and with you leaving me, I got behind"

"David you lost your job through your drinking " she snapped.

Getting his back up, "Well what did you expect me to do" he snapped back.

"Look I am not here for an argument, but before we get down to nitty gritty, I want you to tell me why you blamed me for our break up?"

"What are you talking about " he asked his voice raised this was not going the way he had planned.

"I am asking a simple question, why did you tell people that we split because I was having an affair/" she asked simply.

"I did not" he answered quickly.

"Stop right there ,you either answer the question or I m going straight to a solicitor to sort our finances out, do you understand" he could hear the anger in her voice,

Defeated again he said "I was drunk.

"So you think it`s ok to slander your wife, when we both know the reason we split was because of your unreasonable behaviour, caused through your drinking" she sighed.

"Oh that's it put all the blame on me" he whinged.

She could feel herself loosing patience, gathering up the paperwork "You will be hearing from my solicitor"

Panic setting in he grabbed her arm."I`m sorry please stay and yes lets talk".

Looking at the defeated eyes she had once adored Nodded.

"I`ll have that coffee now" she said .He nodded with a look of relief on his face.

His hands were shaking as he put the kettle on, but not from the drink but through the fear that she would walk out and he would never see her again.

"Sugar " he asked his voice shaking.

Nodding she answered "Two please"
Sitting at the table she was thinking they had turned into complete strangers.
But she wanted an answer.
"I am waiting for an answer" she said as he passed her the coffee,
Looking into the coffee he replied "There is no answer , you had left and it was the first thing that came into my drunken aching head, I was broken still am " he said choking up.
She had no feeling of pity for him.
After the months of humiliation he had put her through it reminded her of his behaviour after Joe`s death.
Which every time she thought about it welled anger up inside.
Breathing deeply, "Thank you for being honest, I`m here to discuss the property and what you propose to do "
He could not believe the coldness in her voice. It was as if they had never been.
He thought this is the end and he would just have to accept it.
"I cant afford to buy you out, and even if I could I would not want to live here without you" he answered looking at her for just a flicker of emotion.
Looking back was the most frosty pair of eyes he had ever looked into.
"I`ll deal with the estate agents, get the ball rolling, and you can live here as long as you keep up your part of the mortgage ,otherwise you will have to share with a stranger as I will have to rent out my part".
Looking surprised "Got it all worked out "He answered.
"Life is too short for delaying the inevitable" she smirked "Joe`s death thought me that".
Embarrassed he looked away.
Finishing her coffee she got the paperwork together.
He wanted to say something but could not think of a thing at that moment in time.
She got up to leave ,as she was leaving he stood up calling her name "Maria".
Turning to him seeing the regret and pain in his eye`s.
Softening just for a moment she smiled saying "Look after yourself""
She was gone.
                    Arriving home Mandy and Don was there cuddled up on the couch, looking as snug as bugs in a rug.
She smiled as she walked in hanging her coat up and removing her high heels.
"Cuppa" she asked. "Please " they both replied.
"How did it go ?" asked Mandy.
Maria turning on her way to the kitchen replying "Ok , were selling the house".
"Christ has he agreed to that?"asked Mandy unravelling herself from Don.
Mandy following her into the kitchen, wanting the details.
Filling her in on the events of the afternoon, pouring the water into the cups,
Looking at Mandy she said "I`ll be seeing a solicitor tomorrow, and that will get the ball rolling."
Mandy put her arms around her sister, saying "Well done".
Maria stood stirring the tea bag in the cup, said "It was horrible, it was like I was talking to a stranger".
"Well at least it is coming to an end" replied Mandy.
"Oh I nearly forgot to tell you I have got an interview for a job, next week" said Mandy excitability
Maria looked at her "Oh Mandy that is wonderful news".
Mandy filled her in on the details, of her new job working in a factory in the new estate the far side of town.
"They money is good" she said as she carried Don`s tea into him."Thank you "he said.

"Good news " smiled Don as has sipped his tea.
"Yes" smiled Maria, feeling very bewildered.
The end of it , that's what Mandy had said, so why did she feel so empty?
Well at least it was moving I the right direction.
        The house sold a couple of months after been put on the market.
They got a fair price for it and they both ended up with a few bob in the bank.
There was still the aloofness from some of Marias neighbours and David 's friends towards her.
But she had learned to ignore, and get on with her life although it was still in the back of her mind to move, London she was thinking where she went on honeymoon with David.
Her and Shelly was still in contact, she had been shocked over her and David splitting up, but then life must go on.
        Passing the travel agents one day after work Maria wandered in picking up some brochure taking them home she was sitting browsing through them when Mandy walked in.
"What you got there?" she asked plonking her self beside her..
"Oh I was just thinking of having a little break" she smiled.
"I think that is a wonderful idea" said Mandy.
Maria looking her smiling said "Are you trying to get rid of me?"

"No " she replied "I think now you have got a few bob you should do something nice for yourself with it"
Smiling Maria answered "Yes I think your right it has been a long year"
  A few months later the house was sold. And Maria had a bit of money under her belt.
Mandy left school that summer and started work at the factory
Her and Don's relationship was solid, this taking a great weight off Maria's mind.
With everything stable at home, Maria decided that a break was just what she needed after the year she endured.
She went and booked a holiday to Gran Canaria for two weeks.
        Don and Mandy drove her to Dublin and waved her off.
Landing four hours later she got off the plane to the sun beaming down on her.
A bus ride later, she was at the hotel, booked in, unpacked and took a walk to see Playa Del Lingus.
The contrast to home could not have been so different, it was a very refreshing change.
She had come away to recharge her batteries after the trauma of her marriage ending.
It had been a long year, trying to keep everything together, Mandy couldn't believe that she had just taken off on her own.
But she needed the space on her own to see what direction her life was going.
        That evening she went to the dinning room for dinner ,afterwards
Going back to her room with a bottle sitting on the balcony watching the sun go down.
Feeling very at peace, inside herself because at home she felt uncomfortable and under pressure.
 The break up had drained her and peoples reactions had shattered her emotionally.
        Waking up the following morning heading out on the balcony feeling the sun on her face made her feel more alive than she had for a long time.

Heading into town after breakfast, she took in the shops and quaint restaurants,
She was mesmerised, by the language of the people, taking in the local sights and the beach.
Walking back towards the hotel she spotted an Irish bar, she sat outside and had a drink.
She looked up to see a tall dark haired man approaching her .

He looked foreign, but when he spoke she realised he was Irish.
"Hi anyone sitting here " he asked in a Dublin accent.
Smiling shaking her long dark hair she smiled at him "No"
"Mind if I join you?" he asked in a cheeky voice.
Noticing her empty glass asking "Can I buy you a drink"
Nodding shading her from the sun she answered "Please".
Her eyes followed him to the bar, he was a very attractive looking bloke, his skin was very
deeply tanned and very muscular legs.
He bought the drinks and sitting beside her, the sun catching the tiny specks of grey hair on
his side locks.
"When did you arrive" he asked taking a sip of his pint?
"Yesterday" she smiled.
The conversation flowed between them, she discovered that he came out here four months
ago for a weeks holiday and decided to stay.But was returning to Dublin at the end of that
week.
"How long are you here for ?" He asked.
"Two weeks" she answered.
"Where are you staying?"
"At the Plazza Palace" she replied.
Looking at her watch she smiled, "Well it was lovely meeting you but I have to go its feeding
time at the zoo" she laughed as she finished her drink.
"Oh don`t go , let me buy you lunch, its` the first day I have had off in two weeks and I
would love to spend it with you"
Thinking to herself why not, he was good company and as she had just got here he could
show her the hot spots.
He took her to a lovely Spanish restaurant, then on a boat ride, she loved it.
Standing in the boat the wind running through her hair the sun on her face, looking behind
her to see him smiling at her.
Leaving the boat back to shore they walked along the beach, he took her hand and she
allowed him.
It felt the most natural thing in the world.
There had not been anyone since David, Johnny was on the scene,
He still popped in to visit but she had not encouraged him since that kiss, well over a year
ago .
She knew he liked her and she liked him but she felt it was too soon after David.
Plus in a small town she did not want to give the locals anymore ammunition to fire her way.
But here she was in a foreign country with no one to answer to, on
holiday, with sun, sand and sangria
She looked at him as they walked along stopping to have ice creams.
Sitting on the beach wall paddling her feet in the water she asked "Are you married?"
Shaking his head a look of sadness crossed his eyes "No I`m not but I do have a son"
"Have you how old?"
"Oh he is coming up four now", he answered
"Where does he live?"she asked curiously.
"With his mum, in Dublin" he answered regret in his eyes.
"Is that why your going back to Dublin?
Nodding he answered "Yes I really miss the little man".
"You never married the mum then?" She asked.
"Your bloody inquisitive " he laughed.
Shrugging her shoulders smiling " Well if you don`t ask you never find out."

"True , it`s a bit of a story too long to go into all the detail`s but basically she had an affair with my best friend, and that killed it". he answered.

  Looking at her he asked" Are you married?"even though he had noticed there was no sign of a wedding band.

"Yes I am married but we split up just over a year ago". she answered.

"That must have been hard, a country girl coming from the bog" he laughed.

She gave him a playful punch, and said "Just cause you're a Dublin Jackeen"

He smiled at her and said seriously "It must have been really difficult for you, because my sister Eileen split from her husband, me Ma nearly done her nut in.

"Yes it still is hard "There such a lot of narrow minded people and the fact that I`m catholic doesn`t help"

Shaking his head he said "I know what you mean, when Kitty got pregnant with Paul there was such an uproar you would have thought I`d killed the pope"

They laughed at this statement.

"Right now we have the histories out of the way, how about a walk up the hill there is a amazing view "he said..

Smiling she answered "Show me the way".

A ten minute walk they were up the hill looking at one of the most breath taking views Maria had ever seen in her life.

"Beautiful isn`t it "he smiled down at her.

Nodding she looked at him "Yes it is magnificent" she answered in awe.

She was getting tired after the heat of the sun, she said "I think I`ll  go back to the hotel for a siesta, that`s what the call it " she said smiling at him.

"That sounds like a plan "he said smiling at her.

"You're a cheeky one " she answered.

"Well as you said earlier if you don`t ask you don`t get"

"Well your not getting" she answered smugly.

Taking her in his arms he kissed her gently.

Pulling away he looked at her surprised at her reaction.

She was feeling a bit disorientated with the situation, having just arrived at her destination, Everything was strange and then meeting Antony it was just too much too soon.

Looking at him "I have not been with anyone since David "she said meekly.

.He understood completely, as he had not been involved himself.

Taking her by the hand he said "I have not been involved since Kitty either."

"What you have been here four months and your telling me there has not been anybody?"

"I`m not saying I haven`t had sex what I`m saying is there has been no one special"

."I`m really tired" she answered not really wanting this conversation.

."Ok " he said smiling down at her "I`ll walk you back to the hotel".

There was an awkward silence between them as they wandered down the hill.

                "I`m feeling a bit vulnerable at moment, so excuse my reaction" she said ruefully.

"I might have been coming on a bit strong" he said smiling at her.

Guiding his hand into hers he squeezed it.

Looking at him she was feeling comfortable again.

As the approached the hotel there was music coming from The Irish Rovers pub.

"Fancy a drink?" He asked her his brown eyes dancing at her.

She suddenly found a new lease of life the tiredness she was feeling when they were on the hill suddenly disappeared .

She smiled and said "Yes why not".

They got inside the bar there was a live Irish band on stage.

Soon they were dancing and singing and the crack was mighty.

They left the pup later that evening both of them feeling very merry.

Antony being the perfect gentleman walked her to the entrance of the hotel.

Giggling she kissed him and said "Thank you for a wonderful day".

He looked into her brown eye's thinking I don't want it today to end but he didn't want to push his luck.

"Tomorrow is my last day at work so if you like when I have finished I can take you out to dinner" he said.

"I think that would be great" she answered blowing him a kiss as she walked into the hotel.

He watched as she went inside , not enjoying that feelings she was stirring inside.

Walking away thinking come on boy you have been there and you didn't like the aftermath of the vehement.

Feelings that Kitty had killed inside of him two years previously.

He had given her his innermost self, blinded by the love he had felt for her.

The had been together just over a year when she fell pregnant.And his son had been born.

The happiness he felt well he had never knew such emotions run through his body

He worked hard in an Italian restaurant in O Connell street in Dublin, Kitty had very high standards and liked the finer things in life.

So while he was working to provide for her and his son she was out playing the field.

Paul had just turned two at the time.

Antony found out she was sleeping with his best friend.

His stomach turned over now with the pain and torture he had felt.

The sick empty feeling that he awoke to every morning in the pit of his stomach.

He thought he was going to die, ended up getting into the drug scene for a time.

That's why he took some time out ,coming out to Gran Caneria, had just been the break he needed to get his head straight.

The change had done him good, and yes there had been women since but then we all have needs.

But not once did he allow his heart to even flicker,

He was having an argument inside of himself on the way back to his room, Christ you have only just met her and she is causing stirrings that you thought had died inside.

Grabbing a beer from the fridge, he lay there thinking about those sexy brown eyes and the radiant smile .Soon he was sleeping.

New chapter

Maria headed into her room thinking of the wonderful day she had had.

Here she was in a foreign country, the sun shinning , boating, eating delicious food and enjoying it all with a wonderful man.

Sitting on the bed hugging her legs underneath her, she couldn't remember ever feeling like this not even with David.

This is pure madness, you have only just met him but the feeling of desire she had for him, well was just breath taking.

She couldn't sleep with the excitement of seeing him tomorrow.She felt sixteen again.

Closing her eyes she was remembering her first love THE LIAM STORY

She nodded off and was awoken by the noise road sweepers.

NEW CHAPTER

The sun was beaming in through the patio doors, Making a coffee she went outside and sitting there with a cigarette she watched Playa Del Ingles wake up.

She had breakfast and taking a book went out by the pool.

Falling asleep she awoke with a shadow shading her.

Looking up she saw Antony standing over her.

"Hello" he said looking at the slim, well trimmed body the long dark hair spread over the back of the deck chair.

"Hello" she said stretching her body out "I wasn`t expecting you until later"

"Oh I`ll go and come back then" he answered smiling.

"No " she replied patting the seat beside her.

Sitting beside her he said in a sad voice "I`m going to miss this going back to the big smoke"

Nodding she answered "Yes it will be strange for you, but at least you will see Paul again".

Looking at her he said "Yes I have spoken to him over the phone but it`s not the same as getting a huge cuddle from his Da"

."Fancy a walk" he asked.

"Yes " she smiled wrapping her sarong around her.

Walking hand in hand they headed to the beach.

The sun was baking down on them.

"Have you got any sun cream " he asked looking at her pale delicate skin.

Shaking her head she answered" `No I left it at the hotel."

"Let`s get you some then or you might burn to a cinder" he said smiling down at her.

She was feeing her shoulders burning "Good idea"

Finding some on the front he sat her down and rubbing it into her shoulders . She looked into his eye`s as he finished he bent down to kiss her.

This time she responded to his surprise, holding her face in his hands pushing his luck he asked could he take her back to the hotel.

Smiling Maria she did not have to think about it for to long and nodded.

He lifted her up and said "I was hoping that would be the answer."

He then led her back to the hotel.Getting the key`s from reception feeling this was right.

Giving him a seductive look she led the way to her room.

Taking her in his arm`s kissing her passionately removing her bikini top he gently laid her on the bed. Looking at him she let a moan of excitement out.

Staring into her eye`s kissing her neck ,his tongue travelling down her body until she was screaming out in passion he entered her and as they became one.

Falling asleep in each other`s arm`s Antony awoke first and couldn`t believe that she had said yes.

Going into the shower he felt so alive something he hadn`t felt in a long time.

Maria woke up to hear him singing in the shower.

Rolling over in the bed with a huge smile on her face, she felt fulfilled and relaxed.

He came out of the shower towel drying his hair, a huge grin on his face.

"You look like the cat that has had the cream" she said smiling at him.

Falling on the bed beside her he answered "And you Madame look like a very contented lady"

"Well that`s because I am" she said with a twinkle in her eye.

Holding her hand thinking out loud "You have awoken a part of me that I thought had died."

Lying beside him stroking his arm "Why do you say that?"

"Because that is how I`m feeling I never thought after Kitty I would want another woman in my life"

"Oh so I`m in your life now am I?" She laughed.

Looking at her seriously nodding "Yes if you want to be".

This remark surprised her.

She looked at him with a beam on her face "I think I would like that very much".

Rolling over he said with a cocky smile "I think I`d like that as well".

They next four day`s were precious Antony showed her parts of the Island tourists normally never frequented.

Making love to her on a secluded beach. He surprised her with his tenderness and warmth.
Neither of them could comprehend, what was happening to them .
Antony thought he would never be able to fill the emptiness in his life that Kitty had caused.
Maria in her wildest dreams never thought that her break away would have led to romance as
it was the last thing on her mind.
Lying together in their own paradise each not wanting to leave the other to
break the magic that had enveloped them .
Getting up on one elbow, stroking her hair kissing her "You are beautiful" he said simply.
There last day together he hired a motor bike and he showed her the whole of the Island.
It was an experience she would never forget, there last five day`s had been like a fairy tale
that she knew was going to end in a matter of hour`s.
Heading back to the resort on the motor bike she clung on to him as if she never was going to
let him go.
Reaching their destination he pulled in and she got off the bike shaking her long dark hair,
looking at his watch, he said "We have got two hours of this heaven left".
"I know" she answered sadly.
Taking him by the hand leading him to her room she gently closed the door.
She undressed him and kissed him teasing him with her tongue until he was morning so
loudly that she put her hand over his mouth .
He gently pulled her from him and started to kiss her top of her head to toe the tip of her
toe`s.
They climaxed and lying in each arm`s in the aftermath of their love making,
Maria looked at him with tears in her eye`s.

He gently wiped them away and said "Baby, don`t cry because it`s over smile because this
could be the future?"
Staring at him, kissing his hand as he gently held her face.
Sighing she said "I wish".
Dream`s can come true" he said smiling at her.
"But for now we just have to put it on hold for a bit because you baby have got another week
in this paradise, and I have to go back to reality."
Sitting with her arm`s wrapped around her knee`s
"So we will be seeing each other again"
"Without a doubt " smiling at her as he gathered up his thing`s.
Sitting beside her holding her hand, kissing her gently on the forehead.
 "This is the phone number of my work , you can contact me on when you get back" he said.
"See you soon", he smiled as he left.
Going on to the balcony, sitting with a coffee, she watched as he left
the hotel and got on the coach.
Thinking don" t cry because it`s over smile because it happened.
Grabbing her towel and sun cream she headed down to the pool, she loved reading
Finding it very hard to focus she went for a walk along the beach.
It seemed like a dream she thought as she looked out at the sea.
Everywhere she looked she could see his face and that cheeky grin,.
She walked along, thinking get your bloody head out of the cloud`s.
So she gave herself a reality check and then having a little skip along the sand, she thought
how lucky she had been to have had felt the magic that she had shared with Antony over the
last few day`s.
 So heading back to the hotel room grabbing her bag, she decided to go shopping for
something for Mandy.

Browsing around the market`s she found just what she had been looking for.
Heading back to the hotel just in time for dinner.
                            Later that evening she went and bought herself a bottle and sitting on the balcony until the early hour`s, watching the night life go by.
The next few day`s she spent by the pool reading or chatting to whoever was beside her.
One evening a couple of day`s after Antony leaving, she decided to ring him.
Heading to reception asking if she could use the phone, they showed her were she could make a phone call from.
Dialling the number, when she heard a Dublin accent on the other end, she asked to speak to Antony.
 "Darling he hasn`t worked here for over four month` s", was the reply she got much to her disappointment.
She hung up thinking another one bite`s the dust, feeling destroyed inside.
She went to the pub next door where Karaoke was played twenty four hour`s a day.
The atmosphere was pumping lot`s of people there singing and dancing.
The drink flowing, so she joined them.
Getting chatted up by lot`s of different bloke`s she got very drunk.
Next morning she woke up to the sound of someone snoring beside her.
Opening her eye`s she saw a bloke with blond hair and a stripped t shirt and shorts on lying beside her.
Looking down at herself seeing she still had the dress on she had worn the evening before.
With no recognition of the evening before, getting out of bed feeling ill and not just through the amount of alcohol she had consumed.
She went to the bathroom washing her face, looking in the mirror she did not like what stared back at her.
Hearing him move she came out of the bathroom.
 "Do you have a drink my mouth feel`s like sand paper" he asked?
Nodding she poured him some water.
"Cheers Bab` s" he said, in an English accent.
"Christ you can dance" he said with a smirk on his face.
Feeling embarrassed she looked away opening the patio door she went outside leaning over the balcony.
Following her he put his arm around her, she quickly pulled away,
Taken aback by her attitude, he said "Well you weren`t pulling back last night".
"That was then this is now" she replied.
"Ok ,ok I can take a hint ,I know where I`m not wanted" he said sarcastically.
Looking at him she said "I`m just in a bit of a dark place at the moment, I was just drowning my sorrow`s yesterday".
"Find them fuck them and forget them that`s my attitude, even though I thought you were up for it, once we got back here you threw yourself on the bed and cried so I lay beside you to comfort you the next thing you were snoring and I was a bit the worst for ware myself so I passed out beside you nothing happened," he smiled" no hard feeling`s".
She was so relived she saw it written all over her face, even though her clothes were in tact she still had doubt`s in her mind.
Smiling at him holding her hand out said "No , no hard feeling`s and thank you for being honest"
"I`m Andrew by the way" he said finishing his water.
Not answering she opened the door.
Holding his hand`s up leaving "I`m out of your hair mate "he said leaving "You look after yourself"

He was gone , closing the door she thought you bloody idiot, here you are in a strange country getting pissed out of your head, ending up with stranger`s in your bed, for fuck sake Maria get you head together.

Showering she felt the tear`s flow down her cheek`s.

She was feeling rough from the drinking she had done the day before and was wishing that Antony was still with her.

Then she remembered the phone call ,her stomach turned over.

There all the same manipulative calculating, liar`s the whole lot of them sweet talk you until they got there wicked way and then it was Ta Da.

Well she had ,had enough from now on she was steering clear of the male species.

Spending the rest of her holiday licking her wound`s, soon she was packing her suitcase for home.

Saying goodbye to Gran Canary, she was on the plane heading home.

Four hour`s later she was going through custom`s hearing her name being called ,looking up to see Mandy and Don waving.

Don taking her suitcase Mandy hugged her asking if she had ,had a good time.

"For god`s sake Mandy she has just got off a bloody plane give her a chance to get her bearing`s."Mandy just scowled at him.

"Let`s have a drink before we head home "said Don "By the way you look great"

Mandy looking at her tan smiled and asked "Is it was all over".

As they were approaching the bar she heard a familiar voice calling her .

She looked around to see Antony standing with a bouquet of flower`s in his arm`s.

And a young boy by his side.

"Maria " he said as he ran up to her.

She was speechless, Mandy turned to see this handsome stranger, Don turned and said "Antony,"

She had turned pale under the tan, this was the last person she expected to see.

"What are you doing here" she half stammered with the shock.

"Waiting for you " he answered simply but getting a feeling rejection, this was not what he had planned.

Going over to her he asked "What`s the matter", the little boy said "Da I need a wee wee".

Looking down at him he said "Ok son" picking him up he said to Maria "Just wait I`ll be back"

Maria watched as he picked the little boy and headed toward` s the toilet`s.

Don looking at Maria with a very confused look on his face, "How do you know Antony".

"Oh I met him holiday" she answered vaguely.

"Come on sis spill the bean`s" Mandy said curiously.

She saw Antony coming holding his son in his arm`s back looking uneasy.

Seeing her still standing there he grinned at her.

Her heart skipping a beat, when she saw that wonderful grin but she thought play it cool.

Don getting the feeling they needed some space said" Maria we will be in the bar"

 Grabbing Mandy by the hand guiding her reluctantly to the bar.

He stood there and asking again "What`s the matter?"

"I tried phoning you a couple of day`s after you left, but to no avail".

Looking relived he said "Let me explain", looking at his son he said.

"Do you want to go and see Don and Daddy will get you a coke"

He nodded saying "Ok Da".

Looking at her he said "Ill be two minute`s".

He hurried back and taking by her arm said "Let`s get a coffee"

She nodded as he lead her to the coffee shop.

MARY D / MARIA THE IRISH COLLEN / PAGE 183

Getting the coffee`s she got them a seat.
He came back "Before I explain I have to tell you ,you look great"
She could feel herself weaken, smiling she answered "So do you"
Running his finger`s through his hair, "Christ were do I start".
"At the beginning would be good," she answered sharply.
"Look I know your annoyed, but let me explain",
Nodding giving him the go ahead.
"I arrived back and went to my sister`s Betty just to see if she could me up for a bit until I got back on my feet."
"Well she lives just a few door`s away from Kitty and Paul, on the way there I popped in to see the little man"
"To be told that if I hadn`t come back she was going to give Paul to her Ma to look after as she had ,had enough". He stopped taking a sip of coffee.
He carried on "She has found a new man who is loaded and he doesn`t like kid`s" he said bitterly.
"So" he sighed "To make a long story short, I`m am now a full time Da".
She looked at him in disbelieve, "God how could she do that".
Shrugging he answered "I don`t know, I have always know she is money oriented but this takes the biscuit".
"Fucking hell Antony" she said touching his hand feeling a bit guilty about how annoyed and disappointed she had felt.
"That`s why you couldn`t get me at the restaurant." He finished simply.
"So what`s happening now?"
"Well Betty has agreed to let us stay at her` s so I can get back to work and get a few bob together to find us somewhere to live, she is great my sis you will have to meet her".
                              "We better get back to Don and Mandy and you can introduce me to your little man" she smiled.
"Come here " he said taking her in his arm`s he kissed her with such passion it left her feeling dizzy.
"I have missed you even with everything going on you were playing a major part inside this" He laughed pointing at his head.
"Me too" she said smiling up at him.
Going into the bar Mandy looked to see them kissing as the came towards them.
She was full of questions, Laughing Maria and Antony filled them in on their encounter.
She was fascinated with the story.
Hugging her sister she said "Oh sis I`m so pleased for you!"
"Well it`s very early day`s yet" Maria replied looking at Antony.
Who looking back at her winked saying "I would call it lucky day`s"
"What`s lucky day`s Da", asked Paul, trying to climb into his Da` s lap.
Antony picking him up replied ,"Everyday is a lucky day as long as I have you and this young lady around to share them with"
"Is Maria your new girlfriend" he asked shyly.
Hugging Paul looking at Maria his eye`s sparkling he said "Yes I hope so".
Don looking at Anthony knew his friend had ,had a tough time of it said "Fancy having to go the whole way to Spain for you two to find each other",
"She was well worth the trip", smiled Antony.
"Yes well it was luck because if I had been a week later we would not have met" smiled Maria.
"I`m glad my Da has got a pretty girlfriend like you" smiled Paul joining in.
"And I`m glad he has got such a handsome little man" she answered .

"How old are you ?" She asked
"I'm four nearly five" he answered in his still babyish voice
He climbed down from Antony's lap and climbed on to Maria's.
"Christ your honoured" Antony said with a surprised look on his face.
Maria looking at Antony replied "He has good taste just like his Da" giving him a cuddle..
"Listen to her "said Mandy."Think the tan is gone to her head"
They all laughed .
Looking at the time Don said" Well I hate to spoil the party but if we don't want to hit the rush hour we better go soon"
Don nodding at Mandy said to Maria "We will meet you outside".
Maria nodded "Ok ".
Maria gently letting Paul down, looked at Antony and knew deep inside that they would certainly be seeing a lot more of each other.
He looked at her and whispered in her ear" I could easily fall in love with you".
Paul noticing his Da whispering said "Da what are you saying".
"Nothing for you to worry your little head about" he said.
"So when will I see you again?" he asked.
"Well where do we meet that is the real question" she answered.
"Well I know we live in different parts of the country but that is a minor detail."he said as he brushed away a piece of hair that had fallen on her face.
Look I feel as if I'm in limbo land at the moment", he said on a more serious note.
"Give me your phone number and I'll phone you tomorrow keep you in the picture as they say" he grinned.
Saying good bye looking into his brown eye` said "I'll see you soon."
"What about me " said Paul. Bending down to kiss him she said "I'll see you soon too"
Don pulled up at the entrance and she jumped in the car. And waved to Antony and Paul until they were out of sight
"Well that's one for the book's "said Mandy.
"Yes " Maria answered her head whirling, Falling asleep on the journey home.
Don stopped on the way picking up a takeaway.
Getting inside they sat up chatting until the early hour's.
Don filled them in on how long he had known Antony, but how they had lost contact ad hadn't seen each other for over a year.
"It's a small world" he said after he had finished his story.
Yawning Maria said "That it is I'm off to bed, goodnight you two"
"Sis" Mandy shouted after her "Yes" she answered "It's good to have you home".
Maria smiled to herself as she climbed into bed, and couldn't decide if it was good to be home or not.
But she did know somewhere she would love to be and that was wrapped around Antony waking up to that lovely grin and the way he always pecked her nose.
Soon she was sleeping.
Life soon went back to it's old routine, Work and trying to make time to see Antony. Which wasn't very often, he had found a job but nowhere to live for Paul and himself.So they only got to spend one weekend a month together and that was at Maria's flat.
  But they spoke regularly on the phone.
Time ended up being very precious to them both.
It was coming up to Christmas and Maria decided as a surprise for Anthony to book a hotel in London for them the weekend.
So on her next visit she told him about it.

He was well chuffed at the thought`s of spending a weekend away together.

Grabbing her and swinging her around he kissed her and said it was the best Christmas present anyone had ever given him.

The week`s passed and one evening when Maria and Mandy were cooking dinner there was a loud banging at the door.

Maria answered it to find David holding himself up in the doorway.

"What do you want?" She asked in a very unfriendly voice.

"That`s not very nice, coming from my wife" he slurred.

She was about to close the door in his face but he wedged his foot in it.

"Get your fucking foot out of the door way or it won`t just be your head that is bleeding" she screamed at him.

Mandy hearing the screaming came out in the hall, "What does he want?"

Looking behind her she answered "Fuck know` s"

Pointing at Maria he answered Mandy "That`s my wife"

"It was David but not anymore", she snarled back at him .Maria still trying to release his foot from the door .

Mandy finding a second wind pushed him out of the way as Maria slammed the door shut.

"Fuck`s sake that`s the second time in a week ", she was getting tried of his antic`s.

"And he came last weekend when you and Antony went out" Mandy said.

"Why didn`t you tell me?"Maria asked getting annoyed.

"Because Don told me to keep that sipped" she said making an action across her mouth, "because Antony doesn`t like Women been picked on"

"That`s fair enough" she replied because she was seeing little enough of Antony as it was without her x husband sticking his ore in.

"I just wish he would get himself a life" she sighed. Then the banging started again.

"Right that`s it, I have had enough", she went to the door finding Don there.

She looked at him in relief, "Thank Christ it`s you"

"Why who were you expecting" he asked seeing how harassed she looked.

"Who David was here a few minutes ago " she answered.

"He is being a right pain. You should report him" said Don.

"Oh I can`t be bothered," she sighed "Look Antony and I are off to London boxing day and I can`t be bothered with the hassle"

The phone ran, it was Antony, he told her there was a chance that he might be able to get him and Paul in the new year.

"Oh that is good new` s " she answered.

"When do you finish work?" He asked.

"Tomorrow, Christmas eve" she answered, "And then there is just two more day`s until we go to London" she answered excitably.

"I know, anyway baby I`m just off to work, ring you tomorrow".

Next morning it was Christmas eve, they salon was buzzing ,Maria was missing Joe. It was the first Christmas without him.

They held a minute`s silence in his memory.

And after work they had a drink for him holding up their glasses in the Bridge House.

Mandy and Don arrived and they all ended up getting a bit drunk.

Christmas morning Maria got in her car and went to see Sean and Paul, bringing Christmas present`s and something for her Ma and Da.

They were very antagonist toward` s her so she didn`t stay long.just making sure that her two younger`s brother`s were ok.

Getting back to the flat ,Mandy and Don having just woken up, they opened their Christmas present`s.

Don arrived out of the bedroom carrying a packet, and passing it to Maria.

She looked at him with a surprised look on her face.

"It`s from Antony" he smiled.

A look of pleasure passed over her face as she ripped it open.

It was a beautiful gold chain and cross with ear ring`s to match.

"Oh Mandy look " she smiled holding it up.

Mandy nodding but not showing much interest as she was busy opening her present`s from Don.

They had a lovely day eating too much and drinking too much, doing just what Christmas was all about.

Next morning Maria having packed the night before headed to Dublin.

Meeting Antony at the air port, hugging him and thanking him for her present.

They boarded the plane and were soon landing in Heathrow airport.

Grabbing a taxi the headed into Langham Place as they were staying at The Langham Hotel.

"This is lovely "said Maria very happy with her choice of venue.

Antony looking around smiling down at her agreed.

They unpacked and Maria said I`m off for a shower.

Running after her Antony joined her going inside taking the shower gel from her gently soaping her body.

Teasing her massaging her breast`s until the nipple`s were totally erect gently soaping her between the leg`s until she climaxed.

Returning the indulgence soaping his chest teasing him until he could stand it no more and entering her body, they became one.

Breathless they came out of the shower, he grabbing a towel wrapping it around his waist.

Maria taking one of the hotel bathrobe`s, wrapping her long hair in a towel.

He was lying on the bed smoking a cigarette, as she approached him, putting the cigarette out holding his arm`s out to her, she went straight into them.

"I have missed you so much " he whispered .

Looking at him she replied "I miss you too darling.

They lay there enjoying the moment, he gently dislodged himself from her saying "I`m famished let`s get dressed and get something to eat."

Realising how hungry she was, smiling at him pulling a bodysuit on she said "Good idea".

Watching her dressing smiling he said "Your one sexy lady".

Wriggling her bum at him, smiling back at him she said "I know".

Kissing her on the lip`s he said "Later and that`s a promise " pulling a shirt and jean`s out of his suitcase, got dressed.

Going downstairs finding the bar they ordered some drink`s.

"I can`t believe this " he said smiling down at her.

"What" she asked taking a sip of her drink.

"That I am in London for a whole weekend with the woman of my dream`s."

"Well believe it " she answered with them brown sexy eye`s.

The waiter had come to take their order`s.

Soon they were eating, and decided to take a walk afterwards.

 Maria saying that tomorrow they would be meeting Shelly.

"How did you meet her" he asked as they walked along hand in hand.

"It`s a long story" Maria answered

"Go on I have time".

So he heard the story of Shelly.

"She sound`s like a character" he said.

"Oh Shelly is that all right" she smiled.

Getting back to the hotel they went to the bar for a nightcap.

Finishing their drink`s they went to their room where they made love had a few more drink`s and talked into the early hour`s.
        Next morning Maria was awoken by the phone, reception telling her there was someone at desk asking for her by the name of Shelly.

Antony looked at her as she jumped out of bed shouting "Shit, shit".

"What`s up baby" he asked yawning.

"Shelly is downstairs" she answered pulling some legging`s on and a top.

Pulling a brush through her hair, she ran out the door.

Getting to reception there she was standing as gorgeous as ever.

"Shelly" she shouted as she ran across the room towards her.

Shelly turning seeing her holding her arm`s out to her friend,

"Hi " said Shelly as she hugged her .

"Come on upstairs, I just woke up" Maria said her eye`s overexcited .

Running upstairs as they entered the bedroom Antony was still in bed.

Turning over smiling he sat up yawning" Hello I`m Antony apologies about the circumstances, but she insisted on keeping me up half of the night".

"That`s her " she smiled, "Pleased to meet you" she said holding her hand out.

Shaking her hand "I would turn around, if I was you don`t want you going into shock" he laughed as started to emerge from the bed.

"Oh Shelly I`m so glad to see you" Maria said.

"I`m going for a shower" said Antony.

"Do you want a hand?" Asked Shelly laughing.

"Come on then" he teased.

"Oh he`s not shy then" said Shelly.

Maria shaking her head said "Right I want to hear about this new man in your life".

Shelly cocking her head, to one side "Oh Maria he is gorgeous, and we really connect."

"Where is he now?" She asked.

"Well there is one bit I forgot to mention," she said holding her head to one side biting her

bottom lip.

 Maria looking at her inquisitively she carried on to tell her that he is married.

"Oh Shelly you know your barking up the wrong tree there" she answered immediately.

"I was expecting that reaction, but it`s my life" she answered uneasily.

"Oh look who am I to judge", Maria answered.

This lightened the atmosphere, and they carried on comparing note`s on what path`s there

lives had taken since they last seen each other.

Shelly already knew about the David saga from Maria over the phone.

Antony arrived out of the shower dressed.Shelly giving Maria a nudge.

"Who I thought I was going to get a free view" she said laughing.

"Oh don`t mind her she is just full of hot air" answered Maria.

They went downstairs for lunch, then they did some sight seeing, Maria insisted on seeing

Madame Tossuards again.

Antony thoroughly enjoying himself, this making Maria feel she had definitely made the

right choose of what activity they done that day.

Afterwards they went and had dinner in a lovely restaurant that Shelly new.

Soon it was time to say goodbye.

Maria promised to keep in contact as they said their farewells.

Going back to the hotel ,Antony putting his arm`s around her outside.

Said `"Thank you I have had the most incredible time, this is the best Christmas present

ever"

She looked at him smiling "I have enjoyed your Christmas present as well".

Picking her up carrying her into the hotel whispering "It`s not over yet".

Giggling in his arms as they approached the room.

Opening the door he gently put her on the bed, and started to undress her.

Removing her leggings and top kissing her neck she was moaning, he let his tongue do the

rest of the walking removing her knickers, pouring some baby oil on her he massaged into

her , gently pushing him away ,she whispered "Now it`s your turn".

Removing his jeans pouring some baby oil on his leg`s she started to massage them.

Her fingers doing a lot of the slipping and sliding, as she gently remove his pants.

Putting his erect penis in her mouth, teasing him with her tongue, she looked up to see him

staring down at her and the pleasure in his eye`s telling her everything she needed to know.

Eventually becoming one they lay totally fatigued in each others arms afterwards.

Laying there in the aftermath of their loving Antony stroking her hair, she was wishing that

this moment would never end.

That evening after having dinner the went for a walk he kept kissing head

and making sure she was warm enough.

Voicing her thoughts she said "I want this to go on forever. "

"Dito" he answered smiling down at her.

The following morning they headed back to Heathrow and were in Dublin within the hour.

Maria was really sad leaving Antony, he promised he would ring her as soon as he got back

to work, the following evening.

Saying goodbye she caught the train back to Athlone.

Getting into the train station, she started to make her way back to the flat.

From across the street she heard her name being called.

Looking across she saw a very drunken David coming out of the pub.

Hurrying along trying to avoid him, catching up with her.

Slurring he said "Hear you have been away lover boy"

With no intentions of listening to him she ignored him and she walked on.

Shouting at her "Have you heard your old Da has snuffed it ".

Turning around frozen to the spot she said "What did you just say"

"Ha that caught your attention" he was now swaying with a smirk on his face.

Screaming at him she repeated "What did you say?"

 "You heard me The fucker is dead."

"Fuck off you drunken idiot" she answered running the rest of the way back to the flat.

Getting into the flat shouting Mandy`s name Mandy appeared her face snow white.

Mandy sobbing looking at Maria said "Daddy is dead".

Maria standing there a thousand thoughts running through her mind.

Not really knowing how to feel relief or regret.

Taking her by the arm leading her into the kitchen sitting her down said "What`s happened?"

Mandy through the sobbing blurted out that their Ma had got home and found him lying on the floor dead.

Feeling absolutely nothing at all, trying to console her sister, the door knocked.

She went to find Don there.

"What`s happened?" He asked his eye`s searching for Mandy.

She ran from the kitchen as soon as she heard his voice crying "Daddy is dead".

Don looking at Maria seeing no reaction at all, asked "What happened"

Maria seemed to be dumb struck, so Mandy continued to tell him what happened.

Maria finding her voice asked "Who let you know?"

Mandy answered "Sean rang yesterday"

"And you have been on your own " Maria asked looking at Don.

"I was in Dublin with my parents" he answered.

NEW CHAPTER

Next day Mandy and Maria headed home.

Finding Catrine in bed after being sedated by the doctor.

Sean and Paul were in the kitchen with Father O` Grady who was there to help organise the funeral.

And there`s Da` s body laid out in Sean`s bedroom.

Tommy had already picked out his plot where he was to be buried.

So this making thing`s a lot simpler for the family.

The funeral mass was to take place at St Mary`s Church at 12 O Clock the following day.

The wake was that evening in the house as neighbours and friends came to pay their last respects.

Maria and Mandy prepared food while Sean and Paul went and organised the drink`s.

Catrine making a miraculous recovery, was able to participate in the farewells to her husband
Tommy.

Maria and Mandy stayed the night and Maria went into the village later that evening to use

the public phone to call Antony

He was shocked by the news and by Maria`s attitude.As he thought he would

be consoling her.

But instead she was totally aloof and emotionless over her fathers death.

Telling her he would get a train down the following morning.

She was very insistent that she could manage on her own

A little taken aback, he put it down to shock.

She said she would be returning to Athlone immediately after the funeral and would ring him
later.
Following morning as they removed Tommy`s body from the house all the

friends and neighbours gathered outside, Catrine the grieving wife in the funeral car.And
Maria,

Mandy Sean and Paul walked behind the hearse to the church.

He was buried at the local cemetery, as his body was put in the ground Mandy , Sean Paul

and Catrine shed tears while Maria stood there motionless.

They all went back to their family home and Maria making excuses headed back to Athlone

leaving Mandy with the family.

Driving back towards home she didn`t know weather laugh or cry, she felt torn inside.

She felt sad for her sister and brothers her Ma would lap up the sympathy for as long as she

could.But she felt as she had watched her Da being buried that a secret was being taken from
this world to be hidden away forever.

Pulling into the side of the road, Maria sat with her hands clenched on the steering wheel until her knuckles went white.

Relief flowing from within, for the first time in her life she felt released from her inner demons.

She had felt all through her life like damaged goods and now with the source gone she could repair herself. The torment was no longer there.

NEW CHAPTER

Mandy arrived home the following morning to find Maria back at work.

She could not understand her sister, she had shown no emotion though out the whole ordeal.

Walking up to the salon she went in to find Maria being her usual cheerful self with the clients.

Turning surprised to see Mandy standing there, Maria went over to her saying,

"Are you ok sis I was not expecting you back until later or even tomorrow".

Mandy looking at her thinking it was shock, replied "Yes I'm ok, I just couldn't stand it without you"

Maria nodding understood what she meant, "It's ok it over now" she said smiling at Mandy.

Mandy did not understand this strange behaviour, it was so unlike her sister to be so cold and unemotional.

"Did Don turn up yesterday?" Asked Maria as she was combing out Mrs Kenny's hair.

Nodding Mandy answered "Yes he got a flat tyre on his way to the funeral" she replied.

"Oh dear who has died" asked Mrs Kenny blessing herself.

"Our Father " answered Mandy .

"Christ you never said Maria" .

"Oh Mrs Kenny I do not bring my personal problems to work" she answered.

"Dear oh dear Maria that is not a problem it is a great loss" answered Mrs Kenny.

"Yes but it is also a fact of life" said Maria choking up "Look at Joe a young life taken for no reason ".

Mandy listening and watching looked at Maria wondering who these tears were for their Da or Joe.

The phone rang "Maria asked Mandy to answer it as they were two staff down that morning.

Mandy ended up staying working alongside her sister for the rest of the day and could see

why Maria had come back to work so soon , as it kept the mind occupied.

And stopped you pondering.

Maria locked up after they had finished and took her sister for a drink.

Mandy grabbing a seat looked around to see who was about. Seeing Johnny she waved.

Johnny went over to her and said "I`m so sorry to hear about your Da Mandy".

Nodding at him she could feel tears pricking the back of her eyes,

Maria arrived back with the drinks smiling "Hello Johnny long time no see"

He smiled at her and said "So sorry about your Da ".

Putting the drinks down "Well that's the one thing we are all guaranteed in this life is to die,

look at Joe, dead for no reason " she said simply.

Mandy looking at her asking "Why do you keep bringing up Joe since Da died"

She looked at Mandy sadly answered "It just brought back how much I miss him".

Mandy nodded trying to make logic of her answer.

The door opening Mandy looked to see David walk in.

Maria following her stare sighed saying "Christ this is all I need".

He went over to them and said "Sorry about the old man".

Maria glaring at him said "Piss off I have had enough grief from you".

Looking down at her he slurred "That`s not a nice way to be greeted by your wife".

Maria losing it shouted, "I`m your fucking wife in name only, and that won`t be for much

longer if I have anything to do with it".

"Why what are you going to do, get a divorce across the water " he answered reeling all over
the place.

"Yes that is the plan" she shouted shoving him out of the way.

Johnny standing up said "Look David I think you should leave".

Maria turning around said "I`m the one who will be leaving".

Mandy looked at her shocked.

"What do you mean" she asked.

"Nothing " she snapped."I`m going home".

Mandy grabbing her bag left with her.

Getting back to the flat, Maria dropping her bag and kicking off her shoe`s.

Mandy following her asking" What that was all about".

Maria sitting in the chair wearily "I have been thinking about this for a while actually quite a lot"

"About what" asked Mandy,

"Look you now what a pain David has been since we broke up"

She nodded.

"I`m going to move to London a fresh start, a new chapter, I have enough of David and the narrow minded people and their sneaky remarks".

"Does Antony know?" She asked.

"No I haven`t mentioned it to him yet" she answered.

With that the phone ran, Mandy answering calling Maria said "It`s for you".

Maria going out in the hall looking at Mandy, she whispered "It`s Antony".

Mandy ear wigging and heard Maria finish the conversation, "Yes there is something I want to talk to you about".

Going back into the living room she said to Mandy "He is coming down tomorrow".

"What Antony?" she asked.

Nodding she answered "Yes I`m going to talk him and see if he is interested in coming with me"

"Oh Maria are you sure this is what you want?"

Maria nodding at her was never more sure about anything in her life she new that her sister

was completely safe now, that Tommy had been removed from this world.

"Yes," she answered "I think it`s time I let my little sister grew up".

Holding out her arm`s Mandy went straight into them, she hugged with such affection,

thinking at last she could breath easy.

The door went Mandy answering it to find Don standing there.

Filling him in on Maria`s plan`s.

Don turning to Maria said "This is a bit sudden".

No " she answered shaking her head "When David and I went to London on our honey

moon ,I didn`t want to come back".

"You never told me that" said Mandy in a surprised voice.

Maria looking at her said "What was the point in talking about something that wasn`t going

to materialise."

She continued saying "Anyway you both can have this place for yourselves, as soon as I`m

out of your hair"

Mandy looking at her smiling said "We were talking about moving in together"

"Well there you go problem solved" she said.

Don smiling said "I`m am really pleased, I presume Antony is going with you".

"He doesn`t even know about her thoughts" replied Mandy.

Maria looking at her said "No but he is arriving down tomorrow, and I`ll ask him then".

Next day Antony arrived, him and Maria, driving him to the village where she

grew up.

Taking him to one of her favourite spot`s which was by a stream, sitting on the wall he put

his arm around her.

Asking how the funeral went, she slowly answered, "It was ok".

Antony having never met any of her family apart from Mandy, "Is this where your Ma lives?"

"Yes, I will take you to meet her one day, not today because she will be in bed sedated".

Antony feeling relived answered "That`s ok" he was not very good in these sort of circumstances.

"I need to ask you something?" she said cuddling up to him.

"Ok " he smiled.

"I`m moving to London and I want to know if you want to come with me?" She blurted out.

He was totally taken aback with this statement, "Where has this come from?"

"To be honest I wanted to move there five year`s ago but David wasn`t up for it".

"It`s always` s been in my mind since I first went there" she answered.

He had not been expecting this.

"Look I know it is a big ask" she said sensing apprehension.

"Darling I would say yes without even thinking about it but I have got the little man to think about" he answered.

Laughing at him she said "You don`t think for one moment I was going to ask you to go without Paul?"

With relief in his eye`s he hugged her and said "I know, but I have to get Kitty`s approval".

Maria looking at him "When did she last see him" she asked.

Looking rather embarrassed he answered "Two month`s ago".

Sighing she said "Well it`s not as if we are going a million mile`s away"

"And I`m sure if she want`s to see him, she`ll make the effort".

Nodding he said "It will be a big upheaval for him".

Smiling she answered " Upheaval, it will be an adventure of a life time for him".

Hugging her he said that`s what "I love about your so optimistic".

"I know " she smiled as he started tickling her.

Looking into the stream she said "I`ll take that as a yes then".

Grabbing hold of her looking into her eye`s "Let`s do it".

Nearly falling off the wall laughing she said" Oh yes".

 The next few week`s flew by, Shelly on the other side had found them a

two bedroom flat, Paul a school .

Maria handing her notice in at work, Mandy was feeling a bit nervous about life without her

sister.

Maria reassuring her that she would only be a phone call or a flight away.

The big day arrived, everyone at the airport Mandy, Don ,Antony`s two sister`s and Kitty

who stuck her head in to say goodbye.

Boarding the plane Antony and Paul gone ahead Maria look behind to see a forlorn figure in

the back ground standing with a can in his hand, that she recognised as her estranged

husband.

A couple of hour`s later they were with Shelly at their new flat , and The New Adventure

began.

NEW CHAPTER

The flat was already furnished , with six month lease on it.

Paul started school the following week and Antony started work on a local building site, as a
hod carrier.

 Maria getting a part time job in the local hairdressers.

So she could look after Paul.

They soon settled into their routine as a family.Maria adjusting to being a step Ma.

Her and Paul soon bonded and became very close.

She still could not get her head around how any Ma could give her child away especially

Paul.

He was so loveable and she adored looking after him.

Next job on Maria`s agenda was to get a divorce, seeing a solicitor getting the ball rolling

Her was no problem has they had over a year separated.

Antony returning from work one evening, Shelly had popped by and Maria

had invited her to stay for dinner.

Paul was setting the table as he liked helping, talking nine to the dozen to Shelly about

school.

Antony had one of his work collages with him Rickie, introducing him to Maria and Shelly.

"Hello very pleased to meet you" he said in an Indian accent.

"You talk funny" laughed Paul.

Looking at the little boy he replied "Do I".

"That`s because he is from India " smiled Antony.

Going over to Maria putting his arms around her "Have we got enough for Rick to join us".

Smiling she answered "Yes I can make it stretch".

"Paul set another place for Rickie" she said going into the kitchen.

Rickie excused himself saying he was just going to the shop.

Arriving back with flowers , chocolates and a couple of bottle`s of wine.

Sitting down to dinner Shelly chatting him up, Rickie lapping it up, as he did

not normally get much attention from women.

Having a good laugh until Rickie produced some marijuana and started to roll a cigarette.

Maria face nearly hit the ground.

"What do you think your doing" she shouted.

"I`m just doing us a joint" he answered smiling.

"Not in my home you don`t" she answered furiously.

Shelly half pissed "Maria chill out the man is just making himself at home".

Paul picking up that there was something a miss, started to cry.

Antony really annoyed at Maria`s reaction "Fuck`s sake Maria, he is only having a joint".

Picking Paul up she said "Say goodnight to everyone".

Putting him to bed he asked why she shouted, "Because the man was going to smoke something nasty and I don`t like the smell".

Turning his light out she went back into the living room to see Rickie was gone.

"Thank` s for that you have just made me look like a right idiot" said Antony raising his voice to her.

She was very taken aback as he never raised his voice to her.

"Since when has it been alright for anyone to produce drug`s in front of your son", she answered him back in a loud voice.

Shelly picking up there was going to be a domestic, gathering her thing`s made a quick exit.

Antony did not have an answer for that question.

Picking up his jacket said "I`m going to the pub".

As he walked out standing in front of him, asking "And who is going to look after your son".

He knew he was defeated, looking down into the brown eye`s that just melted him.

Putting his arm`s around her he apologized, "I`m sorry baby it`s just that Rickie and I sort of connected and I just wanted to make him feel at home.I wasn`t thinking"

"Christ Antony that`s the one thing I don`t want in our live` s is bloody drug`s of any shape or form" she answered.

Looking at his face asking "Have you ever tried them?"

Nodding he answered "Yes I did ,that`s why I went abroad, to get my head together."

Very surprised at his answer "Why didn`t you ever tell me?"

"Because it`s not something I`m proud of, and it was never brought up in conversation".

She couldn`t get her head around this answer.

Pulling away from him asking "How bad was it".

"Look baby it`s all over with now, I was in a very dark place after Kitty and I split up and I used it as a crutch just to help me get through".

She felt sick and heading to the toilet threw up.

Christ what`s brought all this on she thought.

She had only had one drink.

Coming back into the room he asked "Are you ok"

Looking at him with watering eye`s "I don`t know where that came from, I have not been feeing great lately"

"Oh baby why didn`t you say something?"

"Oh it`s nothing, just probably a bit run down".

They sat the rest of the evening together on the couch, Maria playing over and over the conversation the had just had.

Looking at him she said "Please promise me you won`t ever take drugs again".

Staring down at her, shaking his head "I promise baby you have nothing to worry, I`m not that man anymore"

Satisfied with the answer she put it to the back of her mind.

Kissing her the ended up making love on the couch.

 The following week Maria went to the doctor`s where she still was feeling

sick all the time.

She said to Antony "That she better get herself checked out".

He agreed as it was so unlike her to be off colour.

Her appointment was on Monday just after she had dropped Paul off at school and it was her day off from work.

Her name being called she headed into the surgery.

It was her first time there, as she went she noticed a lot of pregnant women in the waiting room, and it suddenly dawned on her the reason she might be sick.

Her heart beating ten to the dozen, as she walked into to see the doctor.

Telling him her symptoms, she asked if she could be pregnant.

Smiling at her he answered "There is only way to find out"

Handing her a pot he pointed her toward`s the ladies.

She was sweating thinking how could she have been so naïve, Christ all the symptoms were there.

Taking the pot back into the surgery she handed it to the doctor.

Doing the test there and then he looked at her smiling "Yes Maria it is positive."

She did not know whether to laugh or cry, The doctor looking at her face said ,

"A surprise?".

Nodding she answered "You could say that".

Leaving with the phone number of the midwife and leaflets on pregnancy, she wandered around to Shelly`s.

Shelly opening the door taking a look at her face said "Come in ."
"
Cuppa" she asked.

"Please" she nodded.

Bringing the tea into the living room, sitting beside her she asked "What`s the matter".

Maria looked up and blurted out "I`m pregnant".

Shelly nearly spilling her tea said "What. Oh sis that is wonderful news"

Looking at her reaction sitting beside her putting her arm around. "It is good news?".

Maria her head between her hand`s, answered "I don`t know".

"Oh come on, you're a natural with Paul and I`m sure Antony will be over the moon".

"Yes " she answered slowly.

"But we have never even talked about having a baby, It is something I have never thought about". She answered.

"Well it's happening girl whether, you want it to or not" Shelly replied matter of factly .

Maria looking down feeling her tummy said "Yes it is there a little person in there" she smiled.

Finishing her tea hugging Shelly she said "Don't tell anybody".

"I won't mum's the word" she promised.

Maria wandered home smiling to herself "Christ I'm going to be a Ma".

She rang Mandy forgetting that she was at work so leaving a message on the answer machine to ring her.

Then thinking to herself She better tell Antony first.

Walking to the site where Antony worked she saw him hiking brick's up a ladder.

Calling him he looked down and seeing Maria shouting "Two minutes".

Dropping the brick's on the roof top he climbed backdown the ladder as quick as he could.

Wiping his hand's he came over to her with a worried look on his face asking.

"What's the matter ?"

She looked at him with a worried look on her face.

"What is it " he asked taking her hand.

"I'm pregnant" she blurted out.

A huge grin appeared on his face as he picked her up and swung her around.

"Oh baby that is amazing " he shouted.

Letting her down gently he asked "Are you sure".

"Yes that's what the doctor said so it's all confirmed" she answered smiling.

"Oh baby I`m over the moon".

The boss shouting at him he looked down at her kissing her smiling "See you later."

Walking home smiling to herself she knew then that this was going to be a good thing to happen.

Looking down at her flat tummy she could not believe there was a life growing inside of her, and it was a magical feeling.

Passing a baby shop she wandered in picking up baby clothes, imagining her and Antony pushing a pram.

She looked at the time Christ it was time to pick up The Little Man.

Getting to the school she felt like standing on a platform shouting that she was pregnant.

Instead she picked Paul up and they sang the whole way home.

Taking him to the park pushing him on the swing`s in her mind she could see her little daughter or son playing here.

She had never felt so happy or contented in her whole life.

Going home Paul yapping ten to the dozen as he always did.

She remembered she needed to get something from the shop for tea.

Meeting her neighbour Jimmy in there.

"Be the holy God if it`s not herself" he said in his broad Irish accent.

"How are you Jimmy?" Maria asked.

"Christ never better" he replied "Got time for a cuppa"

Smiling she said "Always` got time for a cuppa with my favourite neighbour"

"Flattery will get you everywhere" he laughed.

"And how is young Paul" he asked handing him a pound.

"I am fine thank you" answered a smiling Paul taking the pound.

"Ha your very welcome"

Going into Jimmy's he put the kettle on, "What would the like to drink?"

"Have you got any lemonade?" Paul asked.

"You come into the kitchen with me and we will see what we have."

"How is thing`s with you anyway" he shouted at Maria from the kitchen.

"I have got a bit of good new` s" she answered.

"And what`s that" he asked.

"I`m going to have a baby" she smiled as she went into the kitchen.

" Be the holy mother of God that`s great new` s" he smiled at her .

Little ears picking up on the conversation wandered into the kitchen asking " Maria are you

having a baby"

"Be God there is no fly`s on that fellow" laughed Jimmy.

Maria looking down at him said "Yes".

His little eye`s shining answered "Oh I`m going to have a brother or a sister".

"Well it`s looking that way" replied Jimmy smiling.

Finishing there drink`s they left, Jimmy standing at the gate shouting "You take great care".

Maria and Paul waving at him Paul asking a million questions on the way.

 Antony arriving home to Paul running to the door Shouting "Maria is

having a baby"

Antony looking at her smiling going over to her, kissing her forehead said "Yes we are ".

Paul sensing the happiness went and joined in the hug.

He was full of questions, so after dinner Maria bathing him and getting him to bed,

Sitting on the bed beside him doing her best to answer questions about where baby`s come

from he eventually fell asleep.

Coming into the living looking at Antony wiping her brow smiling saying "Christ that was

hard work".

Patting the couch for her to join him putting her arm around her.

"He`s just overexcited" he said smiling.

"A bit like the Da" answered Maria.

"Oh baby you have mad me so happy" he said smiling down at her like a Cheshire cat.

"I did not think you would be this happy about it" she said .

Looking at her "Why not?"

"Well we never really spoke about adding to our family" she answered.

"Oh baby I have always wanted more kid`s"

Nodding at him sitting back, she said "We will have to look for a bigger place".

"Yes " he answered yawning.

"My baby does work hard" she said.

"I`m bloody so tired this evening,"

"Well go on to bed baby, I`ll clear up down here".

He stood up stretching, "I think I will go on up" bending down to kiss her "Thank you ".

She smiled at him, sitting in peace and quite looking at her tummy smiling down at it

thinking You will be the most loved little baby in this whole world.

 The week`s toddled by, one morning Maria was just getting back from

leaving Paul to school, chatting away to her neighbour Chris when she bent over with a

cramp like pain in her tummy.

"Let`s get you inside" she said helping to hold her up.

"Shall I call the doctor?" Chris asked.

The cramp getting worse, tears stinging her eye`s, she nodded.

Maria sobbing said "Chris can you get Antony"

"I`ll just wait until the doctor get`s here then I`ll go and get him".

Bent over in pain."Get him now" she choked.

Chris seeing how distressed she was said "Ok".

Running up the road to where he was working, calling his name as she approached the site.

Seeing her he knew there was something wrong, shouting at the foreman he went to her.

She filled him in on Maria`s condition they two of them ran back to the house.

Maria was bent over the chair and there was blood stain`s on her dress.

The door knocked, Chris went to answer it, the doctor went straight to Maria and seeing the stain`s on her dress said to Antony "Get her to the hospital".

As soon as she arrived she was taken to theatre, where they removed the remain` s of her dead baby.

Keeping her in overnight for observation. Antony had to leave to pick Paul up.

Leaving the hospital tears of sorrow running down his face. He was devastated.

Thinking why us.

Maria in the hospital bed feeling completely empty, the nurse coming to check on her, she asked if they knew the sex of the baby.

Nodding the nurse said "Yes it was a little boy".

Turning toward` s the wall  clutching the sheet`s to her as comfort she sobbed herself to sleep.

She was discharged the following morning, Anthony picked her up.

Asking did you tell Paul.

Nodding unable to speak, because he felt if he did would break down, and Maria was upset enough.

Getting home taking the tablet`s she was given at the hospital, she went to bed.

Shelly popped around as soon as she heard, Chris their neighbour dropped in.

Antony trying to keep together said he would tell Maria they had been.

He went and picked Paul up from school.

The mothers there sending Maria their best wishes.

He couldn`t get away from there quick enough .

Getting Paul home, finding Maria downstairs looking like a ghost.

Paul running to her crying."What`s the matter " she asked.

"Me Da told me last that the baby died" he sobbed.

Holding back the tears, bending down to the little man hugging him,

She said "Yes darling he wasn`t very well so the angle`s came from heaven"

Not being able to hold the tears any longer, she looked at Antony for help.

He came over and bending down hugging them both.

Tears running down his face.

She took Paul and sat him beside her

And said "But he is a twinkling little star in the sky now, so tonight when it get`s dark we

shall go out and his smiling face will twinkle down at us"

 "What`s his name?"he snivelled.

She looked at Paul and softly said "Antony "

"Just like me Da` s "he said smiling.

 Anthony looked at her in amazement.

Thinking what a lovely way to describe what just happened.

She was so strong even at a time like this.

That evening Antony Paul and Maria went out to see Baby Antony

smiling down from the sky at them.

Paul looking up at the sky, shouting "There he is" as he pointed up to a star that was

twinkling.

Antony squeezing Maria`s hand tear`s in both their eye`s as they held little Paul`s hand

watching the star in the dark sky.

Holding hand`s going home Paul said "He know` s we love him now so he won`t be lonely"

Life went back to it`s usual routine, Maria going back to work a few week`s later.

Antony arriving home from work one evening finding Maria in tears.

"What`s the matter "he asked.

Shouting at him "What do you think is the matter?"

"I want my baby" she said rocking too and foe.

Trying to hold her to comfort her she turned around in a rage,

Telling him to "Fuck off that no one could understand the ache that was inside of her."

Chris knocking on the door ,came in leaving Paul back as he had been playing with her boy`s.

"Maria what`s the matter " she asked seeing the tears pouring down her face.

Maria got up and left the room without saying a word.

Chris looked at Antony saying "She is bound to be still grieving".

Nodding he thanked her for having Paul.

"She will be ok it is just time " said Chris as she walked out.

Maria took to her bed for several week`s after this, not talking or wanting to see anybody.

Antony was finding it almost impossible to cope with the whole situation.

Chris helped him out by taking Paul to school, as he tried to concentrate on work,

Doing his best to multi task but not finding it easy.

He rang Mandy asking for help,

She said that she would not be able to come over at the moment ,but give her a few week`s she might be able to sort something out.

Feeling totally at his wit`s end he rang Catrine thinking that her Ma might help.

After phoning her according to Catrine she still in morning over the loss of Tommy, but more to the point she was so ashamed of the scandal Maria had caused by splitting up her marriage to David and if that wasn`t enough running off to England with a Dublin Jackeen so she declined.

On his way home from work that evening bumping into to Jimmy who stopped to ask how Maria was doing.

Antony nearly in tear`s told him what was happening.

"I`ll come around with you" he said.

"I don`t think that`s such a good idea" replied Antony.

Jimmy looking at him asked "Why not?"

"She doesn`t want to see anybody".

"What a pile of shit" answered Jimmy.

Getting back to the house Antony opening the door ,

Shouting "Darling I`m home".

Getting no response which he was getting used too after three week of purgatory.

"Where is she?", asked Jimmy.

Pointing upstairs he answered "First door on the right".

Jimmy patting him on the shoulder said "I won`t be long".

Opening the bedroom door he called, "Maria are you there".

The room was in darkness, curtain`s drawn .

Hearing Jimmy`s voice she stirred beneath the cover`s.

Pulling the curtains back he looked down to see a shadow of the Maria he knew.

Her face white as a sheet, the long dark hair stuck to her face, and her eye`s were dead.

"Be the lord god almighty ,what`s up with you" he asked in a gentle voice.

Putting her hand over her eyes squinting with the light in the room.

"How did you get in" she asked her voice so low he could hardly hear her.

"Never mind how I got in ,what are you doing to yourself" he asked sitting on the bed beside her.

Her hand pulling the cover's back a bit from her, taking her hand in his.

"Maria oh Maria , how have you got here?" He asked shaking his head.

Looking at his snow white hair and kind eyes, she started to cry.

Holding her gentle in his arms he said "That's it pet let it all out"

She cried so hard that at one point Jimmy thought she had stopped breathing.

Pulling her over beside him pulling her hair from her face,

In the most kindest voice he asked, "What has brought all this on? "

Gathering herself together looking at him looking at her tummy.

"I feel empty, so empty nothing makes sense anymore".

"But my lovely nothing in this world makes sense, but if we were all to take to our bed's well there would be no world out there at all but a whole load of closed curtains".

At this statement she half smiled.

"Now that's better, why don't you get up for a little bit ,your Antony is beside himself with worry " he prompted her.

"I can't" she answered.

"There is no meaning to that I can't, you can and you will, "he said smiling.

Holding out his hand to her helping her out of bed, pulling a dressing gown around her.

He noticed she was skin and bone.

"When did you last have a dinner?" Guiding her gently down the stairs,

Hearing Jimmy's voice, Antony went out in the hall to see him helping Maria downstairs.

 She looked at him and half smiled.

Grinning at her he asking if she would like a cup of tea.

"Be god I'd love one "smiled Jimmy.

Getting her into the living room, he gently put her in the chair.

"Now is `nt that better instead of being in a dark hole, burying yourself"

Jimmy said to her.

Nodding feeling very weak she nodded.

Antony returning with two cup`s of tea, put them on the coffee table.

"Lord this is a grand place you have got here" he said looking around.

Antony nodding asked "Have you never been here before?"

Looking at Maria he smirked and answered "Ser I never got invited in".

For the first time in weeks Antony saw a glimmer of life appearing in her eyes.

"And when did you ever have to be invited in anywhere, your like a tinkers ass you would

make yourself ah home anywhere."she answered weakly.

Antony burst out laughing at this statement.

"Well there no point in letting the grass grow under your feet, now is there?" He

laughed.

 "If you were waiting for some people to invite you in ,sur you would be gone past your sell

by date" he said in that broad Irish accent.

This just creased Maria up.

"Christ you're a tonic" she said getting up to hug him.

"I might be that but I want you to get a good feed into yourself and no more hiding"

He answered.   s

She nodded understanding.

Antony letting him out saying "Your a bloody miracle worker."

"I don't know about that" said Jimmy, "You look after her, she is something special".

Antony nodding answered "Yes she is".

Waving he was gone.s

Antony going back into the living room said "Feeling any better"

She looked at him like a lost soul.

"I don`t know but I`m glad Jimmy popped in, I think I`ll have a bath" she said slowly

getting up out of the chair.

"Baby I have missed you" he said holding his arms out to her.

Going into them she replied "I have missed me too"

She felt like a bag of bone`s in his arm`s.

"Where is Paul" she asked.

"He is with Chris, she has been a God send", he said.

                The next few months went by Maria stitching herself back up.

She went back to work and life fell into the regular pattern.

One evening Antony arriving home from work going to have a shower throwing his jacket

on the chair.

Maria picking it up seeing a piece of screwed tin foil fall out of the pocket,

Picking it up opening it finding some oxo cub`s inside.

Smiling to herself thinking what the hell is he doing with bloody oxo cubes in his pocket.

Putting them in her oxo jar, coming out of the shower Antony seeing the jacket gone from

the chair.

"Maria, what have you done with my jacket?"he asked.

"I hung it up " she answered coming into the living room smiling she said,

"I put the oxo cube`s in the jar, that were in your pocket?"

Panic on his face "Oh did you".

"What were you doing with oxo cube`s in your jacket anyway" she asked.

Thinking quickly he replied "Oh Rickie and I make a Bovril drink out of them,"

"Where did you say you put them because Rickie has a special flavour he like`s and there not really for cooking , there just for drinking".

Going into the kitchen holding the jar up she said "In there".

Waiting until she left he quickly grabbed them out of the jar and put them in his dressing

gown pocket, thinking thank God for that.

NEW CHAPTER

Maria waking up one morning feeling sick, running to the toilet.

Antony hearing her asking "Are you ok baby"

  Smiling she came into the room "You don`t think I`m pregnant "

"Here you are jumping the gun, it`s probably the curry we had last night."

Shrugging her shoulders leaving the room, thinking no more about it.

A few mornings later being ill again Antony having gone to work she decided to see the

doctor.

Later that morning having left Paul to school she headed to the doctors.

Going in seeing the doctor who had seen her when she was last pregnant.

Remembering her she said "Hello Maria how are you".

Looking at him she answered "I think I might be pregnant".

"Well you know the procedure" he said handing her the pot.

Going to the toilet doing her business she went back to him with the pot.

Doing the test in front of her looked at her smiling nodding "Yes it`s positive."

Looking at him with a delighted smile.

Asking what precautions to take this time to eliminate, what had happened the last time.

Reassuring her that she didn`t do anything wrong last time, and to just take things a bit easy.

She was looking for guarantee`s but unfortunately he couldn`t give her any.

  Leaving the surgery she went straight to Antony`s site, seeing her with a huge grin on her

Face, he made his way over to her.

"You look happy", he said wiping the sweat from his brow.

"I`m pregnant" she blurted out.

He looked astonished, "Your what" he answered

A huge smile spreading across her face she repeated.

"I`m pregnant" she said hugging him.

"How do you know" he asked looking at the overexcited face.

"I have just been to the doctor`s"

"Oh baby that is the best new` s" he answered picking her up and kissing her.

Rickie walking by saying "Put her down".

Maria looking at him even though she had not forgiven him, for his antics in her home, was so delighted with her new` s she just beamed at him.

Antony said "She has just found out she is pregnant".

"Oh man that is terrific new` s" he said in his Indian accent.

"I better get back to work, another mouth to feed and all that," Antony said kissing her "And You take it easy"

Half skipping she smiled answering "I will, oh darling I`m not going to tell anybody until I`m out of the danger period"

"Good idea" he smiled, Waving as he got back to work.

The weeks went by and when Maria was sixteen weeks pregnant, She started going public with her news.

Telling anyone that would listen, her friend`s were over the moon for her.

" Will angles take the baby away again?"Paul asked sadly.

Maria looking at him answered "I hope not but we will pray to he angles that this baby doesn`t get sick"

Nodding Paul said" We will ask baby Antony tonight ,to ask the angles to keep this baby safe"

They still went each evening to the park to say goodnight to baby Antony.

Maria gave up work at thirty two weeks into the pregnancy.

She was so happy that she had a chart, that her and Paul marked off each day.

Baby was due date was 28th July.

As they time got nearer Maria was getting Brackston Hicks contractions, so she was panicking

that when she real contractions started she wouldn`t be able to tell the difference.

The midwife reassuring her that she will definitely be able to tell.

The 28th of July came and went, leaving Marie feeling very disappointed and fed up.

The midwife saying that this was common with the first baby.

Sunday morning the 6th August, Maria awoke with very severe

Pain .

Waking Antony she said "I think it`s started".

"Are you sure" he asked looking at her.

Letting a scream shouting "Get the midwife".

Jumping out of bed getting on the phone, saying she will be here in ten minuets.

The midwife arrived and Antony showing her upstairs, she examined her.

She had only dilated two centimetres, Karen looking at Maria,

"There is good news and not such good news" she said smiling at her.

"What " asking Maria with a worried look appearing on her face.

"Well, the good news is you have definitely started labour, but the not so good news is it

is going to be a while yet"

Antony looking on asked Karen "How long are we looking at".

Smiling she answered "How long is a piece of string".

"Well are we looking at hours " he asked.

Karen answered "I honestly don't know but I'll call back this afternoon to check on you"
She said looking at Maria who was doubled up in pain.

Karen looking at her watch timing the length of the contraction, which lasted one minute.

"Keep doing as they told you at the anti natal class, and I will see you later."she said
gathering her bag and leaving.

Antony showing her out, smiling at him saying "Any changes ring me".

Nodding closing the door "I will thank you Karen".

"See you later" she smiled.

Antony going inside, Maria waddling downstairs, Paul smiling at her asked

"If the were going see baby Antony later", Maria had not missed one evening of going to see
the star.

In a way it had helped her to come to terms with loosing him, going to see the star..

Maria nodded "Yes pet we will go later".

Satisfied he went back to his drawing he was doing on the floor.

Maria looking at Antony asking if he would make her a cuppa.

"Of course" he smiled, having a feeling it was going to be a long day.

Karen arrived back that afternoon as promised, examined Maria but there was no change.

"I'll call back in the morning, but if there is any drastic change Call me".

Antony let her out, later that evening Maria Antony and Paul took a walk over to the park.

Paul holding their hands, looking at the sky ,he was always the one to pick out which star
Antony was.

Looking at the star he said" Antony please don't let it be too long until Maria can have the
baby."

Antony looking at Maria burst out laughing said "He is like a bloody old man"

Maria giggled and then grabbed his arm as she felt a contraction coming on.

Paul seeing this ran over asking "Is it the baby trying to get out the magic door again."

Catching her breath she nodded.

"Come on darling we'll get you home" Antony said holding on to her

It was a long night Maria up and down with pains.Antony doing his best to help.But feeling like a spare lemon.

Next morning Karen arrived examined Maria, saying that it was time to go to the hospital.

Antony running across the road telling Chris and could she hold on to Paul after school.

Getting to the hospital she was eight centimetres dilated, her midwife Sarah smiling said,

"It shouldn't be too long now." Smiling at Antony and Maria.

Leaving her with gas and air.

The contractions were getting intolerable, Antony starting to panic went looking for the midwife.

Coming in she examined Maria, saying the contractions were coming a lot quicker and giving her an injection to help her cope with the pain.

Maria looking at Antony sobbing saying "I can't take much more of this"

Looking at her feeing totally helpless as she squeezed his hand, in intense pain.

A couple of hour's later Maria was pushing her baby into the world.

Billy Antony came into the world screaming at 3.37 that afternoon weighing 7lb 12 ozs.

Antony in tears at the end of the bed as he watched his son being born.

He watched as the midwife put his son into his mothers arms, watching as Maria stared at him for the longest time, as he knew her dream had come true.

Tears of joy running down her face as looked down at him she had never experienced the Rush of love and protectiveness that she felt for this little bundle before in her life.

Three day's later Billy and Maria was discharged, and Antony arriving with Paul to take them home.

Paul was totally smitten with his new brother.

He kept holding his brothers fingers, counting them.

Maria thrilled to have her baby son home safe and well, and couldn`t wait to show him off.

As soon as she was up to it she had him in his pram out showing him off.

Billy was a very contented baby, going through the night at three weeks.

They had organized the christening for mid September.

Her Ma, Mandy, Don and brothers were coming over from Ireland along with Antony`s Ma
and his sisters.

The time for the christening soon arriving far too quick for Maria.

Maria busy organising food and drinks for everyone.booking bed and breakfast for her
brothers and Mandy and Don, the two Mothers and Antony`s sisters.

The evening before the families were all arriving, Antony coming home to a house of chaos.

There was bags of shopping Billy crying for a feed Paul wandering around and Maria
looking at her wits end.

"Hi darling " she smiled as he walked through the door.

"Could you take over for a minute I need to nip to the shop for a few bits I have forgotten".

Paul jumping into his arm`s.

Billy still screaming.

Looking at her he said "I`ll nip to the shop, I promised Rickie I`d meet him for a quick
pint."

"Oh thank` s a bunch" she snapped.

Then looking at his face regretting her reaction, he had been like a rock to her since Billy
had been born.

Softening she said "Go on for your pint I`ll go to the shop when you get back".

Antony leaving meeting Rickie in the pub.Rickie giving him a nudge.

They went outside, Rickie rolling a joint, passing it to Antony.

Antony looking at him asking if he had the other.

Rickie nodding taking a packet out of his pocket, passing it to him.

"Usual" Antony asked.

"Yes mate" he answered in his Indian accent.

Taking £30 out of his pocket, handing it to him.

"When are the family arriving" he asked.

Antony putting his eye`s up to heaven, said "Day after tomorrow".

"You will need that then " replied Rickey nodding at his pocket.

Antony smiling replied "Not half".

Maria back home, feeding Billy and Paul bathing him, and getting him into his PJs.

Getting the shopping put away, getting the hover out as Antony walked in.

Taking it from her he said "I`ll do that, you go on and do what you got to do".

Putting her arms around she said" You know you're a diamond"

Looking down at her he answered "I know".

Calling to him as she headed out the door shouting "And modest with it" she giggled.

"Can you get me some can`s "he called after her.

On her way to the shop she met Jimmy.

"Be the lord God if it`s not herself" he said smiling.

"Hello Jimmy" she smiled back.

"Time for a cuppa",

"Would love one" she answered.

Walking in behind him, asking if he was all set for the christening.

"Jesus I wouldn`t miss it for the world" he answered.

Making two teas bringing them into the living room.

"Have a look at the celling "he said handing her the cuppa.

Looking up seeing a huge hole in it.

"Bloody hell what happened?"

"Well there was a leak coming from it since the last heavy rain we had a couple of weeks ago."he answered.

She nodded as he continued, "Me and Bridget was sitting here having a cuppa the other day,

And the next thing we knew there was a fucking leg hanging through the celling with a boot on the end"

Maria nearly choked on her cuppa, burst out laughing.

Chuckling he said "Well it was your woman that live` s upstairs she was walking across the room and where the celling got wet, well it softened the floor, and here was Bridget and me sitting minding our own business and she nearly fell in on top of us".

Maria was nearly wetting herself.

"So now that's the crack" he added.

"Well on that note I`ll be off" she answered "And I`ll see you on Sunday"

Kissing him saying "I love you".

Letting her out the gate "I love you too, and you take great care."

Waving she headed off to the shop.

Getting back filling Antony in on Jimmy latest adventure.

Pouring them a drink, they sat on the sofa laughing their heads off, at Jimmy.

Finishing their drink`s, he got up to pour them another, sitting back relaxing thinking how lucky she is. Her little treasure sleeping upstairs. Along with Paul her little solider.

Antony coming back in from the kitchen smiling at her asking "What are you thinking."

Sitting beside her as she snuggled up to him, kissing him on the cheek.

"I was just thinking that life couldn`t get much better" she answered smiling up at him.

"I could " he answered.

"How" she asked looking at him inquiringly.

"We could win the pools" he answered .

"We have" she answered smiling looking up towards the bedroom upstairs.

Looking down at her smiling stretching he answered "Yes your right".

"You know what our next venture will be" she said.

Looking at her with inquisitively" Ok spit it out".

"Well after the christening we will have to look for somewhere bigger" she answered.

"Yes I suppose that is the next move", he replied yawning.

"Do you think we should look into buying, I still have the money from the sale of my house".

"Do you know that`s not a bad idea" he answered.

The following day Antony was busy, Getting all the relatives from the Airport getting them booked into the B& B`s.

Maria at home preparing the food and keeping Paul occupied, as he was getting over excited.

An hour later with a full house, Mandy her Ma and Antony`s Ma cooing over Billy.

Antony looking at Sean and Paul said "I think a pint is in order".

"Thought you would never ask" Sean said grabbing his jacket.

Maria looking at them said,

"Don't come back here half pissed, there is a christening tomorrow"

Paul coming over to her putting his arm around her said "Don`t worry sis I`ll look after them".

"That`s what I`m worried about" she laughed back.

Catrine and Lizzy offering to look after Billy and Paul if the girls wanted to join them.

Maria declined saying she had some more shopping to do.

"I'll come with you" said Mandy delighted to see her sister.

So they rest decided to join the lad`s.

Mandy looked at Maria saying "I can`t believe how much you both have achieved".

Maria smiling said "Yes, we need to move ,so were thinking of buying next".

"Really" she replied.

"Yes, we thought we would just get the Christening out of the way first".

Mandy was well impressed with London. Her and Don had booked to stay for

two weeks.Their Ma and the rest of the gang were just staying for the weekend.

Mandy started asking Maria if there was much work about?

Maria looking at her nodding replied "Yes there is always work if People look for it".

"Why? "Maria asked as they were leaving the shop.

"Nothing I think I would like to live here" she answered smiling.

Maria looking at her in surprise, "Really".

"Yes" she replied.

"What would Don think about that?"

"Don`t know will have to work on that one" she said smiling.

The following morning the house was hectic, All the family

gathering before the christening.

Billy screaming most of time as he wasn`t used to so much noise, Paul buzzing as well.

Maria thought she was going to go crazy.

Upstairs Antony shouting at her "Where my shirt".

Escaping upstairs she walked into the room and saw Antony brushing something off from

under his nose.

"What are you doing" she asked.

Thinking fast "I was looking for my bloody shirt, stuck my head into the wardrobe and a pile of dust fell on top of me as I pulled my head out" he answered quickly.

"Oh my poor pudding and pie." she answered hugging him.

"How is it going downstairs" he asked changing the subject.

"It`s like a fucking mad house down there," she answered taking his shirt from the back of the door.

"There you go "she said.

Going over to her taking her in his arms he said "I Love you".

Looking at him replying "I love you too, can you bring Billy up so I can get him dressed "s

"Of course, do you want me to dress the little man" he asked smiling at her.

Looking a him smiling "Your a brick".

Heading downstairs he saw what she meant,

The two mothers fussing over Billy,

Sean and Paul having a cure, Mandy looking in the mirror Don standing like a lost sheep in the middle of it all.

"Are you all right there mate" smiled Antony as he patted him on the shoulder.

Smiling back at him holding up his drink, "Yes I`m fine, what time are we leaving?".

"Mandy can you take Billy up to Maria?"

"Of course" she said taking Billy from Cathrine.

"Maria just has to get Billy ready and the we will be on our way".

As he spoke a baby ford car pulled up outside, Antony going to the door having a word with the driver.

Going back inside to get Billy, Don asked "What that was all about?".

Smiling he said "It`s a surprise for Maria, thought we would go in style to the church".

"Well she will love that" he smiled approvingly..

The two mothers sitting with there hats on ,Catrine asking "What time the were leaving"

"As soon as the prince is ready" he replied as he went upstairs to check on how thing`s were

going..

Maria up stair` s trying to consoul Billy who didn`t like being dressed

"Oh Billy it`s all too much for you isn t it" she cooed at him.

Cuddling him he clamed down ,she put on his christening gown which she had made

specially for him, Antony coming upstairs, asking "How are we doing" as he walked into the

Bedroom.

"Antony look" she said looking at Billy.

Antony seeing his son and Maria sitting there looking like a picture , could feel a

lump appear in his throat.

It was a sight he would remember for the rest of his life.

Maria and Billy ready ,Antony looking very handsome in a pale grey suit, with a blue tie.

Maria looking beautiful in a white suit trimmed in navy, and a white hat, showing off the

darkness of her hair and eye`s.

Looking at her saying "I am so proud of you, and you look stunning".

The two of them looking at Billy Maria saying "And we cant leave out the main man"

.

Paul arriving in the room in his new grey pants and white shirt, looking the proper little man.

She kissed him and Antony and said right "Right lets do this".

Antony had ordered taxi`s for the guests.

Maria looking out the window seeing the baby ford turned to Antony asking "What`s this".

"It`s a surprise for the mother of my child" he replied.

Getting in the car Antony. Maria , Paul and Billy.

Paul giggling said "We`re like the queen."

The two Mothers Mandy and Don went in one taxi, Sean an Paul with Rickie and Shelly,

Went in the other.

Arriving at the church, the rest of the guests waiting.

The priest Father Flynn, preformed the ceremony.

As he said the words pouring the holy water over Billy`s head.

"I baptise you Billy Antony in the name of the father and of the son and of the holy spirit amen"

Billy screaming in Maria`s arms, when it was over she cuddled him "Saying there you go your all safe now"

They all congregated back at the house to celebrate.

Jimmy turning up with his accordion, playing everyone`s favourite tunes.

The crack was mighty, most of them getting very drunk, except for the three mothers in the Group.

It turned out to be a very rememberable   day.

The following day Maria said goodbye to her Ma and two brothers.

The day after they said goodbye to Antony`s Ma and sister.

That left just Mandy and Don with them which Maria really enjoyed.

Antony back at work Maria took the time to show them as much as she could of London.

Getting their bearing`s they took time out on their own, and went to see the list Maria had made out for them.

Returning that day Mandy like her sister was full of Madame Tussuards.

"Oh Maria it was amazing" telling her about her favourites.

Maria nodding patiently as she listened thinking that is what I must have been like.

Their last evening there Maria cooked a special meal inviting Shelly and her latest conquest.

The had a really good evening and the next day Maria went to the airport saying goodbye to her sister and Don.

NEW CHAPTER

The following week Maria went to the estate agents to book some viewings to look at houses.

Antony returning home from work that evening to a table full of brochures from the estate Agents.

Sitting together that evening working out figures, Maria had plans on working from home

As soon as Paul wet back to school

With the money Maria had saved, they could easily afford the deposit.

Working out the mortgage repayments .it was less than what they were paying rent.

Looking at each other they new the were making the right choice.

Antony kissing her said "Now this is the best way forward".

Paul picking up on their excitement wanting to know what was going on?

When the told him he was buzzing singing to Billy were buying a new house.

The following weeks were full of house hunting.the first one they looked at Maria fell in love with.

It was terraced, three bedroomed, a large lounge and kitchen and as Antony pointed out room in the loft for another bedroom.

The viewed a few others but Maria kept going on about the first one.

In the end Antony smiling said "You always get your own way".

"Can we put a bid in" she asked excitingly.

Nodding he said "Yes", going to the estate agents, they put an offer in and receiving a phone call later that evening telling them it had been accepted.

Maria jumping into his arms with excitement, screaming "We done it".

Chris knocking at the back door hearing her scream,

Paul opening the door, blurting out "Were getting a new house".

"Are you now " answered Chris walking in with a smile on her face.

Maria looking overjoyed, filling Chris in on their achievement.

"Oh I`m so pleased, congratulations" she smiled hugging them both.

"What area is it in" she asked.

"It`s not far Bethnal Green" Antony answered.

"That`s great, we won`t be too far away from each other, have you got a moving in date?"

Nodding Maria answered, "Yes end of the month " Billy started crying.

"He`s right on time" smiled Maria as she went to pick him up.

"It`s feeding time at the zoo" said Paul laughing.

Chris laughing said "I know where you got that from"

"Where" asked Maria.

"David three doors down" she answered.

Chris leaving saying if she needed any help.

"Thanks Chris" she smiled.

Maria found it hectic, getting Paul to school, looking after Billy and trying to sort everything out for the move.

As it was getting closer.

By the time Antony got in from work she was ready to tear her hair out.

So he would take over the packing giving her time, to have a bath or just sit and have a coffee on her own.

He would cook the odd meal when he thought it was getting too much for her.

Soon the big day came, Chris having Paul and Billy while the removal men did their job.Maria busy the other end giving out instructions as to where the stuff should

Go.
Antony having had they day off work, helped load the furniture on the van.

It was a hectic day, they decided to stay in the flat that night much to Pauls disappointment.

Waking up early Maria, getting the rest of their stuff together, feeding Billy,

Paul arriving downstairs, his hair standing on end.

Smiling at him Maria saying "Big day today, little man".

Yawning at her his little eye`s lighting up   "Yea" he sang "Were going to our new house

today".

"Yes we are " she smiled as Antony walked into the room.

"Morning", he smiled Billy crying in his arm.

"Daddy were moving today" smiled Paul hugging his leg`s.

"I know " he replied handing Billy to Maria.

"Oh who is a hungry boy then" said Maria smiling down at him.

"Darling everything is done just need`s to go in the van".

"Ok ,Paul are you up for helping Daddy load up the van" he asked.

"Oh yes," he smiled as he said to Billy "We`re going to our new house today".

As Billy was busy eating his food.

        "I`ll just bring the van around" said Antony smiling at Maria.

Nodding as she put Billy back in his play pin.

Knocking at the back door ,Chris came in "How is it going?".

Looking at her Maria answered "Were nearly there".

"Anything I can do?" She asked.

Nodding Maria answered "Yes put the kettle on".

Chris shouting out ,"Tea or coffee?".

Antony coming through the door, "Hi Chris".

"Were ready to set off" he said to Maria.

"Don`t want a cuppa then?" asked Chris.

Paul looking at Antony he replied "Na were very busy men this morning ."

"Come on then son the sooner we get this done the sooner were in".

Paul looking at Chris said "Were very busy" smiling at her with a cheeky grin on his face.

"He ain` t half grown up", said Chris as she looked at Maria.

"I know where does the time go"

"Do you want me to have Billy while you do the last run?"Chis asked as she watched Maria putting him in the play pin.

Maria smiling at her replied "You're a diamond".

"I know " she smiled as she took Billy with his bit`s to her house.

Maria kissing him said "See you later little man".

Looking around the house making sure she hadn`t forgotten anything.

Going from room to room saying goodbye.

Antony arriving back with Paul running into the flat his little eye`s shining at Maria saying !"I seen it".

"Have you", she answered carrying some boxes out to the van.

"Ill help " Paul said taking one of the boxes from her.

"Don`t go doing yourself an injury" she smiled at him

As she watched him struggle with the box.

At last with all the boxes on board, Paul waving at the house, Maria Going to Chris`s to pick Billy up.

Getting in the van beside Antony smiling, checking Paul had his seat belt on, she sighed "Were off".

Paul leaning over to Billy smiling saying "Were going to our new house now".

Antony smiling at him answered "Yes were off on our new adventure."

Getting to their destination they went into the house.Paul running all over the place like a lunatic.

Maria shouting at him to clam down, trying to get Billy to sleep so she could carry on with her unpacking.

Antony picking him up and turning him upside down, saying he would flush him down the toilet if he didn`t behave.

Maria looking at him putting her eye`s up to heaven "Your making him worse" she said.

Antony looked at Paul and said "I think Maria is getting mad at us".

Giggling Paul said "I think she is".

Maria laughing at them grabbing Paul and tickling him,

"Why would I get mad with my little solider?"

"Because I`m making noise" he screamed trying to wriggle away from her.

"Ok play time over" she said.

Antony smiling said "Ok little man, now you bring that up to your room".

Getting overexcited again "Which one is my room?".

"Come on I`ll show you" she said as she took his hand.

Counting each step as they always did when they were climbing step`s

Getting to the last step he turned and said, "Is this it?"

"Oh wow" he said, his little eye`s opening wide.

There had been a new bed delivered with his favourite cover`s on it Action man.

They had also carpeted the bedroom in a blue carpet with matching carpet and curtains.

Standing at the door his eye`s opened and his little mouth, letting go of her hand.

Running jumping on the bed, singing at the top of his voice.s

Maria laughing, hugging him had a very good feeling about this house.

       The next few weeks flew by, unpacking, getting everything in place.

Paul went back to his old school, so there was no upset in that department.

Billy was starting to crawl, so was getting into everything she needed eye`s in the back of her head.

Maria asking Antony for some money one morning, as she was running out of nappies, was very surprised, when he said he didn`t have any.

Antony had always looked after the finical side of thing`s, not that Maria wasn`t capable of dealing with thing`s but she felt it was a man`s thing with Antony.

Lucky she had hair to do that morning after getting Paul to school and Antony had gone to work.

Getting home the phone was rang, it was Mrs Hogan cancelling her appointment.

Fuck she thought, she needed nappies and to get some food in.

She had never had reason to doubt Antony in any way as to where their money went.

With that the post came seeing a bank statement on the floor which was in both their names, She normally wouldn`t have bothered to open it, leaving it all to Antony.

Tearing it open, Antony`s wage`s were paid straight into the bank, and her hairdressing money she put into the bank.

Going through the bank statement with a fine tooth comb, there was their mortgage, gas and electric, which went out on directs debits.

There was garage and shopping out goings, then she saw a lot of cash transaction`s, which were been taken from the account on a different days of that month.

And it was adding up to quite a lot of money.

Between Antony and her money there should have been £1350 in the account in total.

Minus the bill`s that totalled £645

Adding up the petrol and shopping, for the month which added up to just under £400.

Which should have left them with over £300, for spend` s for the month.

There was also an overdraft facility on the account, of £200 which had also been spent.

Maria waited until Antony came home from work after raiding Paul`s money box to buy nappies for Billy.

When he arrived through the door she was so angry that she slapped the bank statement straight on him.

"Hey what`s the matter" he asked his heart skipping a beat looking at the bank statement in her hand.

"What`s the matter " she screamed, "We have no money left and were only half way trough the month."

"Your joking " he answered taking the bank statement from her.

"No I`m not what`s all these cash withdrawal` s" she asked her face red with anger.

Looking at her having to think very quick, he glanced through the statement, saying,

"There must be a must be a mistake, I`ll go to the bank first thing in the morning".

"There fucking better be " she replied.

"What have you been using all this cash for anyway?" She asked.

Looking at the bank statement again, seeing the amount`s that had been withdrawn,

"I can account for three of them " he answered,

Looking at him waiting for an answer,

"Rickie needed to borrow some cash, for a tool , he needed for work", he said as he pointed to one of the transactions.

This accounted for £70.

"And I had to buy a new hod, as I broke the one the boss gave me".

"You never told me" she answered.

"Darling I didn`t even think" he smiled.

This accounting for another £100.

She seemed satisfied with the explanation, as he promised to go to the bank first thing in the Morning.

Changing the subject kissing her "Asking where is Paul"

Smiling at him she replied "His at his new friend's across the road".

"That didn't take him long" he answered feeling relieved that she believed him.

Next morning he went to the boss asking him for a sub, getting a £100

Went straight to the bank and put it in.

Ringing Maria and telling her there had been a mistake made on the bank's behalf and now

there was a £100 there.

"Well thank Christ for that " she answered him, down the phone.

"Well have to keep an eye on our bank statements from, now on" as she put the phone down.

Relived that it had been an error made by the bank.

The phone rang it was Mandy telling her that her and Don was coming over to live.

Maria over the moon that her sister was going to be living in the same place near her again.

Screaming down the phone in excitement.Maria telling her she would go t the estate agents to

see what was for rent in the area.

The phone ringing again was some of her clients delighted to hear she was back working

again

Overall it was turning to be a good day.

Antony returning from work to find her singing to Billy as she was feeding

Him.

Looking at him as he came over to kiss her, telling him the news about Mandy and Don.

He was pleased .

Paul arriving from his new friend's, full of the woe's of his day.

Having dinner Maria looking around the table and down at Billy in his low chair as he was

splashing food everywhere, thinking how happy she was

NEW CHAPTER
The following week was hectic Mandy and Don arriving she had spruced out the spare room

for them to help them until the got settled.

Paul overexcited at seeing them again, filling them in on his new friend`s and that he was still at the same school talking ten to the dozen.

Mandy was so pleased to be back with her sister, as she had missed her more than she thought she would.

Her and Don went flat hunting, with success on the first day.

Finding a nice two bedroomed flat not far from Maria and Antony.

Antony got Don a job on the building site and Mandy got herself a job in the local supermarket.

They soon settled into every day life.

Don noticed that Antony and Rickey were as thick as thief`s on site they were like each other`s shadow.

Going to the bog one day he discovered why.

They were snorting some cocaine, Antony rubbing the remains from under his nose as he saw Don approach.

Antony smiling at him saying "It`s just a little pick me up",

Ricking offering him a line, Don looked very surprised, declined.

Using the loo he went back to work without even looking at Antony.

Later at lunch Antony approached him saying,

"We`ll keep what you seen under wraps don`t want the girl`s worrying".

"You mean Maria" he glared back at him.

Nodding he answered "Yes, look Don it was just a little pick me up, it`s not a regular thing"

Don looking disgusted at him replied "It`s none of my business but I wouldn`t like to be in your shoe`s if she find`s out".

"There is nothing for her to find out mate, as I said it`s just a chill out pill that I do to take the edge off thing`s" he said smiling.

Don shrugged as he walked away.

Rickie smiled at him and said "Don`t worry my friend we all have to let our hair down sometime"

Antony answered "Your dead right there".

Walking home from work Don asked Antony "How long you been taking the chill out pill`?"

Laughing Antony looking at him, "You make it sound as if I have a habit or something".

"Well have you?" Don asked looking at him seriously.

"Oh for Christ sake, look you were not here when Maria lost the baby, I needed something to help me cope."

"But that was well over a year ago" Don answered sadly.

"Yes that was then and this is now, and at this moment in time, I have pressure coming out of my ears you have got no idea , what it was like for me ,Maria going into deep depression after loosing the baby locking herself away for week`s leaving me to look after Paul keep a Job going, he was my son as well, when you have been there come and talk to me."Antony replied angrily.

Getting home that evening Mandy was there, and asked where Don was.

"Oh I had to stay back and give the boss a hand, he is probably gone home" he said putting his work bag away.

" Oh I thought he would be with you " replied Mandy disappointed.

"I`ll go then" she said.

"No ,no you can`t go" said Paul" You promised to come see Baby Antony with me "

Maria looking at Mandy said" You can`t go back on your promises in this house"

Mandy smiling said "Ok I`ll ring Don and him to meet us in the park"

Getting off the phone she said "He is too tired, said to send his apologies".

"Daddy, Maria, Billy , you and I will go and say goodnight to Baby Antony" said Paul in a matter of fact voice.

Mandy smiling said "Ok then" not having the heart to let the little man down.

Antony grabbing a beer from the fridge sitting outside lighting a cigarette,

Maria wandering out asking if he was ok?

Looking at her smiling "It`s just been a shit day at work".

Paul running out saying "Were ready"

"Just let me get Billy`s jacket on" as she went into the house putting him in the buggy.

Heading across to the park Paul on Antony`s shoulders, Maria pushing the buggy Mandy nattering away, about the colour she was going to paint their bedroom.

They noticed a cop car pull up beside them and one of them getting out.

"Evening sir is your name Antony MacGee?"

Antony looking at the copper nodded.

"Could you put the boy down sir"

Taking Paul from his shoulders passing him to Mandy.

"What`s all this?"asked Antony.

"Mr MacGee I`m arresting you on suspicion of handling class A drugs".

Antony going snow white in the face answered "What" as the copper produced handcuff`s, and putting them on Antony.

Maria and Mandy standing totally bewildered.

Paul started to cry as the police man put Antony into the police car.

Maria finding her voice, started to scream "What are you doing?"

Paul crying "I want my Daddy "s

Maria screaming at Antony as the police car pulled away, he looked back at her with a total look of guilt on his face.

Maria and Mandy left looking at each other in total disbelief, Paul distraught, frightened and crying his eye`s out.

Billy picking up on the commotion, was screaming in the buggy.

Mandy trying to take control of the situation, taking Paul by the hand, nudging Maria, "Let`s get home", she said.

NEW CHAPTER

Returning home Mandy rang Don telling him what had happened.

"I`ll be there in five" ha answered putting the phone down.

Paul hysterical, Maria trying to console him and Billy as she sat there with the two of them in her arms.Wondering what the hell had just happened.

Don arrived and looking at the situation, sat beside Maria asking "What happened?"

Maria in a trance, couldn`t talk so Mandy explaining to the best of her ability.

Shaking his head, he looked at Maria and said "I knew something like this would happen."

Staring at him in disbelief "You knew",

He stared at her nodding, "I knew he was taking drug`s".

He explained how he had found out.

"And you didn`t think to tell me" said Maria, handing Billy to Mandy.

Paul looking confused sobbing asked "What`s drugs".

Maria picking him up answered "There nasty tablets.now we will get you to bed".

"I don`t want to go to bed I want my Daddy" he sobbed.

Don taking him from Maria said "I know you do but Daddy will be home soon come on and I`ll read you a story."

Waving at Maria and Mandy he said "Goodnight".

Coming downstairs Don asked, "What the copper`s had said?"

Maria answered "Nothing, nothing at all they just handcuffed him put him in the car and drove away".

"Right get on the phone and tell them who you are and ask what is going on" said Don.

She did as she was asked, talking to a Sargent Hobb` s hoping he put her in the picture.

Maria was told that he was helping them with enquiry`s so she was no wiser than before she made the call.`

Maria was so distressed and confused with what had gone on, Mandy decided to stay the night with her.

Mandy leaving the next morning as she had to go to work.

Maria carrying on her usual routine in a daze, getting Paul to school, looking after Billy.

She cancelled her client`s that day, telling them that she was poorly.

Picking Paul up from school there was a few comment`s from the other mother`s ignoring them she walked with Paul and Billy home.

Getting Paul his tea and Billy in his play pin playing with his toy`s, there was a knock at the Door.

It was Chris, saying that she heard what had happened and offering her help.

Maria bursting into tear`s sobbing "What am I going to do".

Chris holding her trying to console her , making a coffee Maria said,

"I did not see this coming " she sighed.

Chris leaving saying "You know where I am."

Billy crying taking him out of the play pin sitting on the couch with him in her arm`s.

Paul coming over sitting beside them asking "When is Daddy coming home?"

Shrugging she answered "Soon".

Later that evening, Mandy popping in "Any new` s ?"

Maria shaking her head "No".

She went into the kitchen Mandy playing with Billy, the front door went.

Antony appeared at the kitchen door, Maria looking at him a thousand questions going on in her head.

Paul running to him "Daddy daddy"

Antony picking him up said "Hello son"

Mandy watching, Maria looking at her she knew it was time for her to go.

Saying a quick" Goodbye" she was gone.

"Paul go upstairs and run yourself a bath" she said ,He started to protest but knew by the tone in her voice that it would be to no avail.

Paul having left the room she looked at Antony and said "You have some explaining to do."

Holding his head down he answered "I know".

Getting impatient she said "Well come on then".

He started off with the death of baby Antony telling her how hard it had been, how it had all been to much for him and Rickie suggesting a little pick me up to help him through.

She couldn`t believe her ear`s "You took drug`s to get over Antony`s death, you fucking arse hole and your calling that an excuse."

"I had you down for a lot of thing`s but not weak" she screamed at him.

Trying to hold her she shrugged him off, "Look baby let me explain",

Tears` of frustration running down her face.

"Explain what? How your son had to watch his Da been dragged into a police car

Handcuffed. Over a drug offence".

She was loosing it, the shock , the pain of the lie`s it was all hitting her at once.

She was putting two and two together and coming up with four.

Looking at him saying "There was no error made at the bank you were covering for the

Money you were buying drug`s with, lying to me" she was choking, sobbing in disgust and anger.

"Letting me and the kid`s go without so you could feed you habit, how low can you stoop"

she whispered.

She was looking at him as if he were a stranger pure disgust on her face.

He couldn`t bear to look at her, he knew he was in shit with a capital S, but he also knew that

if he didn`t get out of London he would be going down for a nice stretch.

"Baby let`s go back to Dublin and make a fresh start, leave all this crap behind."he said with

a certain amount of panic going on in his voice.

Looking at him in disbelief, "What crap," she shouted "The fucking crap you have been putting

into your body, Have you forgotten we have just bought a house, your son is just settling into

school" she screamed at him.
Looking at her with panic in eye`s, "If we don`t go back I`m looking at doing time".

"Your what" she was sobbing now, "What are you not telling me?"she questioned him.

"Look baby you have to trust me on this , but we need to go".

Totally bewildered and confused she answered "Trust you, now there`s a laugh ,you can go ,

my life is here now not back in Ireland"

"Is that your final answer?" he asked.

Nodding sobbing she asked "What have you done".

Staring out of the window he answered "The less you know the better, I`m leaving in the

morning".

She couldn`t take it in, her world was turning upside down and she had no say or control

over what was happening.

"Your leaving us?" She was devastated, destroyed "What about Paul?"she whispered.

"He will be coming with me" he answered simply.

Her head pounding, Paul walked into the room all freshly washed with a towel wrapped around his waist.

"Look Da I did this all by myself" he said proudly pointing at the towel.

Antony looking sadly at him said "Well done son".

Paul sensing the atmosphere looking at Maria asking "What`s the matter".

Getting up from the chair ,taking Billy putting his jacket on putting him in his buggy,

Looking at Paul she whispered "You had better ask you Da".

Walking out leaving a very confused little man staring at his father.

Walking around to Mandy`s with Billy, Mandy opening the door she knew by her sister`s face that there was something serious taking place.

Maria walked inside Don was in the living room, Mandy calling him, he came out taking one look at Maria`s face, Mandy said "Take Billy".

Doing as he was asked picking Billy up and taking him into the living room with him.

Maria went into the kitchen with Mandy, she put the kettle on.

"What`s happened?" Mandy asked her sister.

Maria told everything that had happened.Mandy stood there not saying a word.

She was in shock, nearly as much as Maria at the new` s.

Don coming in to see if there was a rusk for Billy, Mandy quickly filled him in.

Don went pale at the new` s "Jesus Christ what shit has he got himself into"

Maria sitting down holding her head in her hand`s looked at him and answered, "You know as much as I do."

"I`m going around to have a word with him", he said grabbing his jacket.

Don arriving at Antony`s finding him, getting Paul to bed.

Coming down the stairs Don looked at him, asking "What the fuck is going on?"

Antony staring at him, answered "I have fucked up majorly".

Don standing with his hand`s in his jacket pocket`s, said "Well come on don`t leave me in the dark".

Huffing he said "Well you know I was taking a bit of a pick me up",

Don nodding "Well I couldn`t afford it as Maria was checking the bank."

"Go on" Don answered .

"Well Rickie told me that if I helped him shift it I could have my quota for free".

Don shaking his head answered "So you started dealing".

Antony nodding his head "That`s the long and short of it".

"You stupid idiot", replied Don."What happened at the cop shop?"

Letting out a huge sigh" I`m in court on Friday".

"Fucking hell that`s three day`s away" said Don.

"That`s why I have to get out, there going to throw the book at me, I`ll go down if I stay.

"Have you told Maria?"

"Not in so many word`s I have told her I have to leave", he replied biting his bottom lip.

"I don`t have any choice, I cannot go to prison" he answered.

"Where are you going to go?" Don looking at him dubiously.

"Back to Dublin, I`ll have to take Paul back with me" he said tear`s appearing in his eye`s.

"Christ you have really done it this time, look at what the two of you have achieved" he said

pointing around the room.

Looking totally pitiful nodding he said" I know but I can`t stay here I`d be looking at a

stretch of minimum three year`s".

Mandy made the coffee, and looked at Maria saying "What if he goes?".

The pain in Maria face was like looking at a tortured soul.
ss
"Mandy I cannot think," she sobbed, "Christ it was a couple of day`s ago I was looking at

my life and thinking I couldn`t be happier."

Billy started crying Mandy went and got him from the front room.

Maria seeing him made her cry harder, "And he is taking Paul with him".

Mandy staring at her "He can`t do that!"

It was just beginning to sink in the reality of the situation, Maria staring at her sister

whispering, "Yes he can, oh I can`t believe this ", she was crying again.

Don arrived back with a look of shock on his face,

Mandy seeing the look said "Well go on spit it out".

"He is in a bit over his head" he answered.

Mandy not understanding shaking her head "What do you mean".

Maria answered guessing hoping she was going to be so wrong,

"Drug`s and not just consuming?" she said looking at him dubiously.

He nodded, and as he had promised that he would not tell her, he reckoned he had said

 Enough.

"So he is going "Mandy said .

"Yes" he nodded "he doesn`t have any choice"

This statement hit home with Maria.

"Doesn`t have any choice ,We all have choice, and he has  chosen drug`s over me and his

two boy`s ,and that`s the facts` of the matter" she chanted furiously.

She left shortly after walking home to find Antony packing.

Looking up as she walked in, he begged her to go with him.

Her heart was crying go, but her head was saying go to what a life of drug`s even thought she

adored the ground he walked on, and never in a thousand year`s thought she would be put in

this position "You broke it and I can`t mend it" she answered simply as tear`s spilled down

her face.

Getting Billy to bed Paul was already asleep, she went back downstairs .

He was standing staring out the window.

"Want a cuppa" she asked, shaking his head "No ta" .

Looking at the bag`s she saw some of Paul`s clothes.

The reality of what was happening hitting her in the face like a cold bucket of water being thrown over her.

He turned around and said "It doesn`t have to be like this, you can come with us"

"Don`t make this any harder than it has to be, you are the cause and the me and the boy`s are the victim`s in all of this" she answered trying her hardest to hold it together.

Holding his head down "I know and how can I say sorry".

"You should never have to say sorry to someone you love" she answered.

Tear`s in his eye`s he asked again "Please come with us".

"To what?" she asked, "A life of drug`s wondering if your taking or not taking".

"I never had Billy to be brought up in that environment, or for his Da to be druggie"

"Baby please don`t break us up is this what you really want, Billy being brought up in a one parent family?"

"That is a very unfair question, you know when I had Billy, I thought we would be together forever and longer" she answered the tear`s falling down her face.

"Please baby please " he begged, he was on his knee`s.

Knowing she would break if she stayed in the room a minute longer,

Shaking her head she answered "I can`t take the risk and I will never ever stop you seeing Billy".

The following morning she watched as he packed Paul and his stuff in the car, Paul thinking he was going on an adventure.

She hadn`t asked what he had told him, mainly because she had , had enough of his lie`s.

She went to the gate as they pulled away, saying to Paul that she loved him and that there was always a bed for him no matter where she lived.

Looking at her with a confused look on his little face, turning to Antony

He asked "Da we are coming back?"

Antony his voice breaking as he looked at him said "Get in the car son we have a long

journey ahead of us."

He stared at Maria and said "It doesn`t have to be like this", tear`s running down his face.

She nodded as she tried to answer as she thought she was going to choke, tear`s pouring

down her face.

"Yes it does have to be like this, I could not live with you in a wonder land, as I said, you

broke it and I cannot mend it, I don`t think you can even mend yourself".

He looked at Billy in her arm`s taking him from her he hugging so tight that Billy started to

cry.

Kissing him he passed him back to Maria, sobbing he got in he car letting the car window

down he waved to her and his son as he drove away, shouting "I will always love

you".
                                        Going back into the house her heart in her stomach she closed

the door, putting Billy in his play pin with his favourite toy she lay on the couch, sobbing

Feeling her heart break into a thousand pieces.

Looking around the room remembering the first day the had seen this house, the dream`s

shattered to bit`s.

                                The Friday after Antony leaving she had the police knocking on the
door

looking for Antony, with a warrant for his arrest. Telling them that he had gone leaving no

forwarding address.

The policeman introduced himself as P.C.Ward, leaving a card with her said

"If you hear anything let me know".

Closing the door, falling down behind it she sobbed crying out Antony`s name her heart felt as if it was going to shatter and break into tiny pieces with pain, that was going on inside it.

Billy started crying and gathering herself up off the floor taking a huge breath, went in picking him up cuddling him to her, sobbing to her baby son we will be ok.

The following weeks she spent trying to figure out how she was going to keep a roof over her and Billy's head's. With Antony gone she was on a very low budget.

Speaking to her friend Chris ,telling her that her sister was looking for somewhere to rent.

She decided to rent out Paul's bedroom, and by doing this she was able to keep the repayment's on the mortgage up to date, and keep her head above water.

Her own work picked up and her and Billy, were coping well.

They house next door to her had been vacant for some time, a few month's after Antony had left a lady with her two children moved in.

They became friend's and got very close as Angie's husband had walked out on her for a younger bit of fluff.

It was soon approaching Bill's first birthday, there had been very little contact from Antony since he had left, so when Billy's birthday arrived, Maria was pleasantly surprise to find a card and an enormous Teddy Bear from Antony and Paul.

He rang that day, hearing his voice, the pain stabbed her right in the heart.Maria was very emotional after getting off the phone from him.

She had asked how Paul was getting on, he told her he was back with his mum.

Angie getting home from work that evening, finding Maria in tear's.

Listening to what had upset her, she said "I think we should have a girl's night out".

Maria had not been out since well before the birth of Billy.

Saying she would think about it she had not allowed herself to dwell on Antony, since he had gone finding it too pain full instead, she had put all her energy in Billy and her work.

Mandy popping around that evening finding her sister upset, Angie making coffee's,

Angie filled her in on Antony`s phone call, and said that she thought her and Maria should have a girl`s night out.

Mandy totally agreeing with her, saying that she should get out and not just fill her life up with Billy and work, that she it wasn`t healthy.

Maria looking at them both agreeing, just to get them off her back.

Mandy saying she would look after Billy so she could go out and enjoy herself without worrying.

So this became the hi light of Maria and Angie`s life going out every other Saturday.

Angie meeting a bloke called Sean, the forth night the went out.

Maria was really pleased for her, but Maria enjoying her Saturday night`s out, still went out once a month, normally with Mandy.

Then Sean and Angie split so it went back to the two girl`s going out .

It was coming up to Christmas and Maria couldn`t believe where the time had gone it was over a year since Antony had gone.

She was looking forward to it, Maria had not met anyone, well no one that had interested her, she was still getting over Antony, and in her mind, she intended to stay single that way , she wouldn`t get hurt or pick the wrong man she had decided that all men were liar`s , drinker`s or druggy` s. And by staying on her own she would not be putting herself at risk to being hurt again.

Christmas came she spent with her sister and Don, Billy being spoilt rotten, they had a really nice day and her Angie and Mandy were going out on new year`s eve.Don had volunteered to do the babysitting.

New year`s eve , Mandy came and took Billy around to Don early so they could have a few drink`s and make an evening of it.

Mandy having bought Maria a lovely black strappy mini dress and some thigh boot`s for Christmas insisting she wear them on the night.

When she arrived down in her new gear Mandy and Angie let out a whistle of

Approval.

"It`s not too revealing "she asked looking down at herself.

Mandy looking at her replied "Sis I have not seen you look this good in

age`s".

"Oh thank` s " she smiled.

"You look amazing", said Angie.

All ready they left and did one or two pub`s before hitting the night club.

Having had a drink`s before the left the house, they three of them were fairly merry before

the got to the night club.

Maria and Mandy really enjoyed dancing, and they were able to turn a few head`s with they

move`s they made.

Mandy getting out of breath leaving Maria on her own to continue dancing.

Angie was being chatted up, when Mandy returned to the bar, so getting the drink`s in

turning to toward` s the dance floor to see a nice looking man watching her sister with great

interest.

Maria coming off the dance floor , standing beside Mandy , he approached her.

Mandy giving her a nudge whispering "He has been checking you out".

Maria feeling a bit dizzy from dancing and the amount she of drink she had consumed,

Could just barley make out a figure coming toward` s her.

"Hi, I`m Mark" he smiled .

Mandy not feeling much better than Maria, said "You have to excuse us but we have had a

little too much to drink."

"Well it is new year`s eve" he answered.

Angie making her way over to the girl`s slurred she was going. Her conquest standing beside her.

Maria nodding tried to interduce her to Mark but couldn't remember his name.

Mandy offering to but him a drink , declining he answered "I don't drink".

"Well that make's a nice change", she slurred at him.

The evening coming to an end, he offered the two sister's a life home.

Mandy saying "Yes please", as Maria seemed to have escaped to another planet

        Next morning Maria awoke with her sister beside her snoring.

Getting out of bed, her head banging she made her way downstairs, taking some paracetamol

Angie seeing her light on, came knocking at her door.

Maria bursting out laughing, at the state of her.

"Oh it's not funny" she said grabbing the tablet's from the side.

"I have been sick" she said "Who was that bloke, I woke up this morning to find an invader on my couch".

Maria creased up at this description, answered "Well at least he wasn't in your bed".

Angie opened her eye's in shock at the thought of it, she was nearly ill again.

With that the heard a morning noise behind them, as the both turned to see a very hung over Mandy walk through the door.

Taking the paracetamol from Angie she swallowed two, looking at them with bloodshot eye's.

"I'm never drinking again" she whinged..

"Christ if I had a pound for every time I said that " replied Angie.

"Who was that fella that left us home?"asked Mandy.

Maria looking very confused asked "What fella?"

"Some bloke that was trying his hardest to get off with you", she replied

"I can't remember" Maria answered.

"Well he gave us a lift home, and said he would pop by soon", Mandy informed her.

"Fucking hell", replied Maria having no recollection of this what so ever.

"I`ll just give Don a ring make sure Billy has behaved himself".

Don answered the phone telling her he`s fine that he will bring him back around in a bit and pick Mandy up.

"He was a bit of all right," continued Mandy.

"Oh shut up, Ill probably never see him again" she yawned.

Don arriving not long after this, dropping Billy off and having a cuppa listening to the banter of the girl`s night out.

Looked at Billy saying "Is your mummy going to get a new boyfriend?"

"Oh piss off" she answered "That`s the last thing I my mind" .

"Well we will see, it`s about time you had a bit of fun in your life Antony has been gone over a year."Don replied in a serious tone.

"I don`t need a man to have fun" she answered.

   "Ok, ok I was just saying", he new how touchy Maria could be on the subject of Men.

NEW CHAPTER

Two day`s later Maria standing in the kitchen, heard a knock at the front door.

Going to answer it finding a very handsome man there , she smiled as she asked if she could Help.

"Hi" he smiled back at her, "I`m Mark the one who gave you a lift home new year`s eve."

Taken totally a back as she had no memory of ever seeing him before,

Smiling he said, "Can`t you remember?"

Shaking her head in embarrassment, she replied "No".

She seemed a bit uneasy with the situation, "Look I can call back at a more convenient time if that is ok."

"I don`t mean to be rude, you gave us a lift, home thank you, why are you calling?"she asked curiously.

He looked at her with sexy brown eye`s and the longest eyelashes she had ever seen on a man.

"Well ok I would like to get to know you, maybe take you out for a drink or dinner maybe " he answered a little clumsy.

Smiling thinking, Don is right I should have a bit of fun in my life, why not he was good looking and seemed pleasant.

But then a bit of panic set in, as she had not been on a date in years and there had not been anybody since Antony.

In an unsteady voice she said "What a nice idea, but I don`t think so".

He looked very disappointed, "Can I have your phone number then?"

She stood staring at him, "You don`t take no for an answer, do you" she asked.

Looking at her shaking his head, he smiled at her with laughter in his eye`s,

"No not really, especially when I see someone that I would really like to get to know".

he answered seriously.

Billy started to cry in the background, "I have to go " she said starting to close the door.

He put his foot in the door way and looking pleading at her "Can I have your number".

"You are very persistent" she said in flattering voice.

He knew she was beginning to thaw.

Giving him the number she closing the door she noticed he was driving a BMW.

Angie arriving home that evening from work doing her usual detour via Maria`s.

"Well have I got new` s for you " Maria greeted her.

"What "replied Angie she loved a bit of gossip.

Maria filling her in on her on her mystery caller.

Angie standing with her mouth open, "Well what can I say, you don`t even have to leave the House, what does he look like?"

"He is about 6ft dark brown hair, the sexiest brown eye`s and the longest eyelashes I have ever seen on a man" she sighed.

"Are we a bit smitten" Angie asked looking at her dubiously.

Maria raising her eye`s to heaven "Don`t be silly woman it was just a bit of a surprise that`s all"

"Oh yes" Angie teased "that`s how you noticed the eye colour and the long eye lashes is it".

"Oh come off it , he probably won`t even ring", she replied in a stand offish voice secretly hoping he would.

Later that evening the phone rang and she heard Mark`s voice down the phone.

"Hello it`s your stalker here" he laughed.

Pretending not to have a clue as to whom was on the other end asked "Who".

"It`s me Mark, don`t tell me you have forgotten me already" he was a bit taken aback.

"Oh I just wasn`t expecting you to ring so soon" she answered.

"Look I`m only just around the corner can I pop in for a coffee" he asked.

Silence on the other end he added "Please."

She looked around the room thinking Billy is in bed so what would she be doing for the rest of the evening watching a bit a of telly and then bed.

"Ok then, I`ll get the kettle on" she said checking herself out in the mirror as she went into the kitchen.

No sooner had she put the water in the kettle, he was knocking the door .

"Hi " he smiled the brown eye`s twinkling at her.

"Hope I`m not interrupting your evening"

Shaking her head "No , no it`s fine come in "she said feeling rather shy not a feeling she was often familiar with.

He looked around the room and commented "Very cosy" he said as he followed her into the Kitchen.He noticed the play pen.

"I see there`s a baby in the house" he smiled.

"Yes my son Billy" she replied proudly.

"How old " he asked.

"He is sixteen month`s now" she smiled.

"And the Dad, I`m not been nosy but I don`t want to step on anybody`s toe`s".

"Oh he hasn`t been on the scene for a while "she answered in a sad tone.

"Do you take sugar" she asked as she flicked her hair across her shoulder something she done when she was uneasy.

Sensing this he asked what part of Ireland she came from.

Passing him his cuppa she answered "County Westmeath".

Noting the blank look on his face she asked if he had ever been to Ireland?

Shaking his head he said "No".

She really enjoyed his company that evening discovering he ran his own roofing company, he was Samaritan and he did not drink or do drug`s.

Which was a huge plus in Maria`s book`s especially after David and Antony.

She also found out he had a daughter Lilly that was a year older than Billy.

She wanted to ask more about but felt since she couldn`t as she wasn`t giving to much information out about her past, she felt she didn`t have the right to ask him.

They evening finished when he received a call form the Samaritans.

Giving her a peak on the cheek promising to ring soon he was gone.

Closing the door she felt good, and thinking what a breath of fresh air to meet someone, that she seemed to have a lot in common with, and even if it never went anywhere at least she could have a friendship.

He rang the next day and wanted to pop and see her that evening .

But she said she had her sister coming around as she thought he was moving far too quickly.

He knocked the following afternoon saying he was just passing, so he had coffee.

And met Billy whom he made a big fuss of.

He turned to Maria and said he was having Lilly that Friday would it be ok to bring her around to meet Billy.

Hesitating she answered "No not at the moment".

Asking "Why?" As he looked at her with them beautiful brown sexy eye`s.

"Don`t you think it is a bit quick for meeting your family"

Smiling he said "Look I get the picture I think, you have been hurt, but life is too short for not taking a gamble, don`t you think, I think your great and I think you like me?"

He looked at her giving one of his puppy dog look`s that would melt an ice maiden.

Maria was still very wary and was no where near to letting her guard down, no matter what puppy dog eye`s he could pull.

Giving the right answer she said "Maybe another time".

He knew there was no point in pushing her or he might loose whatever chance he might Have.

Smiling at her he answered "Your right".

He left shortly after saying goodbye to Billy, and said he would phone later.

He didn`t not that evening or the following evening.

Angie called as usual for her daily fix of coffee, finding Maria looking a bit down.

Asking what the matter was ?

Maria told her about the conversation she had, had with Mark two evening`s before and that he hadn`t called.

"Told you, you were a bit smitten" she smiled.

"No I`m not smitten but I`m disappointed that he hasn`t been in touch" she answered.

The phone rang just as the two of them were putting the world to right`s.

Answering Angie saw a smile cross Maria`s face, she gave her the thumb`s up.

Getting off the phone Maria smiling said "He has been on a job with one of his Samaritan case` s".

"So everything back on tract" Angie asked raising her eye brow`s.

"Think so", Maria giggled.

"You like him, don`t you?"

"Do you know I hate to admit it , but there is something about him", Maria answered as she flicked her hair over her shoulder.

"So when is he popping around?" Angie asked picking up her bag to leave.

"A bit later", picking Billy up saying, "Right mister let`s get you fed and bathed. "

Angie leaving shouting "Enjoy".

She got Billy fed and bathed and after he had, had a play got him to bed. He was now in his own room, which Maria had decorated in Thomas the tank engine, which he loved as he entered the bedroom he tried making booing sounds, which made Maria laugh thinking how quickly they grow up kissing him good night saying "I love you my little boney woney" she had nick named him but for their ear`s only.

She heard the front door go as her lodger came in , she was a dream Maria hardly knew she was there, she worked night`s and slept most of the day.

Going downstairs she saw her coming up, looking up she said "Hi Maria just back to get changed."

"You carry on " Maria replied "I just jumping in the shower".

"See you later ", she called as she left.

Maria coming out of the shower wondering what to wear.Then thinking Christ woman he is just coming around for a coffee.

Looking through her wardrobe, taking out a black jumpsuit, she looked thinking casual.

Slipping into it satisfied it did the trick, sitting at her dressing table, applying her eye make up and lippy, it dawned on her that she did like him and thought about what he had said that life was a gamble, he was stirring feeling`s that she thought had perished.

These thought`s were actually alarming her,

Removing the lippy with a tissue she looked at herself

 She could feel tear`s stinging at the back of her eye`s as she remembered how Antony used to awaken feeling`s in her and take to height` s she had never know existed.

She could feel her shield raising back up, looking down at the jumpsuit she pulled it off , pulling on a pair off jean`s and a sweatshirt on.

Hearing the doorbell ring, pulling herself together she quickly pulled the hairbrush through her hair and ran downstairs to answer the door.

He was standing there with that wonderful grin of his, and a bunch of flowers in his hand`s.

"Hi, I want you to know I was not ignoring you" he said in such haste, that it made her laugh.

"It`s ok it`s no biggie, you explained over the phone, come in " she said.

"These are for you "he smiled passing the flowers.

"Thank you, I`ll just put them in water" she smiled heading into the kitchen.

Following her he walked up behind her in the kitchen and put his arms gently around her as she was filling the vase up with water.

She froze just for a moment, as she had not been expecting this .

Feeling her tense he let go and apologised immediately.

Turning to face him "Look there no need to apologise I just wasn`t expecting you to touch me" she said simply.

Putting his hand`s up, "It`s my fault I wanted to see you , and I`m probably jumping the gun just a tiny bit" he smiled putting his hands in his pockets.

Looking at him thinking what is wrong with me, "Coffee " she asked?

"Thought you would never ask " he answered in that smooth voice of his.

"Been busy" he asked.

Nodding she answered "Yes I`m always busy, between looking after Billy running my business it can get a bit hectic."she smiled flicking her hair over her shoulder.

"You're a very self sufficient woman" he said admiringly.

"Always had to be " she answered smiling at him, as she poured the water into the coffee cup`s.

"Not many women I know like you" he answered .

"How many do you know?" She asked laughing.

Shrugging "One or two, but not one like you" he smiled.

"What do you mean?"

"Well look at you ,your gorgeous, got your own business, and obviously a clever person, with a brain that works "he laughed

"Do you mind if I ask what about Lilly`s mum?"she asked.carring the coffees into the living room.

Sitting beside her he replied "There isn`t very much to tell really".

"Well there must be a tiny bit of history, after all you had your daughter with her" she asked curiously.

Putting his coffee down he said "Ok I met Karen shortly after I joined the Samaritans, she

was a client and needed some outside help which we provide if we think it necessary"

This explanation increased Maria`s curiosity even more,

"Go on " she said putting her arm on the back of the settee.

"Well I went out on the call, I met Karen and she was in a very dark place, and a few weeks

later I was in the mall in town, saw her had a coffee and things just started from there."taking
A of coffee he continued.

"We got together and not long after to be honest it was three months she was pregnant with

Lilly, wow was that a surprise" he said as he stretched his legs out.

She looked at him soaking every word in as he was speaking.

He look at her and said "I thought I was doing the right thing, so I asked her to live with me"

"I was still living at my mum`s , and when she found out let`s just say she wasn`t a happy

bunny"

"Why? " asked Maria,

"That`s a long story and one I don`t want to go into right now" he answered.

"Ok " she nodded understandingly.

"Well I got us a flat it wasn`t in the best part of town, unfortunately but it did until I could

afford something bigger and better, which is where l live now" he said with an amount of

pride in his voice.

This statement really taking Maria by surprise asking "Where did Karen and Lilly go?"

" She moved back to her mum`s, " he answered

"Carry on " she said.

"I don`t mean to be nasty ,when I say this but Karen wasn`t the brightest button you could

press" and after she had Lilly,

"Well to be honest all she wanted was money to buy them the latest matching outfits so she

her could push Lilly about town looking like Cindy dolls", he sighed.

"Well I thought she would at least cook a meal or do a bit of shopping once in a while, but when I got home from work to an empty flat every evening she would be at her mums, as you can imagen this caused arguments so one day I came home to find a note saying she had left and gone back to her mum`s" he said sitting sadly looking into the cup.

"How long ago was that?" Maria asked.

Looking up at the celling "Must be about fourteen months now" he replied half smiling at her.

"Do you see much of Lilly?"

Thinking she seen a glisten of tear`s in his eye`s as he answered,

"Not much as I would want but I see her as often as I can, with work and of course Karen has another boyfriend so it is when their not doing something with her, "he answered sounding very dejected.

Looking at her he said seriously "That make you feel better now that you know something about me"

Getting up from the couch she said "Yes it does you see we all have past`s and that is what makes us who we are today, another coffee" she asked smiling down at him.

"Only if I can have a cuddle when you come back," he answered.

Looking back at him thinking he has not had it easy and he obviously loves little Lilly.

Smiling she nodded and coming back with the coffees he put his arm over her shoulders this time she did not object.

He whispered "Now you know some of my life history can I ask where Billy`s Dad is?"

Nodding she answered "Yes you can but it is still very raw subject".

"How long has he been gone?" He asked in such a gentle voice, that she felt very much at ease.

Filling him in on Antony and Paul came out a lot easier than she thought it would have been telling him.

The intense pain that had been there since they left seemed to have eased or subsided or maybe it was because she was comfortable telling him.

After finishing her story, she looked at him seeing a lot of sorrow in his eye`s towards her.

"I don`t want your pity, " she said rather harshly.

"Hey darling I wasn`t letting off pity signals ,I was thinking what a fool he was to throw you and your son away for drug`s."

Nodding she answered "I`m sorry I snapped but I cannot stand pity, its over its done he

broke it and it couldn`t mended ".

"Very wise word`s "he answered.

Looking at the clock he asked if she fancied a takeaway as he hadn`t eaten.

Smiling she said "Yes that would be great, thank you".

Coming back with a Chinese, he also bought a bottle of wine.

Having the plates warming up under the grill, she had set the table, seeing the wine she took some wine glasses out.

"Thought you said you didn`t drink" she said smiling.

Shaking his head he answered "I don`t".

Looking puzzled, pointing at the bottle raising her eyebrows she asked "Why bother buying it then"

"I thought you might enjoy it" he smiled.

"That`s really kind, but I`m not a wine drinker but my friend next door is so it won`t go waste" " she smiled back.

Looking disheartened, "Oh I`m sorry what is you like" he asked.

"Being totally honest I only have a drink once or twice a month and that`s when me and Angie that`s my friend goes out" she answered.

"Have you ever drank?" She asked .

Swallowing a mouthful of his food, "Once and it was and experience I didn`t care to repeat."

Finishing her meal she sat back in the chair and said "That was just what the doctor ordered and unexpected, thank you " she said smiling at him.

"My pleasure" he said raising his glass of lemonade at her.

She was feeling very relaxed in his company, and had thoroughly enjoyed their evening.

Afterward` s they sat listening to some music, Mark putting his arm around her, holding her close as they drifted off to the sound of Chris Rea.

Maria closing her eye`s had not felt this contented in a very long time.

As the song ended he lifted her chin and kissing her on the lip`s.

Pulling away he looked at her with such longing in his eye`s asking "Is it ok".

Opening her eyes looking at him feeling his breath on her face, she nodded.

Pulling her closer, kissing her passionately, she responded with such intensity it left them feeling breathless.

"Shall we take this upstairs", he whispered in her ear.

She had never been so sure of anything in her life, her body yearning him.

Taking his hand she lead him to her room.

"Just a moment", she said as she disappeared to check on Billy in the next room.

He was sound asleep.

Coming back into the bedroom he had removed his shirt revealing a very fit body and was laying on the bed with just his jeans on.

Looking at the trim top half of his body, she slowly began to remove his jeans.

Exposing long muscular legs, reaching towards her he removed her clothes.

Both totally naked now he started kissing her lips, her throat, and as his lip`s reached her breasts her nipples erect, his tongue playing with them she moaned.

Looking at her face smiling he ran his tongue down her tummy and got to her magic spot between her legs.

Crying out in pleasure as she reached her peak, turning over she started kissing him and looking at him with provocative, voluptuous eyes smiling she whispered,

"Now baby it`s your turn" she kissed the inside of his thighs massaging them as she travelled up towards his erect penis teasing him with her tongue, licking it as if it was her favourite ice cream. until she could see the sperm glisten on top, she then climbed on top and as he entered her and they became one my God did it feel right.

Afterwards lying beside each other, holding her hand turning toward` s looking  into her eye`s.

He whispered "Your beautiful."

Falling asleep, Maria waking up first the next morning looking beside her seeing the long eye lashes snoring gentle beside her.

Smiling she got out of bed and could hear Billy in the other room.

Going to him "Morning Booey " she smiled at him taking him downstairs changing his nappy and feeding him she heard Mark come into the room.

Looking up she smiled "Morning".

Going to her he kissed her and saying "I`m late sorry baby I have to go, call you later."

"Ok " she answered, "see you soon".

Her day was hectic she had a load of hairdressing on. Needed to get some shopping in, the day flying by Angie popping in after work,

"Well" she said smiling at Maria "Did I see a BMW parked outside this morning"

Maria looking at her replied "Yes you did, oh Angie we had a lovely evening".

Filling her in on the meal, telling her about his daughter,

"Oh " she said "Got a pressie for you" she went onto the kitchen bringing out the bottle of wine.

"He bought that last night ,but as you know I don`t drink wine, so I told him it wouldn`t go
to waste" passing her the wine.

"Oh thank you very much, all donations greatly accepted, fucking hell Maria this isn`t cheap
Plonk,. "smiling as she put it in her bag.

Angie hugging her saying "I`m so pleased Maria it`s about time you had some fun in your
life."

"Right I better get next door" she sighed.

As soon she left the phone rang, it was Mark, asking him where he was he answered "Just
open your front door."

Going to the door there he stood with flowers and chocolates in his hands.

Smiling the brown eyes twinkling at her" Hi gorgeous, how has your day been?"

He asked as she let him in.

Filling him in asking if he would like a coffee, "Please" he answered as he bent down
talking to Billy who was toddling about with his teddy under his arms.

"What are you doing this weekend?" he asked as she brought the coffee`s in.

"Nothing planned except for work", she answered sipping her coffee.

"Can you get a babysitter?"

"Yes I can ask, Mandy why?"

"I would like to take you for dinner and afterward `s to somewhere special" he answered.

"That sound`s great," she said picking Billy up.

Looking at Billy "Let`s get you bathed and then it`s bedtime" she said kissing him.

"Say night to Mark, make yourself at home" she said to him.

"Have you eaten "he asked as she went out the door.

Shaking her head "No not yet" she answered.

"Fancy a chip supper?" he asked.

Smiling giving him the thumbs up smiling "Love one".

"Won`t be long " he shouted up the stairs.

Bathing Billy she was singing as he splashed about.

Getting him out of the bath drying him and getting him into his night clothes.

Bringing him downstairs, letting him have his evening play.

Mark arriving back with their chip supper, she took Billy to bed.

"So where this is this special place your taking me " she asked as they sat at the table eating.

Looking at her he answered "It`s the other side of town near Watford" he replied.

"That`s a long way to travel" she answered popping a chip in her mouth.

Looking at her "It will be worth the trip" he smiled rolling up the chip paper putting it in the Bin.

His pager went off "Oh shit" he said "I have to go God is calling me" he smiled.

"I don`t know if I`ll be able to make it back, it`s a call out but I`ll bell you soon".

Taking her in his arm`s he kissed her. "Mmm that tastes like more" he smiled.

Looking at him she smiled saying "Yes it does" as she brushed her hair out of the way.

"Later hopefully " he said, putting his jacket on and grabbing his key`s

Letting him out the front door she stood waving until he was out of sight.

Going back into the living room, the phone rang it was Mandy.

"Hi sis , ok if I pop around for a cuppa" she asked.

Maria staring at the phone laughing down said "Since when did you have to ask".

"Since a little birdie chirped in my ear telling me you have been a busy little girl" she laughed back.

"Yes come on around", going into the kitchen putting the kettle on.

Looking out the window she saw Angie.Waving at her.

Opening her back door asking "Is it ok to pop around".

Maria repeating to her what she had just said to Mandy "When have you ever

had to ask."

Coming through her door she answered "Thought you might be busy."

Maria putting her eye`s up to heaven, said "Oh for God`s sake".

"Mandy`s on" she didn`t get to finish her sentence, because Mandy walked through the door.

Mandy taking a bottle out of her bag smiling "Thought we could

celebrate Maria loosing her virginity again" she laughed.

Maria looking at her giving her a friendly punch said "What I see the chirping birdie has

been chirping louder than Maria knew", she smiled.

Mandy getting the glasses out of the cupboard "Any lemonade "she asked.

"Yes sis it`s in the cupboard under the glasses" Maria shouted back.

Bringing the glasses and lemonades in she patted the seat beside her indicating for Maria to

sit down.

Angie already comfortable, Mandy pouring the drink`s, looking at her sister said,

"Well come on sis spill".

Maria said "Well as the birdie filled you in on most of it there isn`t a lot for me tell."

Smiling Angie answered "Well I only told that he stayed the night".

Maria told her "That he is a Samaritan, he has a daughter from a pervious relation, he has

own company, he has a great body" she laughed.

They continued nattering into the early hours.

Mandy hugging her sister telling her it was about time she started living her life to the full.

The following day Maria was working she, hearing the front knock,

Excusing herself from her client, going to answer it finding Mark there, standing outside ,

He grabbed her gently, kissing her "I missed you" he said in that husky voice of his."

Pulling away laughing she said "I have a client inside."

"Well " he answered looking at his watch "I have a client to see in ten minute`s but I just popped by to see if I can see you later"

Beaming at him she nodded answering" That would be great, what time?"

"About an hour will your client be gone by then?"he asked kissing her again.

"Yes" she reassured him.

Turing giving her the thumbs up "See you in a bit. Oh shall I bring an Indian" he asked as she was just going back indoor` s.

"Yes that`s great" she shouted closing the door.

Finishing her client , letting her out getting Billy in the bath , getting him his tea, so he was ready for bed by the time Mark got there.

The phone rang it was Mark saying he was running late.

"No Prob`s" she answered thinking that would give her time to shower and do her hair.

Billy in bed she ran a bath ,getting out putting her make up on ,taking the black jumpsuit out smiling to herself. put it on and was feeling good.

Going downstairs pouring herself a drink admiring herself in the mirror, putting some music on thinking life is good.

A while later Mark knocked on the door, opening it he let a wolf whistle out.

"Wow baby you look good enough to eat" he said kissing her.

Shaking her long dark hair, she said "Come in".

Indian in one hand dropping it on the floor he took her in his arm`s and they headed upstairs.

Lying her on the bed he kissed her from head to toe, sucking her toe`s licking her finger`s,

His head going between her leg`s she was soon moaning, pulling his body towards hers entering her she gasped.

Falling back all the energy drained from her.

"God that was unreal" he panted.

Looking at him putting her hand`s under her head, she agreed.

"You're an amazing woman" he smiled.

NEW CHAPTER

Saturday came and Maria had bought a new dress for her surprise evening out.

Mandy arriving around to pick Billy up as he was staying at her and Don`s tat evening,

Maria coming downstairs in a new Red strapless mid length dress, with a slit in the side up to the top of her thigh, Red high heeled strapless sandals, her long dark hair pulled to one side, silver ear rings and matching chain.

Mandy looking as she walked into the room ,

Smiling "My God sis you look beautiful" she gasped.

Maria looking in the mirror laughed "I don`t scrub up to badly."

"That dress is absolutely amazing" she said.

Mark arriving Mandy letting him in, walking into the living nearly doing a double take when he saw Maria.

"Bloody hell am I in the right house, you look incredible," he said, taking her arm and leaving the house looking very proud.

Taking her to one of the most popular most expensive restaurant in town, they had a wonderful meal, they staff new him in there he was on first term names with them.

Afterward` s bringing the car around, opening the door he said

"Darling this is just a taste of what I have planned for us this evening" he said smiling at her as they drove toward` s Watford.

Sitting beside him in his BMW, looking at him, overpowered by his presence.

Sitting back really enjoying the ride.

As they pulled in a car park Maria looked up to see the lights of a Casino.

.She was very surprised, Looking at him she laughed "Is this the surprise"

Answering he said, "Yes only the best for my lady in red".

Every one seemed to know Mark there, there were very glamourous women and Maria was

so glad she had splashed out on the red dress.

They had an amazing evening, she was mesmerized by him as watched him on the tables

winning.

Smiling at her as they drove back in the car asking if she had enjoyed the evening.

Nodding smiling back "It was amazing, do you go there often "

Nodding he answered "Now and again it help`s me meet people and promote my business".

"You know that word of mouth is the best advertisement in the world.so I do a bit of

networking and you have to go where the money is".

Looking at him in total agreement she answered "Yes but money cannot buy you

the important things in life".

Looking at her he asked "What do you mean,"

Explaining she answered " Health, Family and Love" she smiled ,
CLINK
Holding her hand , kissing it , he was thinking I`m on to a winner here.

The following weekend she met Lilly, a beautiful little doll like child.

Maria fell in love with her and her and Billy got on.

Maria and Mark were spending as much time as they could together.

Maria suggested that Mark make arrangements with Lilly`s mum that they could maybe

spend time with her once a month.

But it never seemed to materialise, so they saw Lilly on the odd occasion when Lilly`s mum

wasn`t busy taking her here or there with the latest boyfriend. Maria felt very sorry for

Mark, as this seemed to upset him.

Then one day when she was shopping she heard this little voice calling "Maria."

Looking around she saw the doll, "Hello Lilly" she said.looking up seeing a very attractive

blond standing beside her.Presumeing that this was Karen as the two of them were wearing

identical clothes.

Lilly looking at the blonde said "Mummy can I go and see Billy?"

"Hello, I`m Maria, Billy`s mum" said Maria in a friendly voice.

"Hi I`m Karen" she answered.

Lilly pulling her mum`s hand repeating "Can I go and see Billy" she demanded.

Maria sensing that Karen was finding the situation very awkward,

Nodding she said "Yes".

"Well it isn`t my place but Billy and Lilly get along so well I was just wondering if maybe if

you wouldn`t mind of course, if Lilly could spend an odd Sunday with us?"

"No problem I`m always` s saying to Mark he should spend more time with Lilly"

Maria so surprised answered "That`s great how about this Sunday"

Smiling she said "Yes just get Mark to confirm"

So when Mark dropped over that evening Maria informed him that she had met Karen and

she had agreed that the could have Lilly that weekend.

"You are amazing how did you manage that?" He asked, and in the next breath he continued

"Shit did you say this Sunday"

Nodding she said "Yes".

"Oh baby I`m going to price a huge job this weekend" he sighed.

"Well don`t worry" she smiled, "She can come and play with Billy I can look after her"

"Oh Baby that is so kind I couldn`t ask you to do that, she can be a little madam"

"Look it`s no trouble at all and I`ll cook us a nice Sunday lunch".

"Darling I would love that but I want to be here I don`t want to miss out on any of the fun

now do I" he answered with those puppy dog eye`s that she could not say no too.

Looking at Maria`s disappointed face he added "How about if I arrange it for the following Sunday"

" Yes but what if she wants her to go out with her and her boyfriend" she asked.

"Oh I think she is between boyfriends at the moment" he added.

"Ok then darling that`s fine" smiling as she kissed him.

   The following weekend Mark brought Lilly over and the four of had a whale of a time.

So it became a regular thing that Lilly came and visited Maria and Billy once a month.

Maria loved it, as it was company for Billy and her and Mark felt like a real family

New chapter.

The rest of the year just whizzed by, Maria working Billy`s second

birthday, came and went ,this time without any contact from Antony,

It was coming up to Christmas and Mark seemed to be snowed under with work.

One afternoon as Maria was letting one of her client`s out this Man approached her.

"Hi my name is Clark, I believe your Mark`s girlfriend" he said smiling at her.

Looking at him curiously she answered "Yes".

"I noticed his car parked here put two and two together" he said smiling.

"Well your good at counting then" she answered.

"He always has a good looking piece of skirt, looks like he got one with a brain as well "he laughed.

Maria looked at him her curiosity getting they better of her.

"Your a friend of his then?" She asked.

"Well we know each other, I was just wondering if he had got any work?"he asked.

"Well I do know he is a bit snowed under at the moment, give me your telephone number and I`ll let him know you called".

With that a car pulled up, looking Maria said "Oh there he is now".

Getting out of the car she waved at him, walking up the path,

Clark turning around said "Hi Mark long time no see" holding his hand out.

"Christ Clark thought you were locked up" Mark answered taking his hand and shaking it.

Maria turned to Mark asking if he would like to bring him in for a cuppa, as it was freezing

out.

Before Mark could answer Clark said "That really descent of you I could murder one".

Following them inside Maria turning to Mark saying ,"Darling could you pop over the shop

and get some milk" remembering she had none.

Nodding he went to the shop.

Clark looking down said "Hello there" to Billy.

Billy giving him a big dribbling smile, offering some of his rusk.

Clark laughed, said "No thank you".

Maria smiling from the kitchen, asked "Sugar, I`m Maria by the way".

Holding his hand out he said "Pleased to meet you".

Sitting at the table Maria not short in coming forward,

Asking "How do you know Mark?"

"Oh we went to school together" he answered taking a sip of his coffee.

Thinking about it she hadn`t met many of his friends.

"So you reckon he could have some work for me?" He asked

"Well I think so because between his Samaritans and work, well he is a busy man"

"Oh he is still riding that bike" he smirked.

"What do you mean" she asked.

Before he could answer Mark arrived back with the milk.

"There you go " he said.

"Do you want a drink darling" she asked smiling at him.

Nodding "Please" turning to Clark he asked, "When did you get out?"

"Last week" he answered, "So I thought I`d look up some old mates that owes me favours"

Mark giving him an odd look, "Well your in luck as it happens, I could do with a hand at the moment, when can you start?"

Maria bringing the coffee`s through, smiling there you go "Mark I`m just going to bath Billy."

"Well I just popped in to tell you I`m on call tonight, so I won`t be around later."

Clark finished his coffee thanking her, said "I can start in the morning".

"Ok I`ll see you outside the tavern about seven" Mark answered.

Clark left.

"That was short and sweet" smiled Maria.

Kissing her "Look darling I never mix business with pleasure" he smiled.

"Bell you later, see you later Billy" he said as he left.

Strange Maria thought as she took Billy up for his bath.
                    NEW CHAPTER
          Maria getting the Christmas tree up and her decorations Billy was

mesmerised with the whole thing this was the first Christmas that he was old enough to take

any notice and Maria was really enjoying it.

Mark arriving one evening asking if he could take her Billy and Mandy and Don out for

Christmas lunch.

Maria getting totally overexcited ringing Mandy and asking her , getting off the phone she

nodded at him saying "Oh darling there over the moon thank you."

Patting the couch where he was sitting he invited her over . Sitting beside her he said "There

is something else I want to ask you?"

Looking at him she asked "What? "

Getting off the couch he got down on one knee, taking a box out of his pocket, opening it he asked "Maria darling my beautiful girl will you do me the honour of becoming my wife?"

She was totally taken aback she had not been expecting this.

"Oh my God" she screamed, "Oh my God ",looking at the diamond that was shining up at

her ,looking into to them brown eye`s that she had learned to trust and love, tear`s of happiness

in her eye`s she said "Oh yes Mark oh yes."

Taking the ring out of the box slipping it on her finger it fitted perfectly,

Looking at her "You have just me the happiest man on earth."
s
Taking her upstairs making long slow passionate love to her he looked into her brown eye`s

and said "Ever since the first time I set eye`s on you I knew you were the one for me and the

more I got to know of you the more I fell in love with you I adore every inch of you ."

"And you woke a part of me that I thought I would never feel again, and I love you" her eye`s

glistening with tear`s as she said this.

Mark looking at her, she could see and feel the tenderness and devotion rush through her

pouring from him.

Lying back in his arms stroking his chest she said "I never thought I could be this happy."

Sitting up asking him "Can I ring Mandy".

Smiling at her he said "Of course you can."

Jumping out of bed, grabbing her dressing gown she ran downstairs.

Dialling Mandy`s number, Mandy picking the phone up the other end "I`m engaged " she

screamed down the phone.

"What " her sister shouted "were coming around".

Mark appearing at the door she turning around her eye`s shinning in delight with this huge grin

on her face saying" Their coming around," running upstairs to get dressed.

Maria just had time to get her clothes on before she could hear her sister downstairs., calling her.

"Mark just popped to the shop" she smiled as she grabbed Maria`s hand to have a look at the

ring .

"Oh Maria, it`s gorgeous , I`m so happy for you" she smiled with tear`s in her eye` s.

Don walked in with a huge grin on his face "I believe congratulations are in order"

Mark coming back from the shop with a bottle of vodka and a bottle of champagne.

Walking in with a huge grin on his face, he opened the bottle of champagne and asked Don to

get the glasses.

Thought we would need this for a toast, he said not able to conceal his happiness.

Angie knocking at the back door having seen Mandy and Don going in, popping her head

around the door asking "Can anyone join?".

Maria standing there beaming, looking radiate and Mark beside her looking like the cat that

got the cream, smiling at her said "Come and join us" said Mark.

Looking very surprised asking "What`s all this?"

Maria smiling at her holding out her finger, showing her the ring,

Gasping she looked "Oh Maria I am over the moon for you", she said hugging her.

"When did this occur?" She asked,

"About an hour ago" Maria answered looking overwhelmed.

Mark with a grin on his face said "Well a tiny bit longer than that."

They all laughed,

Mark passing the glasses around, filling Maria`s up first ,making a toast to

"Maria my beautiful fiancee, thank for agreeing to become my wife".

Maria responding replied "Thank you for asking me."she smiled kissing him.

Mark who hated the taste of drink, taking a sip and passing it to Don.

"When is the big day" asked Angie taking a sip from her glass.

Maria looking at Mark questionably, "As soon as possible, "he smiled hugging Maria closely to him.

"Well go on then "prompted Mandy, "Give us a little idea so I can start shopping".

Maria looking at her said" You won`t have to shop your my bridesmaid."

Mandy hugging her big sister staring up at her saying "I`m so pleased for you."

Mark asking "Maria how does valentine`s day sound?".

Thinking she answered "Yes that sound`s really good", kissing him.

They all enjoy their celebration drink`s and before they left Mark asked Don if he would be best man.

Don looking very surprised "Yes I`d love to it would be a pleasure ,but wouldn`t you rather have one of your own mates?"

Smiling hugging Maria he answered "I`d rather keep it in the family, so to speak".

Christmas came Mark taking her Mandy and Don and Billy out for Dinner.Neither Mandy or Maria had ever been out for Christmas dinner before.

After dinner in the restaurant Mark announced that he had booked this venue for there wedding reception.

It was a top class restaurant and there was a venue out the back for wedding reception`s

Maria looking at him wide eyed whispered "Can we afford it ?s".

Smiling at her he answered "Let me worry about that".

"Oh Mark it`s going to be the best" she smiled ,beaming at Don and Mandy.

"Only the best for my lady", he smiled holding her hand.

Mandy and Don smiling at her so glad thing`s had worked out for her .

Don shaking Mark`s hand saying "Fair play Mark, your one in a million".

Christmas out of the way, Maria started planning their wedding.

Maria seeing a dress design for both her and Mandy she decided to get them made.

Picking an Ivory silk material for her dress, which was cut off the shoulders waisted and then flowed into an A line skirt which was shaped like a heart so that when you walked it showed your legs off just above the knee.

She picked the same design for Mandy`s dress just changing the colour which Mandy chose a deep pink.

Lilly was to be a flower girl, and she would be wearing ivory with a deep pink sash and a pink ribbon braided through her hair.

Mark and Don, were going to be wearing black morning suit`s Don `s having a deep pink sash and dickie bow to match the bride maid and Mark `s in Ivory to match the bride. And Billy in a morning suit with the pink accessory `s as page boy.

Having the table`s trimmed in the deep pink and the flowers in Ivory and pink .

Mark was footing the bill for everything, so Maria said she would pay for the honeymoon, Which he eventually agreed to, so she booked them a two week honeymoon trip to Gran Canary island`s.

Chris her friend offered to make the wedding cake, as a wedding present.

All her family were coming over from Ireland , and Mark`s Da was with his wife arriving from Japan with Mark`s two step brother `s .Whom he had never met.

Toward` s the middle of January, Maria and Mark hadn`t seen a great deal of each other since new years eve which was there first anniversary of meeting.

Mainly because it was one of the busiest time`s of the year Christmas and January for the Samartins and since Mark had managed to have almost the whole of Christmas off he was on duty ,every evening for weeks without a break.

Maria just seeing him whenever he had a moment to pop by if he was passing.

So after he had done his shift she made a lovely meal for them the first evening he had off.

He arrived in a new shirt and jeans which she immediately noticed.

Admiring his new out fit, he smiled saying he had picked them up in the sale.

Billy was already asleep, so he took her in his arms and carrying her upstairs,

lying her on the bed, he made love to her with such haste that it was over before it began.

Falling back he said "I'm sorry darling but I thought I was going to explode if I didn't have

you."

She smiled glad that he had missed her.

Lying beside him they started talking about money not a subject they often discussed.

She asking questions that seemed to make him uncomfortable.

Telling her that after his mum had died he had left him a substantial sum of money and there

was no need for her to worry.

Feeling comfortable with this explanation he changed the subject to children another subject

they had just briefed on in passing.

Looking at her he said "I would love to start a family as soon as we are married."

She was very surprised as she presumed he felt the same as her, because she had Billy and

he had Lilly, that was enough.

Being totally honest with him "I never wanted anymore children after having Billy ".

"Why ?" He asked looking surprise.

"Mainly because I don't carry baby's very well, I'm always throwing up plus I didn't have a

very easy birth with him ". She answered.

Looking at the devastated face, smiling at him she said "But I think it would be lovely for us

to have our own baby".

"Oh darling thank you " he said letting out a huge sigh of relief.

Thinking about what she had just said, she cringed because after she had , had Billy the pain

had been so intense, giving birth to him that she had wanted to die.and she remembered saying to   Antony never again and she meant it.

But then she had thought that her and Antony would have been forever, and she had never thought that she would be in another relationship where a child would have to be an option.

But then as she had learned through her life , circumstances change and the way her life had changed in the last year, well she certainly never thought she would be planning a wedding.

And to a dream man like Mark or any man for that matter, looking at him beside her he said smiling at her .

"We will produce the most beautiful baby", as he started kissing her neck.

Making love to her this time, such tenderness as he touched her magic spot letting his tongue slide in and out, flicking it until she was screaming as she climaxed, as he entered her and they became one she lay back thinking I have died and gone to heaven.

Panting he turned over to her saying "It only get`s better".

Looking at him she said "I don`t ever want this magic to die".

He stared back at her and said "Nothing is going to destroy what we got baby".

                              Coming off the pill immediately, as she had told him it takes her a long time to conceive.

There was just four week`s left to their big day.

Mark had taken responsibility of the majority of the wedding planning , and just leaving the finer detail`s to Maria and her sister which they seemed to be dealing with very nicely.

The final fitting of the dresses day arrived Maria and Mandy leaving Billy with Don getting in the car heading to Mrs French the dress maker`s.

They two of the, were so excited when she took the dresses out.

Maria trying her` s on first, it was perfect, They whole thing fitting her to perfection.

Mrs French had added a few extra`s putting some pearl`s around the down the bodice and adding train of very fine silk lace on the back . Which totally enhanced the dress.

Mandy trying her dress which need a little adjusting on the hip`s, which Mrs French did on the spot for them.

Mandy and Maria left, Mrs French wishing her all the happiness in the world as she waved them goodbye paying her and giving her a bit extra, the sister`s leaving arm in arm singing There was a nice little pub just down the road and Maria suggested that the have their tea there.

"That sound`s good sis "said Mandy smiling.Getting a table Maria getting the drink`s in, getting Mandy a wine and herself an orange juice, grabbing the menu`s she sat down.

"I`m so pleased with the job Mrs French has done", she said looking very satisfied with her choice.

"You look absolutely stunning in it", Mandy answered taking a sip of her drink.

"An so do you sis you look really good, that shade of pink is beautiful," Maria smiled

"Who ever thought this time a year ago that you would be getting married" said Mandy looking at the menu.

"I know I never thought there would have been anyone after Antony" she smiled.

"Do you ever think about him?"

"Well of course I do, he is Billy`s Da and to be honest he was the love of my life".

"So what`s Mark?" She asked frowning.

"My darling Mark is the man of my dream`s" she smiled.

"He is perfect he adores me he love`s Billy, he doesn`t drink , he doesn`t do drug`s he is kind and most of all I love him and trust which was very hard for me after Antony" she answered letting out a very contented sigh.

Mandy looking at her smiled answering "I`m over the moon for you sis if anyone deserves happiness it is you".

Maria looking at her smiled and said "Thank you".

Driving home Maria said "Mandy I have never been so happy as I am now and it is all down to Mark", she smiled.

Mandy squeezing her hand, "Well we haven`t got long to wait now."

"Getting home Don had got Billy to bed"

Showing Don the dresses, looking saying" Your both going to look stunning".

Laughing together, they sang "We know".

Don laughed back saying "And the two of you is as vain as each other."

Three day`s before the wedding Mark`s Dad and his wife and boy`s arrived from Japan.

Maria had invited them to her` s for dinner the eve of the wedding.

She got on very well with Mark`s Dad, Derek and his wife Ahee.

His brother`s were twin`s and she found them adorable.

Every thing sailing along , soon it was the big day.

Maria`s family arrived from Ireland, and she had booked them into the local hotel.

NEW CHAPTER.

The morning of the wedding arrived Maria ,Mandy ,Catrine Lilly and Billy had stayed at Maria`s the night before, so that morning it was hectic at her`s .

Unlike her first wedding she had hired a hairdresser to come and do the hair`s.

Maria didn`t know what car she was going in as Mark wanted it all to be a surprise for her.

The flowers arriving, Maria said to Mandy it was time to get dressed.

Maria getting into her suspenders and ivory silk laced top stocking`s, with matching lace bra and knickers.

Mandy carefully helping her into her dress, holding her breath as she pulled over her head.

The dress on, Maria looking in the mirror very pleased with the image that reflected back.

Then Mandy, putting the finishing touch` s to Maria`s attire putting her tiara and silk veil on her head as her long dark hair flowed down her back in curls.

Mandy looking at her taking her breath away.

Maria you look so beautiful, she gasped

Turning around smiling she said "So do you."

"Maria the car is outside " her Ma shouted upstairs`.

Maria and Mandy went to the window, peering out, Maria let a gasp there outside her house

was a black limousine.

And behind it was a baby ford for the brides maids.

All trimmed in pink and ivory,

"Oh my God " said Mandy, "Are we going in style or what."jumping up and down in

excitement.

Heading downstairs Catrine had dressed Billy and Lilly, the looked like two little doll`s.

Maria seeing Billy had tears in her eye`s in his tailed morning suit and the pink sash and

a tiny pink dickey bow.

And Lilly in her ivory lace dress with the pink sash, and pink ribbon braided through her

hair.

They two of them looked absolutely adorable.

Maria said she would take Billy and Lilly in the car with her.

So Mandy and her Ma going in the baby ford.

Maria her brother Sean who was giving her away sat in the back of the limo and Lilly and

Billy sat in the front.

"Be Jesus I have never been in a car like this before" said Sean as he sat beside his sister.

"Neither have I", replied Maria.as she gazed around it.

"Posh " she said smiling at Sean.

"Well you wouldn`t see one of these back home", he answered.

"I feel like a penguin, in this suit" he said, as he was making himself comfortable.

"Well you don't look like a penguin, you look great" she smiled.

"So do you " he answered back in a whisper. Sean was a man of few word's.

Arriving at the church , Sean helping Maria out of the car, Lilly and Billy looking so

and adorable.

As soon as the car pulled up all their friend's and family went into the church.

Hearing the choir as soon as she was at the door of the church Maria started tremble.

Sean who was not a very emotional individual at all, squeezed her hand and turning behind

he winked at Mandy, looking at Billy and Lilly he felt a lump in his throat.

They started the walk up the aisle, every one turning to stare.

Maria could sense the aura they were causing.

Looking ahead she saw Mark ,as he turned and smiled at her.

That smile of his did it every time she could feel her heart fluttering.

As she got near him she saw him whisper "I love you".

Her brother handing her over to Mark as the reached they altar.

Mandy removing her veil from over her face.

The sermon began, It was a church of England wedding .

Which wasn't really that much different from the roman catholic.

As they took their wedding vow's Mark looking into her eye's and as she stared back into his

she could see the love that was in them just for her.

Ceremony over, they walked back up the aisle Billy holding Maria's hand and Lilly in

Mark's arms.

Maria's hand through Marks arm she looked at him her eye's shining with happiness as she

looked down at Billy.

For the very first time in her life she felt whole, nothing missing inside she was complete.

Heading to the wedding venue, Mark having organized the whole celebration .

They family and friends headed in after the photographs, and Maria and Mark walked into a round of applause.

The whole place looked amazing, The top table was decorated in Pink and lace ivory Tablecloths. And the present from Chris the wedding cake looked prefect in the centre.

There were fresh pink and ivory roses on all the table`s , it looked amazing.

The meal was delicious catering for all taste`s.

Mark had hired a band for the reception, and there first dance was to "Can`t live without you".

As Mark held her in his arm`s, looking down at her she looked into his eye`s and the love flowed between them, you could almost touch.

He gently started singing in her ear "I can`t live if living is without you."

Looking at him smiling, her eye`s shining , holding his face her hand`s saying "I Love you".

As the evening came to an end, everybody going outside to wave goodbye, as they headed to Heathrow airport for their flight to go on honeymoon.

Fight`s all running on time, arriving at their destination on schedule..

Getting booked into their hotel, taking a stroll through the Playa Del Lingus stopping at one of the many on restaurants the front, for dinner.

Going back to the hotel, holding hand`s kissing each other as they walked.

Totally wrapped up in each other, nothing or nobody else mattered.

Going back to the hotel room "Mark taking her in his arm`s, looking into them brown, sexy eye`s which was what he had fallen love with at the start".

He starting undressing her kissing every part of her ,sucking her nipples until the were tingling, kissing and licking her magic spot, until she was climaxed.

She rolled on to her back and bringing him toward `s her she licked his erect penis

until it was glistening on top she then guided it into her, and slowly pushed her body up and

down , looking down at him he was lying with his eye`s closed, and has he came ,his body

trembling beneath her.

Lying beside him in the aftermath, of their lovemaking, both feeling breathless.

They slept.

The rest of the week they spent sunbathing , taking in the sight`s.

The second week , they hired a car and touring the whole of the island.

Stopping at a local supermarket, buying some sandwiches and drink`s, finding a secluded

spot,

Sitting looking out at the sea Maria dabbling her feet in the water, he came up beside her

sitting , putting his arm`s around her, kissing her passionately, removing her swimwear,

making love to her in the warm water the sun beaming down on them.

After ward`s Mark saying "What a lovely place this would be to conceive a baby."

Maria looked at him answering "Yes it would".

Maria went shopping for Billy, Mandy, Lilly and Don.

Mark having no interest in shopping, stayed by the pool soaking up the sun.

On there last night there Mark finding out there was a casino near the hotel, they went,

Unlike the night they went to the one, outside of London, he lost money and quite a bit.He

was not a happy bunny leaving.

Maria was seeing a slightly darker side to him.

Maria packing their stuff when they got back, so as everything would be ready for the

morning.

Laying on the bed he watched her pack, he seemed to have clamed down a bit after his loss.

"Baby I`m sorry for losing it, but I get rightly pissed off when I loose, at the table`s" he said holding his arm`s out to her.

She went into them saying "But you must know it is all part of the game".

"Yes but I am a sore loser" he smiled.

Taking her in his arm`s making love to her .

Next morning they were up and heading back to the
airport.

Flight`s again all running on schedule, Maria was looking forward to getting home as

She was missing ,Billy she did not voice this to Mark, as she didn`t want him to think she was

worrying.

Mandy had looked after Billy while the were away.

Getting a taxi from the airport, they were soon pulling up out side Maria`s .

This was where they decided to live, for now. Because Mark wanted to live in a better area

eventually.

Pulling up outside, Maria ran in and Billy seeing her started to scream.

Picking him up hugging and kissing him taking out a huge blow up fish she had bought for

him along with some shorts and t shirts and a few other item`s.

Kissing Mandy she asked how he had been .

Mandy looking at her answered "He has been good as gold, wow look at the colour of you"

she smiled kissing her sister, and giving Mark a peck, welcoming them back.

Maria taking out a beautiful bracelet and matching ear ring`s for her.

And bottle of Pernod and some cigarettes for Don.

Mandy after spending two week`s at Maria`s said her goodbye`s to Mark, Maria and Billy.

Mark was on the phone ,Maria turning to him saying "I`m just going to bath Billy."

Nodding he shook his head smiling,

Billy seemed to have got so big, she had bought him new p j` s with, seashell`s and fish on them looking down as she put them on him he said "Fish " pointing at them with a huge dribbley smile.

"Oh you are my clever boy", she said smiling.

Bringing him downstairs, giving him his tea and playing with him . Saying good night to Mark, she put him to bed.

Coming back downstairs Mark seemed a bit preoccupied, looking at him as she was tidying Billy`s toy`s away, asking "What was the matter."

Sighing he said "It`s coming back to reality" smiling at her.

Knowing that everything was not fine, she probed a bit further.

Looking at her he answered "Oh it`s money darling, I`m going back to work tomorrow".

They had decided to keep Maria`s lodger on for now, as Maria said that was their mortgage paid.

Going over to him putting her arm`s around him, He looked at her saying "Nothing for you worry about ", he said kissing her and taking her upstairs

The following morning getting Billy up getting his breakfast, getting him dressed, Mark arriving down kissing her .

Offering to make him some breakfast he declined, saying he had a job to go back and price.

Holding her in his arm`s he kissed her, saying "I`ll try and not be too late, Love you ".

With that the door knocked, Mark answered it and she heard Clark there.

Sticking her head around the living room door she said "Hi Clark".

"Hello Maria ,I believe congratulation`s are in order," he answered smiling.

Right we`re off said Mark "See you later, darling".

Maria with Billy in toe helping, started unpacking the wedding present`s.

Finding some lovely ivory satin sheet`s and duvet cover`s, taking Billy upstairs she striped the bed .

Standing back admiring her creativity, she had also been given some pale heart shaped cushion`s which she scattered on the bed putting the finishing touch`s.

Picking Billy up saying, "Isn`t that pretty" she said smiling at him.

Turning at the door , looking at the bedroom, feeling really pleased with her effort`s

Thinking of their love making the night before, she was singing carrying Billy downstairs.

Going to the freezer taking some mince out she started cooking a bolognese for their tea that evening.

Her phone started ringing, it was her client`s , asking how the wedding went.

The ecstatic tone to her voice telling the whole story, they were really pleased for her, taking their appointment booking`s, hanging up . Billy sitting on the floor with a rusk ,

Smiling at him she said let`s go to the park.Putting his warm winter jacket on and her coat she headed to the park pushing Billy on the swing`s.

She had a flashback of her and Paul , sitting here looking for Baby Antony in the sky.

This memory making her feel very overcome and sad, but with a sigh looking at Billy thinking

life can throw what ever dice there is to throw, and she will just stare it in the face and carry on.

Looking up at the sky she was thinking, I`m so lucky she had got everything she had ever

Dreamed of. Billy putting his hand`s up wanting to get out.

Taking him out saying "Have you had enough", she asked and started walking home.

Meeting Jimmy hearing his laugh before she saw him.

"Jimmy", she called crossing the road

Looking up seeing her he said "Be the holy mother of God if it`s not herself"

He answered smiling.

Jimmy had not been able to make it to the wedding, because he had gone back to Ireland to visit his family.

And how is the little man himself, he asked putting his hand in his pocket taking out some money and handing it to Billy.

"Have you time for a coffee" he asked her.

Nodding smiling she answered "Of course always have time for you darling ".

She filled him in on the wedding and the honeymoon, looking so happy, he said

"Well I`m glad it all went well, I suppose the next thing on the agenda is a little one."

Looking at him shocked asking "How do you know ?"

"Lord God it`s the next natural step". he smiled.

Laughing smiling she said "Yes your right"

"Right I`ll be off got a hubby to look after now " she said smiling.

Walking to the gate with her she kissed him and he said ,

"You take great care," and tossing Billy`s hair he said you little man don`t spend all that at once. he smiled standing on the path the looking after them.

Watching her as her and Billy skipped up the road her singing to him.

Walking back inside remembering her the day Antony had taken him to see her where she had

locked herself away from life .

Thinking to himself ,that`s what make`s life exciting, the unknown one door closes and another one open`s.

Maria getting home ,Angie popping around for her daily intake of coffee and to hear about the honeymoon as she hadn`t seen Maria since she got back.

Knocking on the door going in she looked at Maria with an envy,

"Hi ya welcome home " she said smiling."look at the colour of you I feel like a milk bottle."

Sitting at the table Maria filling her in on the honeymoon.

Hearing the front door go Angie looking as Mark came in "Christ look at you ,I was just saying

to Maria I feel like a milk bottle.

Admiring his arm he answered "Good isn`t it" he smiled proudly.

"Oh it`s good to have you both back it hasn`t been the same" she said hugging them.

"How did the job go " Maria asked.

"I think I have got it" he smiled "Clark helped, I think the old gal fancied him."

"Where is it "asked Angie.

"It`s near Watford, just up the M25".he answered."I`ll tell you something she has a few bob

which I won`t mind relieving of some of it " he laughed.

"How big is it ?" asked Maria.

"Let me put it to you this way, there is ten stables to be roofed, all the guttering`s to be

replaced and the main house which is a converted barn, she want`s that reroofed as well.

"It`s a huge contract, and there is a lot of money to be made, time wise I reckon I`m looking at

the best part of a year`s work".

"Let`s hope you get it " smiled Maria.

"I reckon it`s in the bag especially the way she was looking at Clark and he played a winner."

He said looking very pleased with the out come.

Angie being nosy asking "How old is she."

Shrugging his shoulder`s he answered, "Well she is no spring chicken, I suppose I`d put her

in her early fifty` s".

"Bloody hell" said Maria as she got up to check on dinner.

"How old is Clark?"she asked as she was taking the cutlery out of the drawer.

"Well we went to school together, so he is the same age as me 28" he sniggered.

Leaning back in his chair staring out at her in the kitchen.

"What does she look like?"asked Angie.

"Well how do you describe something that look`s like nothing?" He asked looking at Angie.

"Oh come on you can do better than that," prompted Angie.

"Well she is very skinny, short mousey coloured hair, glasses, what do you call it when you have
got dint`s in your face like pot hole`s, very well spoken which is about her only asset."

"What" asked Maria smiling.

Angie frowning looking totally puzzled, answered "Oh you mean the scars, from acne as a

teenager."

"That`s the one " he laughed.

"Christ she sound`s like a right stunner". smiled Angie.
.
"At least you have no worries of Mark running off with that" she laughed

"What`s her name?" asked Maria

Mark getting up from the chair putting his arm`s around Maria answered"

"Why would I want shandy when I have got champagne at home, her name is Lisa Potter," he

said smiling at Angie.

Angie laughing saying "Well that sort`s of suit`s considering the pot mark`s on her face."

The three of them creased up laughing.

"Well I better go home after that bit of excitement " she said still laughing going out the

door "I`ll see you tomorrow".

"See you Ang" smiled Maria.

The phone rang Mark picking it up, Maria looking to see a huge grin on his face, putting the

phone down, he picked her up kissing her he said, "That was her, yes, baby I have done it ,we`re
in the money I got the job".

Maria hugging him saying "Oh darling that is amazing."Thinking we might need it as she had

been sick again that morning.

"This is the start of our social climb?"he smiled.

CLINK
THE START CHAPTER
The following week`s flying by, Maria had never seen him so hyped up.

Saying to him one evening "That he reminded her of a buzzing bee."

Smiling at him saying "I`m so proud of you."Laughing he answered, "You want to see the

bank balance."

"As I have said to you before money don`t buy the important thing`s in life,"

Staring at her he said, "I know that darling but it does make life a hell of a lot easier".

Nodding she agreed and said "I`m just going to get tea on".

Maria turning to him said "I think I might have some new` s "

Putting his arm`s around her kissing neck asking "And what is that, My baby girl?"

"Well after you went to work yesterday and also this morning , I have been sick ".

Staring at her he said "No !!",

Smiling she said "I have made a doctor`s appointment for the morning".

"Oh bloody hell darling that is the icing on the cake "Taking her in his arm`s

 Hugging her he said "I love you so much."

"I can`t come with you but you phone me as soon as you have been to the doctor`s".

"I will" she smiled reassuring him.

                        Mark heading off to work the following morning, as she waved him
off,
CLINK
He shouted back, "Bell me with the positive new` s" smiling she said ,

 "Yes I will" standing there with her finger`s crossed.

Singing as she got Billy ready to go to the doctor`s,

Walking the she stopped at the shop to get Billy some jelly tot`s his favourite.

Sitting in the waiting room chatting to the other patient` s until her name was called.

Seeing the same doctor that she seen before, looking up saying "Hello Maria ".

"Hello " she answered .

The doctor looking at Billy ,said "Wow isn`t he getting big".

"How old is he now?" He asked giving him a lollypop.

"He is two and a half", Maria nodding replied "I don`t know where the time goes".

"What can I do for you, "he smiled.

"I think I might be pregnant" she answered.

Taking out the bottle smiling "You know the drill". He said passing it to her.

Doing the deed bringing the bottle back to the doctor, she sat biting her lip.

Finishing the test he looked at her smiling "Yes you were right," examining her he said your just 9 week`s. "

Booking her in for her antenatal giving her the 21st of November as the expected date of the new arrival.

Beaming at him she thanked him taking Billy by the hand she went via Jimmy`s house.

Knocking opening the door seeing the bright brown eye`s staring at her.

"What", he asked as he let her in.

"I`m pregnant" she answered beaming at him.

"Be the holy God that is great new` s" he answered."Quick, but great new` s".

He added turning to her asking if she wanted a cuppa.

Declining she shook her head "No thank` s, I just had to tell somebody."

"Oh right , well I won`t bother putting the kettle on then" he smiled.

Walking her to the gate waving after her telling her to take great care.

Getting home phoning Mark, telling him the new` s.

She could hear the excitement in his voice, he was thrilled.

"See I had a feeling that day we made love on the beach in Porto Rico" he laughed down the Phone.

Saying that he would try and finish work early.

Looking at Billy she said "Your going to have a brother or sister".

Picking him up dancing around the room with him.he was giggling.

"Let`s go to the shop`s and get something nice for tea tonight".

On her way to the shop`s she bumped into Chris.

She had not seen her since the wedding.

Going for a coffee, filling her in on the honeymoon, and she added beaming that she had

some amazing new `s.

Chris looking at the face, said "Your pregnant".

Maria looking at her said "How did you know?".

"Just a wild guess" she laughed, adding "I`m so pleased".

Billy getting restless, started wandering around the coffee shop.

"Well that`s my que to go", she smiled.

Making arrangement`s for Chris to pop around the following week.

 Popping into the supermarket picking up some steak`s as they were Mark`s favourite.

Getting home giving the place a good going over, ringing Mandy asking her to pop in from

work on her way home .

At 5.30pm Mandy walked through the back door, seeing Maria sitting on the sofa reading to

Billy.

Putting the book down she looked at her sister saying "Guess what".
.
Mandy picking Billy up saying "Who getting to be a heavy boy ".

Maria looking at her the excitement in her shining eye`s .

"Well what is it "Mandy asked.

"I`m pregnant" she screamed.

Mandy looking at her in amazement, "Oh sis that is wonderful new` s".

Maria dancing around the room singing Billy picking up on the excitement started running around like something possessed.

"Oh bloody hell I have started him off" smiled Maria as she picked him up.

Getting him some jelly tot`s out of the cupboard.

He clamed down.

Sitting at the table with a cuppa Maria filling her in on the date`s.

The door opening Mark walking in with a huge bouquet of roses asking "Where is my clever Girl," smiling passing them to her kissing her.

Mandy looking at her thinking she has got it all, she was really pleased for her.

The following week`s passing with Maria being sick every morning, and just feeling generally yuck.

Mark commenting one morning as he passed the bathroom pulling her head out of the toilet she answered "I told you I don`t carry baby` s very well."

"See you later " he called as he closed the door.

Picking Clark up complaining to him about what he had to wake up to every morning.

Clark looking at him thinking you have not changed much still the same self centred money orientated prick he had always been.

It never ceased to amaze Clark how men like him always ended up with the best looking women,

They just seemed to fall at their feet, and Maria now she was something else, she ticked every box , good looking, funny, kept a lovely home, could have had any man she wanted but what did she pick. Fucking Mark, who now she was up the duff would probably stray somewhere else.Why he had ever married , Clark would never know, men like him never settled down.

They seen something in a skirt that they wanted, and that was it their dick overtaking the brain.Clark looking at him said "You haven`t changed much."

Mark pulling in to pick the new labourer up, asked "What do you mean?"

"Hello Mark," this Irish accent greeted him.

"Morning Sean , this is Clark", he said as he pulled off n the van.

"Oh your Irish, so is Mark`s wife is Irish" said Clark,

"Well I did not know that" said Sean, "But then we didn`t really have a chance to talk."

"Where is she from Mark?"he asked.

"County Westmeath",

"Be the lord God , it`s a small world, I`m from Galway which isn`t far from there at all."

Clark laughed "I love the accent".

"Well I can`t help it, the way I talk".

Pulling into The Barn that`s what Clark had christened it, Sean said,

"Christ almighty this is a big place" Taking in the Ferrari and the Porsche that were parked

outside..

Clark nodding "Yes it is that all right".

Getting out of the car, Mark headed towards the house shouting at Clark, that all the new

material`s were in the far barn, and to start on the end stable.

"Where`s he going "asked Sean.

"In to see the spider", laughed Clark.

Sean looking at him with a puzzled look on his face.

"Who" he asked.

"The governor, The woman that own`s this place" he explained.

"She`s a man eater, tried it on with me but I was having none of it I think she would try to
snare anything."

"Well be God she better not try and do anything with me, cause my Betty would have her
gut`s for garters"
s
Clark fell about the place laughing.

Clark thinking he is going to be fun to work with, heading for the stables.

Mark appearing saying "Right lad`s, you get a start on the job "I`m going with Mrs Potter to get some more material`s".

"Ok boss" answered Sean "Everything is under control".

"Glad to hear it" replied Mark getting in the Ferrari with the spider, Mark driving.

"Be God she does , she look`s like a frigging spider skinny and shapeless, "Sean said as he

watched them drive off.

Maria at home wasn`t having a very good time, she was feeling more ill than normal, and Billy wasn`t helping as he was at the terrible two`s stage.

Getting dinner ready for when Mark arrived home later.

Even the cooking of the food was making her heave.

Mandy ringing saying she had a day off from work,

Maria telling her she was feeling so ill , asking if she could have Billy for a few hour`s.

"No prob`s sis, I`ll be with you in 5" she said.

"Coming through the door looking at her sister she said "Christ you do look rough".

"I had forgotten how bad this feel`s," she said getting a few bit`s ready for Billy.

"I might just go to bed",

"When have you got hair`s to do ", Mandy asking not envying her.

"Tomorrow ", she answered, going as white as a sheet.

Mandy helping her upstairs`, saying she would lock up.

Maria looking so vulnerable under the cover`s Mandy asking if she could get her anything

before she left.

Shaking her head she half smiled at her and said "Thank you".

Mandy looking back at her thinking , hope this doesn`t run in the family.

Maria dosed for the rest of the afternoon, glad of the peace and quite.

Mark arriving back, a few hour`s later ,helping the spider get her shopping in from the car.

Sean watching saying to Clark, "I would keep an eye on them two".

Clark watching thinking your not wrong there, as he watched the spider bringing in bags, as she purred at him.

Looking at the lad`s she asked "Coffee boy`s."

"I wouldn`t mind a cup of tea, Mrs P please" Clark answered.

"Coming right up" she smiled as she swayed her skinny bum their way.

"Be the lord God she think`s her shit doesn`t stink" said Sean as he watched go into the house.

Adding "I would not touch it with a forty foot pole".

"You can see now why I declined" said Clark as he watched the two of them going into the

house.

Clark and Sean carried on working, "What is Maria like?"Sean asking just out of curiosity.

Clark looking at him replied "She is a top girl too good for him."

"You don`t think much of him then, "said Sean.

"Went too school with him, always` up his own arse, had to be the best at everything or else

he would sulk, and leaving school had to have the best".

"Oh I know the type, always have the best looking woman, on their arm a flash car

tossing the cash about".

Clark smiling at him giving him the thumb` s up "That`s the one".

"When did he marry Maria?"

"A couple of month`s ago"

"Well she will bring him down a peg or two" Sean said "Her being Irish"

"I doubt that she is totally smitten, she adore` s him I have seen it. "

"Look we all get a mist over our eye`s sometime` s, but given time ,it lift`s and that`s when

we pull the curtains back and we can see the wood for the tree`s" Sean answered as he passed Clark the last piece of guttering.

Mark arriving out of the house unloading some material`s, putting it down looking at the

lad`s ,

"Well that`s it for today tomorrow we will get the rest of the guttering on and then we will be on to the next stable" he said looking pleased at how the job was going.

Travelling home that evening Sean asked Mark "Have you ever been to Ireland",

Shaking his head "No I haven`t but I would like to go one day see where my lovely wife

Originate` s from."

"But that won`t be for a while yet not until after the little one is born" he added.

"Oh your wife is pregnant?"said Sean.

"Yes and don`t I know about it," Mark sighed.

"Now don`t be like that, God I wouldn`t like to have a babby growing inside of me, with all

the ailment`s that goes with its, I actually feel sorry for women and all they go through".

 said Sean in his broad Irish brogue.
s
Clark totally agreed with him saying "Wise word`s" looking for a reaction from Mark.

He didn`t even bat an eye lid.s

Dropping the lad`s off.He headed home finding Maria in bed and Mandy there giving

Billy tea.

"Hi Mark " greeted Mandy.

"Maria was having a really bad day today so I took over for her" she said smiling.s

Smiling he answered "She is lucky to have you, you're a sweetheart, I`m just going to nip out I`ll get us a takeaway, would you like something".

"I have got dinner ready at home " she smiled.

Looking in the kitchen Mandy seeing that Maria had everything prepared for their evening

meal,

She said to Mark "Maria has everything prepared I can finish it off if you want".

Hearing a noise behind them turning around to see a very pale looking Maria standing in the

doorway.

Mark going over saying "Is my baby girl not feeling well" he said as he kissed her.

Shaking her head she said "I have had a dreadful day".

Come on baby come and sit down, "Ill go and get us a takeaway."

Looking at him she smiled "That would be nice".

Mandy turning to them saying "I`ll not off tomorrow I`m at work sis, but afternoon, Ill pop in
and see how your doing."

Billy was in his P j` s all ready for bed, smiling hugging her sister saying "Thank you sis".

Smiling Mandy went home ,Mark leaving with her to get the takeaway.

Looking at Mandy he asked "How long did this go on when she was pregnant with Billy.

"Through the whole term, "she answered, "So your in for a rocky ride".

"Cheer`s" he smiled, walking to the takeaway thinking bloody hell another seven month`s of

misery to look forward to..

The following month`s got no better Maria having to stop work,

Mark working every hour God sent, which started getting up Maria `s nose , but if she

complained he would take her in his arm`s and reassuring her that he was doing it for them

to give them a better quality of life, and that he wanted them to be financially secure

As soon as possible.

He would then take her in his arm`s and make love to her telling her how important she was

to him and how much he loved her.

The summer months Maria found the worst it was a scorching hot, and she would just

Sit inside the cool, counting the week`s until it was time to bring her baby into the world.

Mark was hardly spending any time at home, as he was so busy at work.

When he did, he ran around Maria , making sure she wasn`t too hot ,buying her a fan.

Billy`s third birthday arrived, again no contact from Antony, which in a way disappointed her as he was his son.

Maria had 15 week's more to go before the birth. Time now dragging,

Billy started nursery in the September, in the morning's for 4 hour's.

She found this a great help because when he got home he would need a nap, so it took some

of the pressure off having to entertain him.Normally she enjoyed the time but being so ill, it

had not being easy.

Mark when he was there doing his best, but with the work he had on, so she

spent most of the time on her own or just her and Billy ,Mandy popped in most evening's and

Angie for her daily gossip.

She didn't even have to cook for Mark as he was eating out most evening's .

This Mrs Porter he was working for having a lot of contact's in the building trade, so two or

three evening's a week he didn't get home until late.

Unknown to Maria he was having an evening at the casino, once or twice

A week. And as Mrs Porter enjoyed a little gamble and did most of the paying for the

evening out.

Well it beat going home to moaning every evening. So Mark was spending a lot of time with

the Spider.

Mark looking at it as a way to pass the time, before Maria had the baby and they could get

back to normal. They had not had sex in week's because anytime he touched her she was

either uncomfortable or had just been sick and not finding this a turn on, he would give her a
cuddle and get some kip in, as between work his visit's to the casino.

And he did need sleep.

As the week's went on he was spending more and more money at the casino, thinking as he

went along, that once the baby was born he would pack it all in.

He drove Lisa home after the casino as he drove either the Porsche or Ferrari there.

Getting back one evening his car would not start, she offered for him to stay the night , in

spare room of course she added, purring.

The following day was Saturday so the would not be working, as Lisa gave Clark and Sean

the taxi fair home when they were going to a "meeting".

Looking at her the tiny beady eye`s as she had a few drink`s when the got to the casino.

Declining he answered, "Thank you for the kind offer but as you know my wife is pregnant

and I get little enough time with her as it is."

"Fine "she answered snarling, "Go on back to the pregnant Irish pig."

Totally shocked with her reaction, he didn`t not want to upset the spider as there was more to
the job than work.

He had the perk`s of driving her car`s spending her money at the casino, dinner`s and been

made feel like a king which wasn`t very often that happened, and especially in the last eight

month`s he felt like an outsider in his own home .With Mandy and Angie buzzing around

Maria as if she was a china doll.

And then him getting the brunt of it, having to put up with the narky comments about how

little time he was spending with her, when all the time he was trying to do the best for them.

And being expected to look after Billy when she was not up to it.

He didn`t think married life was going to be a bed of rose`s but he didn`t thing it was going to
be like school having to account for all your action`s.

The spider spitting feather`s, looking at her with the puppy dog eye`s that always` s

seemed to work on women.

Cuddling him she begged him not to go, looking at the time he answered ,

"Just let me ring Maria",

Nodding getting her hope`s up, she said I`m just jumping in the shower.

Phoning home telling Maria that the car had broken down and that Mrs Porter had kindly

offered to put him up for the night, that she would take him to the garage, in the morning and
he would be straight home.

Maria not feeling very happy about the situation then remembering his description of her agreed.

Having had a hard day the baby kicking her, feeling sick again Billy playing up, looking at the time she thought I'll just go to bed.

Back at the barn thing's were heating up , Mark having hung up saying "I love you" to his wife.

Turning around to see the spider standing in a towel two matchstick's leg's sticking out from underneath. .

The face that was normally caked in make up was now naked, emphasizing the pot mark's on her skin which looked scaly.

Looking at her he could feeling the hair's stand on his arm's.

Taking a bottle of brandy from the cupboard, asking if he fancied one.

Nodding he thought he had to have something to take the edge off of this situation.

Taking out the Waterford crystal glasses pouring them a large one each.

Looking at him with her beaded like eye's, scaly pot marked skin, he downed the drink in one.

Pouring him another, he necked it straight down after the other.

Not been used to alcohol, it went straight to his head, the following morning he awoke with the spider beside him, snoring her scaly pot marked head off.

His head pounding he had absolutely no reconciliation of the evening before or how he got into Lisa's bed.

Climbing out of the bed heading for the shower, feeling sick, finding a spare toothbrush, brushing his teeth, he was sick in the sink.

Turning around seeing the matchstick's climbing out of bed, naked made him feel worse.

Looking at him through the slit beaded eye's and the scaled skin,

Grabbing him from behind saying "Who was a naughty boy last night?"

Pushing her away saying "I have to go".

Not liking this action she said, "Don`t push me out of the way , like a bit of rubbish."

Looking down at her thinking your old enough to be my mother, thinking what the hell have I done.

Then thinking of his beautiful wife at home not far away from giving birth to his child.

He cringed inside , not something he done very often.

Lisa did not have time for anybody unless she was the centre of attention.

Going towards him, smiling she said "You don`t have to feel guilty, nothing happened"

"Not that I said no, but your head hit the pillow and you were zonked".

The relief written all over his face, she looked disappointed.

Not wanting to spoil their working relationship, he apologized for been so harsh,

Just remembering that his car was outside broken down.

He said "I`ll have to call the A.A."

"Why don`t you, take my car and go back and see her and while your gone I`ll call the

A.A.so when you pop back it will be all done for you" she smiled.

He couldn`t resist the thought`s of driving the Ferrari home and parking it outside.

"Are you sure" he smiled.

Pulling her silk dressing gown around her , "Of course Mark anyway I can help , you know

that."she smiled thinking by the time he came back she would have some supper ready and

made herself look good and then they might be able to finish what she had started.

Passing him the key`s smiling saying "See you later baby". smacking his bum on the

way out.

Waving good bye seeing the beady eye`s luring at him.

When he was gone calling one of the catering company`s that

she often used, ordering dinner for 5.oopm.looking at the clock it was now 10.00am.

Grabbing the bottle of brandy, pouring herself a large one she thought she had time for a
s

Siesta before he came back ,looking at the bottle seeing their was only a dribble left in it.pouring the rest in her glass. Setting the alarm she snuggled under the cover`s, and was soon sleeping.
CLINK
Pulling up out side their house, seeing Angie flicking her curtain`s he waved.

Opening her door looking out she said "Bloody hell Mark your coming up in the world.

Grinning he replied "Wish it was mine"

"Who`s is it" Angie asked being her usual nosy self.

"It`s Mrs Potter`s the woman I`m working for".

"Why have you got it?"

"Mine broke down" he smiled.

Going inside Maria and Billy were still sleeping upstairs.

Making a cuppa thinking about the previous evenings, stirring the tea bag in the cup.

Now he new why he didn`t drink.

Hearing stirring coming from upstairs.

Putting a tea bag in the other cup for Maria.

She came in with Billy by the hand, looking really tired and pregnant

"Hi darling , sorry I didn`t get home last night, "he said hugging her.

Hugging him smiling she saying "Just don`t make a habit of it".

Seeing the Ferrari, parked outside she asked "Where`s our car?"

"Mrs Porter kindly lent it to me , because the A.A. couldn`t get out until this afternoon."

"And I didn`t want to leave my baby girl on her own for much longer", he said hugging her.

"That was kind of her, thought you were taking it to the garage? ".

"It was but Mrs Potter lent me her A. A. card, save me a bit of money " he said .

"Here baby I`have just made this for you" he said passing her the tea.

"Thank you darling ", she said taking Billy`s breakfast cereal down.

"Fancy a drive in it" he asked.

"Not right now , I`ll see how I feel later".

Nodding he said "Ok baby I`m just going to catch up on some paper work".

Maria getting on with her day the best she could as she wasn`t feeling on top of the world.

Mandy popped around, What`s with the Ferrari outside " she asked picking Billy up.

Maria explained about the car breaking down and Mark staying the night at Mrs Potter`s.

Many raising her eye brow`s "What he stayed there".

Nodding Maria who was going to be sick again running upstairs.

Mark hearing her ,thinking Christ ,how long more of this did he have to endure this?

Leaving his make shift office, which was a corner of their bedroom, going to the

bathroom door calling "Are you ok darling?"

Maria waddling out water running out of her eye`s "I will be when this little one arrive` s".

"Would you like to go out to lunch today?" he asked.

Shaking her head she replied "Darling I haven`t even got the energy to get dressed."

"Ok " he smiled hugging her .

Going downstairs seeing Mandy there he said "Hi want a cuppa".

Nodding she smiled "Yes please.nice car"

Putting a tea bag in the cup he answered "Yes , wish it was mine".

"She must have a few bob," said Mandy.

Nodding "Yes she has " he said going into the living room, Billy started whinging because

nobody was paying attention to him.

Maria coming in picking him up asking "What`s the matter?"

Mandy looking at her sister said "Do you want me to take him around to mine for a bit?"

Maria nodding looking at gratefully, "Do you know I love you."

Smiling Mandy said "I`m only doing this so that when it`s my turn you can do the same for me" she laughed.

"That goes without saying" ,she answered giving her sister a hug.

"Right I`ll get on with my paper work", smiled Mark glad that Billy was going out.

"When is the car going back" Maria asked.

"Oh I`ll pop it back this afternoon, so I`m all yours "he said putting his arm`s around Maria,

Saying "Bloody hell woman your growing ", turning she gave him a playful slap saying

"I am with child".

Mandy picking up Billy said "Right we will see you later, say good bye to mummy".

Waving his hand he said "Bye bye mummy". Maria hugging him and kissing him saying,

"You be a good boy , see you later".

Maria closing the door after them ,looking at Mark said "Darling I need to go back to bed".

"You go baby ,I`m going to go into Watford pick up some material`s and then I`ll go on to

Mrs Potters and pick up the car, You go and rest and I`ll see you later." He said giving her a

big cuddle.

Looking at him she said "I`m so lucky to have you".

Smiling down at her he answered "You will always have me, how many more week`s is it ",

asked feeling her tummy .

"Three more and our baby will be here", she said smiling.

Taking her by the hand he brought her upstairs lying beside her until she fell asleep.

Feeling better than he had done earlier, he went and had another quick shower, thinking of

the narrow escape he had had the evening before.

Shuddering at the thought of what could of happened, he put on his new jeans and shirt and

headed to the casino.

Pulling in in the Ferrari, a few people turned to have a look.

Getting out he stared at them, dangling the key`s walking toward` s the casino hearing

someone call his name .Looking he saw a guy he barley recognized walking toward` s him.

Seeing the vacant look on Mark`s face, he said it`s me Ronald, Ronald Barker you did an

extension for me about a year ago.

Remembering him putting his hand out, asking how he was.

"I`m good, nice wheel`s " Ronald said, nodding at the Ferrari as they walked toward` s the

Casino.

"Thank` s " Mark replied.

Christ he loved this feeling , thinking of what Maria always said, money can`t buy you the

important thing`s in life well he knew different.

          Back at the barn Lisa woke up remembering her hot date that afternoon,

rolling out if bed she jumped in the shower opening her wardrobe, wondering what to wear,

opening her drawers she took out a black laced designer bra and matching knickers, putting

them on she looked down at her shrinking, sagging boobs what was left of them, wishing the
were more of them and that they were upright and firm.

Staring at her reflection, her hip bones sticking out her rib cage showing, her neck looking

like a turkey`s throat. That was why she always wore turtle neck`s,

But today she decided on a little black, skimpy dress that she thought might do the trick at

luring Mark into bed.

Drying her short cut hair filling the cracks in, spraying some of her expensive perfume on,

giving a tiny twirl, she went downstairs waiting for her prey.

          Going to the tables , he played the afternoon away loosing a lot

of money on his way.

Not a happy bunny as he got in the Ferrari, putting the music on and heading towards the

barn.

Getting there he parked up and went to start his car but to no avail.

Really pissed off he went and knocked on the spiders door, opening it with a smiley grin on her face she said "You weren't long".

Looking at her, he guessed what she was anticipating.

"Did you ring the A.A." he asked rather impatiently.

Shaking her head "No I forgot" she giggled,

Not at all impressed looking at her asking If it was alright to use her phone, he asked.

Not liking his attitude, she winged "What's the big hurry," going toward 's him putting her arm's around him.

Undoing himself from her he answered, "Maria isn't very well and I need to get home to her"

"Oh come off it , it's not her first pregnancy , she's a dab hand at it, she doesn't need baby sitting."she answered sharply.

Sighing looking around at what she had wondering why hadn't he got this .

Having seen this look a thousand time's before, from many a conquest, she had conquered.

Thinking yes, he like's the bait.

"Oh come here I know what you could do with" she grinned, removing his shirt.

"A nice massage ", she purred.

Giving in he let her lead him upstairs.

He removed his jean's and his leg's which was very pleasant to the eye.

She started by putting some oil on him, massaging it into his thighs and the lower part of his legs,

Much to his surprise he could feel himself stir, then thinking he had been a long time since he had had sex no wonder the old boy was reacting.

Turning over and to her delight, seeing his erection gently removing his underwear.

Putting her mouth over it she started licking it as soon as she did this he ejaculated.

Pulling himself up feeling totally embarrassed,

Smiling lying beside him , looking at him "Haven`t had it for a while?"

Nodding he answered "Can`t remember the last time".

Removing her dress, exposing her expensive black underwear, taking his hand and guiding it towards her special spot, she started rubbing herself with his hand.

Closing his eye`s pretending in his mind that this was his wife he was soon back in form.

They spent the rest of the evening upstairs.

Maria waking up , looking at the time calling Mark`s name,

Getting no reply she wandered downstairs and then remembering that he was gone to

Watford to pick up their car.

The phone ringing it was Mandy saying she would be bringing Billy back soon.

Mandy arriving not long after this with Billy, asking how she was feeling.

Then noticing Mark was missing asking where he was?

Looking really pale she answered, "Oh he is gone to Watford, he had to pick up some

material`` s" she said trying to smile.

"When did he go ?"she asked.

"Well he came and lay down on the bed with me after you left, he left not long after" she

yawned.

"Are you ok if I go?"Mandy asked looking concerned, she didn`t think Maria was coping

very well, and she wasn`t looking great.

"You go on I`m fine" she answered.

"Na I`ll stay until Mark come`s back Don is gone to badminton anyway",

There was a knock and Angie walked in.

"Hello , Christ did you see the car Mark was driving", she said

"Yes " they both answered at once laughing.

"Where is he", was her next question.

"He is gone to leave the car back" Mandy said.

Back at the barn, The spider laying body stretched out on the bed, in the aftermath with a sense of elation, knew this little fly, had strayed into her web .

It had been worth the wait.

.Mark in the bathroom. sweat pouring down his forehead, started to tremble, the vision of what had just happened, seemed unreal.

Jumping in the shower started to scrub himself, thinking this must be how someone feel`s after they have been raped.

He walked back into the bedroom looking at the ancient miniature sagging udders flopped out in full view.Taking in the pot holed scaly face and the skinny chicken like leg`s!"

Thinking what the fuck have I done.

Turning to him, playing her final card!

"Darling I thing you have married below yourself ,your meant were for bigger and better

thing`s?"
CLINK
She said in her purring voice.

Looking at her questioningly, "What do you mean.?"

"Look darling I have a proposition, next weekend I have all my business associates arriving

for our annual meeting, and I would really like to introduce you to them, "she purred flicking the chicken like leg`s in the air, with their red painted toe nail`s and a tiny diamond ring on

the big toe..

His ear`s picking up immediately, sitting on the end of the bed he smiled,

"I`m listening darling"

Filling him in on the meeting ,who was going to be there, where it was being held.

Looking at him saying `"You could have what I have got, and more, lot`s more, the world is

your oyster Mark!."

This was music to his ear`s, looking at her through totally different eye`s, all of a sudden the

pot hole`s on her face seemed to disappear, the scale tuned to a silk gloss , and she looked

very ,very appealing.

Putting the chicken like legs, on the floor which didn`t look so bad in the dime light pulling

her black silk dressing gown around her, pouring herself a glass of champagne from the a

drink`s compartment beside the bedside cabinet offering him a glass.

Refusing graciously, looking at the clock, spotting him clock watching , this action

Pissing her off, thinking in her mind this fucking Irish wife has to be terminated.

Bending on her knee`s beside him she started to kiss him.

Kissing her back with his eye`s tightly closed.

Gently pulling away he said "Darling I have to go."

Sulkily she said "Do you have to."

Giving her the puppy dog look, he nodded looking regretful.

"Your life is going to change Mark and with my help I`m going to help make you a very

wealthy man, that my darling is where your destiny lays".

Sipping her champagne, purring she said "You know the small minded say money doesn`t matter,
and that it cannot buy you happiness do you know why that is?"

Pulling his jean`s on shaking his head , trying not to look at the chicken leg`s.

Smiling she said "Because they haven`t got any, and have no idea how to make money , there

out there in their nine to five job`s, or worse still on benefits bringing home a pittance, just

getting by , never knowing what the real world is all about.Where as you lover are hungry

very , very hungry, I can see it in your eye`s." She said finishing her drink and pouring

another

"And I can help fill that hunger pang, or quench your thirst" .

His mind taking another line of thought, not looking at the outside but falling for the inside.

Her mind her way of thinking , that was better than any smiling blond or red head pushing themselves on you.s

"So you go on back to your tiny life, with what prospects? Another whinging mouth to feed."

"You think about what I said and just make sure your there next Saturday 3 .00pm and then you will be able to fill your belly, see the way to fulfil all your dream`s," she purred.

Sowing the seed`s she smiled at him saying "Right you better go then The Irish tart is awaiting to deliver your sprog, I`ll see you Monday, oh and darling take the Ferrari, I`m sure you can think of something to tell The Wife, close the door on the way out" s

Looking at her seeing the power she had , he wanted that feeling.

Getting in the Ferrari, his mind in turbulence, starting the ignition he headed home.

Maria ,Mandy and Ange, were drinking tea discussing name`s for the baby when the phone rang.

Maria answering it ,it was Don looking for Mandy, passing her the phone.

Hearing Mandy say "Oh God are you ok?".

Turning to Maria and Ang she said "Don is at the hospital,"

"What`s happened", Maria asked.

"He has broken his wrist playing badminton", she answered tear`s in her eye`s, Mandy wasn`t very good at dealing with any kind of upset.

"Do you want me to take you to the hospital?" Ang asked.

Shaking her head "No Kevin is with him, he is going to be discharged soon I told him to come here" she said looking at Maria.

"Come here sis "Maria said holding her arms out, going into them she burst into tear`s.

The door went and Mark walked in, seeing Mandy in tear`s, putting his car key`s down.

Asking" What`s the matter?"

Maria looking at him said "Don has broken his wrist and he is at the hospital."

Mark taking control of the situation said "Do you need to get to the hospital?"

Mandy still crying Shaking her head, "No his friend Kev, is bringing him back".

With that Don walked through the door, Mandy seeing him ran to him "Oh Don I was so worried about you".

Smiling he said "I`m fine. "

"Well you don`t look fine, "said Mark.

"I`ll be out of action for six week`s apart from that I`ll live",

Mandy gasped "Out of work for six week`s what are we going to do?, the rent is due tomorrow."

Mark coming to the rescue, said don`t worry "I can tide you over for a bit".

Maria looking at him with a smile on her face thinking, I love you he was one of the kindest men she had ever met in her life. Always there to help.

Mandy looking at him Mark all of a sudden turning from her sister`s adoring husband into her hero.

Don said "I can`t let you do that ,we have a bit of saving`s ,we will be ok."

Mandy looking at him asking "What saving `s you spent it on your badminton fee for signing up and your racket, the short`s and top`s the shoe`s, that you insisted on having" she Answered.

Looking at him whispering "Idiot".

Mark stepping in saying "Look we`re family , and I insist".

Maria her heart filling up with pride, standing beside Mark smiling said,

"You heard the man we`re family" she said looking at her Mark adoringly.

Mark kissing her on top of the head smiling saying "I`m starving shall I get us a takeaway?"

Mandy said "Yes and we will pay for it ".

"Absolutely not, you need to save the pennies" he smiled.

Going over to him hugging him saying "You're the best brother in law anybody could ask for".

Laughing he replied "I wouldn`t go that far".

Watching Maria looking at him thinking how much she loved him.

Billy started whinging again ,Maria asking what`s the matter, sitting him beside her. ,

Cuddling up to her smiling, she hugged him as she felt her other little one move inside of her.

Looking around her ,she had never felt happier, she had everything.

Getting Billy to bed ,after Mandy and Don saying a thousand thank you `s to Mark before they left.

Maria sitting beside him on the couch , having a cuddle, looking at him saying "I love you so much and I`m so proud of you", she smiled, taking his hand putting it on her tummy as she felt their baby kick asking ,

"Did you feel that?"

Nodding at her kissing her he said "Yes my darling I did".

"Not long more to wait", she said looking adoringly at him.

Turning her toward` s him he kissed her and as she responded he gently took her by the hand and lead her upstairs, laying her on the bed, taking her clothe` s off , kissing her and make love to her.

Laying in his arm`s , she looked at him and said "Darling I don`t ever want this magic to go".

Stroking her hair he whispered "I`m not going anywhere, were together forever and longer".

Looking at him she believed every word and soon was sleeping in his arm`s
                    Monday morning arriving Maria getting Billy off to school was feeling a lot better, so she went and did a bit of shopping, the weather a lot cooler and she was glad.

Mark picking Clark and Sean up, heading to Watford, the lad`s seeing him driving the Ferrari.

Clark nudging Sean saying "I wonder how he paid for that privilege."

Sean looking at him asking "What".

Clark shaking his head laughing, got in the car "Morning " said Mark.

"Morning " said Sean, "Did you have a good weekend?"

"Not really," replied Mark "The bloody car broke down, Maria isn`t feeling a 100%"

"Now look you don`t have to tell me about women being pregnant, when my Betty was carrying , she was sick for the whole nine month`s, and to be honest with you I wished I could have helped but what can you do " he said in his Irish brogue.

Sighing Mark replied "Well there is just under Three week`s and then we can back to normal living."

"God but it`s worth it , when you see that little babby and you think I helped make that, there is nothing in the world compared to that feeling, I don`t care what anyone say`s"

Clark watching Mark closely seeing nothing, no reaction at all, smirked and patting him on the shoulder saying "Not long and you will be feeling like that".

No comment.

Pulling into the barn Clark waving as the spider opened the door, Coming out going over to the car saying to Mark that the A.A. should be here shortly.

"Thank` s for that" he answered smiling, thinking shit he was hoping she was going to let him keep it ,but no such luck. Well not keep but a long term lend?

Seeing the disappointed look, she smiled to herself , thinking a little more ammunition she had to fire in the game.

Smiling at him as the A.A. pulled in, putting her hand out for the key`s to the Ferrari.

Reluctantly passing then over, "Fancy a cuppa she asked?".

Feeling rather pissed off, he nodded and said "I`ll be in as soon as I get the lad`s set up."

Looking at Clark and Sean asking if they would like a tea,

Clark smiling giving her the thumb`s up,

She went into the house, minute`s later returning with the hot drink`s.

"Your` s is inside," she said rather shortly.

Going into the house she collard him in the hall and kissing him passionately,

Taken by surprise by her aloofness earlier, he responded.s

Smiling she said "Let`s take this upstairs`".

Reluctantly he followed her upstairs knowing that the lad`s were only outside.

Feeling a bit uneasy, Looking at her he asked "Don`t you think were taking a bit of a risk?".

Looking at him saying "Look darling life is a bit of a risk" she loved playing with fire.

 Pulling him on the bed "It`s like I said, you married beneath yourself, your meant  for bigger and better thing`s".

Afterwards she lay beside him panting, he got off the bed and getting dressed she said

"Don`t forget the meeting on Saturday."

"This could change your life, never having to worry about money again , the ball is in your

court and it is up to you to snap the opportunity",

"You know the score Maria is due in just under three week`s, I can`t just up and leave and

I`m the one that wanted this baby, " he sighed wandering around the room.

Sprawling on the bed the chicken leg`s waving in the air, saying "Well it`s is totally your

choice."she smirked so confident , that she had snared him.

Thinking she is right sitting on the bed, looking at her she could see he needed some

prompting.

"Look Mark you have two choice`s, you either stay in your miniature world, with the Irish

earth mother, and her illegitimate child and her soon to be legitimate child, or you take the

world that you know is there, waiting to grab you, you see life is very simple it is people that complicate it, you see what you want and you go after it letting nothing stand in the way." she said simple.

Nodding he agreed, knowing the world he wanted to live in.finding it very difficult to make this choice , her seeing the hesitation , getting off the bed , saying "Look Mark I know your torn at the moment , but if you want to fulfil your dreams, you need to make the right choice, for you now", she said.
ANG
Thinking of his wife as she had cuddled up to him last night, trusting and believing every word he had said to her, and the buzz he had felt when she had put his hand on her tummy feeling his unborn child kicking .

"If it is the child your concerned about leaving you could always go for custody" the spider suggested.

Looking at her thinking out loud he answered "What , and how am I supposed to look after a new born and work , your encouraging me to, get my business off the ground, and in the next breath your saying for me to take my baby from it`s mother, I have got no idea about Babies."shaking his head in confusion.

Shrugging she answered "Well I was just thinking out loud, and you have to remember, that I don`t work and I would love to help you, so if it`s the baby that is worrying you, well there is your answer."

A thousand`s thought `s running through his head, she was complicating this more than he needed.

"What are you saying that the baby and I could move in here?"

"Why not I have seen the pit , that you live in, drove by it the other day and I think the baby would have a much better opportunity, of having a comfortable life here with us."

"Have you really thought about this ?"he asked.

"Darling I have thought about nothing else since I spotted the hunger in your eye`s."

Knowing she was planting huge seed`s that she was hoping would grow and materialize

."I`ll tell you what you take the Ferrari and hold on to it for a while , get the feel of it "she

said smiling .Dangling another carrot in front of him.

"Whoop`s I nearly forgot I bought you a little present", leaning over the chicken leg`s

swinging high in the air, pulling a box out of the bedside cupboard.

Passing it to him, he opened it seeing a Gold Rolex watched laying inside, he gasped.

Smiling he said "It`s is beautiful, I have always wanted one" bending down to kiss her.

Laying there she purring, she said "That is just a taster of what you could have."

Clark knocking the door , made them both jump, Getting up ,running downstairs, opening

the door .

Clark standing there said "We need a hand with the guttering ,"

"I`ll be there in a tick , just helping Mrs Potter get something out of the loft" he answered.

Clark walking away thinking "I bet you are", with a smirk on his face.

"Is he coming " Sean shouted trying his hardest to hold on to a piece of guttering.

Looking behind Mark running toward` s them.

"I`m here" he shouted.

"Fucking hell boss thought I was going to do my back in there".

The spider poking her face out through the door asking if the boy`s would like another hot
drink

Both of them giving her the thumb`s up, she wandered back inside.

The day finally finishing ,Mark going into the spider`s asking "Is it ok to take the car".

Smiling at him as she stood, with a look of control about her.

"Of course, I never say a thing I don`t mean" she purred.

On the way home Mark stopped at the garage coming out with a bouquet of flowers.

"Guilty consciousness" smirked Clark as he got in the car.

Turning around he said "What, did you say?"

"Nothing just wondering what`s with the flower`s,"

"Because my wife is carrying my baby and she hasn`t been feeling very well, not that it is any of your business."he replied sharply.

sssssse
"Now I think that is a lovely gesture, it show`s her your thinking about her "said Sean dryly.

Letting the lad`s out at the pub, Sean turning saying "See you in the morning boss".

Nodding ,he drove away,

Sean turning to Clark asking "What the fuck is between you and him?"

"Nothing " said Clark "Fancy a pint?"

"Yes might as well see were home a bit earlier, Betty will think I`m still at work".

"She has you right under the thumb" said Clark smiling.S

"She has not, but you have to have a bit of respect for your wife ,feeling`s and all that", he answered in that Irish brogue of his which always made Clark smile.

Mark arrived home to Maria in the kitchen cooking dinner doing steak and chip`s his favourite.The aroma hitting him when he opened the door.

Hearing the door ,calling "Hi darling, dinner is nearly ready."

Walking in it was lovely seeing her with a smile on her face, instead of lying in the couch looking pale and ill.

Putting the flower`s on the table he went over taking her in his arm`s kissing her saying

"Cor you look and smell lovely", kissing her neck, he added "Good enough to eat"

Billy was sitting on the kitchen floor playing with his toys.

"Mark " he said holding up a lorry to him.

Bending down he said," Have you been a good boy for your mummy today"

Nodding his head with his baseball hat on his head, which Maria had bought for him earlier and was now refusing to remove.

He looked at Mark and said "Yes I have been a good boy".

Maria smiling at the two of them feeling good that day, she hugged him saying "I Love you".

Looking into the brown eye`s that were shinning at him like a stars shine`s bright at night.

Billy grabbing his jeans , he picked him up and giving him a hug ,said "Let`s set the table

for mummy."

Putting him down ,getting the cutlery out he went into the dinning room and set the table.

All of a sudden, it dawned on him what he was doing ,playing with fire.

And who was going to get burned, looking over his shoulder at Maria who was chatting to

Billy, and dishing up dinner.s

Then his line of thought, strayed to the spider and what she was offering, and how often in a

lifetime did you get an opportunity like that.

At the end of the day you only have one go in this world, so what path was he going to

Travel. That was the question???

His head in tatters, he couldn`t really see which direction to steer the ship, taking the

flower`s from the table bringing them out into the kitchen , Maria smiling "Oh darling their

are lovely" she said taking them from him, and putting them in water.

Spending the rest of the evening the two of them cuddled up together Maria nattering on

about name`s.

His mind thinking of the Rolex she had given him today, and the Ferrari outside, and all the

other thing`s that his heart desired.

NEW CHAPTER

The rest of the week Maria was feeling on top of the world ,the sickness had

subsided and the weather was cool which helped.

Mandy popping in every evening after work just to make sure Maria was ok.

Mark handing Maria a cheque to give to Mandy, looking at it seeing it was made out for

£600.

"Can we afford this", she asked frowning.

Taking her in his arm`s "Of course we can. The lodger`s rent is due end of this week, and you look after the mortgage and bill`s with that, and what I give you so don`t worry we are fine.

Sometime` s she wandered where the money came from , as there was takeaway`s almost

every evening for the past seven month`s, as she had been to ill to cook.

 Mark was always buying clothe` s,  he always` s left a spare fifty in a jug in the

kitchen for the in case she needed anything.

But then as he said she always looked after the bill`s

So she didn`t question his movement`s on money, as she knew he didn`t like to be

Scrutinised.

Friday evening arrived and Mandy popped in , Maria handing her the cheque, her eye`s

lighting up when she saw the amount.

"Oh Maria tell him thank you, this should tie us over until Don get`s back to work, he is

legend ,"she smiled.

Billy still wearing his baseball cap, Mandy laughing when Maria told her he wears it to bed.

Maria turning to put water in the kettle, suddenly bent over the sink with a sudden gripping

pain.

Mandy seeing her sister bending over ran to her "What`s the matter?"

Maria tear`s streaming down her face with the sudden pain, yelling in panic ,

"I think I have started" .

Mandy looking at her in disbelieve, "You can`t be , your not due for another two week`s"

Maria sitting as the contraction subsided, "Christ Mandy that was a contraction, and a real

one , I remember from Billy".

The door opened and Angie walked in, seeing Maria , Mandy looking at her saying "She think`s she has started"

Maria now standing feeling perfectly ok " No I might be wrong just panicking".

"Whew, thank God for that", said Mandy.

"Well" Angie said "It could have been we`ll stay for a bit just to make sure your ok".

Mandy offering to bath Billy, shaking his head he said "No I want my mummy to do it."

Maria smiling at him said to Mandy "You go and run it" hugging him "Ok mummy will

bath you".

They phone going it was her Ma," Mandy answering it blurting out that Maria might have

Started.

.Hanging up Maria turning to her annoyed.

"For fuck`s Mandy what did you do that for I`m fine, she will be on telephone every five

minutes "

Mandy knowing what her Ma was like biting her bottom lip saying "Sorry."

Maria raising her eye`s to up heaven, "Oh don`t worry it is done now".

"I`ll just go and bath Billy ", she said getting him upstairs and putting him into his fish P.J`s

Bringing back downstairs` Billy laying on the floor with his lorry.

Am hour later Maria got another contraction, which lasted a bit longer than the first,

Angie saying that she thought she had started, but it would be a while yet in her reckoning,

Laughing Mandy said "So you're a midwife now".

They laughed at the expression on Angie ` face as she tried to explain .

Maria said " I`ll just time them, getting a pad and paper so she could write the time`s

Down."

An hour later Mark walked through the door, thinking of the

meeting tomorrow to see Mandy and Angie with the clock on the table and pen and paper.

"What`s all this " he smiled.

"Maria think`s she is going into labour", Mandy blurted out , this time she without receiving a scolding from Maria, because she was getting another contraction.s

Looking at Mark putting his key`s on the table going to her, asking should he call the Midwife?

Breathing the pain away, shaking her head, panting she said "No it`s too early."

Mandy looking at the pad, saying the last one was an hour ago.

"We`ll wait until there about fifteen minute`s apart.then we will call her".

Mark said "Ok darling ", giving her a cuddle.

Mandy suggesting that she take Billy , for the night,

Maria agreeing that is a good idea, Angie saying she was going next door but if they needed anything knock. ss

Mark reassuring her he would let her know of any development` s. she left.

Mandy gathering Billy`s thing`s together, telling him he was going in an adventure.

Maria getting emotional ,tear`s in her eye`s telling Billy to be a good boy, said to Mandy .

"Thank you sis, don`t know what I`d have done without you" hugging her .

Mandy hugging her back whispered "I Love you, and you`ll be fine."

They left.

Maria smiling at Mark saying "It might be a long night,"

Putting his arm`s around her reassuring her he will be with her every step of the way.

Kissing him she said "I know" , and she had never been so sure of anything in her life.

The contraction`s going into to slow mode, were few and far between, scattered, looking at Mark who looked exhausted, saying "You should go to bed out darling I`ll call you if anything happen` s," she said.

"You come with me " he smiled.

"Ok " she nodded .

Getting into bed , he was sleeping as soon as his head hit the pillow.

Maria laying beside him looking at the long eye lashes smiling at him kissing him on the cheek, snuggling down beside him.

Not long before she felt another contraction coming on.

Getting out of bed so as not to disturb, her hubby, going downstairs she spending the night pacing up and down, by 6.00am she thought she better call Mark as the contraction's were coming every 20 min's.

Going into the bedroom calling his name , he awoke .

"What's the matter" he whispered.

"It's time to call the midwife ," she said .

Jumping out of bed, pulling his jean's on running downstairs ringing the midwife.

Maria knowing the drill went and had a bath, shaving herself, having packed what she knew she would need.

The midwife arriving , examining her nodding saying "Yes sweetheart it is time to go to the hospital".

Mark behind her thinking it's the fucking meeting today.why couldn't it have waited for another day how inconvenient, what the fuck am I going to do.

"How long do you think it will be "he asked hoping to hear maybe the next day.

No such luck, The midwife reckoned it would be later that afternoon.

Smiling at Maria he asked "Did you here that,"

Nodding the pain in her face, telling the story.

Getting to the hospital an hour later , Maria had asked for the epidural, the midwife getting the injection and inserting it into Maria spine.

Mark was busy setting up his video equipment, as he intended filming the whole birth much to Maria's surprise as he hadn't discussed this with her.

The epidural taking effect immediately, she was sitting up in bed saying to Mark ,why she

didn`t have this with Billy it would have changed her whole outlook on childbirth.

The midwife kept monitoring her, and at 12.15pm she asked her to start pushing Maria

staring at Mark, she started pushing as he videoed it.

At 1.08pm Baby Tessie Mary was born into the world weighing 7lbs 14ozs, as she was put on her mum, tear`s of joy rolling down Maria`s face and as she looked at Mark who was still

videoing , staring down at her daughter, she opened her little eye`s Maria noticed she had one brown eye and one blue . Smiling at Mark she said look , putting the video to one side

walking over to her kissing her saying

"Well done darling".

The midwife was still at the end of the bed between Maria`s legs`,

Maria looking down saw her pressing a buzzer, panic setting in she asked "What was

happening ", the midwife taking the baby from her passing her to her Dad as Maria

watched, two men come in dressed in surgery uniform`s, taking her from the bed strapping

her to a trolley, crying she was shouting "What is happening ",

The midwife seeing the anxiety, telling her to be calm but they were taking her to theatre for

an emergency operation. Because her Placenta had stuck to her, uterus and it was very

dangerous. So they were taking her to remove it .

Looking back as she was wheeled out of the room to see Mark standing with baby Tessie in his arm`s looking totally bewildered, watching as his wife sobbing "Mark, Mark" was wheeled away.

Panic setting in asking the midwife what was happening?

The midwife explaining that her life was in danger explaining about the placenta, going into

shock he started shaking, the midwife taking the baby from him saying she was taking her to the nursery.

Still crying his name "Mark ,Mark "as she was wheeled into theater she didn`t remember a

single thing after this .

Mark standing frozen to the spot, the midwife taking the

baby saying that if he wanted to he could go to the waiting room he could wait for his wife There.

Looking at his watch it dawned on him thinking he could still get to the meeting, asking the midwife "How long she would be in theater," the midwife replying she had no idea.

Saying he was going home to get something to eat as he was hungry and he would be back later. Going outside lighting a cigarette, getting his car going to meet the spider for the meeting.

Looking down at his attire realizing that he was'nt dressed appropriately for the occasion.it was 2.00pm . Ringing the spider telling her what had happened and that he was on his way.

Reaching his destination finding the spider, pacing the living room, looking at him smiling "It`s a good job I took it upon myself to buy you this" she said holding a Grey suit up, with a pale blue shirt and navy tie. Smiling at her saying "You're a gem".

Not even mentioning his wife or the new born, they got in the car and headed to the meeting, feeling a bit out of his comfort zone, but soon began to relax as the spider introducing him to people of authority from all walk`s, this made his mind up that this was his destiny lay, as to what direction he wanted his life to go.

Drinking champagne and smoking cigar`s, he was feeling whole , knowing that this was what had been missing from his life.

The spider watching closely, thinking Yes the bait has been taken, eaten and devoured, she was beginning to relax, very happy with seed`s she had sown.
ANG
                          Three hour`s later Maria was taken back to the ward, the surgery being a success.

She was still sedated, when brought back to the ward, when she awoke later that night, totally confused as to her where about` s.

Crying out her husband`s name "Mark", the night staff hearing her, going over to her asking how she was feeling.

Tear`s running down her face, sobbing "Where`s my husband ?"

Mary the midwife`s name said "I believed he went home , he was hungry"

Asking how the pain was looking at her saying she was just uncomfortable.

Looking at the end of the bed seeing her baby girl laying there, she asked if she could

cuddle her?

Mary taking her daughter to Maria she held her in her arm`s looking at the tiny finger`s and

the perfection of what her and Mark had made.

Looking down at her whispering to her " Hello Tessie I`m your mummy, and you are

so beautiful, my baby girl, "kissing her on the head.

Back at the barn the spider and Mark having celebration drink`s

as to the success of the evening, Mark having made a huge impression on her associate`s.

Purring the spider saying "Darling I think you know where your destiny lay`s"

Sighing running his hand`s through his hair he said "I better go and see Maria and

my daughter ."

"Where the fuck do your priority`s lie, after the successful day we have just had ,what are

you thinking?"

Staring at her wondering if she had a heart, seeing the look ,changing her tactics

"I know it has been a very emotional day but look at the positive, you know now what your

capable of achieving and how to do it, so it is making your mind up time."
CLINK
"Is it a life of minimal prospects, with what`s her name and the sprog or is it going to be a

whole new chapter of life your going to choose" she asked opening a bottle of champagne.

The greed taking over, knowing that his wife was laying in a hospital bed, just after giving

birth and nearly loosing her life, he knew she had pulled through as he had phoned the

hospital unknown to the spider.

Knowing he had come to another crossroad's and wondering what direction to take when deep inside there had never been any question.

Passing him a glass of champagne, looking at her smiling, clicking his glass,

"To us" he toasted.

Purring lifting her glass up grinning she clinked "To us".

"What are you going to do about "Her,"

Knowing she was referring to Maria, shrugging he said "Not sure yet,"

"You will know, when it is time to fly, make sure it is sooner rather than later" she answered.

"In the mean time you just make sure, you contact those business acquaintance, and keep them sweet" .she said undoing the button's of his new shirt.

"And now I think you and I deserve a bit of fun," smiling down at her, unbuttoning her blouse ,seeing the cow udders poke out at him, closing his eye` s tightly, putting his mouth over them summing up all his courage to give them a nibble.

Maria and his new born daughter the last thing on his mind.

Maria having decided to breast feed baby Tessie, was sitting up putting her on her breast.

Tessie latching on immediately, as she looked at her daughter feeding whispering "Where is your Daddy?"

Looking at her baby she knew that this was her life totally complete, and there was nothing else she could ever ask for .

Smiling to herself, wondering what Billy would think when he saw his new sister.

Calling Mary ,the midwife went over to her.Asking if she could have a pain killer as her tummy was really hurting .

Looking at Tessie she said she would put her back in her crib as she had fallen asleep

"She latched on well", Mary said smiling at Maria.Giving her an injection, telling her to get some sleep.

Mary going back to the desk asked Sally, who had been on the day shift if there was a husband?.

Nodding signing herself out for the day, "Yes ,he was here for the birth and abandoned ship after she was taken to theater, hasn`t been seen since, Oh he did ring to see how the op went, see you in the morning."

Mary thinking that was big of him , this job really opened your eye`s as to what pig`s men really were, nothing surprised her.

Doing her night round noticed that Maria was still awake staring at her daughter sobbing into her pillow.

Mary going over whispering "Are you ok" so as not to disturb the other patients.

Looking at her Maria asking if her husband had been in, tears rolling down her face.

Shaking her head she said "No but he did call , now you get some sleep, you have been through a lot today and her ladyship will be wanting feeding soon , try and rest."

Closing her eye`s wandering where Mark was ,she slept.

She was awoken a few hour`s later by Mary to feed Tessie.

Feeling groggy, looking down at her tiny daughter as her little head went toward` s her Breast.

Kissing her head as she was feeding, thinking about Billy, her whole heart filled up with love and pride, then her thought`s wandered to Mark and she smiled thinking how proud he was going to be having a new daughter.

Thinking of his face as she was pushing their daughter into the world, as he had put the video aside to "Telling her well done".

And the pride in his voice, she knew how proud he was of her.

That had been a surprise him videoing it ,she did not want anyone to see her giving birth in all her glory, no thank you very much.

Looking at Tessie her heart filled with love for this little girl she had just brought into the

world,

Sleeping for a little while she could not wait until the morning when Mark would come and

pick them up.s

The next morning Mark`s phone ringing telling him his wife was being discharged

that afternoon leaving the spider sleeping ,heading home ,finding Mandy back with Billy,

Thinking fast smiling portraying the doting father, and adoring husband apologizing to
Mandy telling her that ,Maria had a baby girl yesterday and had to have an emergency op

early yesterday afternoon and he could not, phone her because after Maria had been taken to

theater, he had an emergency call out from Samaritans` and ended up staying with the client

all night as he was going to take his own life, saying this holding back the tear`s

Mandy turning saying, "Oh Mark, how do you cope your such a strong man"?

Sighing at her saying,"I was so torn ,but the nurses assured me that she was in the best of

hand`s and for me to do what I had to do once I explained. And I kept in contact with the

hospital through the night making sure Maria and the baby were ok."

s

Admiringly she hugged him and asked" When were they coming out.?"

"Today at one o clock" he answered.

Billy looking for a drink, Mandy bending down to him saying "You got a new baby sister".

Looking at her he started crying "I want my mummy"

Mark looking at him thinking Oh no not this drill again.

Playing the game he bent down to him and said "Mark is going to pick up mummy and your

new sister later"

Billy looking totally confused cried louder "I want my mummy.

"He know`s something is going on, normally when he come`s to mine he is good as gold, but last night he kept waking up looking for Maria."

Mark getting him a bag of jelly tot`s out of the cupboard " calmed him.

"Shall I stay here while you pick Maria and the baby up"

Smiling "Yes that would be great ,but I better bring Billy"he answered.

"I`m going to the shop to get some flower`s ",said Mandy.

Taking his wallet out handing her £40, he said get them out of this and get me 20 red roses.

"Oh she will love that "

Getting in the car Mark and Billy headed off to pick up, his Maria and his daughter.

The morning after Maria delivering Tessie, the nurse waking her .

Doctor arriving around very pleased with her recovery said "She could go home that

Afternoon, but she was to get plenty of rest".

Asking the nurse to ring her husband to tell him that she was going home that afternoon.

Mark and a very excited Billy walking into the ward, Billy seeing his mum running toward`s

Her calling "Mummy ,mummy" as she was standing with his sister in her arm`s.

A huge smile on Maria `s face as he approached her, Billy she smiled as she bent down to

introduce him to his sister.

Billy staring at the baby in Maria`s arm`s,he kissed her and said smiling at Maria,

"My sister" looking at Mark pointing.

Mark nodding at him, telling her how amazing she had been the day before, filling her in on

his "call out".

Apologizing repeatedly for not having been there the evening before.

Smiling she answered "It`s ok were all in one piece and I`m ok and so is Tessie".

"Tessie " he smiled.

Looking at him she said "If you remember we agreed if it was a boy ,you would name him ad

if it was a girl I had the privilege, so say hello to Tessie" she smiled.

Looking into the shining proud brown eye`s , he smiled saying "It suit`s her," kissing her on the cheek , taking his daugther in his arm`s kissing her and whispering "Hello baby Tessie", looking at Maria telling her how proud he was of her.

Putting his arm around her carrying his new daughter in her car seat, Billy holding onto Maria`s hand as if he was never going to let her out of his sight again.

Maria sitting with Billy in the back holding Tessie in her arm`s smiling at Billy as he held her hand and watched as she griped his finger.

Thinking he will always look out for his baby sister, as they grew up.

Getting home, Mandy the first to greet her sister and her new niece. Billy trying to tell her that she was his sister.

Maria smiling at the excitement , said to her sister "Let me introduce you to your niece, Tessie" as she passed the baby to her.

Mandy taking Tessie tear`s in her eye`s saying to Maria ,"She is so beautiful and perfect"

 Maria sitting looking at her two children ,Nodding smiling at her sister answered saying, "Yes she is".

Mark coming through with the roses,smiling at him, thinking she was going to burst with happiness.

Billy really scrutinized her , looking at her finger`s and trying to count them.

When Tessie cried he was shocked at the noise she made

.Smiling at Maria saying "She is loud mummy."

Mandy looking at Maria saying "When is the christening going to be, cause me Ma will be asking as soon as she hear`s the baby is born"

Mark looking over his shoulder, said "Christ she has just been born",

Mandy answering "Look Mark were Irish so the next thing is the christening".

Raising his eye`s up to heaven "Ok , but you live in England now."

Mandy smiling at him said "Yes but we are still Irish."

Maria feeding Tessie replied "I will need to ring Father Doyle, tomorrow and get a date".

Mandy asking Maria had she told her Ma ,shaking her head, "I have just given birth , give me a chance " she said laughing.

The phone ringing Mandy answering , turning laughing down the phone

"Yes Ma she had a little girl yesterday",

Passing the phone to Maria , she filled her in on the events of yesterday.

NEW CHAPTER

The following day`s Mandy spent as much time as possible with Maria, Billy and her new niece, having taken time off work , helping her get the christening sorted.

Mandy noticing that Maria was getting very snappy , when she questioned this Maria shrugged it off saying she was exhausted.

The date set for three week`s later, Mandy going back to work,

,Maria finding it hard with Billy who was insisting on helping, Tessie being a crier

Keeping her awake most of the night ,which was getting on Mark`s nerves because he needed sleep and went to work every day.

Maria would stay downstairs with Tessie so as not to disturb him.

Tiredness getting to Maria she became snappy to Mark, in the evening`s.

 Mark arriving home one evening Maria at her wit`s end, crying telling him she had to get some sleep and he would have to cut back on his work to try and help, because after all she was also his daughter.

Taking her in his arm`s, saying as soon as the had got the main part of the job out of the way he promised he would have some time off to help.

Tears of exhaustion running down her face she sobbed,

"Your not listening.I need help now".

Looking at her thinking, bloody hell your the mother, kissing her saying you go to bed and take Tessie with you and Ill sleep down here tonight .

Running his finger`s through his hair he said" Shit",looking at him ,

He picked up Tessie and taking her upstairs put the sleeping Tessie in her crib,

Cuddling her he said ,

"I just remembered I need to pick up some tools for work in the morning, won`t be long"he said kissing her as he watched her drift off.

Getting in the Ferrari he drove to see the spider.

Getting to the barn, Mark complaining to the spider, about Maria whinging in his ear all the time, she has organized the christening for three week`s time,  and she want`s him to spend more time at home.

The spider`s ears picking up , "I think the time has come for you to fly"

Mark thinking your not wrong there, her staring at the discontented face.

The spider tuning around smirking, saying ,"Why don`t you take a little time out for yourself and stay here for a few day`s"

Looking at her saying" That`s just what I need. A bit of space away from a crying baby , a whinging toddler and a moaning wife."

Going over to him putting her arm`s around him she said "You my darling need a bit of T.L.C. " kissing his neck.

This sending shivers down his spine,the hair standing up on the back of his neck,

 Staring at the udders, dangling under her blouse.

The spider noticing the effect she was having on him, taking him by the hand ,

" Saying come on baby I know you want me, I can see the effect I`m having on you" she purred.

Alarm bell`s ringing as she had totally misread the situation, but when need`s must , you

don`t kill the goose that lay`s the golden egg. Smirking to himself as he followed her upstairs.
 CLINK
Panting afterward`s she leaned over him purring, the chicken legs waving above him like

deflated balloons in the air

"So what`s this with the christening it`s a big Irish thing,isn`t it?"she said as pulled open her

her drink`s cabinet taking a bottle of brandy out pouring herself a large drink.

Shrugging he answered "It`s a load of garble,I`m not in the least bit religious if it was down

to me, it wouldn`t be happening," sss

 Purring she said "Your too soft you want to put your foot down "

"Well it is all organized,now " he shrugged.

Purring she said "I think you should get it out of the way and think about packing your bag`s

From the whole intolerable episode,that is stopping you from becoming the man you really

want to be " as she lay sipping her brandy, looking at the empty hungry space in his eye`s,

Nodding he said "Yes" pulling his jeans on.

Finishing her brandy he looked at her asking "Did you ever want children".

Seeing a far away look come into her eye`s nodding "Yes I did once,but that was a long time

ago,and as I said , if you wanted to bring Tessie with you there would not be a problem."

He was really having to think about this, saying "What`s the point ,I would never get custody

of Tessie, the law is always on the mother`s side."

The spider her eye`s shining answered "Not if you could prove the Irish tart to be unfit".

"How could I do that?" he asked, thinking do I really want to be saddled with a baby.s

Stretching her chicken leg`s out on the bed she asking,

"How do you think she will react it when you leave."

A wary look passed over his eye`s, answering "I know she is a very emotional woman and

family means a lot to her,I think it would end her world losing me".

"That is how we do it then" answered the spider.

Frowning at her "What do you mean?"

"Well you have just told me that she is a very emotional woman, at this moment in time her

hormones are all over the place, so is probably as vulnerable and weak as she will ever be

Leaving her, could just ignite a fire, that could just send her out of control" she smiled

Grinning back at her thinking , he could fulfill his dreams without losing anything.

By gaining , a luxury home any amount of money that could accomplish whatever he

wanted.

Thousand`s of thought`s running through his mind, none of them for his wife.

Returning home going upstairs finding Tessie,crying and Maria dead to

the world.

Picking his daughter up ,waking Maria to feed her saying crossly,

"Didn`t you hear Tessie cry?"

Maria awaking bag`s under her eye`s from exhaustion,said

"I thought you were downstairs, and don`t use that tone of voice with me" nearly in tear`s.

Handing her the baby, putting her on her breast to feed.

"I told you, I had to pop out you never seem to listen these day`s" he snapped.

A tear slowly ran down her cheek s
ANG
Staring at him, she sobbed "I have had no sleep for nearly two week`s, I have just given birth

and nearly died in the process,I have had no help from you if it had not been for Mandy I

don`t know what I would have done"

Staring at her in total disbelieve he replied sharply,

"I am the one who keep`s this family together financially, I have to work ,keeping our head`s

above board, what is it you want from me blood"he snarled.

Sobbing as they never rowed,holding her arms out to him, he dismissed this action.

Leaving the room, "I`m going to get some sleep".he said coldly.

Tessie sucking on her breast as tear`s of dismay flowed down her face.

Billy came wandering into the room, as the noise had disturbed him.

Seeing his mummy crying , he ran to her asking "What`s wrong mummy"

Pulling back the quilt so he could get in beside them.

Smiling she said"Mummy is just really tired "

He looked at Tessie feeding and putting his little arm her saying ,

"I love you mummy", this made her cry harder.

Tessie having finished feeding ,Maria put her back in her crib.

Looking at Billy who had fallen back to sleep. She went downstairs where Mark was

wrapped up in a quilt snoring.

Mark was not sleeping but thinking in his mind that this had to be the end of the game for

him ,had enough of playing the doting husband, the perfect step dad and her now trying to

control him.

Looking around him he decided she could have the house , even though it was her`s to start

with, why should he bother trying to get half of it.that was all she was going to be left with.

Going back upstairs so as not to disturb him, laying wondering where that explosion had

erupted from.

Exhaustion taking over she fell into an uneasy sleep.

Waking a few hour`s later by Tessie crying to be feed.

Billy moving beside her,cuddling him as she fed Tessie,

Taking the two children downstairs, Mark still sleeping, putting her finger up to Billy

whispering for him to be quite, as she got his breakfast.

Mark waking to the sound of Tessie crying sat up and said "Have you fed her"

Maria putting Billy`s breakfast on the table, nodding, sighing replied,

"Yes, I don`t know what she wants`?"

Mark taking her out of the crib she shut up.smiling down at her saying

"That`s what she wanted a cuddle from her daddy"

Maria looking at them last night`s explosion forgotten , smiling going to him hugging him,

Pulling away from her, handing her Tessie, saying "I`m going to be late for work."

Billy sitting at the table Maria surprised at Mark`s reaction,asked

"What`s the matter darling,"

"Isn`t it obvious,I`m at my wit`s end with you , as he continued Maria did not hear a word of

his last sentence because Tessie was screaming in her ear.
CClink
Taking one last glance, just for a moment as he left, at his beautiful Maria with the long dark

hair, and those sexy brown eye`s which were at that moment full of tear`s,holding his

daughter in her arms, and her little Billy, who was a lovely boy,she had for a while had they

whole of his heart, had shown nothing but kindness and love, just one thing missing money.

And he was gone.

Maria standing with Tessie screaming in her ear, Billy crying because he had split his bowl of

cereal, she thought her head was going to explode.

Going out the back door as Mark pulled away,Angie just leaving for work asking

"What was wrong?"

Maria just burst into tear`s.Angie looking at her said "I`m late for work but I`ll pop back at

lunch time."

She went back inside trying to put into context what had just happened.

Clearing the breakfast bowl off the floor, getting Billy ready for nursery, she carried on with

her day.

Returning from nursery she tried calling Mark, but it went straight to answer machine.

Angie came home at lunch time as promised , listening to Maria and her tale of the evening before.

Crying she sobbed"This is so unlike him, we never row and last night he was so abrupt to me"

"Maybe he is having problem`s at work and doesn`t want to bother you with them" she answered hoping this would clam her down.

"I have tried ringing him but to no avail" she whispered.

Angie going back to work,Maria carried on with her day picking Billy up, doing some

shopping and meeting friend`s who had not seen Tessie.
CLINK
Getting home she cooked dinner feeding Tessie ,Mandy popping in on her way home from

work, looking at her sister knowing everything was not up to scratch, asking what was the

matter.

In tear`s again she filled her in on the evening before.

Mandy hugging her saying "It`s probably just something to do with work!"

Wiping her eye`s Maria said "I hope so"

Mandy leaving said "Call me".

Angie popped in after work , asking "Any new`s"

Shaking her head she got Billy his tea.

Angie leaving "I`m just next door" hugging her.

Feeding Tessie getting Billy to bed, she rang Mark again.still no answer.

Putting the telly on she sat there just staring at it listening for his car to pull up.

She nodded off and was awoken by the phone,

Smiling thinking it was going to be Mark, but instead to her disappointment hearing Mandy`s

voice.

Telling her she still had not heard anything in spite of all her efforts trying to phone.

"Don`t worry sis he will between home with his tail between his leg`s soon "

Hanging up Tessie waking for another feed , sighing she fed her.

Ringing him again still nothing, going upstairs,she lay on the bed listening to her daughter

breathing.

Half dosing listening for the key to go in the door.

Woken up by Billy climbing into bed beside her.Looking at his little face hugging him .

Tessie waking up a few hour`s later needing feeding.

Looking at the clock it was 2.30am, as she put Tessie back in her crib.

Going downstairs again trying his phone still no answer.

Sitting there trying to think what to do next,going upstairs into his office part of the bedroom

Seeing his tea cup on the desk, with "To the best husband" on it looking through his files.

Crying wondering where the hell he could be.deciding to ring the police who told her there

had been no reports of any accidents in the Watford area, who then advised her to ring the

hospital, again there was no joy.

Pacing the floor tears rolling down her face she kept looking at their wedding picture.

By the following morning she was nearly on the verge of hysteria.

Tessie crying again wanting another feed, Billy arriving downstairs, saying "Mummy I`m

hungry"

Taking a deep breath,doing her best to keep things on a normal keel, getting Billy`s breakfast,

She could feel Billy watching her as he was a very sensitive little boy putting Tessie on her

breast smiling at her saying "Who is a hungry girl".

In her mind the next knock at the door was to tell her that her darling Mark was dead.

There was no other explanation for it.

Her phone rang her hand shaking she answered it, it was Mandy, breaking down telling her

he had`nt come home the evening before, Billy seeing his mummy crying started crying

"I thing I'm going mad " she sobbed "His dead I just know it".

Mandy getting off the phone ringing work telling them there was a family emergency, going straight around to Maria`s.

The sight of her sister frightening her.

The pain in her eye`s she looked like a shell of the person she had seen yesterday.

"Hugging her telling her there would be a simple explanation for this, asking her where he was working "

Sobbing she answered Watford, "Do you have a name "Mandy asked patiently.

Shaking her head holding her head in her hand`s she sobbed "I can`t think"

Billy crying his head off , Mandy picking him up he screamed,

"I want my mummy".

Mandy handing him to Maria thinking ,Where is he, hoping in her heart of hearts that her sister was wrong.

Mandy ringing Don as he had the day off came straight around.

Seeing the state of Maria asking "What`s happened".

Mandy filling him in, saying I`m sure there is a simple explanation to all this.

Maria hearing this said "I just want to know he is ok".

Don asking Maria where he kept his file`s on his work.s

Telling him the were in the corner of he bedroom, he ran upstairs, and finding the file on Mrs Potter bringing the number downstairs asking Maria if she wanted him to ring it nodding she whispered "Yes" Tessie started crying.

"I`ll just take her upstairs, wait until I come back "

Putting her down she was soon sleeping.

When Maria returned , Don made the phone call,

This very posh female voice answering on the other end of the phone,saying "Yes I shall just get him for you"

Don looking at Mandy whispering "His there".

Maria sitting with her head in her hand`s, tears pouring down her face with relief

Heard Don say "Your what" turning to Maria he passed her the phone the line was dead.

"He has been cut off" she cried.

Don taking the phone from her redialing, getting an engaged tone, redialing again.

Looking at Maria and Mandy he must have taken the phone off the hook.s

"What did he say?"asked Mandy.

Unable to get the word`s out, he was just standing there speechless.

Mandy going over to him asking again "What did he say?"

Swallowing hard, tear`s in his eyes looking at Maria repeating,what he had just been told,

"He has left you" he said simply.

Maria turning pale asked "What did you just say?"

Mandy turning to Don looking as pale as her sister,said "You must have heard him wrong"

Shaking his head slowly looking as shocked as they were feeling.

Breathing deeply said"He said he has gone and is not coming back."

Billy having picked up on the atmosphere, was crying his little eyes out.

Maria holding on to him as if her life depended on it.ss

"He is gone , gone where ?" Mandy asked in total shock ,looking at her sister, who looked as

if she was about to pass out, Mandy taking Billy from her telling Don to get her a drink.

Tessie was now crying upstairs ,Don went and got her.

Taking in the scene Don, standing with Tessie in his arm`s shaking his head thinking how can

he walk out on a newborn daughter,just two and a half weeks old.Maria, who ticked all the

boxes` one of the nicest women any man could hope to meet.

And her little son who was adorable, he must be having some sort of breakdown Don thought.

Mandy holding Billy,who had now got himself into a right tizz, Tessie screaming in Don`s arm`s

Mandy looking at Don wondering what to do next.

Maria collapsed on the chair, staring just staring, not uttering a word.

She was not hearing totally oblivious, to her surrounding`s.

Mandy calling her , Billy crying at her Tessie wailing in Don`s arms she could not hear a thing.

Mandy going over and slapping her gently on the face, waiting for a reaction but not getting any.

Taking Tessie from Don she said "I think we should get a doctor"s

Don looking at Maria who was now siting in a rocking position,she is gone in to shock Don thought.

Getting her a cup of tea with lot`s of sugar in, bending down beside her, trying to encourage her to drink it.

Looking at him asking "Where is Mark?"

Don staring at Mandy, shrugging his shoulders not having a clue what to do next.

Maria looking at them with a totally blank expression on her face asking again "Where is Mark?"

Mandy feeling frightened for her sister,looking at Don again asking should they call a doctor? He really did not have a clue what to do.

Billy was now screaming trying to get on to Maria`s knee, staring at him,as if she didn`t recognize him.

Billy pulling her hair screaming her name "mummy", she suddenly jolting back into the present.

Looking at him untangling her hair from his sticky hand`s, picking him up she stared at

Mandy sobbing, "Please tell me I have been dreaming or having a nightmare".

Don looking at her saying "I think he is having some sort of a breakdown ".

Mandy thinking He better be ,this was so out of character for him , he was one of the most

kind generous men she had ever met and he idolized Maria and the children.

"I`ll go and talk to him " said Don looking at the paperwork he had found on Mrs Potter.

Maria looking at him saying"Shall I come with you".
ANG
Shaking his head "No Mandy can`t feed Tessie can she?"he answered thinking quickly.

Looking at the address, "It`s only up the M25," putting his jacket on, kissing Mandy "

"Won`t be long"

Getting in his car, he drove to the barn.

Passing all the stable`s seeing the Porsche and Ferrari parked beside each other, in the

driveway, outside was a beautiful pond, with a garden that looked very well tended too.

Along the front of the house was an open plan veranda, with sculptured figure`s.

Mark saw his car pulling in."Oh fuck " he said turning to the spider.

Putting her glasses on her head she asked "What the matter?"

"Maria sister`s boyfriend has just pulled up outside"he answered.s

Going to the window peering out ,she saw Don getting out of his car.

Knocking at the door,the spider saying "Well go and answer it then".

His heart beating ten to the dozen, his hand`s sweating, gathering his composer.

"Alright mate?"he said when he opened the door.

Don could not believe the casual approach, "Can we talk?"asked Don.

Don dismissing what he had thought earlier, he did not look or was not acting like a man

having a breakdown.

The spider crawled up behind Mark, purring ,"Hello and who have we got here?"she asked.

Don answering before Mark got a chance"I`m Mark`s wife`s sister`s boyfriend.Don"

"Hi I Lisa"she said putting her hand out.

Looking at Mark scolding him asking"Where`s your manner`s, darling do come in" she

 invited.

He stepped inside to an open plan living room, noticing leather couch`s, the carpet was a pale

cream shag pile and heavy glass coffee table`s you could smell the money

"Coffee brandy "she offered,

"No thank you ,this is not a social visit, I`m just hear to speak to Mark" Don replied.

The spider purring at him "Well carry on we have no secrets, do we darling "she said purring

at Mark.

Mark looking rather embarrassed, shaking his head,

"No we don`t, whatever you need to say you can do it in front of Lisa" he said.

Lisa putting her arm through Marks as she led the way into the living room.

"Sit " she commanded.

Don having never before in the company of someone so dominant, automaticly obeying.

Sitting in the living room feeling very uneasy thinking I should have removed my shoe`s.

It was Don`s turn to feel uncomfortable, Mark taking advantage of the situation

saying "What is it you wanted,Don."

Don staring at him not believing, the question he had just asked.

Licking his lip`s , he answered "I`m not here to play game`s, what did you mean earlier when

we spoke, you said that you had left Maria and the children, and you were not coming back?"

Spider woman intervened, asking "What part if the answer did you not understand?"she

asked sipping her brandy.

Don was a not one to be taken for a fool,looking her directly in the eye he asked

"What has this got to do with you?"

Sitting upright on her couch, putting her brandy down she answered,

"Quite a bit ,as Mark and I are now an item", she replied blowing smoke from her cigarette.

Don nearly choked on a coughing fit, that overtook him after hearing this statement.

Looking at Mark in total disbelief ,thinking she is old enough to be your mum, taking in the pot holed face and the scaly skin , it sent shiver's down his spine.

"Do you know what your doing ?"Don asked changing his mind on the opinion, thinking he must be having a breakdown to even think of poking this creature,

Looking at him he asked if he could have a word in private.

The spider said to Mark "I'll just pop upstairs darling,don't take too long as were going into town to buy Mark a new car", she said purring as she left the room.

Don looked at him with,a look of pure disgust on his face, as soon as he thought the spider was out of ear shot he exploded.

"What the fuck are you playing at" he hissed at him.

Mark could not look at him in the eye.

"I admit ,I should never have married her, or got her pregnant" he answered trying to avoid Don's stare.

"What" said Don "Your not making any sense at all, for God sake you love her, I know you do I was there when she met you, and at the wedding and your trying to tell me that was all fabrication."

Mark staring at him said "Look I'm not cut out to be married, or am I father material"

"I should have know that from having Lilly, the only reason I spent time with her was to keep Maria from ear bashing me ."

A total look of disbelief appearing over Don's face,

Was this the same man that only a few week's ago got him and Mandy out of a hole, and

Mandy singing his praises, so much so she sounded like a scratched record.

Running his hand's through his hair, he was running out of patience.
"Mark you want to see Maria, she thought you were dead,she rang all the hospitals, the police, she is at home now in bits your going to destroy her." he said sitting back on the leather couch.

"Come on your not that unemotional, look you have only been married less than a year, your baby daughter is only a couple of week's old, come home ,we can say you had a bit of a breakdown"said trying to make right of a mad situation .

Mark looked at him so coldly,

"What is the attraction,Christ she is old enough to be your mother"

Mark shrugging his shoulder's making a sweeping gesture with his arm,said

"This is what I want, and she can fulfill my dream's."
ANG
Don looking around him answered,

"So it's fucking money, I had you down as lot's of thing's Mark but not a callous money grabber idiot,how shallow can you be, you are willing to walk away from your beautiful wife ,that most men would give their right arm's for, your adorable little girl and Billy, for thing's, my God ,Mark have you totally lost the plot?" said Don shaking his head in total disbelief.

Staring at Don,saying "I'm not a shallow man ,I just know what I want, and I'm going to have it".

"I'm going back to your wife now, daughter and Billy. What message would you like me to pass on that you have left them because ?"

Looking at the floor, fed up with being questioned, walking away and opening the door, which was Don's cue to leave,

Don turning to him saying "I don't know how you can live with yourself, this is going to destroy them."

With a sneer on his face he answered "Oh I can live with it alright".
CLIING
Closing the door as Don left, watching him drive away, thinking thank God that is over,

The spider having ear wigged in on the conversation, coming up behind him saying

"That was not too painful" kissing him.

Sighing "I don`t think that is the end".

"Don`t worry baby, it does not matter, you have taken the right path now, and yes I`m sure

there will be one or two more pot hole`s for you to jump over, but we must make sure that

your daughter is in the right hand`s."

"What do you mean "

"Well you don`t want your little girl growing up thinking her daddy abandoned her,

look at the life we have got to offer her, she would want for nothing, a good education,

compared to the life she is facing with the Irish tart, what has she got to look forward to

there,Irish stew" she said sneering.

He was not quite ready for, that commitment just yet.

Seeing the worried look sweep across his eye`s,hugging him "The time is not just right

yet, fancy a prawn sandwich?"she asked.

Smiling at her he nodded, "Please".

Don driving back to Maria`s dreading having to tell what he had just witnessed,

Getting there as soon as he walked through the door Maria and Mandy were on top of him,

asking questions

 "Give me a minute"

Maria standing there with so much hope in her eye`s asking "Where is he,"

"You better sit down", Don said his voice on the verge of tear`s.

Maria looking at him concerned, knowing it was not going to be good new`s

Sat in the chair "Well go on tell me , "

"His is not coming back " he said simply.

Maria on the verge of fainting,

Mandy with horror in her voice shouting "Why".

Don knowing how much pain he was about to put upon Maria,

He thought there is no easy way of doing this, so he just blurted it out ,

"His not coming back because he has found someone with so much money, and that seem`s

to be his God".

Maria not grasping this at all screaming pulling her hair, "No. No not Mark he is one of the

kindest most generous men I have ever met.he`s my husband , I have just had our baby"

Screaming at the top of her voice,"No no no"making the sound was like that of a wild animal.

Billy screaming frightened of seeing his mum like this,

There was a knock at the door ,it was Maria`s friend Chris, Mandy opening the door ,

Looking at Mandy`s face she asked" Is everything ok?"

Mandy unable to answer, just waved her to come in.

Chris walking into the living room look at Maria asking,

"Whatever is the matter?"when she saw the state of Maria.

Picking Billy up as he was screaming,

Don looked at her saying "He has left her,"

Chris shaking her head frowning, said"Who Mark?"

Nodding Don answered "Yes".

Mandy said "I can not believe it, Christ I thought he loved her."

Looking at her sister who was sitting rocking.

"Not as much as money, said Don sadly.

"My God, where is he now?"

"Watford,I just drove down to see him, he is shacked up with a fucking old spider woman, she is old enough to be his mother" he said shaking his head in total disbelief.

Chris looking at Maria "My God what is up with him".

Maria rocking too and foe, Billy wriggling out of Chris`s arm`s running to his mum, crying.

Hugging her to him they two of them sat there,Tessie upstairs started crying Mandy going up bringing her down.

Chris looking at Don shaking her head, looking at Maria who was destroyed,

"How do you pick yourself up from something like this?" she asked with tear`s in her eye`s
,
Shrugging his shoulders"I don`t think you can".he answered simply.

"Look at her," she nodded as she watched Maria rocking to and foe holding her little Billy in her arm`s.

"How is she going to cope, a toddler and a two and a half week old baby," said Chris standing watching her friend.

Mandy stayed with Maria for a few day`s watching her wandering around all the life in her blow away totally devastated

Mandy got some baby food for Tessie as Maria wasn't capable of feeding her plus as she had not eaten in day`s her milk was drying up.

Mandy taking the two children for a walk one afternoon , Maria rang her Ma.

sobbing down the phone, she begged her Ma to come over and help her.

Her Ma still had not forgiven her for all the scandal she had caused by leaving David,

So declining regretfully,telling her that she would not be able to travel as her back was playing up.

Maria sobbing down the phone "Please Ma, I`m not able to cope,I have got little Billy and

Tessie,Ma please I`m begging you."

After all her pleading the answer was a simple no, from her mother.

Maria falling on the floor as she had been on her knee`s with the phone in her hand begging

for her Ma`s help.

Crying "Mark , Mark, where are you, why have you done this?"

Mandy arriving back finding her sister in a heap on the floor,Tessie who had fallen asleep

and Billy was tired out , taking the two of them upstairs she put Billy down for a nap and

Tessie in her crib.

Coming back downstairs she held her sister as she sobbed as if her heart was going to break.

Maria did not tell her she had rang her Ma, as she did not want them to be rowing.

Mandy making her a cuppa , saying that she would have to go back to work soon.

Maria trying a smile said .

"Yes you have got your life to get on with ,I bet Don is annoyed at all the time your spending

here."she said in a voice that her sister hardly recognized it was so faint.

"Don`t be silly sis Don understand`s you know he think`s the world of you" she smiled .

"Maria your going to have to start to eating"she said stroking her hair.

Maria looking at her nodding tear`s pouring down her face, she held on to Mandy sobbing.

Coming up for breath she asked,Mandy "What am I going to do?"

Mandy having got no idea on what to say or advise her what to do.

She kept stroking her hair,as her sister feel apart in front of her.

Holding her head up Mandy said to Maria "I`m going to have to go back to work tomorrow".

The phone rang Mandy got up to answer it,a huge surprised look crossing her face,

Looking at Maria she whispered "It`s Mark".

Maria jumping up a glimmer of hope passing through her eyes`as she said

"Hello Mark" with such a softness in her voice, Mandy thinking if that was me I would be screaming down the phone at him.

"You want to what" she asked her voice raising a tone.

"Fine you do that, what time"she asked sobbing into the phone.

Mandy looking at her in bewilderment,"Now what?".

Staring at her she said "He is coming by tomorrow to pick up his stuff".

Shaking her head at her in disbelief,thinking how much more can a human being take?

Mandy said "Sis did you hear what I said, I have to go home tonight"

Maria looking at her "You have been a brick to me " she said hugging her tightly.

"That`s what sister`s are for" smiled Mandy,hugging her back.

"I Love you ,and your going to get through this , because I know my sister and she does not fall down at the first hurdle, she pick`s herself up and hold`s her head high".

Mandy left her telling her she was only a phone call away.

This was the first evening she was on her own, since Mark had left, hearing Billy wake up she went upstairs and going into his bedroom seeing the sleepy head, sitting on the bed hugging him.

"I`m hungry mummy"

Getting him she said "Come on then my little soldier and we will get you something to eat"

Hearing Tessie waken she went and picked her looking at her tiny little finger`s,feeling a lump appearing in her throat, she swallowed it trying not to cry.

Getting Billy his beans on toast cut up into little soldiers just how he liked them and ice cream for afters.

Mandy having made some bottles for Tessie she heated one up.

Knock on the door it was Angie, who had been so shocked by what had happened had stayed out of the way while Mandy was there , Remembering her own breakup.

She looked at Maria as she opened the door,held her arms out to her ,as tear`s ran down her face.

Not saying a word just cuddling her, Maria pulling away to check on Tessie`s bottle.

She filled her in on the phone call from Mark earlier,

Angie listening said "Maybe when he see`s you he might realize what a big mistake he is making."

Maria taking this on board, face lighting up as she was sitting feeding Tessie asked "Do you think so?"

Angie looking at her face thinking I should not have said anything, knowing she was probably giving her false hope,

Angie leaving after having a cuppa, Maria getting Billy to bed singing thinking what she should wear in the morning.

Billy delighted to see his mum back wrapping his arms around her neck saying "I love you Mummy."

Staring down at her little Billy she wrapped her arms around him kissing him a tear falling down her cheek saying and" I love you."

Going back downstairs looking at her daughter sleeping in her crib, smiling thinking Daddy will be home soon, looking at their wedding picture, blowing him a kiss, she went upstairs to pick out what she would wear in the morning.

Picking out a jumpsuit and some ankle boot that she knew he liked ,hugging herself she skipped downstairs, humming their wedding song I cant live if living is without you.

The phone ringing it was Mandy, Maria telling her the children had been fed and were sleeping and that tomorrow she knew that Mark would be back.

Mandy getting off the phone telling Don what Maria had just said,

Shaking his head "What the fuck has put that idea in her head", sighing Mandy replied

"Angie, what do you think is going to happen?" Mandy asked him sitting beside hugging him thinking if this was her she shivered.

"I know people can be heartless and thoughtless but this is cruel, this goes beyond them words, I thought we knew Mark how wrong can you be " he said kissing her on the head.

"I just hope she will be able to ride this wave,"

"This is not a wave darling, this is strong current enough to send her over the edge."

Mandy looked at him,"Don`t say that, she is strong and she has to look after Billy and Tessie".

"I know,".he answered simply.

Maria went downstairs and did a mini spring clean on the place, as she kept looking at their wedding picture, humming their wedding song.

She kept an eye on the clock as she anticipated, her reunion with her husband, in a few hour`s.

Sitting down she saw their wedding video, putting it on watching, as she walked down the isle, holding her brothers arm, seeing Mark look back to see her walking towards him, seeing the love in his eyes, that was shining right at her.

Sitting holding her knees underneath her, rocking tears pouring down her face,knowing in her heart that he had not left, like he said together forever and longer.

Hearing Tessie stir upstairs she fetched her a bottle and went to feed her.

Laying on the bed, staring at her tiny daughter, thinking he could not leave his little girl, singing to her as she fed, opening her tiny eye`s one blue and one brown thinking your are so beautiful.touching her tiny face kissing her, as she dosed off in her arms.

Maria dosed for a few moments looking at the clock thinking it was time for to get ready.

Bathing and getting dressed putting her make up on satisfied with the result, she heard Tessie wake, changing her and dressing her in a lovely pink suit, taking her downstairs feeding her she whispered to her, Daddy is going to take one look at you today and think I`m being so silly .

Billy wandering downstairs, looking at him with his hair up standing on end, he went over to

her .

"Morning son " she smiled as he gave his sister a cuddle.

Tessie fed and in her crib sleeping.

Getting his breakfast, and dressed, he was siting playing with his lorry`s, when she heard a

van pull up.

Going to the window seeing Mark outside, her tummy doing a double summer salt, her heart

pounding,checking in the mirror she wandered outside.

Clark standing there said"Hi Maria,"another man getting out of the van, said

"Be God it is lovely to put a face to a name"he said in a broad Irish accent.

Totally oblivious to Clark standing there, and to Sean who talking to her.

She stared at Mark,saying "Hello".

Ignoring her he said to the lad`s "I want you to get my stuff out of the house."

Clark looking at Maria, putting two and two together asked

"What is going on,"

Sobbing whispering "He is leaving me."

Mark looking at Clark "Just get on with the job."he snapped.

Doing as he was told, he went into the house followed by Mark.

Sean standing there gob smacked, staring at Maria asking "Are you alright?"

Ignoring him she went into the house,seeing Mark getting his tools out of the cupboard under

the stairs.

Sobbing trying to grab him screaming "How can you do this? What is the matter with you?"

He did not look at her ,Billy crying disturbing Tessie she started crying ,

Maria going over to her picking her up,standing in the center of the room with Tessie in her arm`s in her little pink suit .

Tear`s running down her face, Sean had come in asking

"What`s going on?" he asked staring at Mark,  This was a sight that would break anyone`s

heart, turning around, Mark snapped,

"Just get on with the job I`m paying you to do," passing Clark the tool`s.

Sean looking at Maria bringing some of the tool`s out to the van,passing Clark he asked,

"What is he up too?"he asked.

Clark wanting to hit Mark and hurt him how he was hurting his wife,snapping at Sean

He said "What do you think he is doing?"

"Well it look`s as if he is moving out, but what about Maria and that little babby and the little

fella in there?"

 Clark and Sean staring as Mark came out of the house followed by his wife sobbing with

their daughter in her arm`s.

"Mother of God the man need`s his head examined, you can`t just up and leave after your

wife just after having a babby, where is he going?"asked Sean.

Clark shaking his head could not believe how naive Sean could be, sometimes wanting to

grab him and shake him.

"Where do you think? The fucking spider`s, the barn"answered Clark.

Sean staring at him in disbelief, taking in the scene, Maria a lovely looking woman and the

babby a dote,in her arm`s, and her little boy, and him just coldly packing his stuff into the

van .

Sean looking at Mark saying "Don`t you think your being a bit hasty here?"

Mark loosing control shouting "Look if I want your opinion, I`ll ask for it".

Maria following Mark to the van,Tessie still in her arm`s,crying, screaming at him for some explanation, she was frantic for an answer. Mark looking at Clark said there is just a few more bit`s upstairs.

Maria was looking at a total stranger, taking Tessie inside putting her in her crib, she ran upstairs after Mark and Clark, Billy following,

Almost hysterical, shouting at him,

"Mark ,Mark you can not just leave us, is it my fault,I can put right whatever I have done to upset you ,darling please , please don`t go please " she cried as she fell on the floor.

Billy screaming going to his mummy, Clark going to help her up as Mark stepped over her as he took his bit`s down to the van.

Downstairs Sean was standing holding the baby in his arm`s who was crying,Mark walking past not even seeing,

Sean shouting at him"For God`s sake , what the hell are you doing? This is your little babby here and your wife upstairs and the little fella, have you totally lost the plot?"

Mark looked at him saying "You want to shut your mouth if you want to keep your job!"

Sean staring at him "Stick your fucking job where the sun don`t shine, I don`t work for people who treat other people, like shit especially your wife and your little babby you have a fucking heart of stone and no morals, you will have no luck in this world no luck at all,for what your doing here,"he said in his Irish brogue in such an angry tone of voice that even shocked Clark, as he came downstairs.

Maria having picked herself up and holding Billy in her arms as she came downstairs.

Sean was on his phone ,"Yes you know where it is,see you in a second".

Looking at Maria he said "Where can I find her bottle?I have just rang my wife she will be here in a minute"he said.

Maria staring at him,saying" Her bottle is in the fridge, looking at Billy saying stay with your sister.

She watched as Mark get in the van,Screaming" Mark, Mark please, please talk to me,don`t

leave us please."

He pulled away without a backward glance. And was gone.

Leaving Maria and his daughter and Billy, Clark looking back at Maria on her knees on

pavement devastated, destroyed, is no where near to describe, what Clark was seeing.

Staring at him Clark shaking his head, "You are one hard bastard".

Mark nodding"Yes ,I am but at the end of the day, you only get one chance in this world and

you have to grab it."

"Regardless of who you destroy along the way" smirked Clark.

Looking straight ahead, he did`n t answer.

Getting back to the barn Clark helped him unload, his belonging`s which were to be stored in

the garage.

The spider came out with a look of triumph on her face.

Purring at Mark asking "All done darling?"

Clark staring said "Have you no shame".

Shocked at being spoken to like that,"Pardon,"

Smirking at her he said"You heard me spider, you snared him good and proper".

Nodding at Mark saying"Come into my web said the spider to the fly, and what did he do

flew straight into it, small people with such, deformed mind`s".

Mark getting angry said "Keep that up and you won`t have a job".

"I`m walking anyway, hope you two will be very happy in your, twisted world,and in my

opinion Maria and that little daughter has had a lucky escape"

Clark with a look of anger in his eye`s said"I`ll go back to your gaff now to make sure that

your beautiful wife and children are ok, that`s what human being`s do for each other, not

torture, lie and cheat on them",walking away putting his cap on looking back at the spider and Mark, "There is nothing as bad as liars,"as he spat in the pond on the way out.

The spider staring at him, putting her arm around Mark,"Let`s get some lunch".

Maria picking herself up from the pavement something died inside of her as she watched her Mark, her husband the man of her dream`s drive away without a backward glance,tear`s rolling down her face going back into the house, shaking and feeling sick, all her hope`s shattered.

Finding Sean sitting there feeding Tessie and Billy, sitting beside him telling him all about his lorry.

Sean looking at her his heart going out to her,passing Tessie to her as door went , "That will be Betty the wife" he said going to answer the door.

Maria was sitting like as if she had gone into a trance, could not see , could not hear, holding Tessie in her arm`s, Billy taking to her.

Betty walking in ,Sean quickly filling her in on the event`s of the morning.

"Good Jesus Christ" she said looking at the new born babby and little Billy.

"What can we do " she asked looking at Sean.

Shrugging his shoulder`s, "I don`t know."

Betty who was a shy gentle woman,going over to Maria putting her arm`s around her, asking "What can we do."

Maria looking at her the pain in her eye`s unbearable to see,the torment in them you could almost touch.

Betty looking at her so kindly,asked"Is there anyone we can get for you".

Staring at her she whispered"Mark ".

Betty looking at Sean, said"I`ll make some bottle`s for the babby, and get the little fella something to eat."

Looking in her fridge,there was not a lot there as Maria had not been out of the house in since

Mark had gone.

"Sean you need to go and do a bit of shopping" she said making a list.

Clark came to the door , Sean opening let him in.

"What are you doing here" he asked.

Clark looking at him replied"I walked ,I not working for a bastard like that.A fucking liar,

a cheat, with no moral`s"

Going to Maria she looked up and when she saw him burst into tear`s , he sat beside her

holding her, Billy crying again all this, drama he was far to young to take on.

"I`ll take him to the shop" said Betty.

"Come on Billy we will go and get some sweets,where is his jacket".

Maria getting up passing Tessie to Clark,getting out the jacket seeing all Mark`s stuff gone ,

Taking a deep breath, pulling Billy`s jacket out passing it to Betty,saying

"Thank you".

Betty smiling said "We all have our hour of need."

Billy waving goodbye to Maria ,smiling at him she said to Clark,

"What is happening ?"fresh tear`s falling down her face.

Sean saying "I`m going to do a bit of shopping for you and the young one`s"

"I have not got any money," then remembering the £50 Mark always left her for an

emergency ,"Hold on " Going to the teapot, it was empty.

He always leaves some money in here for me.she sobbed, holding the empty tea pot upside

down.

"Clark if I give you my bank card and number can you nip to the bank and get it out ,there is

£200 in there".

Nodding putting his jacket on he said "Yes of course, how much"

"The lot I'm going to need it" she answered.

"Right I'll go and do this for you, and don't worry about the money you can give to me later, tell Betty where I am when she get's back,"said Sean.

Clark and Sean walking out the door out of ear shot ,Sean turning to Clark saying,

"This is an awful state of affairs,what in the name of God is she going to do."

Clark shrugging "I do not know, you want to see the two of them down there in that fucking barn, when I was leaving she was standing there purring at him asking ,what would you like for lunch,"he said trying to put on her high pitched squeaky voice.

" She as bad as him,he has just left his wife and all his thinking about is what, the fucker is going to eat, well that is just about right,no such thing as a guilty conscience, do you know when my Betty has a go at me, I cannot eat nothing me stomach turn's over and close's up,which way are you going? " asked Sean.

"The bank is just around the corner" answered Clark .

"Right I'll take me car, because she has hardly got anything in,"

Clark taking his wallet out saying"Here take this,it will help" handing him £30.

"Your a decent man "said Sean.

Clark going to the bank putting the card in drawing a blank, thinking he had put the wrong number in, trying again nothing.

The account had been emptied, The fucking bastard had not just left them but taken all the money as well.What the fuck was he going to tell Maria , this could certainly send her over the edge.

Taking his own card out he withdrew £200, thinking she has got enough problem's without having to deal with this, at this moment.

CLINK

Betty returning with Billy, she had bought him a new lorry and lot's of jelly tot's, he was well pleased and at least this kept his little mind off the drama's, that were all around him at that moment.

Running to Maria, showing off his new wares.

Smiling gratefully at Betty she kissed her saying "Thank you."

Clark coming back, handing her the money.

Sean arriving in at the same time with the shopping, Betty putting it away.

Billy helping her, she looked at Sean,saying what how wonderful Billy had been,

Sean ruffling Billy hair saying "He is a great little man".

The phone ringing Maria answering,it was Mandy.

Maria sobbing again ,Clark taking the phone from her telling that Sean and him had packed

in working for the arse hole.

Clark hanging up looking at the distressed Maria,smiling said,

"Your sister will be here after work".

Staring at him with a very strange distant look in her eye, she nodded.

Billy coming into the room showing Clark his new lorry,Clark bending down playing with

him on the floor.

Maria watching intently,started screaming ,Betty going and taking the babby from her.

Sean staring at her, sitting beside her saying "There ,there get it all out".

She went to get up and collapsed down beside Sean,Betty passing the babby went over to

Clark.

Betty and said," Come me darling I`ll take you to bed your exhausted" Billy screaming again.

Betty said to him"I`m just taking your mammy to bed so she can have a little sleep,and she

will feel lot better, now you go and play with Clark."

Going to Clark putting his little arm`s around his neck he sobbing saying"Mummy is tired"

Clark nodding has he picked him up he had a lump in his throat, swallowing hard because big

boys don't cry.

Sniffing he said to Sean "Will I make a cup of tea?"

Sean sitting there with a tear running down his face, carrying the babby out into the kitchen, "I have seen some thing`s in my time but this take`s the biscuit, how can he do it, Jesus that woman is broken, and you can not mend anything that is broke."he said sniffling back the tears.

Clark looking at him said "Do you know what else he done, the fucker cleared out their bank account."

"What do you mean, I just seen you give her the money" Sean said looking at him puzzled.

"I took that out of my own account so I did not to have to tell her"Clark answered shaking his head,

"How low can you stoop."he added.

"He is not human, he has not got a feeling inside of him" said Sean shaking his head,

"Did I hear you say her sister is coming around?"

Clark nodded "Yes that the only family she has here".

"Well she has me and Betty now, because she is one of our`s and us Irish always stick together, we might row among ourselves but when the sticks are down we always come up trumps for each other" he nodded.

Betty arriving back down looking at Clark asking could she have a cuppa.

Clark liked Sean and Betty down to earth and no bullshit, smiled glad that lump was going from his throat .

Nodding as he put a tea bag in the cup asked "How is she?"

"She is exhausted,when did he leave?" she asked Clark.

"Not sure,by the looks of things it has been at least a week, cause Sean and I have been getting the bus for the past five day`s him the liar saying he was at meeting every evening"

" I bet she has not had a wink of sleep, the poor darling, and two little one`s to look after"Betty sighed.

"I think her sister has been staying when she can"said Clark.s

"Betty I`m hungry" said Billy,

Sean bending down asking "Would you like some chip`s and maybe a sausage?"

Billy giggling,nodding "And can I have some jelly tot`s" he asked giving a cheeky grin.

Sean smiling down at him said "I`m sure that could be arranged".

When Billy was out of ear shot Sean turning to Clark,saying

"The bastard must be made of stone ,that`s all I can say".s

"Well our main concern is that we get his Ma better" said Betty.

"How are you going to do that, she is broken, and you know you can never fix anything you

break"answered Sean.

"Lord you don`t half some shit sometime`s, now go and get that child his chip`s" she said

giving him a playful slap.

 Defensively he said "Look if I break a china cup and the handle falls off ,you can stick it

back on but it never looks or feels the same again, then you can let it fall again and it smashes,

well that`s what he has done to her, he has smashed her to bits,ripped  her to bit`s and no one

can fix that, I seen in her eye`s, it is going to take her a long time to heal that if she ever

does"

Betty looking at Clark said "She is young and Irish so she is made of strong stuff, she might

never recover completely but she will stitch herself back up in time, but like any deep cut

there is always scars."

Clark looking at her thinking the Irish have a way of describing things,voicing this to Betty,

She replied "That is because we are a simple people we call a spade a spade".

He nodded then understanding.s

Sean arriving back with sausage and chip`s for everyone saying,

"It is fucking freezing out there".

"Well it is the November what do you expect, sunshine " replied Betty taking a chip out of

the wrapper.

"Billy here`s your sausage and chip`s" called Betty, he came in wearing his baseball hat.

"Lord he is a lovely little lad," said Sean.

"He is he is a credit to her and do you know something else ☺ that is what will help her

recover, Billy and her new babby , she will have something to get up for every morning"

"Wise word`s"said Clark.

Shaking her head she said "Na common since".

Maria appearing in the kitchen, as they were eating, Betty grabbing a plate, putting a sausage

and some chip`s on a plate for her.
Not a piece of bread had passed Maria lip`s in over a week.

The thought of food had made her heave,never mind eating it.

But the smell of the vinegar made her mouth water.

Nibbling on a sausage she got it down and too her surprise it stayed there.

Mandy walking in after work introduced herself.

Betty putting her hand out shaking it introducing herself and Sean, Clark then introduced

himself smiling saying they had spoke on the phone earlier.

Mandy turning to her sister saying it is nice to see you eating sis as she hugged her,

Then asking how it went this morning,

Sean nearly choking on a chip answered saying,

"Mandy I have never witnessed anything like it in my entire like life".

Betty seeing Maria put the chip down looked at him and said ,

"Thought you and Clark was going for a pint?"she said quickly.

Mandy winking at Betty smiling,said "Yes go on us girls need a bit of female time".

Taking the hint they left , Tessie started stirring and Billy was sitting with his baseball cap on.

The three of them had a chin wag, Maria ending up in tears.

Her sister looking at Betty a look of pity crossing the two women's faces.

Going totally unnoticed by Maria.

Mandy taking Tessie out of her crib, going into the kitchen heating her bottle.

Betty making some more for the babby.

Billy running around with his lorry flying in the air, Maria just staring .

"This is going to be a very long painful journey for her", said Betty.

Mandy agreeing sighing "Yes and the saddest part is no one or nothing can help".

"Time maybe can ease it but nothing can ever remove the damage he has caused" said Betty sadly.

Mandy getting Billy ready for bed once the lad's returned.

Soon they all said their goodbye's Betty saying that her and Sean would pop in on her the following day. Mandy getting her coat on after letting them out, said

 "You will get through this sis look what's upstairs and in the crib no one can take them away"

Maria taking on board what she was saying, nodding she looked at Mandy and the pain in her eye's was intense, that it took Mandy by surprise.

Tear's pouring down her face Maria sobbed,

"He might as well have broke every bone in my body or tore the skin away the pain might be more bearable,than this, I feel as if I can't breath, as if I'm going to smother or drown, I can't sleep or eat , and I know I should to keep me alive, and the only reason I am still breathing is for my two babies, a part of me has died, and it would have been easier if he had died at least then I would have had a grave to take for me and two babies too, and he would have left me through no fault of his own, and I could have grieved and remembered how much he loved

me and the babies, but what he has done is savage and the pain so inconceivable" she was out

of control the sob`crucifying her body.

Mandy grabbing her shaking her, she was getting really worried about her sister.

Making her sugared tea making her drink it , this seemed to clam her.

Mandy leaving telling her to ring her if she needed her.s

A few hours went by and Maria giving Tessie another feed put in her crib upstairs.

Looking at the piece of paper that Don had taken to Watford finding her phone number on it

taking it down stairs she sat staring.

Feeling exhausted, she put the piece of paper by the phone, and tried bed.

Lying there a million thoughts` running through her head, looking at Mark`s side of the bed ,

the tear`s started , moving over to his side of the bed where his smell still lingered, putting the

pillow over her face sobbing into it.

The ache inside of her, was mind blowing it was as if there was a ten ton rock weighing her

heart down,her insides feeling punctured, damaged.

Eventually dozing into an uneasy sleep, she was awoken not so long after by Tessie needing

feeding.

She could feel every bone in her body paining her as she moved,getting Tessie out of her crib

this even felt heavy to her.

Thinking I have to eat, taking her down stairs, she nibbled on a bit of chocolate as she feed

her.Looking at the tiny life that she was totally responsible for and thinking of her little Billy

upstairs, she had never felt so frightened or alone in her life.

And knew she was not feeling right, out of the corner of her eye she spotted her telephone

number.

Tessie having fallen asleep, she put her n her crib.

Thinking well I can`t sleep so why should they two of them.Her hand shaking, she dialed the number.

Hearing a sleepy female voice answer the phone, she screamed so loudly down the phone she frightened herself.

Slamming the phone down her heart beating nine to the dozen, she lay back panting, but feeling a tiny bit better.

Looking at the time it was 4.10am in the morning, laughing hysterically

Looking at the phone she dialed the number again,the same voice answered ,but this time, it was awake.

"Hello, that the old spider that live`s in a barn, who nick`s other women`s husband`s" she laughed down the phone.

Hearing Mark`s voice coming on the line, shocked her ,even though she knew he had gone ,putting a voice to the other woman and knowing he was beside her well that was making it too real.

She put the phone down, and sat staring at it for such a time, looking at the clock it 6.15am,

Shaking her head her, she could not remember any part of the evening before.

Checking on Tessie who was sleeping and running upstairs to Billy`s room she let out a huge sigh of relief, still having no recollection of getting her babies to bed.

Looking at the phone and the piece of paper, that she had drawn spiders on.

Billy wandered into the room, his hair standing on end which always made her smile.

Going over to her hugging her pulling her face toward`s her he said "Mummy I`m hungry."

Feeling a bit high like you did when your drinking , smiling she said "Soldiers and a boiled egg ".

Nodding he smiled"Yes please mummy."

"Did mummy put you to bed last night" she asked turning to him.

Shaking his head his mouth full of toast,"No auntie Mandy did".

Thinking it is sad when you have to ask you toddler who put him to bed.

Not even a flash back , then she wondered if she had , had a drink, even though she did not keep any in the house, looking in the bin just to check. Nothing.

So why was she feeling so weird she thought.Maybe lack of sleep or not eating.

Trying one of Billy`s soldiers, feeling it stick in her throat, she grabbed a glass of water to wash it down.

Tessie woke and she fed her, thinking I need to do some shopping opening the fridge seeing it full, standing with her back against the wall, racking her brain`s as to when she went shopping, nothing registering.

Her phone ringing it was Betty asking how her night went, and that her and Sean would pop by later , suddenly Betty voice triggered her thoughts back to the evening before.
ANGS

Like a shoot gun going off in her head,flash`s of the evening before hit her,and she remembered the phone call`s.

Giggling to herself thinking I can have fun with, the phone becoming her best friend.

Mandy popped in each evening after work to check on her sister,was worried that she still was not eating.

Angie was on her daily intake of caffeine in Maria`s, one evening when Mandy popped in asking if she would have Billy and Tessie the following Saturday.

Answering "Yes I not doing anything,what are you planing ?"

"Well I think my sister deserves a little break, and Don and I would like to invite her around for dinner, and a few drinks"she said smiling st Maria.

Taken totally by surprise, as she had not been out of the house since Mark departed.which was now coming into the third week,and apart from her not eating Mandy did not think this was healthy.

"Oh" feeling a bit nervous, she hesitated.

Mandy having no understanding of her not wanting to leave the house,saying

"Come on sis the house is not going to run away" she insisted.

So there was not going to be any fuss she agreed.

Mandy saying "Right dinner will be served at eight".s

Her and Angie leaving Clark arrived, much to Billy`s pleasure, who loved it when he arrived.

Jumping in his arm`s Clark smiling at him tossing him in the air,asking ,

How are you champ.as Billy giggled down at him.

"See you" Clark smiled Mandy as she left,waving at her as him and Billy continued playing.

Clark had helped Maria fill out the forms for income support, as she had , had no idea about it.

"Asking if she had heard anything ", smiling she said she had ,had a letter that morning ,

showing it to Clark, he smiled at her, "Great you should have some money soon."

"How are you feeling " he asked as Tessie began to cry.

Picking her up and getting her bottle from the fridge she sat feeding her.

"I`m still breathing, "she smiled.Clark leaving after this,The phone rang it was Betty who had

been a rock to her, popping in most days ,getting her a bit of shopping, she was a true friend.

Every night when everyone was gone , after Billy was in bed and Tessie fed she would play

with her new toy, the phone If Mark answered she would hand up, if Mrs Spider answered

she would give her verbal abuse down the phone until she hung up.

New Chapter

Saturday evening came and Mandy picked her up ,Angie already having taken the children.

Getting to Mandy`s , she had the table all laid out for the three of them.

Hoping to get Maria to eat something,sitting at the table Don asking if she was ok as he put a

bowl of soup in front of her.

Mandy and Don sitting beside her, the started eating, Maria picking up her spoon, dipping a tiny bit of bread into it.

Swallowing it, picking up another tiny piece and getting that down.

Mandy watching her, Don having finished his and Mandy he cleared away the plate`s.

The main course was sausages and mash which Mandy had thought as she had not eaten for so long, should be easy for her to stomach.

Maria did manage to get a little bit inside of her,which pleased Mandy.

Smiling at her saying well done.

The evening continued, Mandy pouring her a drink and Don taking something out of a tin and started rolling it into a cigarette, Maria`s eyes opening saying"Is that what, I think it is?".

Mandy smiling said"Yes it a little bit of pot , and before you go into one, Don and I have a little toke every now and then ,just to relax us and we thought that if you tried a little ,it might relax you and help you to start eating" .

Maria staring at them she could not believe that they were offering her drug`s, not after what she had been through with Antony, and her sister even entertaining this she was shocked.

Mandy seeing the look said"Look sis this is nothing like Antony used to take, it`s a cigarette That relax`s you .Look I would not encourage you to take this if I thought it was going to harm you , have a little drag and see how it makes you feel, if you don't like it fine , but it will not do you any harm."

Maria sitting back , looking at her sister smoking it and then she passing it to Don.

Mandy staring at her saying "Look,I have not exploded, as I just said Don and I have a tiny little bit every now and again, just to unwind,if you want it is like having a drink without the hangover"she smiled.

Maria sat there thinking about it ,sipping her drink ,trusting her sister, she smiled saying , "Ok, go on then",passing it to her she. Taking a drag form the cigarette inhaled it,Mandy watching asking "How does that feel?"

Maria falling to the floor ,holding her head,thinking it was going to explode,flashbacks of her childhood coming at her,like lightening forks falling from the sky.Vomiting on the floor,shaking like a leaf.

Mandy watching not believing the effect the pot was having on her, going to her asking ,

"What is the matter,?"

Maria looking at her tear's flowing ,white as a sheet, with a terrified look on her face.

Mandy getting very worried,picking her up from the floor , getting her on to a chair.
ANG
Maria bending over vomiting,some more,Mandy panicking shouting ,

"What is the matter?"

Maria holding her head up, wiping her mouth,sheer fear and panic, going on in her eye's.

Mandy shocked by the whole episode,didn't know what was going on ,looking at Don for help.

Don going to her asking "Maria talk to me what is the matter?".

Maria rocking to and foe, Don shaking her asking "What is the matter?"

Looking at him ,sobbing she whispered "I'm having flash back's".

Mandy looking at Don asking her "Flashback's? Flashback's of what".

"Me Da " she answered.

"Da,Da what?" Mandy shouted.

Tear's flowing down her cheek's staring at Mandy,

"Da had sex with me"she whispered back.

Mandy looked at her with a look of pure shock,"What did you say?"

"Daddy had sex with me ,he abused me ", she answered.

Mandy totally shocked at this allegation, screaming at her ,

"Your a liar, how can you say such a thing", Mandy's face so full of anger.

Thinking she has lost the plot.

Don staring at Maria knew deep down it was true, because whenever he had seen Maria with a drink inside of her,Don had watched seen her crawl into a corner, curling up holding herself, and this action in itself had made him suspicious of something bad , that had happened to her.

Mandy screaming at her,"How could you say such a thing, God no wonder Mark left you, you're a fucking liar."

Maria looking at her in her eye`s begging her to believe her.

Don watching Mandy`s reaction ,knowing that she had no idea, this confirmed in his mind that his Mandy had not been tampered with. .

Mandy looking at Maria for the first time feeling hate towards her sister.

Visioning her Da even touching her like that, made her feel sick, he would not have done something like that.Not their Da.

"Your losing the plot" she screamed, at Maria ,"I see now why all your relationship`s have failed, because you make stories up, to get attention,yes that`s` it you're an attention seeker. Everything has to be about you, Well I have had enough of your lie`s so get out, go on get the fuck out, I don`t care if I never see you again."

Don not liking seeing his Mandy so upset,went to Maria saying,

"I think you should go home, "

Maria blinded by tear`s looked at Mandy whispered"Mandy I`m not lying,and I protected you from him."

Mandy turning to her screaming at her "I am not listening to any more of your lie`s now go , go on and don`t come back you are not my sister anymore!"

Don getting Maria`s coat, helping her into it , said "I don`t think you should have told her that."

Maria staring at Don they had always been close,saying

"I did not mean to tell her, but it was that stuff you gave me, it just triggered my mind,and the shock, it just came out, you believe me?Don`t you "

Opening the door for her sighing saying "It does not mater what I believe,Maria, take care of yourself and the children". he said closing the door.

Maria walked out of their flat,shaking from head to foot, her head spinning as she walked nearly a mile home in the freezing cold.

Vomiting she collapsed in a doorway, looking at the sky wishing she was dead,then thinking about her two babbie`s getting up, she continued her way home.

Getting there she made a cuppa,feeling as if her head was going to explode,petrifying flashing image`s going on in her head.

Pacing up and down her front room she kept heading toward`s the back window, wanting to put her head through it, with the pain.

Sitting down she saw a little tiny girl ,going to bed and her Da following, the tiny girl shaking, in the bed, as he climbed in beside her.

Squeezing up behind her, putting one hand over her mouth,and the other one on his willy between her leg`s, then she would feel warm stuff coming out of it, as he moaned The Girl, The Girl.Taking his hand off her mouth, he would tell her what a good girl she had been, and not to tell anybody or boggy man would come and take her away.

He would get out of bed, leaving the tiny little girl sobbing, thinking if I make any noise the boggy man will come and get me.So covering herself up with the blanket she would lay there all night listening for any strange sound`s .

Maria sitting on the couch, seeing this in her mind as if she was at the cinema, screaming "Why da, why, I was only a tiny little girl" she sobbed,

Staring at the back window ,sending shiver`s down her, thinking of the thought`s she had ,had of putting her head through.

Then looking at their wedding picture, the two pain's combined, she felt as if she was

losing her mind.

The two main men in her life had,hurt her beyond belief,the first one her Da who should have

protected her, had abused her in the worst way possible, and the second her dream husband

whom she would have trusted with her life, had walked, without a goodbye nothing, after she

had just given him the best possible gift any woman could give a man a child.

Tear's pouring down her face thinking of the word's Mark used to say to her,

Together forever and longer, looking at their wedding picture taking it down and stamping on

it screaming, "You liar, you fucking liar".

Calming down,she was feeling so much anger, she looked and seeing her new friend,her

the phone.

Dialing the spider's number she answered, Maria giving her the most obscene abuse down

the phone she hung up.Redialing she got the answer machine, leaving another obscure

message, hanging up and redialing leaving another.

Her head in turmoil, she realized they had taken telephone off the hook, sitting down,

thinking Why am I here.

Going to bed she falling into a disturbed sleep crying.
                         NEW CHAPTER
            Back at the barn, the spider staring at the fly, did not like the poison the Irish

sparrow was spewing at them.

Getting very upset, the spiders eye's welling up with tear's,looking at the fly, sobbing saying

"I have never in my life heard such vile language, or been so insulted or threatened"

The fly looking at the seething scared spidery face thinking, my pot of gold could disintegrate

If that sparrow is not brought under control, she need's her wing's clipped in.

Lying beside the spider The Fly contemplating, suddenly realized he a pawn, that would kill

two bird's with one stone.

That pawn was little Tessie!.

The spider he knew from conversations they had, would have loved a baby, and the sparrow would be sent into a complete breakdown, with the loss of her daughter.

Knowing this would need careful planning,other's would have to be manipulated without their knowledge Did he care, who got hurt in the process! No.

Need's must, after all he deserved the best and all is fair in love and war.

Cuddling the spider,consoling her he gently whispered to her,

"Don't fret my love, not every bird's nest survives the storm,you should have been Tessie's mum,"

Staring at him she had always yearned a child but had never been blessed.

The glint of expectation in her eye's,did not go unnoticed by the fly.

The spider looking at him through misted eye's,"What do you mean"

"Well if the Maria was not capable, of looking after my daughter how would you feel if she came to us.?"

Holding her breath she thought she had every thing in the world money could buy except someone to call her mummy.

"How can we play this" she asked her eye's glimmering in the hope of a pipe dream.

Putting his arm around her saying "Well the phoning is a start."

New chapter
The following morning reality hitting her like a ton of brick's.

The evening before came crashing down around her, remembering the pot that Mandy had given her, which had been like an injection , that had fueled her mind revealing the hidden secret. The anger Mandy had felt when she had told her of what their Da had done to her, the freezing walk home ,thoughts of ending her life.the phoning. It was all getting far too much for her.

Hearing her door go downstairs, pulling her dressing gown on ,it was Angie and her babies.

Seeing them, she took Billy in her arms and hugged him so tightly, he screamed,

"Mummy your hurting me",putting him down she said "Sorry darling mummy missed you"

"That`s ok" he smiled, fixing his baseball cap on his head.

Taking Tessie from Angie she kissed Tessie,

Smiling Angie asked how the evening went.Maria looked at her with pain in her face .

Making Angie a coffee, she filled her in on their evening.

Angie hardly commenting, Maria standing waiting for a reaction.

Angie said"I knew you told me a long time ago ,when you had ,had a few drink`s".

Maria saying"I have never seen Mandy so angry".

"She will be ok ,Christ she is your sister"said Angie.

"You did not see her, she looked at me as if she hated me" answered Maria nearly in tear`s.

The phone ringing it Betty, asking how her night out went?

Maria telling her it was fine not wanting her to know the hidden secret.

Angie listening said"Why did you not tell her?"

"Because there are thing`s that are left best hidden" she replied.

Angie sort of understanding this statement nodded.

Saying her goodbyes she left.

Maria decided to ring Mandy, there was no reply, leaving a message on her answer machine.

There was a knock at the door it was Sean,coming in Maria making a coffee.

He asked "How thing`s?" .Smiling she told him that Clark, had helped her get income

support, so soon she would have a bit of money coming in Sean smiling at her saying "Clark

is a good man a bit rough around the edges but his heart is in the right place"

Maria totally agreeing with him,Staring at him saying, "Thank you and Betty for everything

you have done for me and the children".

"After what has happened to you, anyone would have helped,"he smiled.

Maria going to him hugging him, hugging her back and there was real affection in that hug.

"Well it will soon be Christmas"he said looking at Billy.

Billy jumping up and down singing,"Yes and Santa will be coming down the chimney".

Sean looking at him laughing asking "What would you like him to bring?"

Billy smiling at him answered "Lot`s of toy`s, "

Sean laughing said"I`m sure we can arrange that".

Maria smiling "Yes he has been the best boy,I`m sure Santa know`s."

Running around the room singing"Lot`s and lot`s of toy`s."

"Everything is so bloody expensive, Betty and I went shopping the other day,because were going back to Ireland for the Christmas, be the Lord of heaven we spent the best part of £300"he said clicking his finger`s"Just like that it was gone."

"I`ll be off and Betty will pop in to see you tomorrow."Smiling thanking him again he was gone.

Angie popping back around seeing Sean gone saying she was going to the shop,did she need anything?

Sean and Betty had stocked her up, shaking her head "No were fine thank`s."

"See you later " she smiled Billy running up to her asking for jelly tot`s.

"Angie" ,Maria shouting out the back,"Could you get Billy some jelly tot`s"

Going back inside she rang Mandy`s, Don answering the phone,hearing Maria`s voice,

"Telling her that Mandy,was very upset and shocked by Maria`s allegation`s, and that she had meant everything she said the evening before,that she knew she was lying, and she did not want anything to do with do with her anymore."

Maria could not believe her ear`s, protesting in tear`s she said,

"Don I`m not lying, please you believed me I saw it in your eye`s, she is my sister and my best friend, I can not loose her as well, please ask her to ring me and we can at least talk."

Hanging up,thinking she had just lost the two people that was her world, her sister and her

Mark,her whole world was falling down around her, and there was nothing she could do.

Tessie started crying ,Billy sitting with his baseball hat on.

Feeding Tessie she had a lump in her throat so big ,she thought she was going to choke.

She had not taken Billy to nursery since Mark had gone ,not wanting to face the world and

the look`s` of pity.Deciding to take the jump and venture out, getting Billy bathed , fed and

dressed, putting Tessie in her pram she walked Billy to nursery.Her mind playing trick`s with

her everyone was staring at her pointing at her, getting to the nursery it was closed, Billy

whinging that he wanted to go in, turning the pram around, she realized it was Sunday,

Looking at Billy, she said "Silly mummy thought it was open, but it Sunday."

Walking back she saw Jimmy standing outside his house.

Seeing her he waved,"Long time no see", he smiled,

Looking at her, he could see there was something very wrong.

"What the matter, "he asked with that kind smile of his.

Maria said simply,"He is gone."

"Who`s gone?"

The lump that had been in her throat earlier, moved and tear`s started to spill down her face.

"Be the holy God , come in " Jimmy said,Taking Billy by the hand and Maria pushing the

pram inside.

"I have just come back from Ireland, I just got back yesterday,now sit down and tell me what

the hell has been going on ?"

Getting her a coffee and Billy a drink and some crisp`s,he sat down as she filled him in on the

past three weeks.

Totally shocked he said,"Where is he gone."

This was a big no, no in Jimmy's book's leaving a woman who had just had a babby for him, and were only married five minutes.

Staring at her thinking this could kill her, Tessie started crying taking her out of her pram , Jimmy looking at the babby, with tears in his eye's.

"He must be having some sort of a breakdown, he can't be right up there," he said pointing at his head," God all mighty, how could he just up and leave, his own new born daughter and this little fella, that is not the actions of someone sane".

Maria looking at him with a distant look in her eye's, staring at him ,and more tear's running down her face , told him about the event's with her sister the previous evening.

Jimmy watching her, as she told him of the abuse as a child,as she sat there wringing her hands.

Thinking this was far too much for anybody, rejection in any form or shape was hard to take but in these circumstances, her just after giving birth,less than a year married.

Jesus Christ, and as for the other stuff she had just told him,well that was enough to blow anyone's mind.

Looking at her and her two babbie's his heart going out to her,passing her some tissue's, Little Billy getting upset because his mother was upset, how the hell do you pick your self up form something like this, he thought.

"Are you alright for money?"he asked.

Putting Tessie back in her pram, wiping the tear's away, looking at him saying,

 Nodding she said,"Yes I'll have to go, Tessie need's feeding,"

Jimmy walking her to the gate ,giving Billy a few quid to get some sweet's.

Looking at her walking with the two children, shaking his head going inside thinking ,

He must be mad.

Maria walking back stopping at the shop, to get Billy his sweets,coming out of the shop she lost her bearing`s for a moment not knowing which direction, to get home.

Looking at Billy she said ,"Where is our house?".

Billy thinking it was a game laughing said "This way mummy."

Looking around her she recognized, the park which was near where they lived, feeling panic,and nausea`s, she got home.

Getting inside she was sick, Tessie screaming Billy sitting with his sweets, looking at the two them thinking,crying what am I going to do.She had nobody,her Mark had walked without a backward glance, as if she was worthless, her Ma turning her back on her,she had never asked for her help before, and now her sister , her best friend.Finding it hard to breath,getting a drink of water, her stomach finding it hard to keep that down.

Her little Billy saying"Mummy"offering her a sweet.

Knowing why she was being sick, it was because she had not eaten in nearly three weeks apart from what she had swallowed the evening before at Mandy`s.

Looking at the wedding picture on the floor where she had flung it the evening before, picking it up putting it under the stairs.

Feeding Tessie she nibbled some of Billy`s sweets.

Angie coming back from the shops dropping off Billy`s jelly tot`s Maria telling her about her loss of memory.

Angie staring at her, saying she thought she should see a doctor.

Maria nodding answered,"It`s because I`m not eating or sleeping."

Angie looking at her saying "Well all the more reason to go see the doctor."

There was a knock at the door, looking at Angie , asking her to get it , Angie coming back behind her a policeman,Maria looking up thinking something had happened to Mark.

Taking the bottle from Tessie, she started screaming, the policeman looking at Maria asking her name,

Telling him he said he needed her to go to the police station with him.

Maria looking puzzled, asking, "What for?"

"It is to do with some very malicious phone call`s that you have been making to a Lisa

Potter."he answered.

Maria staring at him saying "Your joking,"

The policeman who introduced himself as P.C.Roach.shaking his head replying

"No I`m not,"

Asking Angie to finishing feeding Tessie, she looked at P.C. Roach "Has she told you why I

have been ringing her?"

"I would rather do this at the station"he answered.

"I have got a three week baby and a toddler, I can not just go to a police station",

Looking at Angie she asked if she could look after them.

"How long will it take?"Maria asked getting her coat on.

P.C.Roach looking at her saying "You can take the children with you if you want."

Maria looking at him like as if he had grown a head, shaking her head said,

"I`m not taking my three week old baby to a police station."

Saying to Angie "I won`t be long," kissing Billy and Tessie she left.

Billy running after asking "Where are you going mummy."

"The police man just want`s to ask mummy a few question`s, I won`t be long."

Getting in the police car, going to the police station spotting the Ferrari, that Mark used to

drive home in, parked around the corner.

Thinking their here,expecting as she went inside to see them.

She was finger printed and photographed, Maria thinking this a bit extreme for making a few

phone call`s, voicing this she was told it was a serious allegation that had been made against

her, that Lisa Potter was feeling very threatened,she was then shown to a cell, where it seemed like hour`s before anyone came and got her.

Standing on the bench in the cell singing"Stand by your man, what a pile of shite."

NEW CHAPTER

In the Ferrari outside, The spider and the fly, watching as the police, escorted her into the station.

This was the first time the spider had seen Mark`s wife, she was very surprised at how pretty she was.

Looking at Mark`s face seeing a smile come over, he said,"Let`s go get my daughter"

Driving to Maria`s, pulling up , getting out of the car, going in, Billy sitting watching postman pat , Angie nursing Tessie , looking up as he the walked in, with a shocked look on her face.

Billy looking seeing Mark smiling saying "Mark, my mummy is gone too the police station"

Looking at Angie he said "I`m taking Tessie"

Angie staring back saying "You can`t"

Mark smiling said"Oh yes I can , I`m her father and her mother has been arrested.I have every right"

Angie hesitated, before handing Tessie to her Dad, asking "Does Maria know?"

Shaking his head smirking,"She is the one who got arrested, if she had been behaving herself, she would not be in this state,whatever she has coming , she will deserve it, and as far as I`m concerned,Tessie is better off with me, they can throw away the key."

"Can I make you a cuppa" Angie asked hoping to be able to talk some sense into him.

Mark looking at her nodding, taking this opportunity to plant some seed`s against the sparrow.

Putting the kettle on asking "How as she coping?"

Angie thinking,she is broken but not wanting to give too much away answered,

"Well as you can imagine, she is confused as to why you left"

Shrugging "Well we all have dream`s, and to fulfill them,we got to do what we got to do"he said coldly.

"Take you for example, your old man up and left,so you took him to the cleaner`s making sure you were ok, and now you jump the bone`s of any man that look`s at you,so it all worked out ok for you, your living your dream."

Angie looking at him shocked,"What did you just say?"

"You heard ,Maria filled me in on how you cleaned him out , and how you hit the town and screwed any man, that looked at you."

"She said what?" gasped Angie. Disgusted at the what she was hearing, she had thought Maria was her friend.

"That is not true. I did not clean him out, and I do not screw any man that walk`s" she answered.Her face red with anger.

Shrugging heading out the door with Tessie, "Well that what she said, see you Angie" he smirked, he was gone.

Billy crying "Angie where is Mark taking Tessie?"

Angie taking him to her house in a state,angry at Maria thinking the fucking bitch.

Giving Mandy a ring telling her what had happened, Mandy was on a day off from work and said she would be straight around.

Getting there finding Billy upset picking him up, looking at Angie asking

"What has she been arrested for",

Angie replying"Phone call`s," and went on to tell Mandy what Mark said to her in a very angry tone.

Mandy smirking at her saying,"That does not surprise me at all, she is a fucking liar, look at what she said about my Da, I`m telling you my ma or my two brothers want nothing to do with her ever again."

"I know she is not coping very well, but after this she is on her own" said Angie.

"What do you mean?"she is not coping asked Mandy.

Shrugging Angie replied "Well I hear Tessie crying for a time,if I`m there I pick her up, she does not seem to hear her."

"Well I might give social service`s a ring, that what their for, to help when parent`s can`t cope, and since she is not, and she is rapidly loosing all her friends and her family don`t want to know, I don not want to see anything happen to Billy or Tessie, I would never forgive myself"said Mandy in a matter of fact voice.

Getting his daughter in the car, the spider staring at his contented face, smiling at Tessie ,not having had any of her own and always thinking a woman is never complete without a child.

He then spotted Mandy going into Angie`s, turning to the spider saying,

"That`s her sister, I need to have a word,"

The spider having gotten in the back of the car with Tessie,looking down at this tiny bundle of joy thinking if we can hold on to her my life will be complete.

Looking at him with that spidery grin she said "You do what you got to do darling."

Seeing Mandy come out of Angie`s he called her.

Very surprised seeing him, she put Billy in the car and going toward`s him not knowing her feeling toward`s him.

Then thinking of how he had helped Don and her out she smiled, thinking there is alway`s two side`s to a story.

"Hi Mark " she smiled.

"Hi I was just wondering how Don is?" he smiled.

"Well he is not back at work, so we are still struggling a bit,"

"Well I`m sure you know what has happened, but you and Don still mean a lot to me, and if I can help you in any way, well here's my new phone number, actually I can do better than that," he said taking his check book out.

Mandy who had always loved money, said "Oh Mark no I can't, you have already helped us out so much."

Mark knowing that Mandy was the selfish one of the two sisters,stared at her saying "Mandy it is my pleasure, to be able to help you out, and with Maria in the frame of mind she is in, well who knows what she is capable of, you want to hear the phone messages she left, the were, well I cannot think of a word to describe them.And done it front of the children, we did ask her to stop that is why Lisa and I had to do something about them, it was not as if she had not been warned, this has to be stopped"he said smugly.

Mandy nodding taking the check said "I know what she is like and continued to tell him about the dread full allegations she had about their Da" shaking her head saying "My Ma or my two brothers never want to see her again" This was music to his ears.

Getting her back to the barn, inside out of the cold,having invested in baby food and bottle's and anything else they thought, baby Tessie would need.

So the whole world had turned their back's on the sparrow, what a shame he thought smirking to himself, as he put Tessie in her new crib.

Tessie started crying ,feeding her Mark looking down at her the spider saying,

"Your such a natural with her."

Staring down at her , thinking she is the image of her mum.

"Yes she is Daddy's little girl."

Maria eventually being taken from the cell, led into a room with several people in it,introducing themselves individually to her, there was two police member's, a doctor , a psychiatrist and a member of social services.

Sitting there her head reeling, wondering what the hell was going on.

MARY D / MARIA THE IRISH COLLEN / PAGE 387

They questioned her about the phone call's and any other problem's she was incurring.

Looking at them she explained that she had just been married for nine month's, had just given

birth to their baby daughter, and her husband walked out one morning and never came back ,

Learning that he was shacked up with this Lisa Potter whom she had never seen, but had

found her phone number, and decided since she could not sleep why should they." Looking

for a reaction from these people.

Crying she asked "If they were in her position what would they have done?"

None of them making any comment.

Picking up their paper work, they left and Maria was released with a warning no more phone

call's, looking at the clock she had been in there six hours.

Coming out of the police station, it had started to snow.

Walking home looking to see if the Ferrari was still hidden, it was gone.

Getting home finding her home in darkness, going to Angie's.

Angie opening the door with a strange look on her face,

"Where is Tessie and Billy,?"Maria asked with a panicked look on her face.

"Where are they?"she screaming "Answer me where is Billy and Tessie?"

Angie staring at her in an angry voice "Tessie is with her Dad, and Billy is with Mandy"

Staring at her in total disbelief, "Tessie is with Mark , how did that happen?"

Tear's rolling down her face,sobbing she asked ,

"How could you let him take her?"

Angie said "I did not have a choice as he pointed out you had been arrested and

he is her father,anyway what's the big deal you know they are both safe"she answered staring

at her .

Maria the anger over taking her said "How did Mandy get Billy ,"

Angie looking at Maria,"I phoned her" she answered simply.

"Oh cheer`s Angie I`m going back down the police station, to see about Tessie, and thank`s"she said anger in her voice through the tear`s.

"Don`t talk to me like that after what you said about me", shouted Angie.

Maria looking at her with a puzzled look on her face but did not have the time to find out what she was talking about.

Angie closing the door in her face.

Slipping and sliding getting to the police station, P.C. Roach was on the desk, seeing her come in,looking at her crying her eye`s out telling him that her baby was gone and her estranged husband had taken her.

P.C.Roach looking at her with a total look of pity in his eye`s said ,

"I`m sorry, but I did tell you to take her with you, there is nothing we can do, he is her natural father ,it is a solicitor you need to see."

Staring at him she said "You knew what was going to happen!"

"Had my suspicion`s" he answered.

Sobbing she stated,"I`m going home and I know I have been warned not to ring that number, but I`m telling you now that is what I`m going to do ,I need my baby back."

Walking out of the station P.C.Roach staring after her, thinking he had seen many domestic`s, But this was a vendetta against her, he had seen it earlier especially from who he had thought was the estranged husband`s mother, but later found out was his bit of fluff. Him and the lad`s had , had a laugh about that,especially after seeing Maria.

Making her way home she phoned Mandy,Don answered the phone,

Hearing her voice he said coldly "That Billy was asleep in bed end that they would bring him back the next morning".he hung up.

Million`s of thoughts flowing through her mind,a lot of them dark.

Staring out the window, thinking is this my life pain, more pain, abandoned by anyone she really loved or cared about.It was like a huge black shadow, had surrounded her and she was totally lost.And could not see any light at the ending this nightmare.

Making the phone call to the barn, getting the answer machine, very calmly leaving a message,"I want my daughter back,I know she is probably sleeping now, if you ever cared about me Mark,even a fraction of what you told me you did ,you will have Tessie back to me tomorrow" Wanting to say a lot more but after her experience in the cell`s she did not want another episode of being locked away.

 Maria sitting her head in her hand`s, thinking Don did not have one bit emotion in his voice when she spoke to him, it was like as if she had been talking to a stranger.

Was there anyone out there who really cared, because Maria knew if the shoe had been on the other foot and this had been her baby sister, she would never be feeling the way she was feeling right now.If Don had walked out on Mandy , she would have been there for her sister, She had protected her from the day she was born.

Mad wild thought`s running through her mind,she quickly went to the shop which was just across the road and bought herself a half a bottle of vodka, some cigarettes and some jelly tots for Billy.

Panic setting in coming as she walked home she started running, hearing her name being called, turning around she saw Clark running towards her. " I was just coming to your`s" Tear`s in her eye`s letting them in,Clark taking a bottle out of the bag, putting it on the table. "Great mind`s think alike," she sobbed at him.he said holding out his arm`s to give her a cuddle.

And that was just what she needed at that moment in time.

Going into his arm`s crying until there was no tear`s left.

Putting her on the couch he said"Let me get the glasses and you can tell me all about it."

Pouring the whole lot of the nightmare she had been through and then filling him in her

They sat until the early hour's Maria talking Clark listening.

Turning to her at one point saying,"You never know how strong you are until strength is your only option,"putting a friendly arm around her looking into her eye's"Your stronger than you think you are and you will be ok."

Clark leaving,Maria going to bed falling into an uneasy sleep.

        The next morning waking ,staring at the empty cot, tear's stinging her eye's,Looking in Billy's room to an empty bed.

Going downstairs, the phone rang.

Bursting into to tear's at the sound of the kind voice.Betty was at her door in minutes.

Getting there she looked at Maria asking where Tessie and Billy.

Maria in between the sob's filled her in on the day before with the police, and returning home to Tessie been gone,that Mark had come into the house and taken her and that Mandy had taken Billy, and now Angie had turned her back on her.

Betty sitting down looking at the empty crib was speechless, staring at her, saying

"My God what an evil thing to do."

"I need to ring him to see when he is bringing her back", said Maria.

Dialing the number Mark answered, hardly able to talk she hi cupped down the phone,

"When are you bringing Tessie back?"

"Later" was the reply she got and he hung up.

Betty staring at her asked "What did he say?"

Shrugging her shoulder's she answered"Later,that is all he said"

"Betty he is my husband, and it is like as if I never knew him, if someone had told me that my gentle Mark was capable of causing this much pain, well I would have thought they were mad. He is a Samaritan and look what he has done."she was almost hysterical.

Betty getting up she knew she was looking at someone who could easily be tipped over the edge.After all we all can only endure so much rejection and pain, before the mind pulls the shutters down.

Maria pacing up and down was making Betty feel dizzy watching.

Don arrived with Billy knocking at the door, he did not even look at Maria , Billy smiling,saying "Hi mummy."

"Hello darling, mummy has missed you so much" she said picking him up hugging him.

Watching as Don walked away without even saying hello,

Maria feeling the rawness of this action, looking at Betty she said as if in a trance,

"I am totally alone through this,"

Betty hugging her answered"No darling not totally, Sean and I are right behind you"

Billy looking around asking "Mummy where is Tessie"

"She will be home soon"

Putting postman pat, on for him, he was settled ,Betty making a coffee.

Maria kept staring out the window at the sound of any car.

Betty watching thinking it is not only the baby you want's back, her heart bleeding for her.

Betty said to Billy "Do you want to go to the shop?"

Jumping up and down he answered "Yes please."

On their way back they saw Maria standing in the window.

 Billy and her waving to her.

Not seeing them she walked away from the window.

Getting inside Betty said "Did you not see us waving at you."

Maria having a total blank stare shaking her head answered "No."

"Are you ok?" Betty asked.

Hearing the sound of a car going by she ran to the window.

It drove by and Betty seeing the disappointment, in her face.

Billy looking at Maria said "Do yo want a sweet,"

Maria looking down at him picking him up saying "I love you."kissing him putting him down,

.Smiling nodding he went back into Betty "My sister is with Mark."

"I know darling" she smiled.

Betty watching her,thinking she has lost so much weight, her face so tormented.

Asking "Are you eating?"

Maria not hearing,just watching the window.

Betty going into the kitchen saying "I`m going to make us something to eat"

Getting some bread out and making some cheese sandwich`s, and some tea.

Putting it in front of Maria, "Get them inside you,"she smiled.

"Come on sit down ,relax" she encouraged

Billy moving out of his chair saying "Mummy sit here"

Sitting beside him her stomach turning upside inside of her, taking a bit of the sandwich,

nearly choking on it, looking at Betty saying "I can not eat."

Betty going to her whispered "Look at that little man beside you, if you don`t eat he won`t

have a mummy."

Swallowing hard she managed one of the sandwich`s and a tiny piece of cake.

Betty pleased that she had got it down and that it had stayed down.

Hearing a car pull up she ran to the window, seeing Mark pull up.

Running to the door her heart pounding, opening it a huge smile on her face.

Looking at Mark with hope in her eye`s,as he took Tessie out in a car seat, going to the open

door putting her on the floor in the hallway, not even acknowledging, that his wife was

standing in front of him.

Staring at him saying "Mark,"

He did not even look at her, heading toward`s the car without even a backward glance.

"Mark , Mark why are you being like this, Mark please talk to me Mark?"she cried.

He coldly got in the car and drove away, Maria running down the street after him ,shouting

his name, screaming "M A R K" but to no avail.

Falling on her knees holding herself sobbing,"Mark ,Mark."

Betty coming out of the house having seen the whole episode, from the window , running to

Maria, getting her up from the pavement, bringing her back to the house.Half carrying her

She felt like skin and bone under her jumper.

Getting Tessie inside she took Maria upstairs, saying to Billy ,you stay with Tessie.

Billy crying saying "I want my mummy."

Betty looking at him saying "Mummy has just fallen and I`m going to get her into bed so she

can have a little rest, then I will take you to the shop and we will get you some sweets" .

Sniffling he nodded and went back into Tessie.

Betty going back upstairs saying, "I`ll ring Sean and tell him I`m staying with you for the rest

of the day. " looking at a broken doll lying on the bed in pieces.

Stroking her hair,"Maria did you here me?."

Hearing Billy down stairs she went to them ringing Sean, telling him where she was.

Sean arriving not long after her phone call,taking Billy to the shop.

Betty looking after Tessie staring at her asking, "What is your Daddy playing at?"

She had witnessed some ignorant thing`s in her day but what she had just seen was one

the most hurtful, cruel of act`s, upstairs was a young woman, who was destroyed, broken to

bit`s and from what she could see at this moment would not recover, it was one of the most

frightening thing`s she had ever seen.

Sean coming back with Billy in toe,Betty in the kitchen getting a bit of dinner ready for them.

Tessie fed and sleeping ,Billy watching postman pat on the telly, Sean went into the kitchen ,

Betty filling her in on the day before,with the police.

Sean scratching his head , saying "What`s the bollocks trying to do kill her?."

Betty stirring a pot of stew, that she had just made ,answering "I don`t know, but what is upstairs is a broken woman , and I don`t know if she will be able to go on."

"What are you saying?" Sean said .

"Go up and see for yourself," she answered, making some bottle`s for Tessie.

Sean going upstairs knocking as he went into Maria, at first all he could make out was a pile a duvet cover as he called her name, a shadow moved, whispering "Who`s there,"

Going to the side of the bed, sitting down he said "It`s me Sean."

Turning so she could see him, pulling her hair from her face,asking "Where is Billy and Tessie."

Telling her not to worry they are downstairs Betty is looking after them, and she is cooking a bit of dinner, so when your ready come down."

Sean going to get up off the bed Maria grabbing his hand saying,

"Sean what am I going to do?"tear`s of anguish pouring down her face.

Hugging her not having a clue what to answer.

"Betty and I will help all we can, I don`t know what kind of a bollocks he is, anyone would be proud to have you as his wife and as for them two little one`s downstairs, "scratching his head,"All I can say is all they have is you, and your going to have to look after yourself, your going to have to eat or you will die it is as simple as that and then where will they be?"

Maria sitting up in the bed staring ahead, nodding thinking, he is right I don`t want to die.

Dragging herself out of the bed, following Sean down stair`s Billy looking up seeing his mummy running to her to her smiling asking"Better mummy,"

Nodding looking down at him, trying to hold the tear`s back, picking him up saying

"Yes mummy will be fine" smiling at Betty saying "That smell`s good"

Sean winking at Betty, she was so pleased to see Maria.

Going to her hugging her, Sean setting the table Maria turning to Betty,

"Thank you, they seem such small word`s after all you have done" she sighed.

"We don`t want any thank`s, we just want to see you get better."she smiled.

Billy showing her the lorry that Sean had bought for him.

Sean setting the table, the four of them sitting down to dinner. Tessie

stirring, Betty getting up seeing Maria making an effort to eat.

Tessie fed and changed, Betty putting her back in the crib.

Sean looking at Maria, giving her a wink as she had managed some of the stew.

The following day she had left Billy to nursery and as she was feeding Tessie there was a

knock at the door , A Woman standing there introducing herself as,Jane Lodge from social

services asking if she could come in.

Maria standing back to let her in ,sitting down, she said "I am here as follow up visit

to your arrest, plus there has been a complaint made that your not coping very well

with your children, so I`m just here to see if there is anything we can do , and to check and

make sure that the children are safe and been looked after ."

Maria staring at her totally oblivious to the seriousness, of the nature of this call.

"No there is nothing anyone can do Mark is gone,I have sorted out income support, and now

I just have to get on with thing`s."

Asking how Tessie was doing Maria said take a look for yourself, pointing at the crib.s

Jane going over seeing little Tessie lying there ,Jane asking how Billy was doing ,Maria

saying it was a devastating time for all of them but he was fine as long as he had his mum and

his sister.

Tessie started crying , Maria did not seem to hear her for a moment , but then after a small

time went and picked her up.

Smiling at her saying "Is my baby girl hungry."

Jane jotting this in her note`s, passing her their number, left wishing Maria a peaceful

Christmas.After Jane left there was a knock at the door it was Jimmy.

"Who was that "he asked as Maria let him in.

"That was social services."

"What did they want?"he asked,making them a cuppa Marie filled him in her arrest over her

phone call`s and Tessie being taken by Mark.

"Be the Holy God,what is the man playing at?"he asked.

"Look I just popped around to give you this, I did not know what to get you, so

you go and get whatever you want, I`m going to my friend in Wales for the Christmas ."he

said smiling giving her a hundred pound`s.

Looking at the money saying "Jimmy I can not take that,"

"It is for you and them two little ones,I`ll come and see you when I get back" giving her the

warmest smile, hugging her saying "You take care, and don`t go hiding"

Hugging her , he was gone.

Maria looking at the time Christ she was late picking Billy up, getting Tessie in her push

chair, half running to the nursery,getting there finding Billy playing on his own with some

toy`s and the head teacher ,looking really pissed off"

Apologizing to the teacher she took Billy and left.

Getting home,going into auto pilot as she did every day,getting Billy his lunch and making

Tessie`s bottles,Billy watching telly ,Tessie fed and sleeping , she would sit in the window

staring just for a glimpse of Mark , thinking if he drives by,hoping he look in and see her.

And maybe stop and pop in .

Later that afternoon,Clark popped by telling her him and his mum were going up north for

Christmas.

Asking if there was anything he could do, she said she had done everything,

Telling him Betty had been around, she had gone out and bought Billy some toy`'s and

they were wrapped up, and under the stair's until Christmas eve."

Leaving wishing her a nice Christmas,promising to call around as soon as he was back.

Sean and Betty arrived around with present's for Maria and the two children, before the went

to Ireland.

Maria in Betty 's eye`'s still wasn't right,sitting down asking what she was doing for

Christmas, and if she had heard from Mandy? Maria shaking her head, saying she had rang

several; time's but heard nothing back, then voicing her thought's to Betty saying she

reckoned that Mark would at least pop by Christmas day , even if it was just with a present

for his daughter. Betty shaking her head telling her not to get her hope's up hugging her

telling her to take care of herself and the children and that they would be around as soon as

they got back.

Billy and Maria putting the Christmas tree up, ,

Maria not hearing a word from any of her family , guessing Mandy had told them all about,

her confession to her, so they had all disowned her.

This putting her in a darker place, than she all ready was.

Maria had never felt so alone or vulnerable in her whole life. Billy looking at her asking

when Santa was coming ,Maria turning him said "Seven day's"

Getting over excited he was singing and dancing around the place.

Maria seeing a car pull up ran straight to the window, seeing Mark sitting outside, waving

at him running to the door, opening it the car was gone.

Coming back in, thinking "What did he do that for?"

Feeling gutted, her head started, pounding as she looked at Billy,he started whinging,

 Tessie started screaming, Billy going on, she screamed at him "Shut up."

The two of them starting together was doing her head in.

Billy looked at her with a shocked little look on his face, started crying,staring down at him thinking, This is not your fault, she started to cry and hugging him saying mummy is so sorry for shouting at you but I have got a real bad headache, and you and Tessie crying at me at the same time it really hurt`s.

Nodding he looked at her, Tessie was still crying, Maria going to pick her up.

Getting her bottle she sat in the window feeding her, Billy sitting beside her sniveling, Maria feeling guilty ,asked him that after she had fed Tessie would he like to go to the shop? Taking him to the shop with Tessie in her pram she saw the Ferrari, slow down not far away from them.

Staring seeing Mark look in the rear view window, she waved, as they got closer, he pulled away.Maria not understanding what was going on feeling a lump in her throat, going to the shop, walking home she kept looking behind her.

Getting inside she turned the Christmas tree light`s on and this, got Billy very excited.

"Mummy, it is Christmas"he sang.

Maria nodding feeling totally exhausted,putting Tessie in her crib, putting the telly on for Billy, nodded off.

Angie coming home from work, hearing Tessie crying going into Maria`s finding her asleep on the couch , and Billy trying to take Tessie out of her cot.

Angie running toward`s him shouting Maria wake up, Maria having gone into a deep sleep, sitting up suddenly,rubbing her red raw eye`s, "What".she answered.

Angie staring at her asking "Have you been drinking?"

Maria staring at her replying "No, What are you doing here? I thought you were not talking to me "

"How could you sleep through that " she asked, pointing at Tessie who was now wailing in

Angie`s arms.

Looking at Angie tear`s in her eye`s "I have not slept in week`s"

"Maria, I understand that but you can not just go to sleep when you have Billy and Tessie

To look after , and with social services on your case you need to be very careful,"Angie

replied crossly, passing Tessie to her.

Taking Tessie Maria staring at her asking "How do you know that social services have been

here?"

"You know who sent them " said Maria as she went into the kitchen to get Tessie`s bottle.

Angie nodding "Yes it was Mandy,"

Maria totally shocked,stared at her "My own sister" she said as she the bottle fall out of her

hand on the floor.

"Why ,Christ Mandy what did she do that for ?"

"Because she is worried about the kid`s"

"Worried Angie, she has not spoken to me since that night the gave the smoke that ignited

inside my head and the hidden secret was reveled" she said pointing to her head.

Going back into the living room,feeding Tessie she said,

"If Mandy or me Ma was here to help me I would not be falling asleep" she sobbed.

"Do you know how many time`s I have been let down in my life, and this over ride`s all the

other`s?" she sobbed,"And what`s my sister , my best fried doing?calling the authority`s on

me, talk about kicking someone when their down, "tear`s of exhaustion and disappointment

running down her tired worn out eye`s.

Angie staring at her said "Well according to Mark and Mandy you brought all of this upon

yourself."

"Angie I don`t know what I am supposed to have said ,but how can you say that to me, you

know I loved Mark and there was nothing I would not have done for him , and my sister, my world has been torn apart I thought you and I were friend`s" she said breaking down.

Angie shrugging answered"Friend`s do not go around spreading disgusting rumor`s about each other ,I know you said it , because Mark told me, I was just checking to make sure the children were all right"She left.

Maria looking at the closed door a thick fog, surrounding her eye`s misting over she could not see.

NEW CHAPTER

Mark ringing Mandy,asking if the check had cleared,Mandy singing down the phone,"Yes it has and thank you so much."

He then asked if Don and her would like to come to the barn for some Christmas drink`s.

"Well Don is not here at the moment ,but I`m sure he will say yes", taking the address she asked when, and then asking if she could take Angie with them.

Mark replying "Of course," getting off the phone, with a very smug contented grin on his face.The arrangement`s were made for the following evening, at eight.

The spider seeing the look asking"What are you looking so happy about?"

"Let`s just say, I am putting a cat among the pigeon`s so I can fulfill my darling`s dream`s" he smiled.Putting his arm`s around her waist ,

"There is nothing I would not do for my tiger."

Purring staring at him wrapping her stick like leg`s around him, sticking her tongue in his ear, the beady eye`s staring into his,taking her upstairs,closing his eye`s he fucked her.

Angie and Mandy having become buzzing buddy`s and Mandy had added a bit more poison,just to add salt to the wound, by telling Angie a few fib`s about what Maria had said about her.

. Mandy had always been a little bit jealous of her sister,everything she touched seemed to turn to gold and men just fell into her lap.She made friend`s easy and every one loved being around her.

Leaving Mandy feeling like her shadow.

But after what she had accused their Da of, and since her and Angie had got close, Angie telling her one evening after a few drink`s that Maria had told her their father was not Maria`s father, well she wanted to go around and kill her, "What`s the lying bitch, trying to infer now that our Ma was a slut," finishing her drink , she said to Angie "She is the slut and a liar?" Angie thinking yes she is a liar ,look what she told Mark making her out to be some sort of easy lay, and money grabbing bitch.

Finishing the bottle between them, opening a second bottle, by the time that had gone Maria was the most evil cow anyone could know.

Don arriving back Mandy telling him about their invite, the following evening.She had already phoned Angie, who was excited about going to see where Mark had moved on to.The two of them discussing what to wear, and making arrangement`s to meet at Mandy`s the following evening.

The following morning Angie leaving for work, thinking of her evening ahead , from what she had heard Mark had moved on to bigger and better thing`s, an was looking forward to seeing the barn and seeing what the spider looked like.

Maria hearing Angie`s door go looked out and asking Angie asking "What day is it?"she asked in a very weak voice.

Angie staring at her,seeing the red bloodshot, black circled eye`s her hair that did not even looked as if it had been brushed, and dressed in an old dressing gown that had seen better day`s,Billy standing in a pair of pajamas.

Maria was not doing very well, she was so tired and weak sometime`s she did not know what day, or what the time was it.

Managing to look after the children just, she knew she needed help but did not know where to look.

Sighing Angie answering Maria in a very contempt tone,

"It`s Tuesday, the 22nd" picking her bag out heading to her car,thinking I am sure she is

drinking.

Taking Billy back inside getting him his breakfast.

Tessie crying for a feed ,Maria going to the fridge looking thinking shit she had forgotten to

make her bottles.

Picking up the box of baby powder, opening thinking in her mind,This is poison, throwing it

in the bin , getting some mike from the fridge putting it in her bottle.

Feeding her and looking at Billy eating his cereal, saying we need to go shopping.

Forgetting to dress Billy and putting a coat over her dressing gown,putting Tessie in her pram,

she was heading out the door when Billy laughing at her said,

"Mummy you have no shoes on."

Looking down at her feet and seeing the dressing gown under her coat.

Taking them back into the living she started to cry.

Billy going to her saying "Mummy it is ok."

She looked in the pram she could not remember if she had changed Tessie.

Taking her out ,changing her nappy looking,out through the window seeing the sun shining

dressing her in a light dress, getting Billy dressed in shorts and a t shirt, she went upstairs to

get dressed,pulling a pair of legging`s on and a t shirt.

Thinking in he mind it was a warm summers day, she headed out .

Getting across the road Billy, complaining that he was cold,Maria feeling nothing.

Getting to the shop`s she putting the food in her basket,and heading out the door of the super

Market with basket on top of the pram , without paying for it .

As soon as she walked through the manager was behind her.

Recognizing Maria as she used to do his wife`s hair, smiling at her , he said,

"Maria "Looking at him with a vacant look on her face, she answered

"Yes" Billy pulling her saying "He was cold".

"Your walking out without paying for your grocery`s" he said kindly as he had heard what

had happened.

Not knowing for a moment where she was and then realizing, what she had done and

recognizing Matthew, she apologized immediately.heading to the check out.

Matthew following her asking if everything was ok, as he had noticed how they were dressed.

They must be freezing, he thought looking at the little boy in a t shirt and short`s and Maria in

a light t shirt.They baby was asleep.

Maria staring at him saying "Yes were fine."

Paying for her grocery`s, leaving the shop, and heading home, thinking I will give Betty a

ring forgetting she was in Ireland.

Billy was glad to get home saying "Mummy I am very cold ".

Looking down at him realizing he was dressed in summer clothe`s,thinking why have I put

 him in summer clothe`s, then looking in the pram seeing Tessie in a light dress, not

remembering that she had thought it was summer when she had looked out through

the window.

       Wednesday evening arrived Angie meeting at Mandy`s, Angie wearing a

new black skirt and a pale blue silk shirt she had invested in as a present for herself for the

festive season.

Walking in Mandy saying "You look lovely".

"So do you" smiled Angie

Mandy dressed in a black jumpsuit, that Don had bought her for Christmas.

 "I am really looking forward this"said Angie.

Mandy answering"Yes it should be interesting,have you seen madame, next door?"

Angie nodding "Yes seen her yesterday morning, she came out asking me what day it was, she looked as if she had been on the piss."

"Well, if she head`s down that road , with social services on her case, do I need to say more, speaking of which I bought us a tipple, "Pouring them a large vodka and coke each,

"Here`s to the evening ahead" smiled Mandy.

Don coming down stairs looking rather dashing in black trousers and a silk black shirt.

Angie saying "Christ Don you look super"

Smiling he said"Thank you Angie and you don`t scrub up too bad yourself."

Don declined on having a drink as he was driving.

"Oh that is not fair,let`s get a taxi ,I!ll pay so we can all have a nice evening."

"Great, that is kind of you Angie" said Don pouring himself a drink.

Mandy ordering a taxi for half an hour later.

Hearing the taxi pulling up, the three of them, went out and giving the driver the address to the barn.

As they pulled into the estate, seeing the converted barn, Mandy looked at Angie in astonishment,as the taxi pulled up outside, the garden was like something you see on a magazine cover,with the pond, statue`s and the patio with swing chairs and table.

Parked to the side was the Ferrari and Porsche, where there was some shrubs shaped into different shapes.And further down was a line of stables.

Mandy nudging Angie saying "Fucking hell, what is the inside like."

Don already having visited had not really take notice of the place as he had come to see Mark.

Mark hearing the taxi pull up, went to the front door to greet them.

Opening the door, smiling acting as if he was King of the castle, inviting them inside.

Entering they saw the spider,standing there purring, Mark introducing them to her.

"Your welcome to my home,can I get you a glass of champagne", she asked.

Mandy looking at her could not believe her eye`s , this woman was old enough to be his

mother, staring at the scaled skin,the beady eye`s.There was absolutely no shape to her she

was so thin it looked painful .Don nudging her, she smiled answering

"Yes please" watching the spider wander across her living room, to the drink`s cupboard,

which as she opened it was a fridge inside. The living area was decorated to perfection

leather couch `s,glass tables,a huge music system and a television.

Handing them there drink`s, toasting them a very happy Christmas.

They all raising their glasses.

She then led them into the dining room which was set for the five of them.

The table a long glass table with brass swan shaped legs, and a white shag pile carpet.

Their were fresh flowers everywhere,Angie and Mandy felt as if they had entered palace.

She had hired caterers, for the dinner party.

The five of them sitting down, first they were served, prawn cocktail ,followed by steak with

a selection of vegetables, and for there after`s there was a choice of Christmas pudding, or

baked Alaska.

They three of them very impressed, Mandy saying to the spider.

 "What a beautiful home you have got."

Smiling holding Mark`s hand she said "Yes it does us."

Gently pulling his hand away, excusing himself from the table, smiling he said

"The little boy`s room",Don excusing himself at the same time.

Heading upstairs,Don said in a disapproving voice "Christ you have hit the jackpot here."

Mark looking at him, answering "You don`t understand,we all; have dreams and to fulfill,

and we have to do what we have to do"Don washing his hands,

"I suppose so, Mandy is ok now with what has happened, because she has washed her hand`s of Maria,after the explosion about her father, I don`t say a lot, but in my mind you are the most disgusting people,that has ever been put on this earth, you want to see your wife,that is one of the kindest woman I have ever had the privileged of meeting, you have destroyed her." He said simply as he left the room.

Matt thinking he is jealous, because he would never have had the ball`s to do what he had done.

Following him downstairs joining them as , they sat around the table, the conversation was about Maria.

The spider was putting her two and sixpence in , saying "I have only seen her once", going on to tell them about the dreadful phone call`s, that she had made to her. And thinking she was looseing it, had contacted the police, and that was why she was arrested" she said in a matter of fact tone, sipping her after dinner brandy, "To be honest with you I honestly think that Mark`s baby would be better off with us here , she would never go without."she added.

Angie having had a lot to drink slightly slurring ,"Well the way she is handling this I think you might be right, she came out to me yesterday morning, you should have seen the state of her , hair hanging unwashed, her eye`s well she looked as if she had been on the piss, asking what day it was"

Mark`s ear`s picking up ""What you recon she had been drinking?" he asked putting a very concerned tone into his voice.

"Well I did not actually see her drinking , I am just saying she looked like it to me."she he-cupped.

Mandy joining in said "Well that is not all the damage she has done, none of her family ever want to see her again, she came out with the most dreadful allegation about my father and then told Angie that he was not her father, how mental is that, basically saying that our Ma was a slag."helping herself to another drink.

"Well if you think she is drinking maybe I should contact social services" said Mark putting his drink down.

"Already done " slurred Mandy.

This was getting easier for Mark the more he heard the better the book was singing, so the next chapter should be a piece of piss.

Mark who had been drinking water out of what looked like a wine bottle.

said "You have contacted social services?"

Angie piping in"Oh yes she has already had a visit"putting her glass out to Mandy who had taken charge of dispensing of the alcohol.

"What did they do?" he asked.

Shrugging Angie said "Have got no idea".

Matt taking a mental note of this, the evening finishing with Angie ,Mandy and Don getting very drunk and the spider who never seemed to be without a brandy breath, sitting there talking, they greatest load of shit.Mark could not wait for the evening to be over.

NEW CHAPTER

Christmas eve ,her friend Chris knocked on the door, Maria opening it letting her in.

Putting the kettle on Chris noticing, the weight Maria had lost,

Billy running up to her saying Santa is coming.

Looking down at him she smiling"I know",

Having a peak in at Tessie, she said"She is growing",

"Yes , they don`t stay babies, for long"she sighed.

"Is she going through the night yet",

Nodding Maria asking ,did she take sugar?.

Sitting at the table Chris looking at her with concern, "How are you doing?

Shrugging she answered"You know , taking one day at a time and getting through it."

Telling her about, her falling out with Mandy and then Angie, she was in tear`s by the time she had finished.

"Oh Maria, What can I say"

Maria staring at her blankly, swallowing a lump in her throat, "There is nothing anybody can say, " then with a sad look she voice her thought`s.

"I think Mark might pop by tomorrow",a look of hope passing over her eye`s.

Chris tuning toward`s her seeing this look pass through the empty eye`s, gently asking, "What give`s you that idea?"

"Well he can`t ignore us forever, and it is Tessie`s first Christmas" she answered with a far away look in her eye`s.

Chris hugging her knew deep inside,knew that her friend was not right,she did not seen to be in touch, she had lost so much weight and had this vacant disturbed look about her.

Taking some presents out for her and the children, she put them on the table.

Maria asking "What are they for",

"Chris answering "There are for you and the children for Christmas".

Maria nodding looking at her with that vacant asking "When is Christmas?"

"It is tomorrow,today is Christmas eve, Maria are you alright?"

Maria looking at her answered "Of course it is, I have so much going on up here I just forgot for that second", pointing at her head.

Chris leaving telling her if there was anything she needed to call her, wishing her a happy Christmas leaving.Thinking in her mind that she should give Mandy a ring as she did not think it right Maria been left with two children, on her own and especially just after given birth and it is Christmas surly she could find it in her heart to forget whatever disagreement, they had. And it was one of the loneliness time`s for anybody to be on their own.

Billy was getting excited asking "What time Santa would be coming?"

Maria looking down at him saying "He will have been when you wake up in the morning"

Tessie was now going through the night,so Christmas eve evening Maria bathing Billy, as he gabbled on about Santa.

Putting his P.J.s on, taking him downstairs giving him his tea ,bathing Tessie and feeding her getting her into her night clothe`s, putting the two of them to bed.

Going downstairs getting their cloths ready for Christmas day.

Maria going under the stairs, getting the present`s out that she had bought for her two babies, and the rest of the gift`s that her friend`s had brought around.

Taking a chicken out of the freezer to defrost preparing the vegetables and making sure she had Tessie`s bottle`s, having put her back on formula, buying it herself.

Having bought herself a bottle of vodka for Christmas, going into the kitchen pouring herself a drink,she sat looking out through the window, in hope of seeing Mark drive by.

Watching as couple`s walked by hand in hand, going home from doing the last of their Christmas shopping.

A huge lump appearing in her throat ,, thinking that should be me and Mark, tear`s spilling down her cheeks.

Thinking I have always been damaged, remembering her father, how she protected Mandy,David how he had treated her and Antony,who she thought was the love of her life, Tear`s pouring down her face, then her Ma rejecting her,and then Mandy whom had been her best friend as well as been her sister, the biggest crunch of the lot,her Mark the man of her dream`s who she had married for better ,for worst,who she thought would be together forever and longer.

Her head pounding, she kept thinking where had she gone wrong?

Coming away from the window, sobbing she poured herself another drink sitting on the sofa,

her phone rang, her heart pounding as she answered it thinking it was Mark.

It was Betty ringing from Ireland in good spirits,saying that she was thinking about her and

that the would be back the 4th of January, and she would come and see her then.

Asking her how the children are ,Maria telling her Billy was very excited.

Telling her to take care and to make sure and eat, she hung up.

Maria finishing her drink going upstairs to bed,looking in on Billy who was sleeping with his

base ball cap on the end of the bed, she smiled.

Going into her bedroom looking at Tessie thinking how could you just up and leave, more

tear`s rolling down her face,she lay on the bed and the ace inside of her unbearable.

Staring at the pillow where his head used to lay, holding his pillow to her she dosed until

Billy woke her.

NEW CHAPTER
Billy screaming in her ear he has been mummy, come and see.

Maria so tired, Tessie waking, taking her downstairs, feeding her.

Maria doing her best to get into the spirit of the festive season.

Putting the chicken in the oven, having prepared the veg the evening before, she cooked them.

The day progressing every car that went by she was at the window thinking it was Mark.

Dishing up dinner her and Billy pulling cracker`s.

Ringing her Ma in Ireland ,Sean answering asking "What the fuck do you want," sobbing

down the phone saying, "It is Christmas day and I just wanted to wish her a happy

Christmas."

Sean hanging up telling her not to ring her Ma anymore that she was on her own from now

on, after the lie`s she had told.The phone line went dead.

Maria sitting on the couch, her head in her hand`s sobbing, pulling her hair out.

Billy seeing this started to cry, "Mummy , mummy".

Looking at him thinking none of this mess is his fault ,picking him up saying, "Mummy is just sad because my Ma,don`t want to talk to her."Billy looking at her wrapping his arm`s around her neck.

She felt as she was the child and Billy the adult.

Knowing in her heart that Mark did not care about them , if he had he would have phoned them so going under the stairs, dragging their wedding picture out , taking it outside putting it in the bin, getting some firelighters out putting them in on top of the picture, going back inside Billy sitting watching postman pat , Tessie was sleeping.

Looking around her feeling so disappointed, rejected, she did not know what to do , but she knew she had to get him out, out of her home. Getting the bed cover`s from the bed, which she had not changed since he had left, because she knew it would take away his scent.

Taking crystal glasses from her cupboard, which had been wedding present`s and anything else she could see that had been given to them.

Putting them in the bin and set them alight.Watching as the black smoke curled through the air.

In her mind which was nearing it`s cut off point, she was punishing Mark for leaving,she was burning him.

Going back inside, Chris who was out for a walk seeing the smoke went and knocked on Maria`s door, answering it with a far away look in her eye`s.

"Maria what is going on? Are the children ok" nodding she said "I`m burning him out of our live`s" she answered with such a tormented stare in her eye`s that it frightened Chris.

"I am just going to come in" said Chris

Chris following her inside her heart pounding not knowing what she was going to find as she called , Billy`s name he toddled through showing her his toy`s.

Checking Tessie she turned to Maria who could not hear or see for a moment, nearly fainting,

Chris catching her sitting her down making them some tea, Tessie started crying Chris

taking her out of her crib, Billy standing next to Maria, getting Tessie`s bottle out of the

fridge, warming it up for her.

Chris looking at Maria and Billy and Tessie in her arm`s, thinking how could he just leave,

without an explanation his wife just after having a baby, and her young son it was evil, how

could he sleep at night. Hoping that he would have to suffer they same pain on some path of

his life.

Chris staying until it was time for the children to go to bed.

Maria letting her out saying she was going to have a bath and go to bed.

Maria seemed to be in a world of her own ,Chris thinking I should have contacted Mandy

yesterday but when she had got home her mum and sister had turned up, and it had gone

totally out of her mind.

Chris returning home rang Mandy, telling her of the confused state of

Maria`s mind, and about the burning of Mark outside.

Mandy asking if the children were ok. Chris reassuring her that they were fine but she was

really concerned for Maria.Saying that she should go around after all she was her sister, and

whatever their disagreement was about, well she needed her help.

Mandy filling Don in on her sister`s antic`s, Don looking at her saying

"Maybe we should go around there",

Many who was as stubborn as they come disagreed,

"It is not our problem, she has made her bed , so she can lie in it"

"So what are we going to do?"he asked, Don had always liked Maria, but after the explosion,

which really affected Mandy, and her hurt her very deeply, well Don had always been a one

for a peaceful life, so he just kept quite.

Staring at him she answered"I going to ring Mark."

Don thinking under the circumstances that would be the best avenue to go down after all he was her husband.

Back at the range the spider and the fly having had a very lovely meal where just sitting back having a drink, watching some telly when they phone rang.

It was Mandy ringing the barn Mark answering, Mandy informing him of the state Maria had got herself into, and that she was burning stuff at the house.

"Well " he answered "This is what social service`s are being paid for, I will ring them."

Christ he thought this chapter is getting to be a doddle.

Getting off the phone ,getting through to social services,speaking to a Sam Andrew`s telling her that his wife had already had a visit from them day`s earlier, and he had just had a phone call from her sister saying that she was setting the fire to the house, and was drinking and that she could be violent, that she had his baby daughter in the house who was only weeks old and a three year old son.

Sam saying the need to act immediately, as there such young children involved,that she would call the police and meet them at the house.

Mark not particularly,wanting to have to go,asking "Why do I need to be there",

Sam answering "Well you just said , that it is your baby daughter and son that is in the house with her."

"Yes she is my daughter, but the boy is not my son",

"Is there relative that is around that could look after the boy?because I will be looking at having this woman, put into psychiatric hospital, because they are not the action`s of a sane person, can I have her doctors name" she asked.

"Yes she has a sister that I can contact ,I am sure she will take Billy"

Giving her the details she needed, and the address of Maria`s.

"Ok we will meet you outside, in twenty minutes" she hung up.

Mark ringing Mandy telling her what was happening,saying I will meet you outside her`s in twenty minutes.

Arriving at the house, Sam already with the police, asking, has anybody got a key to the house?

Mark answering "Yes, passing her the key, she handed them to the police"

Giving them the order`s to go inside.

Mark and Mandy standing watching, a bit shocked at action going on around them.

Looking at each other as they knew deep down they were responsible for this .

Going upstairs running her bath, her mind now exhausted thinking Mark will be here soon. getting out a black dress that she knew was Mark`s favourite. Sitting at her dressing table not seeing the bone`s that were now sticking out of her body as there was no flesh left to cover them she was gone so painfully thin.

Putting the dress on,hearing the front door go just as she finished applying her make up.

Hearing the front go,

He`s back, she thought hugging herself, opening the bathroom door, seeing two strange women taking her Billy and Tessie out of their bedroom`s, two policemen outside the bathroom door, screaming, going toward`s the women who were taking her children.

The policeman grabbing her as they women walked past with her children in there arm`s

Kicking and screaming , the policeman handcuffed her, taking her downstairs after the children.

She was almost hysterical, screaming kicking, begging these women too put her babies back.s

The policeman surprised at the amount of strength in this tiny woman, as she pulled him down the stairs, screaming after her them.

Mark and Mandy across the road watching as social services took the children toward`s them

Getting her outside she looked across the road to see,Billy crying mummy, mummy, in her sisters arms, his little arm`s reaching out to her. And Tessie wailing in her Mark`s arms.

Mandy getting Billy in her car ,without a backward glance, Billy wailing "I want my mummy".

Mandy explaining to him that mummy is sick and the nice policeman is taking her to hospital and that he is coming to stay with her and Don.He nodded, his little face so very confused.

Mark getting Tessie in his car, the spider smirking saying "That is her out of the way for a while." as she cooed at Tessie.

The policeman holding her head as he put her into the police car, and drove off with her.

Maria staring at her baby sister Mandy putting Billy in her car, and her darling husband Mark putting Tessie in the Ferrari. Not another glance did either of them give Maria. Tear`s of panic and frustration running down her face .

Crying at the police "What are you doing , where are you taking me?"

The snow was falling as the police drove her to the local psychiatric unit, as they led her through the corridor,she was screaming there was snakes coming off the walls wrapping themselves around her, they were choking her, her arm`s swinging trying to remove them. The nurses seeing the distress she was in,after she being admitted she was sectioned,taken to a room where they gave her injections to clam her down and strapping her to the bed for her own protection being sedated, she went into a nightmare, of dreams seeing Mark in front of her laughing , mocking her, her Ma with a big sneer on her face, and Mandy pointing at her shouting "Your on your own now, big sis."

Wakening up the next morning, to pain`s in her leg`s,feeling her wrists and leg`s tied to the bed with straps, shouting "Help,Billy , Billy where are you " sobbing "Someone help me."

"Someone help me please" crying into the pillow.

The nurse on duty and as she walked in "Maria in her delirious state thought in her mind the devil was in the bedroom with her ,panic setting in she pulled the cover over her head. Screaming "Help,help, don`t let the devil take me"

Annie one of the other staff going into the room , hearing the scream`s of Maria, giving her an injection, soon she was back in her, dream`s world of nightmares.

The nurses having a chat between themselves, Annie saying I know her she used to do my mum`s hair.

"She is emotionally drained, and totally under nourished,it look`s as if she has not eaten in month`s, she has just had a baby, has`nt she" said Georgina.

Annie nodding replied"Yes and the husband up and left her, they were not even married a

year and the baby was just week`s old when he did his moonlight."

"What a bastard, it should be him that should be in here" said Annie, "Christ I know some men are pig`s but that take`s the biscuit,"

Nodding agreeing Georgina added "And she has another little boy, and from her record`s she has been arrested, and has now got social services on her back."

"Fucking hell, "said Georgina, "Who signed her in ".

"Guess?"replied Annie.

Georgina staring at her in disbelief, "Your joking first he leaves and then he signs her in here. who is the psycho ?, "she said.

"And her sister, singed the other form. " Annie added.

"Well there is nothing like stoning someone when there down,where is the children now?"

"The baby is with him and her son is with her sister".s

Maria woke up a bit later ,Nurse Annie going to her.They had to put her on a drip she was so dehydrated, on admission.

"How are you feeling" she asked smiling at her in a friendly voice.

Maria looking at her eye`s,so sad and pained "Where are my baby`s.?"she choked.

Annie sitting on the edge of her bed, rubbing her lovely long dark hair, said

"Don`t worry their safe, your baby is with her father, and your son is with your sister."

"Where am I?"staring at the drip in her arm.

"Your in St Gorges Hospital, in the psychiatric unit," she explained.

"When can I go home my babie`s need me", she cried.

"I am afraid you have been sectioned",

"What does that mean?"

"It mean`s that you have to stay here , because people thought you were a danger to yourself"

"What people?" she cried.

"Don`t worry about that now you just get some rest,"she answered kindly giving her another

injection to help her sleep.

Awaking next morning, another nurse had taken over from the night staff.

"Good morning, I`m nurse Janet, how are you feeling?"

Crying "I want my Billy and Tessie"she answered.

"You don`t worry about your children they are fine you just focus on getting better,"

Maria trying to sit up saying "There is nothing wrong with me."

Janet removing the strap`s answered"You were totally dehydrated, exhausted and

hallucinating, when you were admitted last night"

Maria staring at her the nurse her appearance changing in front of her, turning into the form

of her Da , standing over her ,she started to scream,"Get him away from me"in a panic, she

tried getting out of bed .

Janet pressing the buzzer for help, a doctor arrived injecting her, putting the straps back on

her, she fell into a very uneasy sleep.She was having nightmares, about her head bleeding,

dicks being stuck inside of her,Mark ,Mandy and her Ma standing sneering at her, and a huge

spider crawling over her face.

She woke up the sweat running down her face, shaking her heart thumping, screaming terrified.

The doctor was called again who called the psychiatrist,

Spending some time with her, going back to the doctor asking "Did you know she has just got a three month old baby and the husband walked out on her."

"I am just reading up on her notes now " he replied.

"Let her get some rest, hopefully she will sleep, then try and get her to eat, and put her in my diary for first thing tomorrow morning, she is completely exhausted,"

The following morning Maria woke after very disturbed night and nurse Anne came unstrapped her, showing her the bathroom saying she could shower.

Showering getting dressed into her party dress as they had not brought any clothe`s for her.

Washing her knicker`s out and hanging it on the Christmas tree, on her way to the Psychiatrist.

New chapter
Going into the office the psychiatrist introducing himself as Dr Donald Mathews,taking a seat, she sat and described the past few month`s of her life.

She cried a lot through the interview as she described how, she had nearly died giving birth to her daughter, her Mark had walked out on them, just weeks afterward`s his daughter been born, no warning,the break up with her sister also her best friend, ringing her Ma for help and the rejection there, the  burning of the thing`s that were given to her and Mark, the police arriving at her house arresting her in front of her little Billy.

Staring at Dr Matthew`s, licking her lip`s they were so dry, telling him she was damaged and how lonely and cold she had felt.

"He left me , and I don`t know why", she sobbed the pain in her eye`s so vivid.

Dr Matthews then asked her about her childhood, she filled him in on the poverty, never having enough to eat, the cold, the ill treatment from her mother, the sexual abuse from her father, her broken marriage to David,her relationship with Antony, how she had sworn she

would ever have another baby after Billy the pain had been so unbearable."

Her tone changing when she got to Mark, it became soft and full of emotion, How she had

married him and agreed to have a baby.

How happy they had been or so she thought ,and after her daughter Tessie arrived, all her

dream`s having been fulfilled.

Her voice filling with such passion, that it started to quiver, as she mentioned Mark,and

described the day they took Tessie home from the hospital.

Dr Matthew`s putting his pen down, she looked at him and said simply

"I loved him, he was my world"

Dr Matthews mentioned the burning of the pictures and other items in the bin outside,

"He never came back, and they never rang"she answered faintly.

"Who" he asked.

"Mark, it was Christmas day and in my mind he could not have left me and his little baby girl

or Billy on our own , but he did, "she whispered.

"We heard nothing from me Ma or my sister or my two brothers,so I decided to burn him out

of our live`s and I was hoping he was feeling it,"this time speaking with a hint of vengeance

in her voice.

Dr Matthews staring at her asking "Do you not think this action was a bit abnormal?"

Looking directly at him she replied "It eased the pain for a bit".

Shutting his folder, folding his arms he asked "When did you eat last"

Shaking her head "I have no idea, can I ask you a question?"

Nodding he answered "Of course".

"Why am I here"

"Because two members of your family were worried about your safety and the safety of your children".

Staring at him "My husband and my sister, you don't need to answer, they don't even talk to me ,this is a fucking conspiracy" she sobbed.

Pulling his chair back he said "Let's see if we can temp you to eat something."

Leaving the canteen after getting a couple of mouthful of soup down.

He looked at her saying you get some rest,she went to wonder towards a door to go outside to get some fresh air, one of the staff stopped her.

"I just want to get a bit of fresh air"

"Sorry love your under section" he said.

"Where can I go"

Pointing to the smoking room, the living area and upstairs.

Thinking this is one big game that she knew she would have to play, if she was ever going to get out.Going upstairs meeting nurse Anne on the landing,asking "How it went with Dr Matthew's,"Knowing it was a game she smiled and said "It was good"

"You just get some sleep and we will talk some more when you wake up,"she said in a soft voice.

Going to her bed closing her eye's going back into her dream's of nightmare's.

Waking later, nurse Anne.saying she should go and have something to eat.

Maria looking at her nodding even though she did not feel hungry but she knew if she was to get herself better, and get her baby's back she would have to start eating to get her strength back.

Managing a glass of orange juice, and a tiny bit of toast, she went into the reception area ,looking around her there were, people rocking to and foe, all age's one girl Cathy started talking to her.

Telling her she is a hairdresser and making arrangement's for Maria to do it the following day.

Maria looking at a door, going to it kicking it because in her now so tired mind, thinking that

her children and Mark were locked behind it, sitting there waiting for her, underneath

the Christmas tree.

Nurse Anne going to her asking "What`s the matter?"

Turning to her in tear`s saying "Their behind the door waiting for me"

"Who`s waiting?" she asked as she could see how Maria distraught was,

"Mark, Billy and Tessie" she sobbed.

 Taking her upstairs, giving her another injection putting her back into bed, reassuring her

that neither Mark or her children were in the hospital

"Where are they" she asked with a wild look over casting her eye`s.

Anne realizing , she was so exhausted, that her mind was playing, games with her.

Sitting with her until she, went into an uneasy sleep.

This was the pattern for the next few day`s, getting her to slowly eat, and catch up on some

sleep.

Getting out of bed, so weak hardly able to walk, her thighs so bruised , it was painful from all

the injection she had been given.

On the seventh day she began to feel a bit more human and had some visitor`s,

Chris when she arrived could not believe, where they had put her.

And looking at Maria could not believe how thin she had got, and how dead her eye`s were.

Maria seeing Chris, smiling, it was so nice to see a friendly face.

Hugging her Chris saying "It is my fault your in here,"

Maria looking at her answering her "How is it your fault?"

"I rang Mandy, asking her to go around to you, because I was worried, who must have rang

Mark, so here you are." she was almost in tear`s.

Maria looking at her whispering "There in there,"pointing to a closed door.

Chris looking asking "Who is in there?"

"Mark, Billy and Tessie " she whispered.

Chris staring at her answered "I don`t think so"

Maria staring at her saying "I know their in there, I heard Tessie crying and Billy looking for me " she sobbed, her mind so confused.

"Oh Maria , there not in that room , Tessie is with Mark, and Billy is with Mandy"

Staring at her asking "How have I got here?"she asked almost hysterical.

"Can`t you remember Mark left , you looked for help from your mum, and then Mandy had a falling out with you, and you just when down hill from there, which is very understandable. none of us like rejection, but the amount that was thrown at you, well it would be enough to send anybody over the edge."

Looking at Chris saying,"I have lost control,I have to get out of here and I want my children back, at home with me, where they should be "

"What about Mark ," Chris asked.

"With a long lost look in her eye`s, as if she had traveled far away"she answered,with tear`s "He was the man of my dream`s, when I married him ,I thought I had won the lottery,and that we would be together forever and longer, he might as well have cut my arm`s and leg`s off, and left me to bleed to death, it could not have more painful, and then Ma, did not want to know, and when Mandy disowned me, well I thought I was drowning, in a sea with no bottom.It was so unreal,I thought I was in a nightmare that I would wake up from"she was so crying so hard,Chris could feel her pain

Looking at her saying "Now look at me sectioned, in a psychiatric hospital,my children gone, and who care`s, not my dream husband, he and Mandy are they two that got me signed in here, and this is the reality of my life "

Chris listened, and agreed with everything she said, but not voicing her thought`s.

Chris leaving Maria telling her where the spare key was, and asking for she would bring in some clothe's for her.

Chris saying she would and told her she would be in the next day.

The rest of the evening Maria spent on her bed trying to make sense of everything that had happened.

Dozing and waking up with the feeling of not knowing where she was, feeling frightened, and very alone.

The following day she was, beginning to feel claustrophobic, as she had not been outside in seven day's and needed some fresh air inside of her.

Asking Annie if she could go outside, Annie smiling at her saying she had a surprise coming for her, that she knew would cheer her up.

Staring inquisitively, she asked "What?".Anne nodding behind her she saw Billy with her sister and her Ma arriving.

She was finding it hard to walk at this stage, with all the medication that had been injected into her,and the lack of food was beginning to take its toll

Her Ma and Mandy staring at Maria shocked at her appearance,She was painfully thin , no colour in her face it was a grey colour and her eyes were dead.

Maria seeing her Billy hobbled towards him with a huge grin on her face, picking him up and kissing him.

"Mummy", he cried, hugging her back , one of the inmate's going toward's her, his name was Kevin, asking Maria who this was,

Giving the biggest smile, she introduced her pride and joy, her son Billy.

Looking at Billy he asked if he would like to play in the playroom , a bit later after he had seen his mum.

Kevin was a big child at heart and had signed himself in voluntary.

This Maria could never understand in a million year`s.

Nodding,Billy was holding on to Maria `s so tightly, she let him down,looking at him,

hugging him kissing him, Saying "Mummy has missed you so much".

The little face looked at her asking"Mummy when are we going home"

Maria staring back at him answering "I`m not sure, but it will be soon "

"Mummy where is Tessie?" he asked.

"She is with Mark"she answered.

Staring at her Ma and her sister,she led them into the smoking area.

Turning saying "This is the only room I`m allowed into,"

 Her Ma saying "Are you not even going to say hello".

"Hello" she answered.

Mandy saying she needed the loo could not believe the place her sister had ended up in.

It was full of mental people, people that looked like zombie`s, totally lifeless and apathetic,

she felt so uncomfortable.

Bumping into one bloke with a crucifix, the size of a egg hanging about his neck, a rosary

beads in his hands and long hair he looked like Jesus Christ.

Finding the loo and hurrying back.

Her Ma sitting in the smoking room with Maria as Kevin took Billy to the play room.

Maria had a hair brush in her hand so her Ma started to brush her hair.

Maria started to cry.

Cathrine having never been able to deal with any burst of emotion, asked "Why are you

crying?"

Pulling her head away, looking at her Ma , as if she had grown a head.

"Why do you think ? because I`m in a fucking looney  bin, I should be at home with my two children, Mark left and Mandy doesn`t want to know me and you would not come over to me , even though it was not going to cost you a penny, yet here you are, Why?" Maria demanded.

"Don`t I even deserve an answer?"

"Look I told you, my back was playing me up"she answered quickly.

"Don`t give me that shite"

"So how come when I rang on Christmas day, you would not talk to me instead Sean was on the phone saying you wanted to contact me again", she sobbed.

Nurse Anne arrived saying "Maria you have got another visitor"

Chris walked in with a bag of clothe`s for her.

Looking at her mother saying "Hello"

Maria staring at her Ma introduced, her to Chris.

Billy coming back with Kevin saying "I like it here"

Chris laughing, Maria hugging him,"I just pop these up to your room", said Chris.

 Mandy returning back sensing an atmosphere, between them.

Maria asking her "Where is Don"

Mandy ignoring her, thinking have`nt you caused enough trouble?

Saying to her Ma "Do you want to go,

 Maria`s face fell saying "You have only just got here"

Mandy looking at her said "You have no one to blame but yourself."

Chris coming back down overhearing Mandy`s comment, giving Mandy the dirtiest look, shaking her head.

Billy crying saying "I don`t want my mummy in here on her own".

Maria cuddling him saying she had lot`s of friend`s here and she was fine, looking at Mandy asking "When will you bring him in again?"

Shrugging her shoulder`s answering "Tomorrow maybe the next day."

Cathrine frightened that if they stayed she would find out the truth to the hidden secret,

answered "Yes we will go"

Maria could not believe her ear`s,"Christ Ma I have hardly seen him."

Mandy staring at Maria with a look of contempt in her eye`s, saying,

"Go on Maria don`t think of anyone but your self, Ma her back is playing up ,do you care?"

Shaking her head she went got Billy`s coat, who was crying,

 "I want to stay with my mummy"

Cathrine thinking what a state of affair`s, grabbing Billy`s hand, saying

"Come on now .your mammy is not feeling well, and we will come back and see her soon "

Maria looking at her Ma,said"Don`t you think there has been enough lie`s"looking down at

Billy, kissing him said"Darling you go on with Mandy and nanny Cathrine, and mummy will

be home soon."

Watching as the two of them walked away with her son , without a glance back.Billy waving,

saying "Good bye mummy."

"Bye my little soldier" she whispered.

Turning before he could see the tear`s rolling down her face, Chris said

""Nobody deserves this treatment"

"Good bye mummy",she waved back, wondering what she had to do ,to get out of this hell

hole and get her life back on tract.

Kevin having seen what had happened,said "Your family don`t like you very much"

Looking at him replying "You don`t know the half of it".

Chris hugging her saying "I`m only a phone call away"

Maria sobbing, said "It should not be you saying that, it should be them two", she said as she

stared up the corridor.

Chris stayed with her a little longer,

Leaving she said"You be strong darling, you will get through this, just do what ever the tell

you, and get yourself back home"

Maria sobbing her heart out, looking at Chris saying "I will try."

"Look at Billy he is heartbroken to see your in here,there is only one person that can do this

and that is you."

Hugging her as she left, whispering in her ear, "You have got friend`s that care."

"Yes I know but their all away at the moment"

"They will be back soon"

"I try and come over tomorrow if not the day after" Chris promised before she left.

"And Billy and Tessie are not behind that door " she smiled as she left.

Maria smiling,"That was just wishful thinking".

Maria went to the office, Anne was in there with Janet,looking up as

she walked in, "I just thought I should say thank you"

"What for "asked Janet,

"For letting me see my son and now I know that my children are not behind that door , she

said pointing at the door that had been her focal point since she had been admitted.

Smiling at her they said"That`s what we are here for to help"

That evening she was in the smoking room, when Kevin appeared.

They got chatting, telling her that this was the only place in the world he felt safe.

Taking a bottle of vodka out of his pocket he offering her one.

Surprised she said "I did not know that we were allowed that in here"

Staring at her replying were not.

"But if you have a drink don`t take the pills"

What do you like with it, smiling she answered "Coke"

"I will just go and get some"

She had a couple of drink`s with him, hiding the drink`s when they heard the staff approach,

Nurse Anne came in with their medication

She told her she would take them before she went to bed, that she was having a nice time

with Kevin and they made her sleepy.

"That`s ok , "leaving them on the table,glad to see Maria relaxing.

She was going off duty and said she would see them tomorrow.

Maria now feeling like a naughty school girl.

Having had enough left for one more drink.

Maria was feeling that it was not the end, but a huge mountain that she had to climb in her

life that had to get sorted.

She went to put the pill`s in the bin but Kevin stopped her saying

"Don`t the check the bin`s, flush them down the loo"

Smiling at him saying you know the run of the mill here,nodding he answered

"I am part of the furniture"he laughed.

She went to bed thanking Kevin for his company, and lay there thinking

about her visit , from her Ma and Mandy and then smiling to herself seeing her little Billy and

knowing that her Ma and Mandy would look after him ,she dozed.

She was awoken the next morning by a siren going off, getting out of bed still not too steady

on her feet, going into the corridor seeing Cathy being carried out of the bathroom blood

pouring from her wrists.

One of the patients shouting "Cathy has killed herself.

Nurse Anne who was in tears as the two security men carried her out.

She was shocked as she had only being talking to her yesterday, and had made arrangement`s

to do her hair today.   -

The staff were shooing the patient`s back into their bedroom `s

Anne who was passing Maria`s room ,she asked"What has happened?"

Anne sobbing answered "She has just come off suicide watch,but one of us obviously were

not doing our job`s properly "

This really shocked Maria, after the body was taken away they were all sent down to

breakfast.

She sat there wondering how the could face food, Christ one of their in-mates had just killed

themselves only feet away.

Maria going into the smoking room, lighting a cigarette, one of the nurses

coming to her saying Dr Matthews would like to see her.

Nodding following her, smiling as she walked into the office,Dr Matthew`s standing up

asking how she was feeling.

"A lot better " she smiled.

Looking at her saying "I would like to put you on a program that is just to make sure that the

stress you have been under, has not disrupted your brain function."

"What does this consist of"she asked feeling a little apprehensive.

"It is nothing for you to worry about, it is an exercise to make sure that your

brain can still make since of thing`s,because like a motor car, if you run it without oil it can

cause damage it. And with the amount of stress you have been under, well that is why were

taking this precaution."

"Ok when does it start?"

"Tomorrow it will take about one hour, oh and by the way we have arranged a visit from your

baby daughter, this afternoon,"he watched as her eye`s lit up.

She jumped up and gave him a kiss of gratitude."Thank you"

Laughing he said" My pleasure ".

Watching her as she skipped out of the office, he was really not sure in his professional opinion, why she was here and was she right in what she had said that it was a conspiracy against her?.

She had been through so much in such a short space of time, she was exhausted, both mentally physically, and destroyed by her husband emotionally.Making a mental note to have a word at their next meeting which looking through his diary was three days time.

Leaving the office feeling elated, she was going to see her Tessie. It was over a week now since she had seen her baby daughter, which was far too long in Maria`s book`s.

Skipping upstairs, getting changed into a clean pair of legging`s and top, brushing her long hair , going back downstairs she sat staring at the door waiting for her baby.

Her eye`s staring around the reception room, focusing on the Christmas tree, thinking this is one Christmas I will never forget.

Kevin came and sat with her,

Looking sad he said"Have you heard about Cathy."

"I saw her" she answered, as got up staring out the window at the snow.

"It is all part of the course in here" he said standing beside her.

Surprised she asked"Does it happen often ?"

"Not on my watch, this is about the third, since I have been coming here,which is about, well must be coming up to seven years,Who know`s how the mind work`s, it is a very powerful

machine, that is why I come here ,I sometime have very overpowering thought`s

that scare me, so I make my way here, I always feel safe. "

"What are you doing in here?" he asked

"I was taken in Christmas night, and sectioned" she sighed.

"Who did that?"

"My husband and my sister" she answered.

"Christ they must really hate you", he replied.

"It has been a conspiracy, to get me out of the way , so he could have Tessie,"she answered.

"You will be here for a while " he answered.

Maria staring at him asking "How long?"

"Minimum up to three month`s."

Maria looking at him in disbelief, "What they can`t keep me locked up for that long"

"Oh they can and longer if they don`t think your making progress."

Maria staring at him saying "I can`t survive in here that long".

"Well what choice do you have?"

Shrugging she said "I am seeing my baby daughter today,"she said.

"How many children have you got?"

"Two my son, Billy you met yesterday, he is three and my Tessie who is three months

old,have you got any?"

Shaking his head "Never been in the situation to have been that lucky" he said sadly.

Seeing a woman come through the door with a baby in a car seat,Maria running toward`s her,

the woman introducing, herself as Jackie Mill`s from social services.

 Looking down at the baby Maria started to cry panic, setting in saying,

 "This is not my baby."They baby opening her eye`s with the scream , Maria looking into her

eye`s seeing one brown and one blue eye, realized it was Tessie.

Picking her up kissing her she cried"Oh baby mummy is so sorry she did not recognize you,"

Jackie saying "That it was not unusual under the circumstances."

"What do you mean, "asked Maria holding Tessie in arm`s

"Well we have it in your note`s,about the amount of drug`s you have been given and it has

been over a week since you have seen her, and baby`s do change very quick"

Holding her so close having missed the smell of her daughter,staring at the tiny

finger`s,smiling at her, sitting down ,.

The other patients coming over cooing at her, Maria sitting there so proud of her little girl.

Nurse Anne going into the office, seeing if they would allow Maria to go to the front door, with her daughter, when she had to leave.

Getting the go ahead,she approached Maria,telling her that it was Mark`s new partner that had left Tessie to the hospital, and that she had got permission for her to leave her back to the front door,Maria staring  at her with a look of panic on her face, Anne seeing this saying "You don`t have to go, but I think it might help you come to grip with thing`s, help you move forward" she said kindly.

Nodding Maria understanding where she was coming from.

Maria feeding Tessie being, watched closely by Jackie.

Smiling at her saying "I do remember how to feed her."

Jackie reading her not`s, seeing she had been reported for neglect of her daughter,saying she had been dressed in summer clothe`s in the cold winter, reading on seeing that her husband had moonlighted just after she had given birth, and they had not been long married, thinking in her maid that it was a wonder she had remembered to dress herself with a shock like that.

The hour`s that she was given with Tessie just seem like minute`s to Maria .

Jackie staring at her seeing the love in her eye`s, that she felt for her child.

Then having to tell her it was time for her to go "We have to go now Maria"

Anne was in the background, saying to Jackie that Maria could walk her daughter to the door.

Jackie gathering her paper work , Anne and Maria holding her baby making their way to the entrance .

 There was a fish tank, inside the front door with different coloured fish in it,

Maria holding Tessie in her arms who was now becoming aware of what was going on around her, showing her the fish.

Getting a nudge from Anne she looked up toward`s the door to see, a female man like figure appear, through the snow she was extremely thin, very well dressed, in a mink fur coat, dripping in gold approaching.

As she got closer, Nurse Anne thinking how the fuck could one woman do this to another. It was one thing to take another woman's man ,but her baby??.

Maria staring at her, getting a shock looking at the spider's face, she is old enough to be his mother.

Seeing the scaled, pot holed skin ,very cleverly made up, to conceal it.But still noticeable.

 She smiled at Nurse Anne, who just gave her dagger's.

Maria staring at her, only getting a cold stare back, from the spider.

Hugging Tessie saying," You be a good girl for Mark's Granny ,"

Anne and Jackie had to hold back from laughing at this comment.

Passing Tessie to her saying"Don't drop her I know how frail Granny's can be.She is my baby daughter,you take great care of her, I will be out soon to take her home".

The spider going beetroot in the face taking Tessie, without a feeling of remorse,towards Maria walked away.

Maria staring after her, shaking her head,thinking that is what her Mark had left her for.

Anne hugging her thinking she might be small , but she was showing a tower of strength.

If it was me I would be tearing the bitch's hair out.

New chapter

Back at the ranch, Mark was waiting patiently, for the spider's return . It had been the spider's idea to go drop, Tessie off much to Mark's relief, as the day before he had been summons to the office of Dr Donald Matthew's, where he was asked to explain and collaborate, his reasons for having his wife sectioned.

Dr Matthews, informed him that he had grave concerns about validity of his accusations,and in his professional opinion, he did not think that a section order was applicable, in Maria`s situation.

Going back to his car his head reeling thinking,

Fuck this was not going to plan, she was going to be released a lot quicker than he had anticipated. He could see the pawn being moved to the wrong side of the board, This was not the position,he needed to be in, to guarantee winning the game.

His next gambit, would have to be fool proof, to ensure check mate.

New Chapter

The spider having seen, how distressed Mark was,on his return,from the meeting with Dr Matthews`wondering if guilt had set in , she did not want too lose him and her precious baby to the Irish loony that he had married , and there would be no chance of her fulfilling her dream of being a mum.

So gently she suggested, to Mark that she should take Tessie to the hospital.

She was loving being a mum, to Tessie, and had got no intention of allowing anything or anybody to take this away from her, and her friend`s at the golf club could not believe that she had pulled Mark, he looked almost as good on her arm as her fur coat, and now having his baby living with them.Well she was the flavour of the month.

The following morning ,dressing Tessie in her new winter fur suit she had bought for her, she got in the Ferrari and went to the loony bin, where she was taken by social services to see that Irish bitch, even thought she thought in her heart that a loony bin was no place for her Tessie to be visiting.

Sitting in her car thinking,congratulating herself on all her achievements` on having snared the fly and his daughter, and how she was been a good mother to Tessie since Christmas night and she would never go without.Looking at her watch wishing the time away. Watching people go in and out, wondering what it would be like to be locked in a place like this, dismissing the thought straight away.

At last it was time to pick her baby up,going to the entrance she was gutted to see The Irish tart standing there with her baby in her arm`s.Escorted by a nurse and a member of social

services.

Holding her head high she went to take her Tessie from The Irish Thing.

Maria staring at her, The Spider feeling no remorse, as she took Tessie from her mother.

Maria looking at her saying to Tessie "Go to Mark`s new granny, you take great care of

her ,she is my baby, and I will get out of here soon "

That stung, the spider.

Getting Tessie in the car she headed back to the barn.Heading back to the

barn, fuming at the remarks The Irish Tart had commented about her.Pulling in taking Tessie

out of the car, Mark waiting at the window, seeing them, walking outside asking

"Everything ok",

 The Spider not wanting to repeat to Mark what the Irish loony had called her replied

"Yes all went to plan,except that deranged wife of your`s has to be escorted everywhere

By one of the staff, obviously they think she is at risk ,why else would she have to be

supervised,"she snapped.

Mark looking at her saying "We are going to have to find a good solicitor, the best money

can buy."

The day`s dragged into weeks, Maria started eating again, under the

supervision of staff and spent her time doing they patient`s hair, and generally making

themselves` feel better about themselves.She became very popular with the staff and the other

patient`s.The staff realizing she was not a threat to anyone.

There was a solicitor, who normally visited they hospital, once a week, but because of the

Christmas period , he had not been.

New chapter
He was introduced to Maria on the 8th of January 1996, reading her report`s, and after

speaking to her , he realized there had been a total injustice done.

Two day`s later she was put in front of a panel of police, social worker`s, and doctor`s, including Doctor Matthew`s.

They threw question`s at her which she answered honestly.

When they had finished,Maria actually finished the meeting by asking each of them individually, "Does any one of you know how it feel`s to watch your children be taken from their bedroom`s on Christmas day ,or any day for that matter and then for you to be hand cuffed, without any explanation and locked up here."she asked feeling a bit breathless after her input.

There was total silence. They left for a recess, leaving Maria and the solicitor in the room.

One hour later the head of the team came and told her she was being released.

It was 7.00pm,

Maria stared at him saying"What I can go home "

The solicitor shaking her hand smiling at her said "Yes you can go home"

She bowed at the head of the team thanking him.Going back inside with Richard the solicitor ,beaming at him saying "Thank you so much."

"Your a free woman,"he smiled watching her skip up the corridor.

Thinking and a very strong one.

New Chapter

She went to the office Anne was there with the superviser, Anne looking at the excited face

Maria said "I am free, I`m out of here"

The superviser having already been informed, smiled and looking at her said

"We will miss you, you have been like a breath of fresh air to this place."

Maria staring at her answered"I`m not being nasty, I will remember you and all you done to help me, but I won`t miss this"she smiled asking

"Is it was aright to go and pack her thing`s"

Smiling she nodded and said "Yes sweetheart you can go,"

Coming out of the office she saw Dr Matthew`s coming down the corridor.

Calling him he stopped, smiling saying "That was quite a little speech you did in there."

With tear`s in her eye`s she answered saying "I just want to thank you from the bottom of my

heart, for believing in me."she gave him a hug and a kiss on the cheek.

He stared down at her saying "I have never met anyone quite like you before, and I wish you

all the luck in the world"

Going upstairs she bumped into Kevin,telling him she had been released.

Hugging her saying "I wish you all you want from this world and more and it was my

pleasure to meet you", kissing her and there was real affection in that kiss.

Getting her few bit`s together she walked down the stairs thinking it was sixteen day`s ago

since she had walked in here, and to be honest it seemed more like sixteen year`s.

Waving goodbye to Anne, heading to the exit door the cold air hit

her ,looking at the snow falling around her.

Getting to the hospital gate`s she tuned back, all six stone of her.She looked like an

orphaned child from the distance.Thinking Why am I here.

Taking a deep breath she started walking the four mile journey home.

Slipping on the ice, falling hurting her knees, picking herself up, tear`s of relief and sorrow,

in her eye`s, relief to be out of the hospital, and sorrow at how she had ended up there.

She could see Billy`s smiling face and Tessie`s twinkling blue and brown eye in her mind,

and with this vision,putting one foot in front of the other, and started her cold frosty walk

home.

In her mind`s eye, the intensity of the ordeal she had been through,

was begining to make her feel the only reason she was still breathing, her heart still beating,

after the explosion that had ripped her soul apart, shredded her life to bit`s, was the knowledge that soon she would be reunited with her two babies Billy and Tessie, where they

belonged in their mother's arm's, and where they should never have been taken from.

But unknown to her the fuse had not even been ignited

Finished on the 22 02 17 at 11.22pm.s
 s

Maria - The Irish Colleen The Aftermath

Made in the USA
Middletown, DE
16 June 2017